"IMPRESSIVE ... FASCINATING ...

This novel is Carl Hiaasen's latest dangerous weapon—Uzi satire in 9-millimeter bursts aimed at those classic baddies, vanity and greed.... No one has ever designed funnier, more terrifying bad guys."

The New York Times Book Review

"Every once in a while, fortunate readers can feel an almost electric shock from the opening pages of a new book.... The dialogue, madcap pacing and satiric plot twists will bring grins of recognition from Hiaasen fans. First-time readers may note that Stranahan bears some resemblance to Travis McGee."

Chicago Tribune

"Hiaasen spins manic tales in a tangle of wide, eccentric loops that involve a broad range of characters and lasso a variety of sanctimonious and greedy social predators.... The reader's best recourse is not to try to outguess Hiaasen—one can't—but simply to lean back and let him deliver his absurdly comic vision."

The Miami Herald

"Carl Hiaasen is back: bizarre, brutal and blackly comic as ever.... His third thriller just may be the one that catapults him from cult status to national bestseller."

Atlanta Journal & Constitution

"HE OUTDOES HIMSELF....

What makes the story work so well—we're talking page-burner here, a wasted weekend—is Hiaasen's talent for crafting flesh-and-blood characters who, love 'em or hate 'em, keep us wondering: What in the heck can possibly happen next?"

The Orlando Sentinel

"Stranahan has style.... He is insouciance personified, as he glides through the phantasmagoria of sleaze that is author Hiaasen's South Florida."

The Philadelphia Inquirer

"Great, if often grisly fun ... Hiaasen's fiction sticks close enough to fact to make anybody think twice about getting the most routine nip and tuck."

The Wall Street Journal

"With a crisp newspaper style, Hiaasen once again takes readers through the streets of Miami and into the lifestyles of the weird and wacko.... His writing is so concise, so fluid that readers may not realize how much homework he must have done on his subjects."

The Tampa Tribune & Times

"TRULY OUTRAGEOUS . . .

SKIN TIGHT

Carl Hiaasen

FAWCETT CREST • NEW YORK

Acknowledgments

For his advice, expertise, and good humor,
I am grateful to Dr. Gerard Grau, and also to his
former surgical nurse Connie, who is my wife.

1

On the third of January, a leaden, blustery day, two tourists from Covington, Tennessee, removed their sensible shoes to go strolling on the beach at Key Biscayne.

When they got to the old Cape Florida lighthouse, the young man and his finacée sat down on the damp sand to watch the ocean crash hard across the brown boulders at the point of the island. There was a salt haze in the air, and it stung the young man's eyes so that when he spotted the thing floating, it took several moments to focus on what it was.

"It's a big dead fish," his fiancée said. "Maybe a porpoise."

"I don't believe so," said the young man. He stood up, dusted off the seat of his trousers, and walked to the edge of the surf. As the thing floated closer, the young man began to wonder about his legal responsibilities, providing it turned out to be what he thought it was. Oh yes, he had heard about Miami; this sort of stuff happened every day.

"Let's go back now," he said abruptly to his fiancée.

"No, I want to see what it is. It doesn't look like a fish anymore."

The young man scanned the beach and saw they were all alone, thanks to the lousy weather. He also knew from a brochure back at the hotel that the lighthouse was long ago abandoned, so there would be no one watching from above.

"It's a dead body," he said grimly to his fiancée.

"Come off it."

At that instant a big, lisping breaker took the thing on its crest

1

and carried it all the way to the beach, where it stuck—the nose of the dead man grounding as a keel in the sand.

The young man's fiancée stared down at the corpse and said, "Geez, you're right."

The young man sucked in his breath and took a step back.

"Should we turn it over?" his fiancée asked. "Maybe he's still alive."

"Don't touch it. He's dead."

"How do you know?"

The young man pointed with a bare toe. "See that hole?"

"That's a hole?"

She bent over and studied a stain on the shirt. The stain was the color of rust and the size of a sand dollar.

"Well, he didn't just drown," the young man announced.

His fiancée shivered a little and buttoned her sweater. "So what do we do now?"

"Now we get out of here."

"Shouldn't we call the police?"

"It's our vacation, Cheryl. Besides, we're a half-hour's walk to the nearest phone."

The young man was getting nervous; he thought he heard a boat's engine somewhere around the point of the island, on the bay side.

The woman tourist said, "Just a second." She unsnapped the black leather case that held her trusty Canon Sure-Shot.

"What are you doing?"

"I want a picture, Thomas." She already had the camera up to her eye.

"Are you crazy?"

"Otherwise no one back home will believe us. I mean, we come all the way down to Miami and what happens? Remember how your brother was making murder jokes before we left? It's unreal. Stand to the right a little, Thomas, and pretend to look down at it."

"Pretend, hell."

"Come on, one picture."

"No," the man said, eyeing the corpse.

"Please? You used up a whole roll on Flipper."

The woman snapped the picture and said, "That's good. Now you take one of me."

"Well, hurry it up," the young man grumped. The wind was blowing harder from the northeast, moaning through the whippy Australian pines behind them. The sound of the boat engine, wherever it was, had faded away.

The young man's fiancée struck a pose next to the dead body: She pointed at it and made a sour face, crinkling her zinc-coated nose.

"I can't believe this," the young man said, lining up the photograph.

"Me neither, Thomas. A real live dead body—just like on the TV show. Yuk!"

"Yeah, yuk," said the young man. "Fucking yuk is right."

The day had begun with only a light, cool breeze and a rim of broken raspberry clouds out toward the Bahamas. Stranahan was up early, frying eggs and chasing the gulls off the roof. He lived in an old stilt house on the shallow tidal flats of Biscayne Bay, a mile from the tip of Cape Florida. The house had a small generator powered by a four-bladed windmill, but no air-conditioning. Except for a few days in August and September, there was always a decent breeze. That was one nice thing about living on the water.

There were maybe a dozen other houses in the stretch of Biscayne Bay known as Stiltsville, but none were inhabited; rich owners used them for weekend parties, and their kids got drunk on them in the summer. The rest of the time they served as fancy, split-level toilets for seagulls and cormorants.

Stranahan had purchased his house dirt-cheap at a government auction. The previous owner was a Venezuelan cocaine courier who had been shot thirteen times in a serious business dispute, then indicted posthumously. No sooner had the corpse been air-freighted back to Caracas than Customs agents seized the stilt house, along with three condos, two Porsches, a one-eyed scarlet macaw, and a yacht with a hot tub. The hot tub was where the Venezuelan had met his spectacular death, so bidding was feverish. Likewise the macaw—a material witness to its owner's murder—fetched top dollar; before the auction, mischievous Customs agents had taught the bird to say, "Duck, you shithead!"

By the time the stilt house had come up on the block, nobody was interested. Stranahan had picked it up for forty thousand and change.

He coveted the solitude of the flats, and was delighted to be the only human soul living in Stiltsville. His house, barn-red with brown shutters, sat three hundred yards off the main channel, so most of the weekend boat traffic traveled clear of him. Occasionally a drunk or a total moron would try to clear the banks with a big cabin cruiser, but they did not get far, and they got no sympathy or assistance from the big man in the barn-red house.

January third was a weekday and, with the weather blackening out east, there wouldn't be many boaters out. Stranahan savored this fact as he sat on the sun deck, eating his eggs and Canadian bacon right out of the frying pan. When a pair of fat, dirty gulls swooped in to nag him for the leftovers, he picked up a BB pistol and opened fire. The birds screeched off in the direction of the Miami skyline, and Stranahan hoped they would not stop until they got there.

After breakfast he pulled on a pair of stringy denim cutoffs and started doing push-ups. He stopped at one hundred five, and went inside to get some orange juice. From the kitchen he heard a boat coming and checked out the window. It was a yellow bonefish skiff, racing heedlessly across the shallows. Stranahan smiled; he knew all the local guides. Sometimes he'd let them use his house for a bathroom stop, if they had a particularly shy female customer who didn't want to hang it over the side of the boat.

Stranahan poured two cups of hot coffee and went back out on the deck. The yellow skiff was idling up to the dock, which was below the house itself and served as a boat garage. The guide waved up at Stranahan and tied off from the bow. The man's client, an inordinately pale fellow, was preoccupied trying to decide which of four different grades of sunscreen to slather on his milky arms. The guide hopped out of the skiff and climbed up to the sun deck.

"Morning, Captain." Stranahan handed a mug of coffee to the guide, who accepted it with a friendly grunt. The two men had known each other many years, but this was only the second or third occasion that the captain had gotten out of his boat and come up to the stilt house. Stranahan waited to hear the reason.

When he put down the empty cup, the guide said: "Mick, you expecting company?"

"No."

"There was a man this morning."

"At the marina?"

"No, out here. Asking which house was yours." The guide glanced over the railing at his client, who now was practicing with a fly rod, snapping the line like a horsewhip.

Stranahan laughed and said, "Looks like a winner."

"Looks like a long goddamn day," the captain muttered.

"Tell me about this guy."

"He flagged me down over by the radio towers. He was in a white Seacraft, a twenty-footer. I thought he was having engine trouble but all he wanted was to know which house was yours. I sent him down toward Elliott Key, so I hope he wasn't a friend. Said he was."

"Did he give you a name?"

"Tim is what he said."

Stranahan said the only Tim he knew was an ex-homicide cop named Gavigan.

"That's it," the fishing guide said. "Tim Gavigan is what he said."

"Skinny redhead?"

"Nope."

"Shit," said Stranahan. Of course it wasn't Timmy Gavigan. Gavigan was busy dying of lung cancer in the VA.

The captain said, "You want me to hang close today?"

"Hell, no, you got your sport down there, he's raring to go."

"Fuck it, Mick, he wouldn't know a bonefish from a sperm whale. Anyway, I've got a few choice spots right around here—maybe we'll luck out."

"Not with this breeze, buddy; the flats are already pea soup. You go on down south, I'll be all right. He's probably just some process-server."

"Somebody's sure to tell him which house."

"Yeah, I figure so," Stranahan said. "A white Seacraft, you said?"

"Twenty-footer," the guide repeated. Before he started down the stairs, he said, "The guy's got some size to him, too."

"Thanks for the info."

Stranahan watched the yellow skiff shoot south, across the flats, until all he could see was the long zipper of foam in its wake. The guide would be heading to Sand Key, Stranahan thought, or maybe all the way to Caesar Creek—well out of radio range. As if the damn radio still worked.

By three o'clock in the afternoon, the wind had stiffened, and the sky and the water had acquired the same purple shade of gray. Stranahan slipped into long jeans and a light jacket. He put on his sneakers, too; at the time he didn't think about why he did this, but much later it came to him: Splinters. From running on the wooden deck. The raw two-by-fours were hell on bare feet, so Stranahan had put on his sneakers. In case he had to run.

The Seacraft was noisy. Stranahan heard it coming two miles away. He found the white speck through his field glasses and watched it plow through the hard chop. The boat was heading straight for Stranahan's stilt house and staying clean in the channels, too.

Figures, Stranahan thought sourly. Probably one of the park rangers down at Elliott Key told the guy which house; just trying to be helpful.

He got up and closed the brown shutters from the outside. Through the field glasses he took one more long look at the man in the Seacraft, who was still a half mile away. Stranahan did not recognize the man, but could tell he was from up North— the guy made a point of shirt-sleeves, on this kind of a day, and the dumbest-looking sunglasses ever made.

Stranahan slipped inside the house and closed the door behind him. There was no way to lock it from the inside; there was no reason, usually.

With the shutters down the inside of the house was pitch-black, but Stranahan knew every corner of each room. In this house he had ridden out two hurricanes—baby ones, but nasty just the same. He had spent both storms in total darkness, because the wind knifed through the walls and played hell with the lanterns, and the last thing you wanted was an indoor fire.

So Stranahan knew the house in the dark.

He selected his place and waited.

After a few minutes the pitch of the Seacraft's engines dropped an octave, and Stranahan figured the boat was slowing down. The guy would be eyeing the place closely, trying to figure out the best way up on the flat. There was a narrow cut in the marl, maybe four feet deep at high tide and wide enough for one boat. If the guy saw it and made this his entry, he would certainly spot Stranahan's aluminum skiff tied up under the water tanks. And then he would know.

Stranahan heard the Seacraft's engines chewing up the marly bottom. The guy had missed the deep cut.

Stranahan heard the big boat thud into the pilings at the west end of the house. He could hear the guy clunking around in the bow, grunting as he tried to tie it off against the tide, which was falling fast.

Stranahan heard—and felt—the man hoist himself out of the boat and climb to the main deck of the house. He heard the man say: "Anybody home?"

The man did not have a light step; the captain was right—he was a big one. By the vibrations of the plankboards, Stranahan charted the intruder's movements.

Finally the guy knocked on the door and said: "Hey! Hello there!"

When no one answered, the guy just opened the door.

He stood framed in the afternoon light, such as it was, and Stranahan got a pretty good look. The man had removed his sunglasses. As he peered into the dark house, his right hand went to the waist of his trousers.

"State your business," Stranahan said from the shadows.

"Oh, hey!" The man stepped backward onto the deck, forfeiting his silhouette for detail. Stranahan did not recognize the face—an odd and lumpy one, skin stretched tightly over squared cheekbones. Also, the nose didn't match the eyes and chin. Stranahan wondered if the guy had ever been in a bad car wreck.

The man said: "I ran out of gas, and I was wondering if you had a couple gallons to get me back to the marina. I'll be happy to pay."

"Sorry," Stranahan said.

The guy looked for the source of the voice, but he couldn't see a damn thing in the shuttered-up house.

"Hey, pal, you okay?"

"Just fine," Stranahan said.

"Well, then, would you mind stepping out where I can see you?"

With his left hand Stranahan grabbed the leg of a barstool and sent it skidding along the bare floor to no place in particular. He just wanted to see what the asshole would do, and he was not disappointed. The guy took a short-barreled pistol out of his pants and held it behind his back. Then he took two steps forward until he was completely inside the house. He took another slow step toward the spot where the broken barstool lay, only now he was holding the pistol in front of him.

Stranahan, who had squeezed himself into a spot between the freezer and the pantry, had seen enough of the damn gun.

"Over here," he said to the stranger.

And when the guy spun around to get a bead on where the voice was coming from, Mick Stranahan lunged out of the shadows and stabbed him straight through with a stuffed marlin head he had gotten off the wall.

It was a fine blue marlin, maybe four hundred pounds, and whoever caught it had decided to mount only the head and shoulders, down to the spike of the dorsal. The trophy fish had come with the Venezuelan's house and hung in the living room, where Stranahan had grown accustomed to its indigo stripes, its raging glass eye and its fearsome black sword. In a way it was a shame to mess it up, but Stranahan knew the BB gun would be useless against a real revolver.

The taxidermied fish was not as heavy as Stranahan anticipated, but it was cumbersome; Stranahan concentrated on his aim as he charged the intruder. It paid off.

The marlin's bill split the man's breastbone, tore his aorta, and severed his spine. He died before Stranahan got a chance to ask him any questions. The final puzzled look on the man's face suggested that he was not expecting to be gored by a giant stuffed fish head.

The intruder carried no identification, no wallet, no wedding ring; just the keys to a rented Thunderbird. Aboard the Seacraft, which was also rented, Stranahan found an Igloo cooler with two six-packs of Corona and a couple of cheap spinning rods that the killer had brought along just for looks.

Stranahan heaved the body into the Seacraft and took the boat out into the Biscayne Channel. There he pushed the dead guy overboard, tossed the pistol into deep water, rinsed down the deck, dove off the stern, and swam back toward the stilt house. In fifteen minutes his knees hit the mud bank, and he waded the last seventy-five yards to the dock.

That night there was no sunset to speak of, because of the dreary skies, but Stranahan sat on the deck anyway. As he stared out to the west, he tried to figure out who wanted him dead, and why. He considered this a priority.

2

On the fourth of January, the sun came out, and Dr. Rudy Graveline smiled. The sun was very good for business. It baked and fried and pitted the facial flesh, and seeded the pores with vile microscopic cancers that would eventually sprout and require excision. Dr. Rudy Graveline was a plastic surgeon, and he dearly loved to see the sun.

He was in a fine mood, anyway, because it was January. In Florida, January is the heart of the winter tourist season and a bonanza time for cosmetic surgeons. Thousands of older men and women who flock down for the warm weather also use the occasion to improve their features. Tummy tucks, nose jobs, boob jobs, butt jobs, fat suctions, face lifts, you name it. And they always beg for an appointment in January, so that the scars will be healed by the time they go back North in the spring.

Dr. Rudy Graveline could not accommodate all the snowbirds, but he did his damnedest. All four surgical theaters at the Whispering Palms Spa were booked from dawn to dusk in January, February, and halfway into March. Most of the patients asked especially for Dr. Graveline, whose reputation greatly exceeded his talents. While Rudy usually farmed the cases out to the eight other plastic surgeons on staff, many patients got the impression that Dr. Graveline himself had performed their surgery. This is because Rudy would often come in and pat their wrinkled hands until they nodded off, blissfully, under the nitrous or I.V. Valium. At that point Rudy would turn them over to one of his younger and more competent protégés.

Dr. Graveline saved himself for the richest patients. The regulars got cut on every winter, and Rudy counted on their business. He reassured his surgical hypochondriacs that there was nothing abnormal about having a fifth, sixth, or seventh blepharoplasty in as many years. *Does it make you feel better about yourself?* Rudy would ask them. *Then it's worth it, isn't it? Of course it is.*

Such a patient was Madeleine Margaret Wilhoit, age sixtynine, of North Palm Beach. In the course of their acquaintance, there was scarcely a square inch of Madeleine's substantial physique that Dr. Rudy Graveline had not altered. Whatever he did and whatever he charged, Madeleine was always delighted. And she always came back the next year for more. Though Madeleine's face reminded Dr. Graveline in many ways of a camel, he was fond of her. She was the kind of steady patient that offshore trust funds are made of.

On January fourth, buoyed by the warm sunny drive to Whispering Palms, Rudy Graveline set about the task of repairing for the fifth, sixth, or seventh time (he couldn't remember exactly) the upper eyelids of Madeleine Margaret Wilhoit. Given the dromedarian texture of the woman's skin, the mission was doomed and Rudy knew it. Any cosmetic improvement would have to take place exclusively in Madeleine's imagination, but Rudy (knowing she would be ecstatic) pressed on.

Midway through the operation, the telephone on the wall let out two beeps. With a gowned elbow the operating-room nurse deftly punched the intercom box and told the caller that Dr. Graveline was in the middle of surgery and not available.

"It's fucking important, tell him," said a sullen male voice, which Rudy instantly recognized.

He asked the nurse and the anesthetist to leave the operating room for a few minutes. When they were gone, he said to the phone box: "Go ahead. This is me."

The phone call was made from a pay booth in Atlantic City, New Jersey, not that it would have mattered to Rudy. Jersey was all he knew, all he needed to know.

"You want the report?" the man asked.

"Of course."

"It went lousy."

Rudy sighed and stared down at the violet vectors he had inked around Madeleine's eyes. "How lousy?" the surgeon said to the phone box.

"The ultimate fucking lousy."

Rudy tried to imagine the face on the other end of the line, in New Jersey. In the old days he could guess a face by the voice on the phone. This particular voice sounded fat and lardy, with black curly eyebrows and mean dark eyes.

"So what now?" the doctor asked.

"Keep the other half of your money."

What a prince, Rudy thought.

"What if I want you to try again?"

"Fine by me."

"So what'll *that* cost?"

"Same," said Curly Eyebrows. "Deal's a deal."

"Can I think on it?"

"Sure. I'll call back tomorrow."

Rudy said, "It's just that I didn't count on any problems."

"The problem's not yours. Anyway, this shit happens."

"I understand," Dr. Graveline said.

The man in New Jersey hung up, and Madeleine Margaret Wilhoit started to squirm. It occurred to Rudy that maybe the old bag wasn't asleep after all, and that maybe she'd heard the whole conversation.

"Madeleine?" he whispered in her ear.

"Unngggh."

"Are you okay?"

"Fine, Papa," Madeleine drooled. "When do I get to ride in the sailboat?"

Rudy Graveline smiled, then buzzed for the nurse and anesthetist to come back and help him finish the job.

During his time at the State Attorney's Office, Mick Stranahan had helped put many people in jail. Most of them were out now, even the murderers, due to a federal court order requiring the state of Florida to seasonally purge its overcrowded prisons.

Stranahan accepted the fact that some of these ex-cons harbored bitterness against him, and that more than a few would be delighted to see him dead. For this reason, Stranahan was exceedingly cautious about visitors. He was not a paranoid person, but took a practical view of risk: When someone pulls a gun at your front door, there's really no point to asking what he wants. The answer is obvious, and so is the solution.

The gunman who came to the stilt house was the fifth person that Mick Stranahan had killed in his lifetime.

The first two were North Vietnamese Army regulars who were laying trip wire for land mines near the town of Dak Mat Lop in the Central Highlands. Stranahan surprised the young soldiers by using his sidearm instead of his M-16, and by not missing. It happened during the second week of May 1969, when Stranahan was barely twenty years old.

The third person he killed was a Miami holdup man named Thomas Henry Thomas, who made the mistake of sticking up a fried-chicken joint while Stranahan was standing in line for a nine-piece box of Extra Double Crispy. To supplement the paltry seventy-eight dollars he had grabbed from the cash register, Thomas Henry Thomas decided to confiscate the wallets and purses of each customer. It went rather smoothly until he came down the line to Mick Stranahan, who calmly took away Thomas Henry Thomas's .38-caliber Charter Arms revolver and shot him twice in the right temporal lobe. In appreciation, the fried-chicken franchise presented Stranahan with three months' worth of discount coupons and offered to put his likeness on every carton of Chicken Chunkettes sold during the month of December 1977. Being broke and savagely divorced, Stranahan took the coupons but declined the celebrity photo.

The shooting of Thomas Henry Thomas (his obvious character flaws aside) was deemed serious enough to dissuade both the Miami and metropolitan Dade County police from hiring Mick Stranahan as an officer. His virulent refusal to take any routine psychological tests also militated against him. However, the State Attorney's Office was in dire need of a streetwise investigator, and was delighted to hire a highly decorated war veteran, even at the relatively tender age of twenty-nine.

The fourth and most important person that Mick Stranahan killed was a crooked Dade County judge named Raleigh Goomer. Judge Goomer's specialty was shaking down defense lawyers in exchange for ridiculous bond reductions, which allowed dangerous felons to get out of jail and skip town. It was Stranahan who caught Judge Goomer at this game and arrested him taking a payoff at a strip joint near the Miami airport. On the trip to the jail, Judge Goomer apparently panicked, pulled a .22 somewhere out of his black nylon socks, and fired three shots at Mick Stranahan. Hit twice in the right thigh, Stranahan still managed to seize the gun, twist the barrel up the judge's right nostril, and fire.

A special prosecutor sent down from Tampa presented the case to the grand jury, and the grand jury agreed that the killing of Judge Raleigh Goomer was probably self-defense, though a point-blank nostril shot did seem extreme. Even though Stranahan was cleared, he obviously could no longer be employed by the State Attorney's Office. Pressure for his dismissal came most intensely from other crooked judges, several of whom stated that they were afraid to have Mr. Stranahan testifying in their courtrooms.

On June 7, 1988, Mick Stranahan resigned from the prosecutor's staff. The press release called it early retirement, and disclosed that Stranahan would be receiving full disability compensation as a result of injuries suffered in the Goomer shooting. Stranahan wasn't disabled at all, but his family connection with a notorious personal-injury lawyer was sufficient to terrify the county into paying him off. When Stranahan said he didn't want the money, the county promptly doubled its offer and threw in a motorized wheelchair. Stranahan gave up.

Not long afterwards, he moved out to Stiltsville and made friends with the fish.

* * *

A marine patrol boat pulled up to Mick Stranahan's place at half-past noon. Stranahan was on the top deck, dropping a line for mangrove snappers down below.

"Got a second?" asked the marine patrol officer, a sharp young Cuban named Luis Córdova. Stranahan liked him all right.

"Come on up," he said.

Stranahan reeled in his bait and put the fishing rod down. He dumped four dead snappers out of the bucket and gutted them one at a time, tossing their creamy innards in the water.

Córdova was talking about the body that had washed up on Cape Florida.

"Rangers found it yesterday evening," he said. "Lemon shark got the left foot."

"That happens," Stranahan said, skinning one of the fish filets.

"The M.E. says it was one hell of a stab wound."

"I'm gonna fry these up for sandwiches," Stranahan said. "You interested in lunch?"

Córdova shook his head. "No, Mick, there's some jerks poaching lobster down at Boca Chita so I gotta be on my way. Metro asked me to poke around out here, see if somebody saw anything. And since you're the only one out here . . ."

Stranahan glanced up from the fish-cleaning. "I don't remember much going on yesterday," he said. "Weather was piss-poor, that I know."

He tossed the fish skeletons, heads still attached, over the rail.

"Well, Metro's not all that excited," Córdova said.

"How come? Who's the stiff?"

"Name of Tony Traviola, wise guy. Jersey state police got a fat jacket on him. Tony the Eel, loan-collector type. Not a very nice man, from what I understand."

Stranahan said, "They think it's a mob hit?"

"I don't know what they think."

Stranahan carried the filets into the house and ran them under the tap. He was careful with the water, since the tanks were low. Córdova accepted a glass of iced tea and stood next to Stranahan in the kitchen, watching him roll the filets in egg yolk and bread crumbs. Normally Stranahan preferred to be left alone when he cooked, but he didn't want Luis Córdova to go just yet.

"They found the guy's boat, too," the marine patrolman went on. "It was a rental out of Haulover. White Seacraft."

Stranahan said he hadn't seen one of those lately.

"Few specks of blood was all they found," Córdova said. "Somebody cleaned it pretty good."

Stranahan laid the snapper filets in a half inch of oil in a frying pan. The stove didn't seem to be working, so he got on his knees and checked the pilot light—dead, as usual. He put a match to it and, before long, the fish started to sizzle.

Córdova sat down on one of the wicker barstools.

"So why don't they think it was the mob?" Stranahan asked.

"I didn't say they didn't, Mick."

Stranahan smiled and opened a bottle of beer.

Córdova shrugged. "They don't tell me every little thing."

"First of all, they wouldn't bring him all the way down to Florida to do it, would they, Luis? They got the exact same ocean up in Jersey. So Tony the Eel was already here on business."

"Makes sense," Córdova nodded.

"Second, why didn't they just shoot him? Knives are for kids, not pros."

Córdova took the bait. "Wasn't a knife," he said. "It was too big, the M.E. said. More like a javelin."

"That's not like the guineas."

"No," Córdova agreed.

Stranahan made three fish sandwiches and gave one to the marine patrolman, who had forgotten about going after the lobster poachers, if there ever were any.

"The other weird thing," he said through a mouthful of bread, "is the guy's face."

"What about it?"

"It didn't match the mug shots, not even close. They made him through fingerprints and dentals, but when they got the mugs back from the FBI it looked like a different guy altogether.

So Metro calls the Bureau and says you made a mistake, and they say the hell we did, that's Tony Traviola. They go back and forth for about two hours until somebody has the brains to call the M.E." Córdova stopped to gulp some iced tea; the fish was steaming in his cheeks.

Stranahan said, "And?"

"Plastic surgery."

"No shit?"

"At least five different operations, from his eyes to his chin. Tony the Eel, he was a regular Michael Jackson. His own mother wouldn't have known him."

Stranahan opened another beer and sat down. "Why would a bum like Traviola get his face remade?"

Córdova said, "Traviola did a nickel for extortion, got out of Rahway about two years ago. Not long afterwards a Purolator truck gets hit, but the robbers turn up dead three days later—without the loot. Classic mob rip. The feds put a warrant out for Traviola, hung his snapshot in every post office along the Eastern seaboard."

"Good reason to get the old shnoz bobbed," Stranahan said.

"That's what they figure." Córdova got up and rinsed his plate in the sink.

Stranahan was impressed. "You didn't get all this out of Metro, did you?"

Córdova laughed. "Hey, even the grouper troopers got a computer."

This was a good kid, Stranahan thought, a good cop. Maybe there was hope for the world after all.

"I see you went out and got the newspaper," the marine patrolman remarked. "What's the occasion, you got a pony running at Gulfstream?"

Hell, Stranahan thought, that was a stupid move. On the counter was the *Herald*, open to the page with the story about the dead floater. Miami being what it is, the floater story was only two paragraphs long, wedged under a tiny headline between a one-ton coke bust and a double homicide on the river. Maybe Luis Córdova wouldn't notice.

"You must've got up early to get to the marina and back," he said.

"Grocery run," Stranahan lied. "Besides, it was a nice morning for a boat ride. How was the fish?"

"Delicious, Mick." Córdova slapped him on the shoulder and said so long.

Stranahan walked out on the deck and watched Córdova untie his patrol boat, a gray Mako outboard with a blue police light mounted on the center console.

"If anything comes up, I'll give you a call, Luis."

"No sweat, it's Metro's party," the marine patrolman said. "Guy sounds like a dirtbag, anyway."

"Yeah," Stranahan said, "I feel sorry for that shark, the one that ate his foot."

Córdova chuckled. "Yeah, he'll be puking for a week."

Stranahan waved as the police boat pulled away. He was pleased to see Luis Córdova heading south toward Boca Chita, as Luis had said he would. He was also pleased that the young officer had not asked him about the blue marlin head on the living-room wall, about why the sword was mended together with fresh hurricane tape.

Timmy Gavigan had looked like death for most of his adult life. Now he had an excuse.

His coppery hair had fallen out in thickets, revealing patches of pale freckled scalp. His face, once round and florid, looked like somebody had let the air out.

From his hospital bed Timmy Gavigan said, "Mick, can you believe this fucking food?" He picked up a chunk of gray meat off the tray and held it up with two fingers, like an important piece of evidence. "'This is your government in action, Mick. Same fuckers that want to put lasers in outer space can't fry a Salisbury steak."

Stranahan said, "I'll go get us some take-out."

"Forget it."

"You're not hungry?"

"I got about five gallons of poison in my bloodstream, Mick.

Some new formula, experimental super juice. I told 'em to go ahead, why the hell not? If it kills just one of those goddamn cells, then I'm for it.''

Stranahan smiled and sat down.

"A man came out to see me the other day. He was using your name, Tim.''

Gavigan's laugh rattled. "Not too bright. Didn't he know we was friends?''

"Yeah, that's what I mean. He was telling people he was you, trying to find out where my house was.''

"But he didn't tell *you* he was me?''

"No,'' Stranahan said.

Gavigan's blue eyes seemed to light up. "Did he find your place?''

"Unfortunately.''

"And?''

Stranahan thought about how to handle it.

"Hey, Mick, I haven't got loads of time, okay? I mean, I could check out of this life any second now, so don't make me choke the goddamn story out of you.''

Stranahan said, "It turns out he was a bad guy from back East. Killer for the mob.''

"Was?'' Gavigan grinned. "So that's it. And here I thought you'd come by just to see how your old pal was hanging in.''

"That, too,'' Stranahan said.

"But first you want me to help you figure it out, how this pasta-breath tied us together.''

"I don't like the fact he was using your name.''

"How d'you think I feel?'' Gavigan handed Stranahan the dinner tray and told him to set it on the floor. He folded his papery hands on his lap, over the thin woolen blanket. "How would he know we was friends, Mick? You never call, never send candy. Missed my birthday three years in a row.''

"That's not true, Timmy. Two years ago I sent a strip-o-gram.''

"You sent that broad? I thought she just showed up lonely at the station and picked out the handsomest cop. Hell, Mick, I took her to Grand Bahama for a week, damn near married her.''

Stranahan was feeling better; Timmy knew something. Stranahan could tell from the eyes. It had come back to him.

Gavigan said, ''Mick, that girl had the finest nipples I ever saw. I meant to thank you.''

''Anytime.''

''Like Susan B. Anthony dollars, that's how big they were. Same shape, too. Octagonal.'' Gavigan winked. ''You remember the Barletta thing?''

''Sure.'' A missing-person's case that had turned into a possible kidnap. The victim was a twenty-two-year-old University of Miami student. Victoria Barletta: brown eyes, black hair, five eight, one hundred and thirty pounds. Disappeared on a rainy March afternoon.

Still unsolved.

''We had our names in the paper,'' Gavigan said. ''I still got the clipping.''

Stranahan remembered. There was a press conference. Victoria's parents offered a $10,000 reward. Timmy was there from Homicide, Stranahan from the State Attorney's Office. Both of them were quoted in the story, which ran on the front pages of the *Herald* and the *Miami News*.

Gavigan coughed in a way that startled Mick Stranahan. It sounded like Timmy's lungs had turned to custard.

''Hand me that cup,'' Gavigan said. ''Know what? That was the only time we made the papers together.''

''Timmy, we got in the papers all the time.''

''Yeah, but not together.'' He slurped down some ginger ale and pointed a pale bony finger at Stranahan. ''Not together, bucko, trust me. I save all the clippings for my scrapbook. Don't you?''

Stranahan said no.

''You *wouldn't.*'' Gavigan hacked out a laugh.

''So you think this Mafia guy got it out of the papers?''

''Not the Mafia guy,'' Gavigan said, ''but the guy who hired him. It's a good possibility.''

"The Barletta thing was four years ago, Timmy."

"Hey, I ain't the only one who keeps scrapbooks."

He yawned. "Think hard on this, Mick, it's probably important."

Stranahan stood up and said, "You get some rest, buddy."

"I'm glad you took care of that prick who was using my name."

"Hey, I don't know what you're talking about."

"Yeah, you do." Gavigan smiled. "Anyway, I'm glad you took care of him. He had no business lying like that, using my name."

Stranahan pulled the blanket up to his friend's neck.

"Good night, Timmy."

"Be careful, Mick," the old cop said. "Hey, and when I croak, you save the newspaper clipping, okay? Glue it on the last page of my scrapbook."

"It's a promise."

"Unless it don't make the papers."

"It'll make the damn papers," Stranahan said. "Buried back in the truss ads, where you belong."

Timmy Gavigan laughed so hard, he had to ring the nurse for oxygen.

3

Four days after the Mafia man came to murder him, Mick Stranahan got up early and took the skiff to the marina. There he jump-started his old Chrysler Imperial and drove down to Gables-by-the-Sea, a ritzy but misnomered neighborhood where his sister Kate lived with her degenerate lawyer husband and three teenaged daughters from two previous marriages (his, not hers). The subdivision was nowhere near the ocean but fronted a series of man-made canals that emptied into Biscayne Bay. No one complained about this marketing deception, as it was understood by buyers and sellers alike that Gables-by-the-Sea sounded much more toney than Gables-on-the-Canal. The price of the real estate duly reflected this exaggeration.

Stranahan's sister lived in a big split-level house with five bedrooms, a swimming pool, a sauna, and a putting green in the yard. Her lawyer husband even bought a thirty-foot sailboat to go with the dock out back, although he couldn't tell his fore from his aft. The sight of the sparkling white mast poking over the top of the big house made Stranahan shake his head as he pulled into the driveway—Kate's husband was positively born for South Florida.

When Stranahan's sister came to the door, she said, "Well, look who's here."

Stranahan kissed her and said, "Is Jocko home?"

"His name's not Jocko."

"He's a circus ape, Katie, that's a fact."

"His name's not Jocko, so lay off."

"Where's the blue Beemer?"

"We traded it."

Stranahan followed his sister into the living room, where one the girls was watching MTV and never looked up.

"Traded for what?"

"A Maserati," Kate said, adding: "The sedan, not the sporty one."

"Perfect," Stranahan said.

Kate made a sad face, and Stranahan gave her a little hug; it killed him to think his little sister had married a sleazeball ambulance chaser. Kipper Garth's face was on highway billboards up and down the Gold Coast—"If you've had an accident, somebody somewhere owes you money!!! Dial 555-TORT." Kipper Garth's firm was called The Friendly Solicitors, and it proved to be a marvelously lucrative racket. Kipper Garth culled through thousands of greedy complainants, dumping the losers and farming out the good cases to legitimate personal-injury lawyers, with whom he would split the fees fifty-fifty. In this way Kipper Garth made hundreds of thousands of dollars without ever setting his Bally loafers on a courtroom floor, which (given his general ignorance of the law) was a blessing for his clients.

"He's playing tennis," Kate said.

"I'm sorry for what I said," Stranahan told her. "You know how I feel."

"I wish you'd give him a chance, Mick. He's got some fine qualities."

If you like tapeworms, Stranahan thought. He could scarcely hear Kate over the Def Leppard video on the television, so he motioned her to the kitchen.

"I came by to pick up my shotgun," he said.

His sister's eyes went from green to gray, like when they were kids and she was onto him.

"I got a seagull problem out at the house," Stranahan said.

Kate said, "Oh? What happened to those plastic owls?"

"Didn't work," Stranahan said. "Gulls just crapped all over 'em."

They went into Kipper Garth's study, the square footage of which exceeded that of Stranahan's entire house. His shotgun, a Remington pump, was locked up with some fancy filigreed bird guns in a maplewood rack. Kate got the key from a drawer in her husband's desk. Stranahan took the Remington down and looked it over.

Kate noticed his expression and said, "Kip used it once or twice up North. For pheasant."

"He could've cleaned off the mud, at least."

"Sorry, Mick."

"The man is hopeless."

Kate touched his arm and said, "He'll be home in an hour. Would you stay?"

"I can't."

"As a favor, please. I'd like you to straighten out this lawsuit nonsense once and for all."

"Nothing to straighten out, Katie. The little monkey wants to sue me, fine. I understand."

The dispute stemmed from a pending disbarment proceeding against Kipper Garth, who stood accused of defrauding an insurance company. One of Kipper Garth's clients had claimed eighty percent disability after tripping over a rake on the seventeenth hole of a golf course. Three days after the suit had been filed, the man was dumb enough to enter the 26-kilometer Orange Bowl Marathon, dumb enough to finish third, and dumb enough to give interviews to several TV sportscasters.

It was such an egregious scam that even the Florida Bar couldn't ignore it, and with no encouragement Mick Stranahan had stepped forward to testify against his own brother-in-law. Some of what Stranahan had said was fact, and some was opinion; Kipper Garth liked none of it and had threatened to sue for defamation.

"It's getting ridiculous," Kate said. "It really is."

"Don't worry, he won't file," Stranahan said. "He couldn't find the goddamn courthouse with a map."

"Will you ever let up? This is my husband you're talking about."

Stranahan shrugged. "He's treating you well?"

"Like a princess. Now will you let up?"

"Sure, Katie."

At the door, she gave him a worried look and said, "Be careful with the gun, Mick."

"No problem," he said. "Tell Jocko I was here."

"Not hello? Or maybe Happy New Year?"

"No, just tell him I was here. That's all."

Stranahan got back to the marina and wrapped the shotgun in an oilcloth and slipped it lengthwise under the seats of the skiff. He headed south in a biting wind, taking spray over the port side and bouncing hard in the troughs. It took twenty-five minutes to reach the stilt house; Stranahan idled in on a low tide. As soon as he tied off, he heard voices up above and bare feet on the planks.

He unwrapped the shotgun and crept up the stairs.

Three naked women were stretched out sunning on the deck. One of them, a slender brunette, looked up and screamed. The others reflexively scrambled for their towels.

Stranahan said, "What are you doing on my house?"

"Are you about to shoot us?" the brunette asked.

"I doubt it."

"We didn't know this place was yours," said another woman, a bleached blonde with substantial breasts.

Stranahan muttered and opened the door, which was padlocked from the outside. This happened occasionally—sunbathers or drunken kids climbing up on the place when he wasn't home. He put the gun away, got a cold beer, and came back out. The women had wrapped themselves up and were gathering their lotions and Sony Walk-Mans.

"Where's your boat?" Stranahan asked.

"Way out there," the brunette said, pointing.

Stranahan squinted into the glare. It looked like a big red Formula, towing two skiers. "Boyfriends?" he said.

The bleached blonde nodded. "They said this place was deserted. Honest, we didn't know. They'll be back at four."

"It's all right, you can stay," he said. "It's a nice day for the water." Then he went back inside to clean the shotgun. Before long, the third woman, a true blonde, came in and asked for a glass of water.

"Take a beer," Stranahan said. "I'm saving the water."

She was back to her naked state. Stranahan tried to concentrate on the Remington.

"I'm a model," she announced, and starting talking. Name's Tina, nineteen years old, born in Detroit but moved down here when she was still a baby, likes to model but hates some of the creeps who take the pictures.

"My career is really taking off," she declared. She sat down on a bar stool, crossed her legs, folded her arms under her breasts.

"So what do you do?" she asked.

"I'm retired."

"You look awful young to be retired. You must be rich."

"A billionaire," Stranahan said, peering through the shiny blue barrel of the shotgun. "Maybe even a trillionaire. I'm not sure."

Tina smiled. "Right," she said. "You ever watch *Miami Vice*? I've been on there twice. Both times I played prostitutes, but at least I had some good lines."

"I don't have a television," Stranahan said. "Sorry I missed it."

"Know what else? I dated Don Johnson."

"I bet that looks good on the résumé."

"He's a really nice guy," Tina remarked, "not like they say."

Stranahan glanced up and said, "I think your tan's fading."

Tina the model looked down at herself, seemed to get tangled up in a thought. "Can I ask you a favor?"

A headache was taking seed in Mick Stranahan's brain. He actually felt it sprouting, like ragweed, out of the base of his skull.

Tina stood up and said: "I want you to look at my boobs."

"I have. They're lovely."

"Please, look again. Closer."

Stranahan screwed the Remington shut and laid it across his lap. He sat up straight and looked directly at Tina's breasts. They seemed exquisite in all respects.

She said, "Are they lined up okay?"

"Appear to be."

"Reason I ask, I had one of those operations. You know, a boob job. For the kind of modeling I do, it was necessary. I mean, I was about a thirty-two A, if you can imagine."

Stranahan just shook his head. He felt unable to contribute to the conversation.

"Anyway, I paid three grand for this boob job and it's really helped, workwise. Except the other day I did a *Penthouse* tryout and the photog makes some remark about my tits. Says I got a gravity problem on the left side."

Stranahan studied the two breasts and said, "Would that be your left or my left?"

"Mine."

"Well, he's nuts," Stranahan said. "They're both perfect."

"You're not just saying that?"

"I'll prove it," he said, thinking: I can't believe I'm doing this. He went to the pantry and rummaged noisily until he found what he was searching for, a carpenter's level.

Tiny eyed it and said, "I've seen one of those."

"Hold still," Stranahan said.

"What are you going to do?"

"Just watch the bubble."

The level was a galvanized steel ruler with a clear cylinder of amber liquid fixed in the middle. Inside the cylinder was a bubble of air, which moved in the liquid according to the angle being measured. If the surface was dead level, the bubble sat at the midway point of the cylinder.

Stranahan placed the tool across Tina's chest, so that each end rested lightly on a nipple.

"Now look down slowly, Tina."

" 'Kay."

"Where's the bubble?" he said.

"Smack dab in the center."

"Right," Stranahan said. "See—they're lined up perfectly."

He lifted the ruler off her chest and set in on the bar. Tina beamed and gave herself a little squeeze, which caused her to bounce in a truly wonderful way. Stranahan decided to clean the shotgun one more time.

"Well, back to the sunshine," Tina laughed, sprinting bare-assed out the door.

"Back to the sunshine," Mick Stranahan said, thinking that there was no sight in the world like a young lady completely at ease with herself, even if it cost three grand to get that way.

At four-thirty, the red Formula full of husky boyfriends roared up. Stranahan was reading on the sun deck, paying little attention to the naked women. The water was way too shallow for the ski boat, so the boyfriends idled it about fifty yards from the stilt house. After a manly huddle, one of them hopped to the bow and shouted at Mick Stranahan.

"Hey, what the hell are you doing?"

Stranahan glanced up from the newspaper and said nothing. Tina called out to the boat, "It's okay. He lives here."

"Put your clothes on!" hollered one of the guys in the boat, probably Tina's boyfriend.

Tina wiggled into a T-shirt. All the boyfriends appeared to be fairly agitated by Stranahan's presence among the nude women. Stranahan stood up and told the girls the water was too low for the ski boat.

"I'll run you out there in the skiff," he said.

"You better not, Richie's real upset," Tina said.

"Richie should have more faith in his fellow man."

The three young women gathered their towels and suntan oils and clambered awkwardly into Stranahan's skiff. He jacked the outboard up a couple notches, so the prop wouldn't hit bottom, and steered out toward the red Formula in the channel. Once alongside the ski boat, he helped the girls climb up one at a time. Tina even gave him a peck on the cheek as she left.

The boyfriends were every bit as dumb and full of themselves as Stranahan figured. Each one wore a gold chain on his chest, which said it all.

"What was that about?" snarled the boyfriend called Richie, after witnessing Tina's good-bye peck.

"Nothing," Tina said. "He's an all-right guy."

Stranahan had already let go, and the skiff had drifted a few yards beyond the ski boat, when Richie slapped Tina for being such a slut. Then he pointed out at Stranahan and yelled something extremely rude.

The boyfriends were quite surprised to see the aluminum skiff coming back at them, fast. They were equally amazed at the nimbleness with which the big stranger hopped onto the bow of their boat.

Richie took an impressive roundhouse swing at the guy, but the next thing the other boyfriends knew, Richie was flat on his back with the ski rope tied around both feet. Suddenly he was in the water, and the boat was moving, and Richie was dragging in the salt spray and yowling at the top of his lungs. The other boyfriends tried to seize the throttle, but the stranger knocked them down quickly and with a minimum of effort.

After about three-quarters of a mile, Tina and the other women asked Stranahan to please stop the speedboat, and he did. He grabbed the ski rope and hauled Richie back in, and they all watched him vomit up sea water for ten minutes straight.

"You're a stupid young man," Stranahan counseled. "Don't ever come out here again."

Then Stranahan got in the skiff and went back to the stilt house, and the Formula sped away. Stranahan fixed himself a drink and stretched out on the sun deck. He was troubled by what was happening to the bay, when boatloads of idiots could spoil the whole afternoon. It was becoming a regular annoyance, and Stranahan could foresee a time when he might have to move away.

By late afternoon most of the other boats had cleared out of Stiltsville, except for a cabin cruiser that anchored on the south side of the radio towers in about four feet of water. A very odd location, Stranahan thought. On this boat he counted three people; one seemed to be pointing something big and black in the direction of Stranahan's house.

Stranahan went inside and came back with the shotgun, utterly useless at five hundred yards, and the binoculars, which were not. Quickly he got the cabin cruiser into focus and determined that what was being aimed at him was not a big gun, but a portable television camera.

The people in the cabin cruiser were taking his picture.

This was the capper. First the Mafia hit man, then the nude sunbathers and their troglodyte boyfriends, now a bloody TV crew. Stranahan turned his back to the cabin cruiser and kicked off his trousers. This would give them something to think about: moon over Miami. He was in such sour spirits that he didn't even peek over his shoulder to see their reaction when he bent over.

Watching the sun slide low, Mick Stranahan perceived the

syncopation of these events as providential; things had changed on the water, all was no longer calm. The emotion that accompanied this realization was not fear, or even anxiety, but disappointment. All these days the tranquility of the bay, its bright and relentless beauty, had lulled him into thinking the world was not so rotten after all.

The minicam on the cabin cruiser reminded him otherwise. Mick Stranahan had no idea what the bastards wanted, but he was sorely tempted to hop in the skiff and go find out. In the end, he simply finished his gin and tonic and went back inside the stilt house. At dusk, when the light was gone, the boat pulled anchor and motored away.

4

After quitting the State Attorney's Office, Stranahan had kept his gold investigator's badge to remind people that he used to work there, in case he needed to get back inside. Like now.

A young assistant state attorney, whose name was Dreeson, took Stranahan to an interview room and handed him the Barletta file, which must have weighed four pounds. In an officious voice, the young prosecutor said:

"You can sit here and make notes, Mr. Stranahan. But it's still an open case, so don't take anything out."

"You mean I can't blow my nose on the affidavits?"

Dreeson made a face and shut the door, hard.

Stranahan opened the jacket, and the first thing to fall out was a photograph of Victoria Barletta. Class picture, clipped from the 1985 University of Miami student yearbook. Long dark hair, brushed to a shine; big dark eyes; a long sharp nose, probably her old man's; gorgeous Italian smile, warm and laughing and honest.

Stranahan set the picture aside. He had never met the girl, never would.

He skimmed the statements taken so long ago by himself and Timmy Gavigan: the parents, the boyfriend, the sorority sisters. The details of the case came back to him quickly in a cold flood.

On March 12, 1986, Victoria Barletta had gotten up early, jogged three miles around the campus, showered, attended a 9 A.M. class in advanced public relations, met her boyfriend at a breakfast shop near Mark Light Field, then bicycled to an 11 A.M. seminar on the history of television news. Afterwards, Vicky went back to the Alpha Chi Omega house, changed into jeans, sneakers, and a sweatshirt, and asked a sorority sister to give her a lift to a doctor's appointment in South Miami, only three miles from the university.

The appointment was scheduled for 1:30 P.M. at a medical building called the Durkos Center. As Vicky got out of the car, she instructed her friend to come back at about 5 P.M. and pick her up. Then she went inside and got a nose job and was never seen again.

According to a doctor and a nurse at the clinic, Vicky Barletta left the office at about 4:50 P.M. to wait on the bus bench out front for her ride back to campus. Her face was splotched, her eyes swollen to slits, and her nose heavily bandaged—not exactly a tempting sight for your average trolling rapist, Timmy Gavigan had pointed out.

Still, they both knew better than to rule it out. One minute the girl was on the bench, the next she was gone.

Three county buses had stopped there between 4:50 and 5:14 P.M., when Vicky's friend finally arrived at the clinic. None of the bus drivers remembered seeing a woman with a busted-up face get on board.

So the cops were left to assume that somebody snatched Victoria Barletta off the bus bench moments after she emerged from the Durkos Center.

The case was treated like a kidnapping, though Gavigan and

Stranahan suspected otherwise. The Barlettas had no money and no access to any; Vicky's father was half-owner of a car wash in Evanston, Illinois. Aside from a couple of cranks, there were no ransom calls made to the family, or to the police. The girl was just plain gone, and undoubtedly dead.

Rereading the file four years later, Mick Stranahan began to feel frustrated all over again. It was the damnedest thing: Vicky had told no one—not her parents, her boyfriend, nobody—about the cosmetic surgery; apparently it was meant to be a surprise.

Stranahan and Timmy Gavigan had spent a total of fifteen hours interviewing Vicky's boyfriend and wound up believing him. The kid had cried pathetically; he used to tease Vicky about her shnoz. "My little anteater," he used to call her. The boyfriend had been shattered by what happened, and blamed himself: His birthday was March twentieth. Obviously, he sobbed, the new nose was Vicky's present to him.

From a homicide investigator's point of view, the secrecy with which Victoria Barletta planned her doctor's visit meant something else: It limited the suspects to somebody who just happened to be passing by, a random psychopath.

A killer who was never caught.

A victim who was never found.

That was how Mick Stranahan remembered it. He scribbled a few names and numbers on a pad, stuffed everything into the file, then carried it back to a pock-faced clerk.

"Tell me something," Stranahan said, "how'd you happen to have this one downtown?"

The clerk said, "What do you mean?"

"I mean, this place didn't used to be so efficient. Used to take two weeks to dig out an old case like this."

"You just got lucky," the clerk said. "We pulled the file from the warehouse a week ago."

"This file here?" Stranahan tapped the green folder. "Same one?"

"Mr. Eckert wanted to see it."

Gerry Eckert was the State Attorney. He hadn't personally

gone to court in at least sixteen years, so Stranahan doubted if he even remembered how to read a file.

"So how's old Gerry doing?"

"Just dandy," said the clerk, as if Eckert were his closest, dearest pal in the world. "He's doing real good."

"Don't tell me he's finally gonna pop somebody in this case."

"I don't think so, Mr. Stranahan. He just wanted to refresh his memory before he went on TV. The Reynaldo Flemm show."

Stranahan whistled. Reynaldo Flemm was a television journalist who specialized in sensational crime cases. He was nationally famous for getting beaten up on camera, usually by the very hoodlums he was trying to interview. No matter what kind of elaborate disguise Reynaldo Flemm would devise, he was always too vain to cover his face. Naturally the crooks would recognize him instantly and bash the living shit out of him. For pure action footage, it was hard to beat; Reynaldo Flemm's specials were among the highest-rated programs on television.

"So Gerry's hit the big time," Stranahan said.

"Yep," the clerk said.

"What did he say about this case?"

"Mr. Eckert?"

"Yeah, what he did he tell this TV guy?"

The clerk said, "Well, I wasn't there for the taping. But from what I heard, Mr. Eckert said the whole thing is still a mystery."

"Well, that's true enough."

"And Mr. Eckert told Mr. Flemm that he wouldn't be one bit surprised if someday it turns out that Victoria Barletta ran away. Just took one look at her face and ran away. Otherwise, why haven't they found a body?"

Stranahan thought: Eckert hasn't changed a bit, still dumb as a bull gator.

"I can't wait to see the show," Stranahan remarked.

"It's scheduled to be on March twelfth at nine P.M." The clerk held up a piece of paper. "We got a memo from Mr. Eckert today."

* * *

The man from New Jersey did not call Dr. Rudy Graveline again for four days. Then, on the afternoon of January eighth, Rudy got a message on his beeper. The beeper went off at a bad moment, when Rudy happened to be screwing the young wife of a Miami Dolphins wide receiver. The woman had come to Whispering Palms for a simple consult—a tiny pink scar along her jawline, could it be fixed?—and the next thing she knew, the doctor had her talking about all kinds of personal things, including how lonely it got at home during the football season when Jake's mind was on the game and nothing else. Well, the next thing she knew, the doctor was taking her to lunch in his black Jaguar sedan with the great Dolby sound system, and the football player's wife found herself thinking how the rich smell of leather upholstery made her hot, really hot, and then—as if he could read her mind—the doctor suddenly pulled off the Julia Tuttle Causeway, parked the Jag in some pepper trees, and started to gnaw her panties off. He even made cute little squirrel noises as he nuzzled between her legs.

Before long the doctor was merrily pounding away while the football player's wife gazed up at him through the spokes of the walnut steering wheel, under which her head had become uncomfortably wedged.

When the beeper went off on Dr. Graveline's belt, he scarcely missed a beat. He glanced down at the phone number (glowing in bright green numerals) and snatched the car phone from its cradle in the glove box. With one hand he managed to dial the long-distance number even as he finished with the football player's wife, who by this time was silently counting down, hoping he'd hurry it up. She'd had about all she could take of the smell of new leather.

Dr. Graveline pulled away just as the phone started ringing somewhere in New Jersey.

The man answered on the fourth ring. "Yeah, what?"

"It's me. Rudy."

"You been jogging or what?"

"Something like that."

"Sounds like you're gonna have a fuckin' heart attack."

Dr. Graveline said: "Give me a second to catch my breath."

The football player's wife was squirming back into her slacks. The look on her face suggested disappointment at her partner's performance, but Rudy Graveline did not notice.

"About the deal," he said. "I don't think so."

Curly Eyebrows in New Jersey said: "Your problem musta gone away."

"Not really."

"Then what?"

"I'm going to get somebody local."

The man in New Jersey started to laugh. He laughed and laughed until he began to wheeze.

"Doc, this is a big mistake. Local is no good."

"I've got a guy in mind," Dr. Graveline said.

"A Cuban, right? Crazy fuckin' Cuban, I knew it."

"No, he's not a Cuban."

"One of my people?"

"No," Rudy said. "He's by himself."

Again Curly Eyebrows laughed. "Nobody is by himself, Doc. Nobody in this business."

"This one is different," Rudy said. Different wasn't the word for it. "Anyway, I just wanted to let you know, so you wouldn't send anybody else."

"Suit yourself."

"And I'm sorry about the other fellow."

"Don't bring up that shit, hear? You're on one of those cellular phones, I can tell. I hate them things, Doc, they ain't safe. They give off all kinds of fucked-up microwaves, anybody can listen in."

Dr. Graveline said, "I don't think so."

"Yeah, well, I read where people can listen on their blenders and hair dryers and shit. Pick up everything you say."

The football player's wife was brushing on fresh makeup, using the vanity mirror on the back of the sun visor.

The man in Jersey said: "Your luck, some broad's pickin' us up on her electric dildo. Every word."

"Talk to you later," Rudy said.

"One piece of advice," said Curly Eyebrows. "This guy you lined up for the job, don't tell him your life story. I mean it, Doc. Give him the name, the address, the dough, and that's it."

"Oh, I can trust him," Dr. Graveline said.

"Like hell," laughed the man in New Jersey, and hung up.

The football player's wife flipped the sun visor up, closed her compact, and said, "Business?"

"Yes, I dabble in real estate." Rudy zipped up his pants. "I've decided to go with a Miami broker."

The woman shrugged. She noticed her pink bikini panties on the floormat, and quickly put them in her purse. They were ruined; the doctor had chewed a hole in them.

"Can I drive your car back to the office?" she asked.

"No," said Rudy Graveline. He got out and walked around to the driver's side. The football player's wife slid across the seat, and Rudy got in.

"I almost forgot," the woman said, fingering the place on her jaw, "about my scar."

"A cinch," the doctor said. "We can do it under local anesthetic, make it smooth as silk."

The football player's wife smiled. "Really?"

"Oh sure, it's easy," Rudy said, steering the Jaguar back on the highway. "But I was wondering about something else. . . ."

"Yes?"

"You won't mind some friendly professional advice?"

"Of course not." The woman's voice held an edge of concern.

"Well, I couldn't help but notice," Dr. Graveline said, "when we were making love . . ."

"Yes?"

Without taking his eyes off the road, he reached down and patted her hip. "You could use a little suction around the saddlebags."

The football player's wife turned away and blinked.

"Please don't be embarrassed," the doctor said. "This is my specialty, after all. Believe me, darling, I've got an eye for perfection, and you're only an inch or two away."

She took a little breath and said, "Around the thighs?"

"That's all."

"How much would it cost?" she asked with a trace of a sniffle.

Rudy Graveline smiled warmly and passed her a mono-grammed handkerchief. "Less than you think," he said.

The cabin cruiser with the camera crew came back again, anchored in the same place. Stranahan sighed and spit hard into the tide. He was in no mood for this.

He was standing on the dock with a spinning rod in his hands, catching pinfish from around the pilings of the stilt house. Suspended motionless in the gin-clear water below was a dark blue log, or so it would have appeared to the average tourist. The log measured about five feet long and, when properly motivated, could streak through the water at about sixty knots to make a kill. Teeth were the trademark of the Great Barracuda, and the monster specimen that Mick Stranahan called Liza had once left thirteen needle-sharp incisors in a large plastic mullet that some moron had trolled through the Biscayne Channel. Since that episode the barracuda had more or less camped beneath Stranahan's place. Every afternoon he went out and caught for its supper a few dollar-sized pinfish, which he tossed off the dock, and which the barracuda devoured in lightning flashes that churned the water and sent the mangrove snappers diving for cover. Liza's teeth had long since grown back.

Because of his preoccupation with the camera boat, Mick Stranahan allowed the last pinfish to stay on the line longer than he should have. It tugged back and forth, sparkling just below the surface until the barracuda ran out of patience. Before Stranahan could react, the big fish rocketed from under the stilt house and severed the majority of the pinfish as cleanly as a scalpel; a quivering pair of fish lips was all that remained on Stranahan's hook.

"Nice shot," he mumbled and stored the rod away.

He climbed into the skiff and motored off the flat, toward the cabin cruiser. The photographer immediately put down the video camera; Stranahan could see him conferring with the rest of the crew. There was a brief and clumsy attempt to raise the anchor, followed by the sound of the boat's engine whining impotently in the way that cold outboards do. Finally the crew gave up and just waited for the big man in the skiff, who by now was within hailing distance.

A stocky man with a lacquered helmet of black hair and a stiff bottlebrush mustache stood on the transom of the boat and shouted, "Ahoy there!"

Stranahan cut the motor and let the skiff coast up to the cabin cruiser. He tied off on a deck cleat, stood up, and said, "Did I hear you right? Did you actually say *ahoy*?"

The man with the mustache nodded uneasily.

"Where did you learn that, watching pirate movies? Jesus Christ, I can't believe you said that. *Ahoy there!* Give me a break." Stranahan was really aggravated. He jumped into the bigger boat and said, "Which one of you assholes is Reynaldo Flemm? Let me guess; it's Captain Blood here."

The stocky man with the mustache puffed out his chest and said, "Watch it, pal!"—which took a certain amount of courage, since Mick Stranahan was holding a stainless-steel tarpon gaff in his right hand. Flemm's crew—an overweight cameraman and an athletic young woman in blue jeans—kept one eye on their precious equipment and the other on the stranger with the steel hook.

Stranahan said, "Why have you been taking my picture?"

"For a story," Flemm said. "For television."

"What's the story?"

"I'm not at liberty to say."

Stranahan frowned. "What's it got to do with Vicky Barletta?"

Reynaldo Flemm shook his head. "In due time, Mr. Stranahan. When we're ready to do the interview."

Stranahan said, "I'm ready to do the interview now."

Flemm smiled in a superior way. "Sorry."

Stranahan slipped the tarpon gaff between Reynaldo Flemm's legs and gave a little jerk. The tip of the blade not only poked through Reynaldo Flemm's Banana Republic trousers, but also through his thirty-dollar bikini underpants (flamenco red), which he had purchased at a boutique in Coconut Grove. The cold point of the gaff came to rest on Reynaldo Flemm's scrotum, and at this frightful instant the air rushed from his intestinal tract with a sharp noise that seemed to punctuate Mick Stranahan's request.

"The interview," he said again to Flemm, who nodded energetically.

But words escaped the television celebrity. Try as he might, Flemm could only burble in clipped phrases. Fear, and the absence of cue cards, had robbed him of cogent conversation.

The young woman in blue jeans stepped forward from the cabin of the boat and said, "Please, Mr. Stranahan, we didn't mean to intrude."

"Of course you did."

"My name is Christina Marks. I'm the producer of this segment."

"Segment of what?" Stranahan asked.

"Of the Reynaldo Flemm show. *In Your Face.* You must have seen it."

"Never."

For Reynaldo, Stranahan knew, this was worse than a gaff in the balls.

"Come on," Christina Marks said.

"Honest," Stranahan said. "You see a TV dish over on my house?"

"Well, no."

"There you go. Now, what's this all about? And hurry it up, your man here looks like his legs are cramping."

Indeed, Reynaldo Flemm was shaking on his tiptoes. Stranahan eased the gaff down just a notch or two.

Christina Marks said: "Do you know a nurse named Maggie Gonzalez?"

"Nope," Stranahan said.

"Are you sure?"

"Give me a hint."

"She worked at the Durkos Medical Center."

"Okay, now I remember." He had taken her statement the day after Victoria Barletta had vanished. Timmy Gavigan had done the doctor, while Stranahan had taken the nurse. He had scanned the affidavits in the State Attorney's file that morning.

"You sure about the last name?" Stranahan asked.

"Sorry—Gonzalez is her married name. Back then it was Orestes."

"So let's have the rest."

"About a month ago, in New York, she came to us."

"To me," croaked Reynaldo Flemm.

"Shut up," said Stranahan.

Christina Marks went on: "She said she had some important information about the Barletta case. She indicated she was willing to talk on camera."

"To me," Flemm said, before Stranahan tweaked him once more with the tarpon gaff.

"But first," Christina Marks said, "she said she had to speak to you, Mr. Stranahan."

"About what?"

"All she said was that she needed to talk to you first, because you could do something about it. And don't ask me about what, because I don't know. We gave her six hundred bucks, put her on a plane to Florida, and never saw her again. She was supposed to be back two weeks ago last Monday." Christina Marks put her hands in her pockets. "That's all there is. We came down here to look for Maggie Gonzalez, and you're the best lead we had."

Stranahan removed the gaff from Reynaldo Flemm's crotch and tossed it into the bow of his skiff. Almost instantly, Flemm leapt from the stern and bolted for the cabin. "Get tape of that fucker," he cried at the cameraman, "so we can prosecute his fat ass!"

"Ray, knock it off," said Christina Marks.

Stranahan liked the way she talked down to the big star. "Tell him," he said, "that if he points that goddamn camera at me again, he'll be auditioning for the Elephant Man on Broadway. That's how seriously I'll mess up his face.''

"Ray," she said, "did you hear that?"

"Roll tape! Roll tape!" Flemm was all over the cameraman.

Wearily, Stranahan got back into his skiff and said, "Miss Marks, the interview is over."

Now it was her turn to be angry. She hopped up on the transom, tennis shoes squeaking on the teak. "Wait a minute, that's it?"

Stranahan looked up from his little boat. "I haven't seen Maggie Gonzalez since the day after the Barletta girl disappeared. That's the truth. I don't know whether she took your money and went south or what, but I haven't heard from her."

"He's lying," sneered Reynaldo Flemm, and he stormed into the cabin to sulk. A gust of wind had made a comical nest of his hair.

Stranahan hand-cranked the outboard and slipped it into gear.

"I'm at the Sonesta," Christina Marks said to him, "if Maggie Gonzalez should call."

Not likely, Stranahan thought. Not very likely at all.

"How the hell did you find me, anyway?" he called out to the young TV producer.

"Your ex-wife," Christina Marks called back from the cabin cruiser.

"Which one?"

"Number four."

That would be Chloe, Stranahan thought. Naturally.

"How much did it cost you?" he shouted.

Sheepishly, Christina Marks held up five fingers.

"You got off light," Mick Stranahan said, and turned the skiff homeward.

5

Christina Marks was in bed, reading an old *New Yorker*, when somebody rapped on the door of the hotel room. She was hoping it might be Mick Stranahan, but it wasn't.

"Hello, Ray."

As Reynaldo Flemm breezed in, he patted her on the rump.

"Cute," Christina said, closing the door. "I was getting ready to turn in."

"I brought some wine."

"No, thanks."

Reynaldo Flemm turned on the television and made himself at home. He was wearing another pair of khaki Banana Republic trousers and a baggy denim shirt. He smelled like a bucket of Brut. In a single motion he scissored his legs and propped his white high-top Air Jordans on the coffee table.

Christina Marks tightened the sash on her bathrobe and sat down at the other end of the sofa. "I'm tired, Ray," she said.

He acted like he didn't hear it. "This Stranahan guy, he's the key to it," Flemm said. "I think we should follow him tomorrow."

"Oh, please."

"Rent a van. A van with smoked window panels. We set the camera on a tripod in back. I'll be driving, so Willie gets the angle over my . . . let's see, it'd be my right shoulder. Great shot, through the windshield as we follow this big prick—"

"Willie gets carsick," Christina Marks said.

Reynaldo Flemm cackled scornfully.

"It's a lousy idea," Christina said. She wanted him to go away, now.

"What, you trust that Stranahan?"

"No," she said, but in a way she did trust him. At least more than she trusted Maggie Gonzalez; there was something squirrely about the woman's sudden need to fly to Miami. Why had she said she wanted to see Stranahan? Where had she really gone?

Reynaldo Flemm wasn't remotely concerned about Maggie's motives—good video was good video—but Christina Marks wanted to know more about the woman. She had better things to do than sit in a steaming van, tailing a guy who, if he caught them, would probably destroy every piece of electronics in their possession.

"So, what other leads we got?" Reynaldo Flemm demanded. "Tell me that."

"Maggie's probably got family here," Christina said, "and friends."

"Dull, dull, dull."

"Hard work is dull sometimes," Christina said sharply, "But how would you know?"

Flemm sat up straight and flared his upper lip like a chihuahua. "You can't talk to me like that! You just remember who's the star."

"And you just remember who writes all your lines. And who does all your dull, dull research. Remember who tells you what questions to ask. And who edits these pieces so you don't come off looking like a pompous airhead." Except that's exactly how Reynaldo came off, most of the time. There was no way around it, no postproduction wizardry that could disguise the man's true personality on tape.

Reynaldo Flemm shrugged. His attention had been stolen by something on the television: Mike Wallace of CBS was a guest on the Letterman show. Flemm punched up the volume and inched to the edge of the sofa.

"You know how old that geezer is?" he said, pointing at Wallace. "I'm half his age."

Christina Marks held her tongue.

Reynaldo said, "I bet *his* producer sleeps with him anytime he wants." He glanced sideways at Christina.

She got up, went to the door, and held it open. "Go back to your room, Ray."

"Aw, come on, I was kidding."

"No, you weren't."

"All right, I wasn't. Come on, Chris, close the door. Let's open the wine."

"Good night, Ray."

He got up and turned off the TV. He was sulking.

"I'm sorry," he said.

"You sure are."

Christina Marks held all the cards. Reynaldo Flemm needed her far worse than she needed him. Not only was she very talented, but she knew things about Reynaldo Flemm that he did not wish the whole world of television to know. About the time she caught him beating himself up, for example. It happened at a Hyatt House in Atlanta. Flemm was supposed to be out interviewing street-gang members, but Christina found him in the bathroom of his hotel room, thwacking himself in the cheek with a sock full of parking tokens. Reynaldo's idea was to give himself a nasty shiner, then go on camera and breathlessly report that an infamous gang leader named Rapper Otis had assaulted him.

Reynaldo Flemm had begged Christina Marks not to tell the executive producers about the sock incident, and she hadn't; the weeping is what got to her. She couldn't bear it.

For keeping this and other weird secrets, Christina felt secure in her job, certainly secure enough to tell Reynaldo Flemm to go pound salt every time he put the make on her.

On the way out the door, he said, "I still say we get up early and follow this Stranahan guy."

"And I still say no."

"But, Chris, he *knows* something."

"Yeah, Ray, he knows how to hurt people."

Christina couldn't be sure, but she thought she saw a hungry spark in the eyes of Reynaldo Flemm.

The next morning Stranahan left the skiff at the marina, got the Chrysler and drove back across the Rickenbacker Causeway to the mainland. Next to him on the front seat was his yellow notepad, open to the page where he had jotted the names and numbers from the Barletta file. The first place he went was the Durkos Medical Center, except it wasn't there anymore. The building was now occupied entirely by dentists: nine of them, according to Stranahan's count from the office directory. He went looking for the building manager.

Every door and hallway reverberated with the nerve-stabbing whine of high-speed dental drills; soon Stranahan's molars started to throb, and he began to feel claustrophobic. He enlisted a friendly janitor to lead him to the superintendent, a mammoth olive-colored woman who introduced herself as Marlee Jones.

Stranahan handed Marlee Jones a card and told her what he wanted. She glanced at the card and shrugged. "I don't have to tell you nothing," she said, displaying the kind of public-spirited cooperation that Stranahan had come to appreciate among the Miami citizenry.

"No, you don't have to tell me nothing," he said to Marlee, "but I can make it possible for a county code inspector to brighten your morning tomorrow, and the day after that, and every single day until you die of old age." Stranahan picked up a broom and stabbed the wooden handle into the foam-tile ceiling. "Looks like pure asbestos to me," he said. "Sure hate for the feds to find out."

Marlee Jones scowled, exhibiting an impressive array of gold teeth: bribes, no doubt, from her tenants. She shuffled to a metal desk and opened a bottom drawer and got out a black ledger. "All right, smartass, what was that name?"

"Durkos." Stranahan spelled it. "A medical group. They were here as of March twelfth, four years ago."

"Well, as of April first, four years ago, they was gone."

Marlee started to close the ledger, but Stranahan put his hand on the page.

"May I look?"

"It's just numbers, mister."

"Aw, let me give it a whirl." Stranahan took the ledger from Marlee Jones and ran down the columns with his forefinger. The Durkos Medical Trust, Inc., had been sole tenant of the building for two years, but had vacated within weeks after Victoria Barletta's disappearance. The ledger showed that the company had paid its lease and security deposits through May. Stranahan thought it was peculiar that, after moving out, the medical group never got a refund.

"Maybe they didn't ask," Marlee Jones said.

"Doctors are the cheapest human beings alive," Stranahan said. "For fifteen grand they don't just ask, they hire lawyers."

Again Marlee Jones shrugged. "Some people be in a big damn hurry."

"What do you remember about it?"

"Who says I was here?"

"This handwriting in the ledger book—it's the same as on these receipts." Stranahan tapped a finger on a pile of rental coupons. Marlee Jones appeared to be having a spell of high blood pressure.

Stranahan asked again: "So what do you remember?"

With a groan Marlee Jones heaved her bottom into the chair behind the desk. She said, "One night they cleared out. Must've backed up a trailer truck, who knows. I came in, the place was empty, except for a bunch of cheapo paintings on the walls. Cats with big eyes, that sorta shit."

"Were they all surgeons?"

"Seemed like it. But they wasn't partners."

"Durkos the main man?"

"Was no Durkos that I heard of. Big man was a Doctor Graveyard, something like that. The other four guys worked for him. How come I know this is, the day after all the stuff is gone, a couple of the other doctors showed up dressed for work. They couldn't believe their office was emptied."

Graveline was the name of the surgeon who had operated on Vicky Barletta. There was no point to correcting Marlee Jones on the name. Stranahan said, "This Dr. Graveyard, he didn't even tell the other doctors about the move?"

"This is Miami, lots of people in a big-time hurry."

"Yeah, but not many pay in advance."

Marlee Jones finally laughed. "You right about that."

"Did anybody leave a forwarding address?"

"Nope."

Stranahan handed Marlee Jones the ledger book.

"You be through with me?" she asked.

"Yes, ma'am."

"For good?"

"Most likely."

"Then can I ask who is it you're workin' for?"

"Myself," said Mick Stranahan.

Since the day that the Durkos Medical Center had ceased to exist, the life of Nurse Maggie Orestes had gotten complicated. She had gone to work in the emergency room at Jackson Hospital, where one night she had met a man named Ricky Gonzalez. The reason for Ricky Gonzalez's visit to the emergency room was that he had accidentally been run over by a turbocharged Ferrari during the annual running of the Miami Grand Prix. Ricky was a race-car promoter, and he had been posing for pictures with Lorenzo Lamas in pit row, not paying close attention when the Ferrari had roared in and run over both his feet. Ricky broke a total of fourteen bones, while Lorenzo Lamas escaped without a scratch.

Nurse Maggie Orestes attended to Ricky Gonzalez in the emergency room before they put him under for surgery. He was young, dashing, full of promises—and so cheerful, considering what had happened.

A month later they were married at a Catholic church in Hialeah. Ricky persuaded Maggie to quit nursing and be a full-time hostess for the many important social functions that race-car promoters must necessarily conduct. Maggie had hoped she would come to enjoy car racing and the people involved in it, but she didn't. It was noisy and stupid and boring, and the people were worse. Maggie and Ricky had some fierce arguments, and she was on the verge of walking out of the marriage when the second pit-row accident happened.

This time it was a Porsche, and Ricky wasn't so lucky. After the service they cremated him in his complimentary silver Purolator racing jacket, which turned out to be fireproof, so they had to cremate that portion twice. Lorenzo Lamas sent a wreath all the way from Malibu, California. At the wake Ricky's lawyer came up to Maggie Gonzalez and told her the bad news: First, her husband had no life insurance; second, he had emptied their joint bank accounts to pay for his cocaine habit. Maggie had known nothing about the drug problem, but in retrospect it explained her late husband's irrepressible high spirits and also his lack of caution around the race track.

A widowhood of destitution did not appeal to Maggie Gonzalez. She went back to being a nurse with a plan to nail herself a rich doctor or at least his money. In eighteen months she had been through three of them, all disasters—a married pediatrician, a divorced radiologist, and a urologist who wore women's underwear and who wound up giving Maggie a stubborn venereal disease. When she dumped the urologist, he got her fired from the hospital and filed a phony complaint with the state nursing board.

All this left Maggie Gonzalez with a molten hatred of men and a mind for vengeance.

Money is what pushed her to the brink. With the mortgage payment on her duplex coming due, and only eighty-eight bucks in the checking account, Maggie decided to go ahead and do it. Part of the motive was financial desperation, true, but there was also a delicious hint of excitement—payback, to the sonofabitch who'd started it all.

First Maggie used her Visa card to buy a plane ticket to New York, where she caught a cab to the midtown offices of Reynaldo Flemm, the famous television journalist. There she told producer Christina Marks the story of Victoria Barletta, and cut a deal.

Five thousand dollars to repeat it on camera—that's as high as Reynaldo's people would go. Maggie Gonzalez was disappointed; it was, after all, one hell of a story.

That night Christina Marks got Maggie a room at the Goreham Hotel, and she lay there watching Robin Leach on TV and worrying about the risks she was taking. She remembered the State Attorney's investigator who had questioned her nearly four years ago, and how she had lied to him. God, what was she thinking of now? Flemm's people would fly straight to Miami and interview the investigator—Stranahan was his name—and he'd tell them she'd never said a word about all this when it happened. Her credibility would be shot, and so would the five grand. Out the window.

Maggie realized she had to do something about Stranahan.

And also about Dr. Rudy Graveline.

Graveline was a dangerous creep. To rat on Rudy—well, he had warned her. And rewarded her, in a sense. A decent severance, glowing references for a new job. That was after he closed down the Durkos Center.

Lying there, Maggie got another idea. It was wild, but it just might work. The next morning she went back to Christina Marks and made up a vague story about how she had to go see Investigator Stranahan right away, otherwise no TV show. Reluctantly the producer gave her a plane ticket and six hundred in expenses.

Of course, Maggie had no intention of visiting Mick Stranahan. When she got back to Florida, she drove directly to the Whispering Palms Spa and Surgery Center in beautiful Bal Harbour. Dr. Rudy Graveline was very surprised to see her. He led her into a private office and closed the door.

"You look frightened," the surgeon said.

"I am."

"And a little bouncy in the bottom."

"I eat when I'm frightened," Maggie said, keeping her cool.

"So what is it?" Rudy asked.

"Vicky Barletta," she said. "Somebody's making a fuss."

"Oh." Rudy Graveline appeared calm. "Who?"

"One of the investigators. A man named Stranahan."

"I don't remember him," Rudy said.

"I do. He's scary."

"Did he speak to you?"

Maggie shook her head. "Worse than that," she said. "Some TV people came to my place. They're doing a special on missing persons."

"Christ, don't tell me."

"Stranahan's going to talk."

Rudy said, "But what does he know?"

Maggie blinked. "I'm worried, Dr. Graveline. It's going to break open all over again."

"No way."

Maggie's notion was to get Stranahan out of the way. Whether Dr. Graveline bribed him, terrorized him, or worse was immaterial; Rudy could get to anybody. Those who stood in his way either got with the program or got run over. One time another surgeon had done a corrective rhinoplasty on one of Rudy's botched-up patients, then badmouthed Rudy at a medical society cocktail party. Rudy got so furious that he paid two goons to trash the other doctor's office, but not before stealing his medical files. Soon, the other doctor's surgical patients received personal letters thanking them for being so understanding while he battled that terrible heroin addiction, which now seemed to be under control. Well, almost . . . By the end of the month, the other doctor had closed what was left of his practice and moved to British Columbia.

Maggie Gonzalez was counting on Rudy Graveline to overreact again; she wanted him worried about Stranahan to the exclusion of all others. By the time the doctor turned on the tube and discovered who was the real threat, Maggie would be long gone. And out of reach.

She went on: "They won't leave me alone, these TV people. They said the case is going to a grand jury. They said Stranahan's going to testify.'' She fished in her purse for a tissue. "I thought you ought to know."

Rudy Graveline thanked her for coming. He told her not to worry, everything was going to be fine. He suggested she get out of town for a few weeks, and she said that was probably a good idea. He asked if there was anywhere in particular she wanted to go, and she said New York. The doctor said New York is a swell place to visit around Christmas time, and he wrote out a personal check for twenty-five hundred dollars. He recommended that Maggie stay gone for at least a month, and said to call if she needed more money. *When*, Maggie said. Not *if* she needed more money, but when.

Later that same afternoon, Dr. Rudy Graveline had locked his office door and made a telephone call to a seafood restaurant in New Jersey. He talked to a man who probably had curly eyebrows, a man who promised to send somebody down around the first of the year.

On the day that Tony Traviola, the first hit man, arrived to kill Mick Stranahan, Maggie Gonzalez was in a tenth-floor room at the Essex House hotel. The room had a view of Central Park, where Maggie was taking skating lessons at Donald Trump's ice rink. She planned to lie low for a few more weeks, maybe stop in for a chat at *20/20*. A little competition never hurt. Maybe Reynaldo Flemm would get worried enough to jack up his offer. Five grand sucked, it really did.

Dr. Rudy Graveline made an appointment with the second killer for January tenth at three in the afternoon. The man arrived at Whispering Palms a half-hour early and sat quietly in the waiting room, scaring the hell out of the other patients.

Rudy knew him only as Chemo, a cruel but descriptive nickname, for he truly did appear to be in the final grim stages of chemotherapy. Black hair sprouted in random wisps from a blue-veined scalp. His lips were thin and papery, the color of wet cement. Red-rimmed eyes peered back at gawkers with a dull and chilling indifference; the hooded lids blinked slowly, pellucid as a salamander's. And the skin—the skin is what made people gasp, what emptied the waiting room at Whispering Palms. Chemo's skin looked like breakfast cereal, like somebody had glued Rice Krispies to every square centimeter of his face.

This, and the fact that he stood six foot nine, made Chemo a memorable sight.

Dr. Graveline was not alarmed, because he knew how Chemo had come to look this way: It was not melanoma, but a freak electrolysis accident in Scranton, many years before. While burning two ingrown hair follicles off the tip of Chemo's nose, an elderly dermatologist had suffered a crippling stroke and lost all hand-eye coordination. Valiantly the old doctor had tried to complete the procedure, but in so doing managed to incinerate every normal pore within range of the electrified needle. Since Chemo had eaten five Valiums for breakfast, he was fast asleep on the table when the tragedy occurred. When he awoke to find his whole face blistered up like a lobster, he immediately garroted the dermatologist and fled the State of Pennsylvania forever.

Chemo had spent the better part of five years on the lam, seeking medical relief; ointments proved futile, and in fact a faulty prescription had caused the startling Rice Krispie effect. Eventually Chemo came to believe that the only hope was cosmetic surgery, and his quest for a miracle brought him naturally to Florida and naturally into the care of Dr. Rudy Graveline.

At three sharp, Rudy motioned Chemo into the consultation room. Chemo ducked as he entered and shut the door behind him. He sat in an overstuffed chair and blinked moistly at Dr. Graveline.

Rudy said: "And how are we doing today?"

Chemo grunted. "How do you think?"

"When you were here a few weeks ago, we discussed a treatment plan. You remember?"

"Yep," Chemo said.

"And a payment plan, too."

"How could I forget?" Chemo said.

Dr. Graveline ignored the sarcasm; the man had every right to be bitter.

"Dermabrasion is expensive," Rudy said.

"I don't know why," Chemo said. "You just stick my face in a belt sander, right?"

The doctor smiled patiently. "It's a bit more sophisticated than that—"

"But the principle's the same."

Rudy nodded. "Roughly speaking."

"So how can it be two hundred bucks a pop?"

"Two hundred and ten," Rudy corrected. "Because it requires uncommonly steady hands. You can appreciate that, I'm sure."

Chemo smiled at the remark. Rudy wished he hadn't; the smile was harrowing, a deadly weapon all by itself. Chemo looked like he'd been teething on cinderblocks.

"I *did* get a job," he said.

Dr. Graveline agreed that was a start.

"At the Gay Bidet," Chemo said. "It's a punk club down on South Beach. I'm a greeter." Again with the smile.

"A greeter," said Rudy. "Well, well."

"I keep out the scum," Chemo explained.

Rudy asked about the pay. Chemo said he got six bucks an hour, not including tips.

"Not bad," Rudy said, "but still . . ." He scribbled some figures on a pad, then took a calculator out of his desk and punched on it for a while. All very dramatic.

Chemo stretched his neck to look. "What's the damage?"

"I figure twenty-four visits, that's a minimum," Rudy said. "Say we do one square inch every session."

"Shit, just do it all at once."

"Can't," Rudy lied, "not with dermabrasion. Say twenty-four visits at two ten each, that's—"

"Five thousand and forty dollars," Chemo muttered. "Jesus H. Christ."

Dr. Graveline said: "I don't need it all at once. Give me half to start."

"Jesus H. Christ."

Rudy put the calculator away.

"I just started at the club a week ago," Chemo said. "I gotta buy groceries."

Rudy came around the desk and sat down on the edge. In a fatherly tone he asked: "You have Blue Cross?"

"The fuck, I'm a fugitive, remember?"

"Of course."

Rudy shook his head and mused. It was all so sad, that a great country like ours couldn't provide minimal health care to all its citizens.

"So I'm screwed," Chemo said.

"Not necessarily," Dr. Graveline rubbed his chin. "I've got an idea."

"Yeah?"

"It's a job I need done."

If Chemo had had eyebrows, they would have arched.

"If you could do this job," Rudy went on, "I think we could work a deal."

"A discount?"

"I don't see why not."

Idly, Chemo fingered the scales on his cheeks. "What's the job?"

"I need you to kill somebody," Rudy said.

"Who?"

"A man that could cause me some trouble."

"What kind of trouble?"

"Could shut down Whispering Palms. Take away my medical license. And that's for starters."

Chemo ran a bloodless tongue across his lips. "Who is this man?"

"His name is Mick Stranahan."

"Where do I find him?"

"I'm not sure," Rudy said. "He's here in Miami somewhere."

Chemo said that wasn't much of a lead. "I figure a murder is worth at least five grand," he said.

"Come on, he's not a cop or anything. He's just a regular guy. Three thousand, tops." Rudy was a bear when it got down to money.

Chemo folded his huge bony hands. "Twenty treatments, that's my final offer."

Rudy worked it out in his head. "That's forty-two hundred dollars!"

"Right."

"You sure drive a hard bargain," Rudy said.

Chemo grinned triumphantly. "So when can you start on my face?"

"Soon as this chore is done."

Chemo stood up. "I suppose you'll want proof."

Rudy Graveline hadn't really thought about it. He said, "A newspaper clipping would do."

"Sure you don't want me to bring you something?"

"Like what?"

"A finger," Chemo said, "maybe one of his nuts."

"That won't be necessary," said Dr. Graveline, "really it won't."

6

Stranahan got Maggie Orestes Gonzalez's home address from a friend of his who worked for the state nursing board in Jacksonville. Although Maggie's license was paid up to date, no current place of employment was listed on the file.

The address was a duplex apartment in a quiet old neighborhood off Coral Way, in the Little Havana section of Miami. There was a chain-link fence around a sparse brown yard, a ceramic statue of Santa Barbara in the flower bed, and the customary burglar bars on every window. Stranahan propped open the screen door and knocked three times on the heavy pine frame. He wasn't surprised that no one was home.

To break into Maggie Gonzalez's apartment, Stranahan used a three-inch stainless-steel lockpick that he had confiscated from the mouth of an infamous condominium burglar named Wet Willie Jeeter. Wet Willie got his nickname because he only worked on rainy days; on sunny days he was a golf caddy at the Doral Country Club. When they went through Wet Willie's place after the arrest, the cops found seventeen personally autographed photos of Jack Nicklaus, going back to the 1967 Masters. What the cops did not find was any of Wet Willie's burglar tools, due to the fact that Wet Willie kept them well hidden beneath his tongue.

Stranahan found them when he visited Wet Willie in the Dade County Jail, two weeks before the trial. The purpose of the visit was to make Wet Willie realize the wisdom of pleading guilty and saving the taxpayers the expense of trial. Unspoken was the fact that the State Attorney's Office had a miserably weak case and was desperate for a deal. Wet Willie told Stranahan thanks anyway, but he'd just as soon take his chances with a jury. Stranahan said fine and offered Wet Willie a stick of Dentyne, which the burglar popped into his mouth without thinking. The chewing dislodged the steel lockpicks, which immediately stuck fast in the Dentyne; the whole mess eventually lodged itself in Wet Willie's throat. For a few hectic minutes Stranahan thought he might have to perform an amateur tracheotomy, but miraculously the burglar coughed up the tiny tools and also a complete confession. Stranahan kept one of Wet Willie's lockpicks as a souvenir.

The lock on Maggie's door was a breeze.

Stranahan slipped inside and noticed how neat the place looked. Someone, probably a neighbor or a relative, had carefully stacked the unopened mail on a table near the front door. On the kitchen counter was a Princess-model telephone attached to an answering machine. Stranahan pressed the Rewind button, then Play, and listened to Maggie's voice say: "Hi, I'm not home right now so you're listening to another one of those dumb answering machines. Please leave a brief message and I'll get back to you as soon as possible. Bye now!"

Stranahan played the rest of the tape, which was blank. Either Maggie Gonzalez wasn't getting any calls, or someone was taking them for her, or she was phoning in for her own messages with one of those remote pocket beepers. Whatever the circumstances, it was a sign that she probably wasn't all that dead.

Other clues in the apartment pointed to travel. There was no luggage in the closets, no bras or underwear in the bedroom drawers, no makeup on the bathroom sink. The most interesting thing Stranahan found was crumpled in a waste basket in a corner of the living room: a bank deposit slip for twenty-five hundred dollars, dated the twenty-seventh of December.

Have a nice trip, Stranahan thought.

He let himself out, carefully locking the door behind him. Then he drove three blocks to a pay phone at a 7-Eleven, where he dialed Maggie's phone number and left a very important message on her machine.

At the end of the day, Christina Marks dropped her rented Ford Escort with the hotel valet, bought a copy of the *New York Times* at the shop in the lobby, and took the elevator up to her room. Before she could get the key out of the door, Mick Stranahan opened it from the other side.

"Come on in," he said.

"Nice of you," Christina said, "considering it's my room."

Stranahan noticed she had one of those trendy leather briefcase satchels that you wear over your shoulder. A couple of legal pads stuck out the top.

"You've been busy."

"You want a drink?"

"Gin and tonic, thanks," Stranahan said. After a pause: "I was afraid the great Reynaldo might see me if I waited in the lobby."

"So you got a key to my room?"

"Not exactly."

Christina Marks handed him the drink. Then she poured herself a beer, and sat down in a rattan chair with garish floral pillows that were supposed to look tropical.

"I went to see Maggie's family today," she said.

"Any luck?"

"No. Unfortunately, they don't speak English."

Stranahan smiled and shook his head.

"What's so funny?" Christina said. "Just because I don't speak Spanish?"

Stranahan said, "Except for probably her grandmother, all Maggie's family speaks perfect English. Perfect."

"What?"

"Her father teaches physics at Palmetto High School. Her mother is an operator for Southern Bell. Her sister Consuelo is a legal secretary, and her brother, whats-his-name . . ."

"Tomás."

"Tommy, yeah," Stranahan said. "He's a senior account executive at Merrill Lynch."

Christina Marks put down her beer so decisively that it nearly broke the glass coffee table. "I sat in the living room, talking to these people, and they just stared at me and said—"

'No habla English, *señora.'*

"Exactly."

"Oldest trick in Miami," Stranahan said. "They just didn't want to talk. Don't feel bad, they tried the same thing with me."

"And I suppose you know Spanish."

"Enough to make them think I knew more. They're worried about Maggie, actually. Been worried for some time. She's had some personal problems, Maggie has. Money problems, too—that much I found out before her old lady started having chest pains."

"You're kidding."

"Second oldest trick," Stranahan said, smiling, "but I was done anyway. I honestly don't think they know where she is."

Christina Marks finished her beer and got another from the

small hotel refrigerator. When she sat down again, she kicked off her shoes.

"So," she said, "you're ahead of us."

"You and Reynaldo?"

"The crew," Christina said, looking stung.

"No, I'm not ahead of you," Stranahan said. "Tell me what Maggie Gonzalez knows about Vicky Barletta."

Christina said, "I can't do that."

"How much did you promise to pay?"

Again Christina shook her head.

"Know what I think?" Stranahan said. "I think you and Ray are getting the hum job of your lives."

"Pardon?"

"I think Maggie is sucking you off, big-time."

Christina heard herself saying, "You might be right."

Stranahan softened his tone. "Let me give you a hypothetical," he said. "This Maggie Gonzalez, whom you've never seen before, shows up in New York one day and offers to tell you a sensational story about a missing college coed. The way she tells it, the girl came to a terrible and ghastly end. And, conveniently, the way she tells it can't ever be proven or disproven. Why? Because it happened a long time ago. And the odds are, Christina, that Victoria Barletta is dead. And the odds are, whoever did it isn't about to come forward to say that Reynaldo Flemm got it all wrong when he told the story on national TV."

Christina Marks leaned forward. "Fine. All fine, except for one thing. She names names."

"Maggie does?"

"Yes. She describes exactly how it happened and who did it."

"And these people—"

"Person, singular."

"He? She?"

"He," Christina said.

"He's still alive?"

"Sure is."

"Here in town?"

"That's right."

"Jesus," Stranahan said. He got up and fixed himself another gin. He dropped a couple of ice cubes, his hands were shaking so much. This was not good, he told himself, getting so excited was definitely not good.

He carried his drink back to the living room and said, "Is it the doctor?"

"I can't say." It would violate a confidence, Christina Marks explained. Journalists have to protect their sources. Stranahan finished half his drink before he spoke again. "Are you any good?"

Christina looked at him curiously.

"At what you do," he said irritably, "are you any damn good?"

"Yes, I think so."

"Can you keep the great Reynaldo out of my hair?"

"I'll try. Why?"

"Because," Stranahan said, "it would be to our mutual benefit to meet once in a while, just you and me."

"Compare notes?"

"Something like that. I don't know why, but I think I can trust you."

"Thanks."

"I'm not saying I do, just that it's possible."

He put down the glass and stood up.

"What's your stake in this?" Christina Marks asked.

"Truth, justice, whatever."

"No, it's bigger than that."

She was pretty sharp, he had to admit. But he wasn't ready to tell her about Tony the Eel and the marlin head.

As she walked Stranahan to the door, Christina said, "I spent some time at the newspaper today."

"Reading up, I suppose."

"You've got quite a clip file," she said. "I suppose I ought to be scared of you."

"You don't believe everything you read?"

"Of course not." Christina Marks opened the door. "Just tell me, how much of it was true?"

"All of it," Mick Stranahan said, "unfortunately."

Of Stranahan's five ex-wives, only one had chosen to keep his last name: ex-wife number four, Chloe Simpkins Stranahan. Even after she remarried, Chloe hung on to his name as an act of unalloyed spite. Naturally she was listed in the Miami phone book; Stranahan had begged her to please get a nonpublished number, but Chloe had said that would defeat the whole purpose. "This way, any girl who wants to call up and check on you, I can tell them the truth. That you're a dangerous lunatic. That's what I'll tell them when they call up, Mick—*honey, he was one dangerous lunatic.*"

Christina Marks had gotten all the Stranahan numbers from directory assistance. When she had called Chloe from New York, Chloe assumed it was just one of Mick's girlfriends, and had given a vitriolic and highly embellished account of their eight-month marriage and nine-month divorce. Finally Christina Marks had cut in and explained who she was and what she wanted, and Chloe Simpkins Stranahan had said: "That'll cost you a grand."

"Five hundred," Christina countered.

"Bitch," Chloe hissed. But when the cashier's check arrived the next afternoon by Federal Express, Chloe faithfully picked up the phone and called Christina Marks (collect) in New York and told her where to locate her dangerous lunatic of an ex-husband.

"Give him a disease for me, will you?" Chloe had said and then had hung up.

The hit man known as Chemo was not nearly as resourceful as Christina Marks, but he did know enough to check the telephone book for Stranahans. There were five, and Chemo wrote them all down.

The day after his meeting with Dr. Rudy Graveline, Chemo went for a drive. His car was a royal blue 1980 Bonneville, with tinted windows. The tinted windows were essential to conceal

Chemo's face, the mere glimpse of which could cause a high-speed pileup at any intersection.

Louis K. Stranahan was the first on Chemo's list. A Miamian would have recognized the address as being in the middle of Liberty City, but Chemo did not. It occurred to him upon entering the neighborhood that he should have asked Dr. Graveline whether the man he was supposed to kill was black or white, because it might have saved some time.

The address was in the James Scott housing project, a bleak and tragic warren where few outsiders of any color dared to go. Even on a bright winter day, the project gave off a dark and ominous heat. Chemo was oblivious; he saw no danger here, just work. He parked the Bonneville next to a fenced-in basketball court and got out. Almost instantly the kids on the court stopped playing. The basketball hit the rim and bounced lazily out of bounds, but no one ran to pick it up. They were all staring at Chemo. The only sound was the dental-drill rap of Run-D.M.C. from a distant quadrophonic blaster.

"Hello, there," Chemo said.

The kids from the project glanced at one another, trying to guess how they should play it; this was one of the tallest white motherfuckers they'd ever seen this side of the Interstate. Also, one of the ugliest.

"Game's full," the biggest kid declared with a forced authority.

"Oh, I don't want to play," Chemo said.

A look of relief spread among the players, and one of them jogged after the basketball.

"I'm looking for a man named Louis Stranahan."

"He ain't here."

"Where is he?"

"Gone."

Chemo said, "Does he have a brother named Mick?"

"He's got six brothers," one of the basketball players volunteered. "But no Mick."

"There's a Dick," said another teenager.

"And a Lawrence."

Chemo took the list out of his pocket and frowned. Sure enough, Lawrence Stranahan was the second name from the phone book. The address was close by, too.

As Chemo stood there, cranelike, squinting at the piece of paper, the black kids loosened up a little. They started shooting a few hoops, horsing around. The white guy wasn't so scary after all; shit, there were eight of them and one of him.

"Where could I find Louis?" Chemo tried again.

"Raiford," said two of the kids, simultaneously.

"Raiford," Chemo repeated. "That's a prison, isn't it?"

With this, all the teenagers doubled up, slapping fives, howling hysterically at this gangly freak with the fuzzballs on his head.

"Fuck, yeah, it's a prison," one of them said finally.

Chemo scratched the top two Stranahans off his list. As he opened the door of the Bonneville, the black kid who was dribbling the basketball hollered, "Hey, big man, you a movie star?"

"No," Chemo said.

"I swear you are."

"I swear I'm not."

"Then how come I saw you in *Halloween III*?"

The kid bent over in a deep wheeze; he thought this was so damn funny. Chemo reached under the car seat and got a .22-caliber pistol, which was fitted with a cheap mail-order suppressor. Without saying a word, he took aim across the roof of the Bonneville and shot the basketball clean out of the kid's hands. The explosion sounded like the world's biggest fart, but the kids from the project didn't think it was funny. They ran like hell.

As Chemo drove away, he decided he had taught the youngsters a valuable lesson: Never make fun of a man's complexion.

It was half-past noon when Chemo found the third address, a two-story Mediterranean style house in Coral Gables. An ill-tempered Rottweiler was chained to the trunk of an olive tree in the front yard, but Chemo ambled past the big dog without incident; the animal merely cocked its head and watched, perhaps not sure if this odd extenuated creature was the same species he'd been trained to attack.

Chloe Simpkins Stranahan was on the phone to her husband's secretary when the doorbell rang.

"Tell him, if he's not home by eight, I sell the Dali. Tell him that right now." Chloe slammed down the phone and stalked to the door. She looked up at Chemo and said, "How'd you get past the pooch?"

Chemo shrugged. He was wearing black Raybans, which he hoped would lessen the effect of his facial condition. If necessary, he was prepared to explain what had happened; it wouldn't be the first time.

Yet Chloe Simpkins Stranahan didn't mention it. She said, "You selling something?"

"I'm looking for a man named Mick Stranahan."

"He's a dangerous lunatic," Chloe said. "Come right in."

Chemo removed the sunglasses and folded them into the top pocket of his shirt. He sat down in the living room, and put a hand on each of his bony kneecaps. At the wet bar Chloe fixed him a cold ginger ale. She acted like she didn't even notice what was wrong with his appearance.

"Who are you?" she asked.

"Collection agent," Chemo said. Watching Chloe move around the house, he saw that she was a very beautiful woman: auburn hair, long legs, and a good figure. Listening to her, he could tell she was also hard as nails.

"Mick is my ex," Chloe said. "I have nothing good to say about him. Nothing."

"He owe you money, too?"

She chuckled harshly. "No, I took him for every goddamn dime. Cleaned his clock." She drummed her ruby fingernails on the side of the ginger ale glass. "I'm now married to a CPA," she said. "Has his own firm."

"Nice to hear it," Chemo said.

"Dull as a dog turd, but at least he's no lunatic."

Chemo shifted in the chair. "Lunatic, you keep saying that

word. What do you mean? Is Mr. Stranahan violent? Did he hit you?''

"Mick? Never. Not me," Chloe said. "But he did attack a friend of mine. A male-type friend."

Chemo figured he ought to learn as much as possible about the man he was supposed to kill. He said to Chloe, "What exactly did Mick do to this male-type friend?"

"It's hard for me to talk about it." Chloe got up and dumped a jigger of vodka into her ginger ale. "He was always on the road, Mick was. Never home. No doubt he was screwing around."

"You know for a fact?"

"I'm sure of it."

"So you got a . . . boyfriend."

"You're a smart one," Chloe said mordantly. "A goddamn rocket scientist, you are. Yes, I got a *boyfriend*. And he loved me, this guy. He treated me like a queen."

Chemo said. "So one night Mr. Stranahan gets home early from a trip and catches the two of you—"

"In action," Chloe said. "Don't get me wrong, I didn't plan it that way. God knows I didn't want him to walk in on us—you gotta know Mick, it's just not a safe situation."

"Short fuse?"

"No fuse."

"So then what?"

Chloe sighed. "I can't believe I'm telling this to some stranger, a bill collector! Unbelievable." She polished off her drink and got another. This time when she came back from the bar, she sat down on the divan next to Chemo; close enough that he could smell her perfume.

"I'm a talker," she said with a soft smile. The smile certainly didn't go with the voice.

"And I'm a listener," Chemo said.

"And I like you."

"You do?" This broad is creepy, he thought, a real head case.

"I like you," Chloe went on, "and I'd like to help you with your problem."

"Then just tell me," Chemo said, "where I can find your ex-husband."

"How much are you willing to pay?"

"Ah, so that's it."

"Everything's got a price," Chloe said, "especially good information."

"Unfortunately, Mrs. Stranahan, I don't have any money. Money is the reason I'm looking for Mick."

Chloe crossed her legs, and Chemo noticed a very fine run in one of her nylon stockings; it seemed to go on forever, all the way up her thigh. Who knew where it ended? Internally he cautioned himself against such distractions. Any moment now, she was going to say something about his Rice Krispie face—Chemo knew it.

"You're not a bill collector," Chloe said sharply, "so cut the shit."

"All right," Chemo said. Feverishly he set his limited imagination to work, trying to come up with another story.

"I don't care what you are."

"You don't?"

"Nope. Long as you're not a friend of Mick's."

Chemo said, "I'm not a friend."

"Then I'll help," Chloe said, "maybe."

"What about the money?" Chemo said. "The most I can do is a hundred dollars, maybe one fifty."

"Fine."

"Fine?" Christ, he couldn't believe this woman. A hundred bucks.

She said, "But before I agree to help, you ought to know everything. It would be irresponsible for me not to warn you what you're up against."

"I can handle myself," Chemo said with a cold smile. Even that—his fractured, cadaverous leer—didn't seem to bother Chloe Simpkins Stranahan.

She said, "So you really don't want to know?"

"Go ahead, then, shoot. What did Stranahan do to your precious boyfriend?"

"He put Krazy Glue on his balls."

"What?"

"A whole tube," Chloe said. "He glued the man to the hood of his car. By the balls. Stark naked, glued to the hood of an Eldorado convertible."

"Jesus H. Christ," Chemo said.

"Ever seen the hood ornament on a Cadillac?"

Chemo nodded.

"Think about it," Chloe said grimly.

"And glue burns like hell," Chemo remarked.

"Indeed it does."

"So Mick came home, caught you two in the sack—"

"Right here on the divan."

"Wherever," Chemo said. "Anyway, he hauls Mr. Studhunk outside and glues him buck naked to the hood of his Caddy."

"By the testicles."

"Then what?"

"That's it," Chloe said. "Mick packed his suitcase and left. The paramedics came. What more is there?"

"Your male friend—is this the same guy you're married to?"

"No, it isn't," Chloe said. "My male-type friend never recovered from his encounter with Mick Stranahan. I mean *never recovered*. You understand what I'm saying?"

"I think so."

"The doctors insisted there was nothing wrong, medically speaking. I mean, the glue peeled off with acetone, and in a few days the skin healed just like new. But, still, the man was never the same."

Chemo said, "It's a major trauma, Mrs. Stranahan. It probably takes some time—"

He flinched as Chloe threw her cocktail glass against the wall. "Time?" she said. "I gave him plenty of time, mister. And I tried every trick I knew, but he was a dead man after that night with Mick. It was like trying to screw linguini."

Chemo could imagine the hellish bedroom scene. He felt himself shrivel, just thinking about it.

"I loved that man," Chloe went on. "At least, I was getting there. And Mick ruined everything. He couldn't just beat the shit out of him, like other jealous husbands. No, he had to torture the guy."

In a way, Chemo admired Stranahan's style. Murder is the way Chemo himself would have handled the situation: A bullet in the base of the skull. For both of them.

Chloe Simpkins Stranahan was up and pacing now, arms folded across her chest, heels clicking on the Spanish tile. "So you see," she said, "this is why I hate my ex-husband so much."

There had to be more, but who cared. Chemo said, "You want to get even?"

"Boy, are you a swifty. Yes, I want to get even."

"Then why should I pay you anything? You should pay *me*."

Chloe had to smile. "Good point." She bent over and picked a chunk of broken glass out of the deep-pile carpet. She looked up at Chemo and asked, "Who are you, anyway?"

"Doesn't matter, Mrs. Stranahan. The question is, how bad do you want revenge on your ex-husband?"

"I guess that is the question," Chloe said thoughtfully. "How about another ginger ale?"

7

Of the four plastic surgeons who had worked with Dr. Rudy Graveline at the Durkos Center, only one had remained in Miami after the clinic closed. His name was George Ginger, and Stranahan found him on a tennis court at Turnberry Isle in the middle of a weekday afternoon. Mixed doubles, naturally.

Stranahan watched the pudgy little man wheeze back and forth behind the baseline, and marveled at the atrociousness of his hairpiece. It was one of those synthetic jobs, the kind you're supposed to be able to wear in the shower. In Dr. George Ginger's case, the thing on his head looked a lot like a fresh road kill.

Each point in the tennis game became its own little comedy, and Stranahan wondered if this stop was a waste of time, an unconscious stall on his part. By now he knew exactly where to locate Rudy Graveline; the problem was, he didn't know what to ask him that would produce the truth. It was a long way from Vicky Barletta to Tony the Eel, and Stranahan still hadn't found the thread, if there was one. One way or another, Dr. Graveline was central to the mystery, and Stranahan didn't want to spook him. For now, he wanted him safe and contented at Whispering Palms.

Stranahan strolled into the dead lane of the tennis court and said, "Dr. Ginger?"

"Yo!" said the doctor, huffing.

Stranahan knew about guys who said yo.

"We need to talk."

"Do we now?" said Dr. Ginger, missing an easy backhand. His doubles partner, a lanky, overtanned woman, shot Stranahan a dirty look.

"Just take a minute," Stranahan said.

Dr. Ginger picked up two of the tennis balls. "Sorry, but I'm on serve."

"No, you're not," Stranahan said. "And besides, that was the set." He'd been following the match from a gazebo two courts over.

As Dr. Ginger intently bounced one of the balls between his feet, the other players picked up their monogrammed club towels and calfskin racket covers and ambled off the court.

Solemnly George Ginger said, "The tall fellow was my lawyer."

"Every doctor should have a lawyer," said Mick Stranahan. "Especially surgeons."

Ginger jammed the tennis balls into the pockets of his damp white shorts. "What's this all about?"

"Rudy Graveline."

"I've heard of him."

This was going to be fun, Stranahan thought. He loved it when they played cool.

"You worked for him at the Durkos Center," Stranahan said to George Ginger. "Why don't you be a nice fellow and tell me about it?"

George Ginger motioned Stranahan to follow. He picked a quiet patio table with an umbrella, not far from the pro shop.

"Who are you with?" the doctor inquired in a low voice.

"The board," Stranahan said. Any board would do; Dr. Ginger wouldn't press it.

After wiping his forehead for the umpteenth time, the doctor said, "There were four of us—Kelly, Greer, Shulman, and me. Graveline was the managing partner."

"Business was good?"

"It was getting there."

"Then why did he close the place?"

"I'm still not certain," George Ginger said.

"But you heard rumors."

"Yes, we heard there was a problem with a patient. The sort of problem that might bring in the state."

"One of Rudy's patients?"

George Ginger nodded. "A young woman is what we heard."

"Her name?"

"I don't know." The doctor was quite a lousy liar.

"How bad a problem?" Stranahan went on.

"I don't know that, either. We assumed it was a major fuckup, or else why would Graveline pull out so fast?"

"Didn't any of you guys bother to ask?"

"Hell, no. I've been to court before, buddy, and it's no damn fun. None of us wanted to get dragged down that road. Anyway, we show up for work one day and the place is empty. Later we get a certified check from Rudy with a note saying he's sorry for the inconvenience, but good luck with our careers. Before you know it, he's back in business at Bal Harbour—of all places—with a frigging assembly-line operation. A dozen boob jobs a day.''

Stranahan said, ''Why didn't you call him?''

''What for? Old times' sake?''

''That certified check, it must've been a good one.''

''It was,'' Dr. Ginger conceded, ''very generous.''

Stranahan picked up the doctor's graphite tennis racket and plucked idly at the strings. George Ginger eyed him worriedly. ''Do you remember the day the police came?'' Stranahan asked. ''The day a young female patient disappeared from a bus bench in front of the clinic?''

''I was off that day.''

''That's not what I asked.'' Stranahan studied him through the grid of the racket strings.

''I remember hearing about it,'' George Ginger said lamely.

''That happened right before Dr. Graveline split, didn't it?''

''I think so, yes.''

Stranahan said, ''You consider yourself a bright man, Dr. Ginger? Don't look so insulted, it's a serious question.'' He put the tennis racket down on the patio table.

''I consider myself to be intelligent, yes.''

''Well, then, didn't you wonder about the timing? A girl gets snatched from in front of your office, and a few weeks later the boss closes up shop. Could that be the fuckup you guys heard about? What do you think?''

Sourly, George Ginger said, ''I can't imagine a connection.'' He picked up his tennis racket and, with a touch of pique, zipped it into its carry case.

Stranahan stood up. ''Well, the important thing is, you still got your medical license. Now, where can I find the rest of the stooges?''

Dr. Ginger wrapped the towel around his neck, a real jock gesture. ''Kelly moved to Michigan. Shulman's up in Atlanta, working for some HMO. Dr. Greer is deceased, unfortunately.''

''Do tell.''

''Don't you guys have it in your files? I mean, when a doctor dies?''

''Not in every case,'' Stranahan bluffed.

George Ginger said, ''It happened maybe six months after Durkos closed. A hunting accident up around Ocala.''

''Who else was there?''

''I really don't know,'' the doctor said with an insipid shrug. ''I'm afraid I'm not clear about all the details.''

''Why,'' said Mick Stranahan, ''am I not surprised?''

The Rudy Graveline system was brilliant in its simplicity: Sting, persuade, operate, then flatter.

On the wall of each waiting room at Whispering Palms hung a creed: VANITY IS BEAUTIFUL. Similar maxims were posted in the hallways and examining rooms. WHAT'S WRONG WITH PERFECTION? was one of Rudy's favorites. Another: TO IMPROVE ONE'S SELF, IMPROVE ONE'S FACE. This one was framed in the spa, where post-op patients relaxed in the crucial days following their plastic surgery, when they didn't want to go out in public. Rudy had shrewdly recognized that an after-surgery spa would not only be a tremendous money-maker, it would also provide important positive feedback during recovery. Everyone there had fresh scars and bruises, so no patient was in a position to criticize another's results.

As best as he could, Reynaldo Flemm made mental notes of Whispering Palms during his tour. He was posing as a male exotic dancer who needed a blemish removed from his right buttock. For the purpose of disguise, Flemm had dyed his hair brown and greased it straight back; that was all he could bear to do to alter his appearance. Secretly, he loved it when people stared because they recognized him from television.

As it happened, the nurse who greeted him at Whispering Palms apparently never watched *In Your Face*. She treated Flemm as any other prospective patient. After a quick tour of the facilities, she led him to a consultation room, turned off the lights and showed him a videotape about the wonders of cosmetic surgery. Afterwards she turned the lights back on and asked if he had any questions.

"How much will it cost?" Reynaldo Flemm said.

"That depends on the size of the mole."

"Oh, it's a big mole," Reynaldo said. "Like an olive." He held up his thumb and forefinger to show her the size of his fictional growth.

The nurse said, "May I see it?"

"No!"

"Surely you're not shy," she said. "Not in your line of work."

"I'll show it to the doctor," Flemm said. "No one else."

"Very well, I'll arrange for an appointment."

"With Dr. Graveline, please."

The nurse smiled. "Really, Mr. LeTigre."

Flemm had come up with the name Johnny LeTigre all by himself. It seemed perfect for a male go-go dancer.

"Dr. Graveline doesn't do moles," the nurse said in a chilly tone. "One of our other excellent surgeons can take care of it quite easily."

"It's Dr. Graveline or nobody," Flemm said firmly. "This is my dancing career, my life we're talking about."

"I'm sorry, but Dr. Graveline is not available."

"For ten grand I bet he is."

The nurse tried not to seem surprised. "I'll be right back," she said lightly.

When he was alone, Reynaldo Flemm checked himself in the mirror to see how the disguise was holding up. All he needed was a date and time to see the doctor, then he'd come back with Willie and a camera for the showdown—not out on the street, but inside the clinic. And if Graveline ordered them out, Reynaldo and Willie would be sure to leave through the spa exit, tape rolling. It would be dynamite stuff; even Christina would have to admit it.

The nurse returned and said, "Come with me, Mr. LeTigre."

"Where to?"

"Dr. Graveline has agreed to see you."

"Now?" Flemm squeaked.

"He only has a few minutes."

A cold prickle of panic accompanied Reynaldo Flemm as he followed the nurse down a long pale-blue hallway. About to meet the target of his investigation and here he was, defense-less—no camera, no tape, no notebooks. He could blow the whole story if he wasn't careful. The only thing in Flemm's favor was the fact that he also had no script. He wouldn't know what to ask even if the opportunity presented itself.

The nurse abandoned him in a spacious office with a grand view of north Biscayne Bay, foamy with whitecaps. Reynaldo Flemm barely had time to snoop the joint over before Dr. Rudy Graveline came in and introduced himself. Reynaldo took a good close look, in case he might later have to point him out to Willie from the TV van: Lean build, medium height, sandy brown hair. Had a golfer's tan but not much muscle. Overall, not a bad-looking guy.

Rudy Graveline didn't waste any time. "Let's see your little problem, Mr. LeTigre."

"Hold on a minute."

"It's only a mole."

"To you, maybe," Reynaldo Flemm said. "Before we go any further, I'd like to ask you some questions." He paused, then: "Questions about your background."

Dr. Graveline settled in behind a gleaming onyx desk and folded his hands. "Fire away," he said amiably.

"What medical school did you go to?"

"Harvard," Rudy replied.

Reynaldo nodded approvingly.

He asked, "How long have you been in practice?"

"Sixteen years," Dr. Graveline said.

"Ah," said Reynaldo Flemm. He couldn't think of much else to ask, which was fine with Rudy. Sometimes patients wanted to know how high the doctor had placed in his med school class (dead last), or whether he was certified by a national board of plastic and reconstructive surgeons (he was not). In truth, Rudy had barely squeaked through a residency in radiology and had never been trained in plastic surgery. Still, no law prevented him from declaring it to be his speciality; that was the beauty of the medical profession—once you got a degree, you could try whatever you damn well pleased, from brain surgery to gynecology. Hospitals might do some checking, but never the patients. And failing at one or more specialties (as Rudy had), you could always leave town and try something else.

Still stalling, Reynaldo Flemm said, "What's involved in an operation like this?"

"First we numb the area with a mild anesthetic, then we use a small knife to remove the mole. If you need a couple sutures afterward, we do that, too."

"What about a scar?"

"No scar, I guarantee it," said Dr. Graveline.

"For ten grand, you're damn right."

The doctor said, "I didn't realize male strippers made that much money."

"They don't. It's inheritance."

If Flemm had been paying attention, he would have noticed a hungry flicker in Dr. Graveline's expression.

"Mr. LeTigre, you won't mind some friendly professional advice?"

"Of course not."

"Your nose," Rudy ventured. "I mean, as long as you're going to all the trouble of surgery."

"What the hell is wrong with my nose?"

"It's about two sizes too large for your face. And, to be honest, your tummy could probably come down an inch or three. I can do a liposuction after we excise the mole."

Reynaldo Flemm said, "Are you kidding? There's nothing wrong with me."

"Please don't be embarrassed," Rudy said. "This is my specialty. I just thought someone in a job like yours would want to look their very best."

Flemm was getting furious. "I *do* look my very best!"

Dr. Graveline put his elbows on the desk and leaned forward.

Gently he said, "With all respect, Mr. LeTigre, we seldom choose to see ourselves the way others do. It's human nature."

"I've heard enough," Reynaldo Flemm snapped.

"If it's the money, look, I'll do the mole and the fat suction as a package. Toss in the rhinoplasty for nothing, okay?"

Flemm said, "I don't need a goddamn rhinoplasty."

"Please," said Dr. Graveline, "go home and think about it. Take a good critical look at yourself in the mirror."

"Fuck you," said Reynaldo Flemm, and stormed out of the office.

"It's no sin to have a big honker," Rudy Graveline called after him. "Nobody's *born* perfect!"

One hour later, as Rudy was fitting a Mentor Model 7000 Gel-Filled Mammary Prosthesis into the left breast of the future Miss Ecuador, he was summoned from the operating suite to take an urgent phone call from New York.

The semi-hysterical voice on the other end belonged to Maggie Gonzalez.

"Take some deep breaths," Rudy advised.

"No, you listen. I got a message on my machine," Maggie said. "The phone machine at my house."

"Who was it from?"

"Stranahan. That investigator."

"Really." Dr. Graveline worked hard at staying calm; he took pride in his composure. He asked, "What was the message, Maggie?"

"Three words: *'It won't work.'*"

Dr. Graveline repeated the message out loud. Maggie sounded like she was bouncing off the walls.

"Don't come back here for a while," Rudy said. "I'll wire you some more money." He couldn't think clearly with Maggie hyperventilating into the phone, and he did need to think. *It won't work.* Damn, he didn't like the sound of that. How much did Stranahan know? Was it a bluff? Rudy Graveline wondered if he should call Chemo and tell him to speed things up.

"What are we going to do?" Maggie demanded.

"It's being done," the doctor said.

"Good." Maggie didn't ask specifically what was being done. Specifically, she didn't want to know.

After lunch, Mick Stranahan stopped by the VA hospital, but for the second day in a row the nurses told him that Timmy Gavigan was asleep. They said it had been another poor night, that the new medicine was still giving him fevers.

Stranahan was eager to hear what his friend remembered about Dr. Rudy Graveline. Like most good cops, Timmy never forgot an interview; and like most cops, Timmy was the only one who could read his own handwriting. The Barletta file was full of Gavigan-type scribbles.

After leaving the VA, Stranahan drove back to the marina at Key Biscayne. On the skiff out to Stiltsville, he mentally catalogued everything he knew so far.

Vicky Barletta had disappeared, and was probably dead.

Her doctor had closed up shop a few weeks later and bought out his four partners for fifty thousand dollars apiece.

One of those partners, Dr. Kenneth Greer, had never cashed his check—this according to microfiche records at the bank.

Approximately seven months after Rudy Graveline closed the Durkos Center, Dr. Kenneth Greer was shot to death while hunting deer in the Ocala National Forest. The sheriff's office had ruled it an accident.

The hunter who had somehow mistaken Kenneth Greer for a white-tail buck had given his name as T. B. Luckner of 1333 Carter Boulevard in Decatur, Georgia. If the sheriff in Ocala had troubled himself to check, he would have found that there was no such person and no such address.

The nurse who participated in Victoria Barletta's surgery had recently gone to New York to sell her story to a TV producer.

Shortly afterwards, a paid killer named Tony the Eel showed up to murder Mick Stranahan. Tony, with a brand-new face.

Then the TV producer arrived in Miami to take Stranahan's picture for a prime-time special.

All traced to a four-year-old kidnapping that Mick Stranahan had never solved.

As he steered the boat into the Biscayne Channel, angling out of the messy following chop, he gunned the outboard and made a beeline for his stilt house. The tide was up, making it safe to cross the flats.

On the way, he thought about Rudy Graveline.

Suppose the doctor had killed Vicky. Stranahan checked himself—make that Victoria, not Vicky. Better yet, just plain Barletta. No sense personalizing.

But suppose the doctor had killed her, and suppose Greer knew, or found out. Greer was the only one who didn't cash the buyout check—maybe he was holding out for more money, or maybe he was ready to blab to the authorities.

Either way, Dr. Graveline would have had plenty of motive to silence him.

And if, for some reason, Dr. Graveline had been led to believe that Mick Stranahan posed a similar threat, what would stop him from killing again?

Stranahan couldn't help but marvel at the possibility. Considering all the cons and ex-cons who'd love to see him dead—hoods, dopers, scammers, bikers and stickup artists—it was ironic that the most likely suspect was some rich quack he'd never even met.

The more Stranahan learned about the case, and the more he thought about what he'd learned, the lousier he felt.

His spirits improved somewhat when he spotted his model friend Tina stretched out on the sun deck of the stilt house. He was especially pleased to notice that she was alone.

8

Stranahan caught four small snappers and fried them up for supper.

"Richie left me," Tina was explaining. "I mean, he put me out on your house and left. Can you believe that?"

Stranahan pretended to be listening as he foraged in the refrigerator. "You want lemon or garlic salt?"

"Both," Tina said. "We had a fight and he ordered me to get off the boat. Then he drove away."

She wore a baggy Jimmy Buffett T-shirt over a cranberry bikini bottom. Her wheat-colored hair was pulled back in a ponytail, and a charm glinted at her throat; a tiny gold porpoise, it looked like.

"Richie deals a little coke," Tiny went on. "That's what we were fighting about. Well, part of it."

Stranahan said, "Keep an eye on the biscuits so they don't burn."

"Sure. Anyway, know what else we were fighting about? This is so dumb you won't believe it."

Stranahan was dicing a pepper on the kitchen countertop. He was barefoot, wearing cutoff jeans and a khaki short-sleeved shirt, open to the chest. His hair was still damp from the shower. Overall, he felt much better about his situation.

Tina said, "I got this modeling job and Richie, he went crazy. All because I had to do some, you know, nudes. Just beach stuff, nobody out there but me and the photog. Richie says no way, you can't do it. And I said, you can't tell me what to do. Then—then!—he calls me a slut, and I say that's pretty rich coming from a two-bit doper. So then he slugs me in the stomach and tells me to get my butt out of the boat.'' Tina paused for a sigh. "Your house was closest."

"You can stay for the night," Stranahan said, sounding downright fatherly.

"What if Richie comes back?"

"Then we teach him some manners."

Tina said, "He's still pissed about the last time, when you dragged him through the water."

"The biscuits," Stranahan reminded her.

"Oh, yeah, sorry." Tina pulled the hot tray out of the oven.

For at least thirteen minutes she didn't say anything, because the snapper was excellent and she was hungry. Stranahan found a bottle of white wine and poured two glasses. It was then Tina smiled and said, "Got any candles?"

Stranahan played along, even though darkness still was an hour away. He lighted two stubby hurricane candles and set them on the oilskin tablecloth.

"This is really nice," Tina said.

"Yes, it is."

"I haven't found a single bone," she said, chewing intently.

"Good."

"Are you married, Mick?"

"Divorced," he replied. "Five times."

"Wow."

"My fault, every one," he added. To some degree, he believed it. Each time the same thing had happened: He'd awakened one morning and felt nothing; not guilt or jealousy or anger, but an implacable numbness, which was worse. Like his blood had turned to novocaine overnight. He'd stared at the woman in his bed and become incredulous at the notion that this was a spouse, that he had married this person. He'd felt trapped and done a poor job of concealing it. By the fifth go-round, divorce had become an eerie out-of-body experience, except for the part with the lawyers.

"Were you fooling around a lot, or what?" Tina asked.

"It wasn't that," Stranahan said.

"Then what? You're a nice-looking guy, I don't know why a girl would cut and run."

Stranahan poured more wine for both of them.

"I wasn't much fun to be around."

"Oh, I disagree," Tina said with a perkiness that startled him.

Her eyes wandered up to the big mount on the living room wall. "What happened to Mr. Swordfish?"

"That's a marlin," Stranahan said. "He fell off the wall and broke his beak."

"The tape looks pretty tacky, Mick."

"Yeah, I know."

After dinner they went out on the deck to watch the sun go down behind Coconut Grove. Stranahan tied a size 12 hook on his fishing line and baited it with a lint-sized shred of frozen shrimp. In fifteen minutes he caught five lively pinfish, which he dropped in a plastic bait bucket. Entranced, Tina sat cross-legged on the deck and watched the little fish swim frenetic circles inside the container.

Stranahan stowed the rod in the stilt house, came out, and picked up the bucket. "I'll be right back."

"Where you off to?"

"Downstairs, by the boat."

"Can I come?"

He shrugged. "You might not like it."

"Like what?" Tina asked and followed him tentatively down the wooden stairs toward the water.

Liza hovered formidably in the usual place. Stranahan pointed at the huge barracuda and said, "See there?"

"Wow, is that a shark?"

"No."

He reached into the bucket and grabbed one of the pinfish, carefully folding the dorsal so it wouldn't prick his fingers.

Tina said, "Now I get it."

"She's like a pet," Stranahan said. He tossed the pinfish into the water, and the barracuda devoured it in a silent mercury flash, all fangs. When the turbulence subsided, they saw that

the big fish had returned to its station; it hung there as if it had
never moved.

Impassively Stranahan tossed another pinfish and the barracuda repeated the kill.

Tina stood so close that Stranahan could feel her warm breath
on his bare arm. "Do they eat people?" she asked.

He could have hugged her right then.

"No," he said, "they don't eat people."

"Good!"

"They do strike at shiny objects," he said, "so don't wear a
bracelet if you've diving."

"Seriously?"

"It's been known to happen."

This time he scooped up two pinfish and lobbed them into
the water simultaneously; the barracuda got them both in one
fierce swipe.

"I call her Liza," Stranahan said. "Liza with a *z*."

Tina nodded as if she thought it was a perfectly cute name.
She asked if she could try a toss.

"You bet." Stranahan got the last pinfish from the bucket
and placed it carefully in the palm of her hand. "Just throw it
anywhere," he said.

Tina leaned forward and called out, "Here Liza! Here you
go!"

The little fish landed with a soft splash and spun a dizzy figure
eight under the dock. The barracuda didn't move.

Stranahan smiled. In slow motion the addled pinfish cork-
screwed its way to the bottom, taking refuge inside an old horse
conch.

"What'd I do wrong?" Tina wondered.

"Not a thing," Stranahan said. "She wasn't hungry anymore, that's all."

"Maybe it's just me."

"Maybe it is," Stranahan said.

He took her by the hand and led her upstairs. He turned on
the lights in the house and vented the shutters on both sides to

catch the cool night breeze. On the roof, the windmill creaked as it picked up speed.

Tina made a place for herself on a faded lumpy soda. She said, "I always wondered what it's like out here in the dark."

"Not much to do, I'm afraid."

"No TV?"

"No TV," Stranahan said.

"You want to make love?"

"There's an idea."

"You already saw me naked."

"I haven't forgotten," Stranahan said. "The thing is—"

"Don't worry about Richie. Anyway, this is just for fun. We'll keep it casual, okay?"

"I don't do anything casually," Stranahan said, "This is my problem." He was constantly falling in love; how else would you explain five marriages, all to cocktail waitresses?

Tina peeled off the tropical T-shirt and draped it across a barstool. Rockette-style, she kicked her way out of her bikini bottoms and left them in a rumple on the floor.

"How about these tan lines, huh?"

"What tan lines?" he asked.

"Exactly." Tina pulled the rubber band out of her ponytail and shook her hair free. Then she got back on the sofa and said, "Watch this." She stretched out and struck a smokey-eyed modeling pose—a half-turn up on one elbow, legs scissored, one arm shading her nipples.

"That looks great," Stranahan said, amused but also uneasy.

"It's tough work on a beach," Tina remarked. "Sand sticks to places you wouldn't believe. I did a professional job, though."

"I'm sure."

"Thanks to you, I got my confidence back. About my boobs, I mean." She glanced down at herself appraisingly.

"Confidence is everything in the modeling business," she said. "Somebody tells you that your ass is sagging or your tits don't match up, it's like an emotional disaster. I was worried sick until you measured them with that carpenter's thing."

"Glad I could help," Stranahan said, trying to think of something, anything, more romantic.

She said, "Anyone ever tell you that you've got Nick Nolte's nose?"

"That's all?" Stranahan said. Nick Nolte was a new one.

"Now the eyes," Tina said, "your eyes are more like Sting's. I met him one time at the Strand."

"Thank you," Stranahan said. He didn't know who the hell she was talking about. Maybe one of the those pro wrestlers from cable television.

Holding her pose, Tina motioned him to join her on the old sofa. When he did, she took his hands, placed them on her staunch new breasts, and held them there. Stranahan assumed a compliment was in order.

"They're perfect," he said, squeezing politely.

Urgently Tina arched her back and rolled over, Stranahan hanging on like a rock climber.

"While we're on the subject," he said, "could I get the name of your surgeon?"

Even before the electrolysis accident, Chemo had led a difficult life. His parents had belonged to a religious sect that believed in bigamy, vegetarianism, UFOs, and not paying federal income taxes; his mother, father and three of their respective spouses were killed by the FBI during a bloody ten-day siege at a post office outside Grand Forks, North Dakota. Chemo, who was only six at the time, went to live with an aunt and uncle in the Amish country of western Pennsylvania. It was a rigorous and demanding period, especially since Chemo's aunt and uncle were not actually Amish themselves, but fair-weather Presbyterians fleeing a mail-fraud indictment out of Bergen County, New Jersey.

Using their hard-won embezzlements, the couple had purchased a modest farm and somehow managed to infiltrate the hermetic social structure of an Amish township. At first it was just another scam, a temporary cover until the heat was off. As the years passed, though, Chemo's aunt and uncle got authentically converted. They grew to love the simple pastoral ways and hearty fellowship of the farm folk; Chemo was devastated by their transformation. Growing up, he had come to resent the family's ruse, and consequently the Amish in general. The plain baggy clothes and strict table manners were bad enough, but it was the facial hair that drove him to fury. Amish men do not shave their chins, and Chemo's uncle insisted that, once attaining puberty, he adhere to custom. Since religious arguments held no sway with Chemo, it was the practical view that his uncle propounded: All fugitives need a disguise, and a good beard was hard to beat.

Chemo sullenly acceded, until the day of his twenty-first birthday when he got in his uncle's pickup truck, drove down to the local branch of the Chemical Bank, threatened a teller with a pitchfork (the Amish own no pistols), and strolled off with seven thousand dollars and change. The first thing he bought was a Bic disposable safety razor.

The *Philadelphia Inquirer* reported that it was the only bank robbery by an Amish in the entire history of the commonwealth. Chemo himself was never arrested for the crime, but his aunt and uncle were unmasked, extradited back to New Jersey, tried and convicted of mail fraud, then shipped off to a country-club prison in north Florida. Their wheat farm was seized by the U.S. government and sold at auction.

Once Chemo was free of the Amish, the foremost challenge of adulthood was avoiding manual labor, to which he had a chronic aversion. Crime seemed to be the most efficient way of making money without working up a sweat, so Chemo gave it a try. Unfortunately, nature had dealt him a cruel disadvantage: While six foot nine was the perfect height for an NBA forward, for a burglar it was disastrous. Chemo got stuck in the very first window he ever jimmied; he could break, but he could not enter.

Four months in a county jail passes too slowly. He thought often of his aunt and uncle, and upbraided himself for not taking advantage of their vast expertise. They could have taught him many secrets about white-collar crime, yet in his rebellious in-

solence he had never bothered to ask. Now it was too late—
their most recent postcard from the Eglin prison camp had
concluded with a religious limerick and the drawing of a happy
face. Chemo knew they were lost forever.

After finishing his stretch for the aborted burglary, he moved
to a small town outside of Scranton and went to work for the
city parks and recreation department. Before long, he parlayed
a phony but impressive résumé into the post of assistant city
manager, a job that entitled him to a secretary and a municipal
car. While the salary was only twenty thousand dollars a year,
the secondary income derived from bribes and kickbacks was
substantial. Chemo prospered as a shakedown artist, and the
town prospered, too. He was delighted to discover how often
the mutual interests of private enterprise and government seemed
to intersect.

The high point of Chemo's municipal career was his savvy
trashing of local zoning laws to allow a Mafia-owned-and-
operated dog food plant to be built in the suburbs. Three hundred new jobs were created, and there was talk of running
Chemo for major.

He greatly liked the idea and immediately began gouging
illegal political contributions out of city contractors. Soon a
campaign poster was designed, but Chemo recoiled when he
saw the finished product: the four-foot photographic blowup of
his face magnified the two ingrown hair follicles on the tip of
his otherwise normal nose; the blemishes looked, in Chemo's
own distraught simile, "like two ticks fucking." He ordered the
campaign posters shredded, scheduled a second photo session,
and drove straight to Scranton for the ill-fated electrolysis treatment.

The grisly mishap and subsequent murder of the offending
doctor put an end to Chemo's political career. He swore off
public service forever.

They rented an Aquasport and docked it at Sunday's-on-the-
Bay. They chose a table under the awning, near the water.

Chemo ordered a ginger ale and Chloe Simpkins Stranahan got a vodka tonic, double.

"We'll wait till dusk," Chemo said.

"Fine by me." Chloe slurped her drink like a parched coyote. She was wearing a ridiculous white sailor's suit from Lord and Taylor's; she even had the cap. It was not ideal boatwear.

"I used to work in this joint," Chloe said, as if to illustrate how far she'd come.

Chemo said, "This is where you met Mick?"

"Unfortunately."

The bar was packed for ladies' night. In addition to the standard assembly of slick Latin studs in lizard shoes, there were a dozen blond, husky mates off the charter boats. In contrast to the disco Dannies, the mates wore T-shirts and sandals and deep Gulf Stream tans, and they drank mostly beer. The competition for feminine attention was fierce, but Chemo planned to be long gone before any fights broke out. Besides, he didn't like sitting out in the open, where people could stare.

"Have you got your plan?" Chloe asked.

"The less you know, the better."

"Oh, pardon me," she said caustically. "Pardon me, Mister James Fucking Bond."

He blinked neutrally. A young pelican was preening itself on a nearby dock piling, and Chemo found this infinitely more fascinating than watching Chloe Simpkins Stranahan in a Shirley Temple sailor cap, sucking down vodkas. It offended him that someone so beautiful could be so repellent and obnoxious; it seemed damned unfair.

On the other hand, she had yet to make the first wisecrack about his face, so maybe she had one redeeming quality.

"This isn't going to get too heavy?" she said.

"Define heavy."

Chloe stirred her drink pensively. "Maybe you could just put a good scare in him."

"Bet on it," Chemo said.

"But you won't get too tough, right?"

"What is this, all of a sudden you're worried about him?"

"You can hate someone's guts and still worry about him."

"Jesus H. Christ."

Chloe said, "Chill out, okay? I'm not backing down."

Chemo toyed with one of the infrequent black wisps attached to his scalp. He said: "Where does your husband think you are?"

"Shopping," Chloe replied.

"Alone?"

"Sure."

Chemo licked his lips and scanned the room. "You see anybody you know?"

Chloe looked around and said, "No. Why do you ask?"

"Just making sure. I don't want any surprises; neither do you."

Chemo paid the tab, helped Chloe into the bow of the Aquasport and cast off the ropes. He checked his wristwatch: 5:15. Give it maybe an hour before nightfall. He handed Chloe a plastic map of Biscayne Bay with the pertinent channel markers circled in red ink. "Keep that handy," he shouted over the engine, "case I get lost."

She tapped the map with one of her stiletto fingernails. "You can't miss the goddamn things, they're sticking three stories out of the water."

Fifteen minutes later, they were drifting through a Stiltsville channel with the boat's engine off. Chloe Simpkins Stranahan was complaining about her hair getting salty, while Chemo untangled the anchor ropes. The anchor was a big rusty clunker with a bent tongue. He hauled it out of the Aquasport's forward hatch and laid it on the deck.

Then he took some binoculars from a canvas duffel and began scouting the stilt houses. "Which one is it?" he asked.

"I told you, it's got a windmill."

"I'm looking at three houses with windmills, so which is it? I'd like to get the anchor out before we float to frigging Nassau."

Chloe huffed and took the binoculars. After a few moments she said, "Well, they all look alike."

"No shit."

She admitted she had never been on her ex-husband's house before. "But I've been by there in a boat."

Chemo said, "How do you know it was his?"

"Because I saw him. He was outside, fishing."

"How long ago was this?"

"Three, maybe four months. What's the difference?"

Chemo said, "Did Mick know it was you in the boat?"

"Sure he did, he dropped his damn pants." Chloe handed Chemo the binoculars and pointed. "That's the one, over there."

"You sure?"

"Yes, Captain Ahab, I am."

Chemo studied the stilt house through the field glasses. The windmill was turning and a skiff was tied up under the water tanks, but no one was outside.

"So now what?" Chloe said.

"I'm thinking."

"Know what I wish you'd do? I wish you'd do to him what he did to my male friend. Krazy Glue the bastard."

"That would settle things, huh?"

Chloe's tone became grave. "Mick Stranahan destroyed a man without killing him. Can you think of anything worse?"

"Well," Chemo said, reaching for the duffel, "I didn't bring any glue. All I brought was this." He took out the .22 pistol and screwed on the silencer.

Chloe made a gulping noise and grabbed the bow rail for support. So much for poise, Chemo thought.

"Don't worry, Mrs. Stranahan, this is my just-in-case." He laid the pistol on top of the boat's console. "All I really need is a little friction." Smiling, he held up a book of matches from Sunday's bar.

"You're going to burn the house down? That's great!" Chloe's eyes shone with relief. "Burning the house, that'll freak him out."

"Big-time," Chemo agreed.

"Just what that dangerous lunatic deserves."

"Right."

Chloe looked at him mischievously. "You promised to tell me who you really are."

"No, I didn't."

"At least tell me why you're doing this."

"I'm being paid," Chemo said.

"By who?"

"Nobody you know."

"Another ex-wife, I'll bet."

"What did I say?"

"Oh, all right." Chloe stood up and peered over the gunwale at the slick green water. Chemo figured she was checking out her own reflection.

"Did you bring anything to drink?"

"No," Chemo replied. "No drinks."

She folded her arms to show how peeved she was. "You mean, I've got to stay out here till dark with nothing to drink."

"Longer than that," Chemo said. "Midnight."

"But Mick'll be asleep by then."

"That's the idea, Mrs. Stranahan."

"But how will he know to get out of the house?"

Chemo laughed gruffly. "Now who's the rocket scientist?"

Chloe's expression darkened. She pursed her lips and said, "Wait a minute. I don't want you to kill him."

"Who asked you?"

A change was taking place in Chloe's attitude, the way she regarded Chemo. It was as if she was seeing the man for the first time, and she was staring, which Chemo did not appreciate. Her and her tweezered eyebrows.

"You're a killer," she said, reproachfully.

Chemo blinked amphibiously and plucked at one of the skin tags on his cheek. His eyes were round and wet and distant.

"You're a killer," Chloe repeated, "and you tricked me."

Chemo said, "You hate him so much, what do you care if he's dead or not?"

Her eyes flashed. "I care because I still get a check from that son of a bitch as long as he's alive. He's dead, I get zip."

Chemo was dumbstruck. "You get alimony? But you're remarried! To a frigging CPA!"

"Let's just say Mick Stranahan didn't have the world's sharpest lawyer."

"You are one greedy twat," Chemo said acidly.

"Hey, it's one-fifty a month," Chloe said. "Barely covers the lawn service."

She did not notice the hostility growing in Chemo's expression. "Killing Mick Stranahan is out of the question," she declared. "Burn up the house, fine, but I don't want him dead."

"Tough titties," Chemo said.

"Look, I don't know who you are—"

"Sit," Chemo said. "And keep your damn voice down."

The wind was kicking up, and he was afraid the argument might carry across the flats to the house.

Chloe sat down but was not about to shut up. "You listen to me—"

"I said, keep your damn voice down!"

"Screw you, Velcro-face."

Chemo's brow crinkled, his cheeks fluttered. He probably even flushed, though this was impossible to discern.

Velcro-face—there it was, finally. The insult. The witch just couldn't resist after all.

"Now what's the matter?" Chloe Simpkins Stranahan said. "You look seasick."

"I'm fine," Chemo said, "But you shouldn't call people names."

Then he heaved the thirty-pound anchor into her lap, and watched her pitch over backwards in her silky sailor suit. The staccato trail of bubbles suggested that she was cursing him all the way to the bottom of the bay.

9

Tina woke up alone in bed. She wrapped herself in a sheet and padded groggily around the dark house, looking for Mick Stranahan. She found him outside, balanced on the deck rail with his hands on his hips. He was watching Old Man Chitworth's stilt house light up the sky; a cracking orange torch, visible for miles. The house seemed to sway on its wooden legs, an illusion caused by blasts of raw heat above the water.

Tina thought it was the most breathtaking thing she had ever seen, even better than Old Faithful. In the glow from the blaze she looked up at Stranahan's face and saw concern.

"Somebody living there?" she said.

"No." Stranahan watched Old Man Chitworth's windmill fall, the flaming blades spinning faster in descent. It hit the water with a sizzle and hiss.

"What started the fire?" Tina asked.

"Arson," Stranahan said matter-of-factly, "I heard a boat."

"Maybe it was an accident," she suggested. "Maybe somebody tossed a cigarette."

"Gasoline," Stranahan said. "I smelled it."

"Wow. Whoever owns that place has some serious enemies, I guess."

"The man who owns that place just turned eighty-three," Stranahan said. "He's on tubes in a nursing home, all flaked out. Thinks he's Eddie Rickenbacker."

A gust of wind prompted Tina to rearrange her sheet. She got a shiver and edged closer to Mick. She said, "Some harmless old geezer. Then I don't get it."

Stranahan said, "Wrong house, that's all." He hopped off the rail. "Somebody fucked up." So much for paradise, he thought; so much for peace and tranquility.

Across the bay, from Dinner Key, came the whine of toy-like sirens.

Stranahan didn't need binoculars to see the flashing blue dots from the advancing police boats.

Tina clutched his hand. She couldn't take her eyes off the fire. "Mick, have you got enemies like that?"

"Hell, I've got *friends* like that."

By midmorning the Chitworth house had burned to the waterline, and the flames died. All that remained sticking out were charred tips of the wood pilings, some still smoldering.

Tina was reading on a deck chair and Stranahan was doing push-ups when the marine patrol boat drove up and stopped. It was Luis Córdova and another man whom Stranahan did not expect.

"Now, there's something you don't see every day," Stranahan announced, plenty loud. "Two Cubans in a boat, and no beer."

Luis Córdova grinned. The other man climbed noisily up on the dock and said, "And here's something else you don't see every day: An Irishman up before noon, and still sober."

The man's name was Al García, a homicide detective for the Metro-Dade police. His J. C. Penney coat jacket was slung over one arm, and his shiny necktie was loosened halfway down his chest. García was not wild about boat rides, so he was in a gruff and unsettled mood. Also, there was the matter of the dead body.

"What dead body?" Mick Stranahan said.

Badger-like, García shuffled up the stairs to the house, with Stranahan and Luis Córdova following single file. García gave the place the once-over and waved courteously to Tina on her lounge chair. The detective half-turned to Stranahan and in a low voice said, "What, you opened a halfway house for bimbos! Mick, you're a freaking saint, I swear."

They went inside the stilt house and closed the door. "Tell me about the dead body," Stranahan said.

"Sit down. Hey, Luis, I could use some coffee."

"A minute ago you were seasick," Luis Córdova said.

"I'm feeling much better, okay?" García scowled theatrically as the young marine patrol officer went to the kitchen. "Interdepartmental cooperation, that's the buzzword these days. Coffee's a damn good place to start."

"Easy, man, Luis is a sharp kid."

"He sure is. I wish he was ours."

Stranahan said, "Now about the body . . ."

García waved a meaty brown hand in the air, as if shooing an invisible horsefly. "Mick, what are you doing way the fuck out here? Somehow I don't see you as Robinson Crusoe, sucking the milk out of raw coconuts."

"It's real quiet out here."

Luis Córdova brought three cups of hot coffee.

Al García smacked his lips as he drank. "Quiet—is that what you said? Jeez, you got dead gangsters floating around, not to mention burning houses—"

"Is this about Tony the Eel?"

"No," Luis said seriously.

García put down his coffee cup and looked straight at Stranahan. "When's the last time you saw Chloe?"

Suddenly Mick Stranahan did not feel so well.

"A couple months back," he said. "She was on a boat with some guy. I assumed it was her new husband. Why?"

"You mooned her."

"Can you blame me?"

"We heard about it from the mister this morning."

Stranahan braced to hear the whole story. Luis Córdova opened a spiral notebook but didn't write much. Stranahan listened somberly and occasionally looked out the window toward the channel where Al García said it had happened.

"A rusty anchor?" Stranahan said in disbelief.

"It got tangled in this silky thing she was wearing," the de-

tective explained. "She went down like a sack of cement."
Sensitivity was not García's strong suit.

"The rope is what gave it away," added Luis Córdova. "One of the guys coming out to the fire saw the rope drifting up out of the current."

"Hauled her right in," García said, "like a lobster pot."

"Lord."

García said, "Fact is, we really shouldn't be telling you all this."

"Why not?"

"Because you're the prime suspect."

"That's very funny." Stranahan looked at Luis Córdova. "Is he kidding?"

The young marine patrolman shook his head.

García said, "Mick, your track record is not so hot. I mean, you already got a few notches on your belt."

"Not murder."

"Chloe hated your guts," Al García said, in the tone of a reminder.

"That's my motive? She hated my guts?"

"Then there's the dough."

"You think I'd kill her over a crummy one-hundred fifty dollars a month?"

"The principle," Al García said, unwrapping a cigar. "I think you just might do it over the principle of the thing."

Stranahan leaned back with a tired sigh. He felt bad about Chloe's death, but mostly he felt curious. What the hell was she doing out here at night?

"I always heard good things about you," Al García said, "mainly from Timmy Gavigan."

"Yeah, he said the same for you."

"And the way Eckert dumped you from the State Attorney's, that was low."

Stranahan shrugged. "They don't forget it when you shoot a judge. It's bound to make people nervous."

García made a great ceremony of lighting the cigar. Afterwards, he blew two rings of smoke and said, "For what it's worth, Luis here doesn't think you did it."

"It's the anchor business," Luis Córdova explained, "very strange." He was trying to sound all business, as if the friendship meant nothing.

Stranahan said, "The murder's got to be connected to the fire."

"The fire was an arson," Luis said. "Boat gas and a match. These houses are nothing but tinder." To make his point, he tapped the rubber heel of his shoe on the pine floor.

Stranahan said, "I think you both ought to know: Somebody wants to kill me."

García's eyebrows shot up and he rolled the cigar from one side of his mouth to the other. "Who is it, *chico*? Please, make my job easier."

"I think it's a doctor. His name is Rudy Graveline. Write this down, Luis, please."

"And why would this doctor want you dead?"

"I'm not sure, Al."

"But you want me to roust him on a hunch."

"No, I just want his name in a file somewhere. I want you to know who he is, just in case."

García turned to Luis Córdova. "Don't you love the fucking sound of that? *Just in case.* Luis, I think this is where we're supposed to give Mr. Stranahan a lecture about taking the law into his own hands."

Luis said, "Don't take the law into your own hands, Mick."

"Thank you, Luis."

Al García flicked a stubby thumb through his black mustache. "Just for the record, you didn't invite the lovely Chloe Simpkins Stranahan out here for a romantic reconciliation over fresh fish and wine?"

"No," Stranahan said. Fish and wine—that fucking García must have scoped out the dirty dinner dishes.

"And the two of you didn't go for a boat ride?"

"No, Al."

"And you didn't get in a sloppy drunken fight?"

"No."

"And you didn't hook her to the anchor and drop her overboard?"

"Nope."

"Luis, you get all that?"

Luis Córdova nodded as he jotted in the notebook. Shorthand, too; Stranahan was impressed.

García got up and went knocking around the house, making Stranahan very nervous. When the detective finally stopped prowling, he stood directly under the stuffed blue marlin. "Mick, I don't have to tell you there's some guys in Homicide think you aced old Judge Goomer without provocation."

"I know that, Al. There's some guys in Homicide used to be in business with Judge Goomer."

"And I know *that*. Point is, they'll be looking at this Chloe thing real hard. Harder than normal."

Stranahan said, "There's no chance it was an accident?"

"No," Luis Córdova interjected. "No chance."

"So," said Al García, "you see the position I'm in. Until we get another suspect, you're it. The good news is, we've got no physical evidence connecting you. The bad news is, we've got Chloe's manicurist."

Stranahan groaned. "Jesus, let's hear it."

García ambled to a window, stuck his arm out and tapped cigar ash into the water.

"Chloe had her toenails done yesterday morning," the detective said. "Told the girl she was coming out here to clean your clock."

"Lovely," said Mick Stranahan.

There was a small rap on the door and Tina came in, fiddling with the strap on the top piece of her swimsuit. Al García beamed like he'd just won the lottery; a dreary day suddenly had been brightened.

Stranahan stood up. "Tina, I want you to meet Sergeant García and Officer Córdova. They're here on police business. Al, Luis, I'd like you to meet my alibi."

"How do you do," said Luis Córdova, shaking Tina's hand in a commendably official way.

García gave Stranahan another sideways look. "I love it," said the detective. "I absolutely love this job."

Christina Marks heard about the death of Chloe Simpkins Stranahan on the six o'clock news. The only thing she could think was that Mick had done it to pay Chloe back for siccing the TV crew on him. It was painful to believe, but the only other possibility was too far-fetched—that Chloe's murder was a co-incidence of timing and had nothing to do with Mick or Victoria Barletta. This Christina Marks could not accept; she had to plan for the worst.

If Mick was the killer, that would be a problem.

If Chloe had blabbed about getting five hundred in tipster money from the Reynaldo Flemm show, that would be a problem too. The police would want to know everything, then the papers would get hold of it and the Barletta story would blow up prematurely.

Then there was the substantial problem of Reynaldo himself; Christina cold just hear him hyping the hell out of Chloe's murder in the intro: "The story you are about to see is so explosive that a confidential informant who provided us with key information was brutally murdered only days later . . ." *Brutally murdered* was one of Reynaldo's favorite on-camera redundancies. Once Christina had drolly asked Reynaldo if he'd ever heard of anyone being *gently* murdered, but he missed the point.

Sometimes, when he got particularly excited about a story, Reynaldo Flemm would actually try to write out the script himself, with comic results. The murder of Stranahan's ex-wife was just the sort of bombshell to inspire Reynaldo's muse, so Christina decided on a preemptive attack. She was reaching across the bed for the telephone when it rang.

It was Maggie Gonzalez, calling collect from somewhere in Manhattan.

"Miss Marks, I got a little problem."

Christina said: "We've been looking all over for you. What happened to your trip to Miami?"

"I went, I came back," Maggie said. "I told you, there's a problem down there."

"So what've you been doing the last few weeks," Christina said, "besides spending our money?" Christina had just about had it with this ditz; she was beginning to think Mick was right, the girl was ripping them off.

Maggie said, "Hey, I'm sorry I didn't call sooner. I was scared. Scared out of my mind."

"We thought you might be dead."

"No," said Maggie, barely audible. A long pause suggested that she was fretting over the grim possibility.

"Don't you even want to know how the story is going?" Christina asked warily.

"That's the problem," Maggie replied. "That's what I want to talk to you about."

"Oh?"

Then, almost as an afterthought, Maggie asked, "Who've you interviewed so far?"

"Nobody," Christina said. "We've got a lot of legwork to do first."

"I can't believe you haven't interviewed anybody!"

Maggie was trolling for something, Christina could tell. "We're taking it slow," Christina said. "This is a sensitive piece."

"No joke," Maggie said. "Real sensitive."

Christina held the phone in the crook of her shoulder and dug a legal pad and felt-tip pen from her shoulder bag on the bed table.

Maggie went on: "This whole thing could get me killed, and I think that's worth more than five thousand dollars."

"But that was our agreement," Christina said, scribbling along with the conversation.

"That was before I started getting threatening calls on my machine," said Maggie Gonzalez.

"From who?"

"I don't know who," Maggie lied. "It sounded like Dr. Graveline."

"What kind of threats? What did they say?"

"*Threat* threats," Maggie said impatiently. "Enough to scare me shitless, okay? You guys tricked me into believing this was safe."

"We did nothing of the sort."

"Yeah, well, five thousand dollars isn't going to cut it anymore. By the time this is finished, I'll probably have to pack up and move out of Miami. You got any idea what that'll cost?"

Christina Marks said, "What's the bottom line here, Maggie?"

"The bottom line is, I talked to *20/20*."

Perfect, Christina thought. The perfect ending to a perfect day.

"I met with an executive producer," Maggie said.

"Lucky you," said Christina Marks. "How much did they offer?"

"Ten."

"Ten thousand?"

"Right," Maggie said. "Plus a month in Mexico after the program airs . . . you know, to let things cool off."

"You thought of this all by yourself, or did you get an agent?"

"A what?"

"An agent. Every eyewitness to a murder ought to have his own booking agent, don't you think?"

Maggie sounded confused. "Ten seemed like a good number," she said. "Could be better, of course."

Christina Marks was dying to find out how much Maggie Gonzalez had told the producer at *20/20*, but instead of asking she said: "Ten sounds like a winner, Maggie. Besides, I don't think we're interested in the story anymore."

During the long silence that followed, Christina tried to imagine the look on Maggie's face.

Finally: "What do you mean, 'not interested?'?"

"It's just too old, too messy, too hard to prove," Christina said. "The fact that you waited four years to speak up really kills us in the credibility department . . ."

"Hold on—"

"By the way, are they still polygraphing all their sources over at *20/20*?"

But Maggie was too sharp. "Getting back to the money," she said, "are you saying you won't even consider a counter-offer?"

"Exactly."

"Have you talked this over with Mr. Flemm?"

"Of course," Christina Marks bluffed, forging blindly ahead.

"That's very weird," remarked Maggie Gonzalez, "because I just talked to Mr. Flemm myself about ten minutes ago."

Christina sagged back on the bed and closed her eyes.

"And?"

"And he offered me fifteen grand, plus six weeks in Ha-waii."

"I see," Christina said thinly.

"Anyway, he said I should call you right away and smooth out the details."

"Such as?"

"Reservations," said Maggie Gonzalez. "Maui would be my first choice."

10

One of the wondrous things about Florida, Rudy Graveline thought as he chewed on a jumbo shrimp, was the climate of unabashed corruption: There was absolutely no trouble from which money could not extricate you.

Rudy had learned this lesson years earlier when the state medical board had first tried to take away his license. For the board it had been a long sticky process, reviewing the complaints of disfigured patients, comparing the "before" and "after" photographs, sifting through the minutiae of thirteen separate malpractice suits. Since the medical board was made up mostly of other doctors, Rudy Graveline had fully expected exoneration—physicians stick together like shit on a shoe.

But the grossness of Rudy's surgical mistakes was so astounding that even his peers could not ignore it; they recommended that he be suspended from the practice of medicine forever. Rudy hired a Tallahassee lawyer and pushed the case to a state administrative hearing. The hearing officer acting as judge was not a doctor himself, but some schlump civil servant knocking down twenty-eight thousand a year, tops. At the end of the third day of testimony—some of it so ghastly that Rudy's own attorney became nauseated—Rudy noticed the hearing officer getting into a decrepit old Ford Fairmont to go home to his wife and four kids. This gave Rudy an idea. On the fourth day, he made a phone call. On the fifth day, a brand new Volvo station wagon with cruise control was delivered to the home of the hearing officer. On the sixth day, Dr. Rudy Graveline was cleared of all charges against him.

The board immediately reinstated Rudy's license and sealed all the records from the public and the press—thus honoring the long-held philosophy of Florida's medical establishment that the last persons who need to know about a doctor's incompetence are the patients.

Safe from the sanctions and scrutiny of his own profession, Dr. Rudy Graveline viewed all outside threats as problems that could be handled politically; that is, with bribery. Which is why he was having a long lunch with Dade County Commissioner Roberto Pepsical, who was chatting about the next election.

"Shrimp good, no?" said Roberto, who pocketed one in each cheek.

"Excellent," Rudy agreed. He pushed the cocktail platter

aside and dabbed the corners of his mouth with a napkin. "Bobby, I'd like to give each of you twenty-five."

"Grand?" Roberto Pepsical flashed a mouthful of pink-flecked teeth. "Twenty-five grand, are you serious?"

The man was a hog: a florid, jowly, pug-nosed, rheumy-eyed hog. A cosmetic surgeon's nightmare. Rudy Graveline couldn't bear to watch him eat. "Not so loud," he said to the commissioner. "I know what the campaign law says, but there are ways to duck it."

"Great!" said Roberto. He had an account in the Caymans; all the commissioners did, except for Lillian Atwater, who was trying out a phony blind trust in the Dominican Republic.

Rudy said, "First I've got to ask a favor."

"Shoot."

The doctor leaned forward, trying to ignore Roberto's hot gumbo breath. "The vote on Old Cypress Towers," Rudy said, "the rezoning thing."

Roberto Pepsical lunged for a crab leg and cracked it open with his front teeth. "Nooooo problem," he said.

Old Cypress Towers was one of Dr. Rudy Graveline's many real estate projects and tax shelters: a thirty-three story luxury apartment building with a nightclub and health spa planned for the top floor. Only trouble was, the land currently was zoned for low-density public use—parks, schools, ball fields, shit like that. Rudy needed five votes on the county commission to turn it around.

"No sweat," Roberto reiterated. "I'll talk to the others."

The "others" were the four commissioners who always got pieced out in Roberto Pepsical's crooked deals. The way the system was set up, each of the nine commissioners had his own crooked deals and his own set of locked votes. That way the tally always came out 5–4, but with different players on each side. The idea was to confuse the hell out of the newspaper reporters, who were always trying to figure out who on the commission was honest and who wasn't.

"One more thing," Dr. Rudy Graveline said.

"How about another beer?" asked Roberto Pepsical, eyeing his empty sweaty glass. "You don't mind if I get one."

"Go ahead," Rudy said, biting back his disgust.

"Crab?" The commissioner brandished another buttery leg.

"No thanks." Rudy waited for him to wedge it in his mouth, then said: "Bobby, I also need you to keep your ears open."

"For what?"

"Somebody who used to work for me is threatening to go to the cops, trying to bust my balls. They're making up stuff about some old surgical case."

Roberto nodded and chewed in synchronization, like a mechanical dashboard ornament. Rudy found it very distracting.

He said, "The whole thing's bullshit, honestly. A disgruntled employee."

Roberto said, "Boy, I know how it is."

"But for a doctor, Bobby, it could be a disaster. My reputation, my livelihood, surely you can understand. That's why I need to know if the cops ever go for it."

Roberto Pepsical said, "I'll talk to the chief myself."

"Only if you hear something."

Roberto winked. "I'll poke around."

"I'd sure appreciate it," Dr. Graveline said. "I can't afford a scandal, Bobby. Something like that, I'd probably have to leave town."

The commissioner's brow furrowed as he contemplated his twenty-five large on the wing. "Don't sweat it," he said confidently to the doctor. "Here, have a conch fritter."

Chemo was in the waiting room when Rudy Graveline got back to Whispering Palms.

"I did it," he announced.

Rudy quickly led him into the office.

"You got Stranahan?"

"Last night," Chemo said matter-of-factly. "So when can we get started on my face?"

Unbelievable, Rudy thought. Very scary, this guy.

"You mean the dermabrasion treatments."

"Fucking A," Chemo said. "We had a deal."

Rudy buzzed his secretary and asked her to bring him the morning *Herald*. After she went out again, Chemo said, "It happened so late, probably didn't make the paper."

"Hmmmm," said Rudy Graveline, scanning the local news page. "Maybe that's it—must have happened too late. Tell me about it, please."

Chemo wet his dead-looking lips. "I torched his house." No expression at all. "He was asleep."

"You know this for a fact?"

"I watched it go up," Chemo said. "Nobody got out." He crossed his long legs and stared dully at the doctor. The droopy lids made him look like he was about to doze off.

Rudy folded up the newspaper. "I believe you," he said to Chemo, "but I'd like to be sure. By tomorrow it ought to be in the papers."

Chemo rubbed the palm of one hand along his cheeks, making sandpaper sounds. Rudy Graveline wished he would knock it off.

"What about the TV?" Chemo asked. "Does that count, if it makes the TV?"

"Of course."

"Radio, too?"

"Certainly," Rudy said. "I told you before, no big deal. I don't need to see the actual corpse, okay, but we do need to be sure. It's very important, because this is a dangerous man."

"Was," Chemo said pointedly.

"Right. This was a dangerous man." Rudy didn't mention Stranahan's ominous phone call on Maggie Gonzalez's answering machine. Better to limit the cast of characters, for Chemo's sake. Keep him focused.

"Maybe it's already on the radio," Chemo said hopefully.

Rudy didn't want to put the guy in a mood. "Tell you what," he said in a generous tone. "We'll go ahead and do the first treatment this afternoon."

Chemo straightened up excitedly. "No shit?"

"Why not?" the doctor said, standing. "We'll try a little patch on your chin."

"How about the nose?" Chemo said, touching himself there.

Rudy slipped on his glasses and came around the desk to where Chemo was sitting. Because of Chemo's height, even in the chair, the surgeon didn't have to lean over far to get a close-up look at the corrugated, cheesy mass that passed for Chemo's nose.

"Pretty rough terrain," Rudy Graveline said, peering intently. "Better to start slow and easy."

"Fast and rough is fine with me."

Rudy took off his glasses and struck an avuncular pose, a regular Marcus Welby. "I want to be very careful," he told Chemo. "Yours is an extreme case."

"You noticed."

"The machine we use is a Stryker dermabrader—"

"I don't care if it's a fucking Black and Decker, let's just do it."

"Scar tissue is tricky," Rudy persisted. "Some skin reacts better to sanding than others." He couldn't help remembering what had happened to the last doctor who had screwed up Chemo's face. Getting murdered was even worse than getting sued for malpractice.

"One little step at a time," Rudy cautioned. "Trust me."

"Fine, then start on the chin, whatever," Chemo said with a wave of a pale hand. "You're the doctor."

Those magic words.

How Rudy Graveline loved to hear them.

Compared to other law firms, Kipper Garth's had the over-head problem licked. He had one central office, no partners, no associates, no "of counsels." His major expenses were bill-board advertising, cable, telephones (he had twenty lines), and, of course, secretaries (he called them legal aides, and employed fifteen). Kipper Garth's law practice was, in essence, a high-class boiler room.

The phones never stopped ringing. This was because Kipper

Garth had shrewdly put up his billboards at the most dangerous traffic intersections in South Florida, so that the second thing every noncomatose accident victim saw (after the Jaws of Life) was Kipper Garth's phone number in nine-foot red letters: 555-TORT.

Winnowing the incoming cases took most of the time, so Kipper Garth delegated this task to his secretaries, who were undoubtedly more qualified anyway. Kipper Garth saved his own energy for selecting the referrals; some P.I. lawyers specialized in spinal cord injuries, others in orthopedics, still others in death-and-dismemberment. Though Kipper Garth was not one to judge a colleague's skill in the courtroom (not having *been* in a courtroom in at least a decade), he knew a fifty-fifty fee split when he saw it, and made his referrals accordingly.

The phone bank at Kipper Garth's firm looked and sounded like the catalog-order department at Montgomery Ward. By contrast, the interior of Kipper Garth's private office was rich and staid, lit like an old library and just as quiet. This is where Mick Stranahan found his brother-in-law, practicing his putting.

"You don't knock anymore?" said Kipper Garth, eyeing a ten-footer into a Michelob stein.

"I came to make a little deal," Stranahan said.

"This I gotta hear." Kipper Garth wore gray European-cut slacks, a silk paisley necktie and a bone-colored shirt, the French cuffs rolled up to his elbows. His salt-and-pepper hair had been dyed silver to make him look more trustworthy on the billboards.

"Let's forget this disbarment thing," Stranahan said.

Kipper Garth chuckled. "It's a little late, Mick. You already testified, remember?"

"How about if I agree not to testify next time?"

Kipper Garth backed away from the next putt and looked up. "Next time?"

"There's other cases kicking around the grievance committee, am I right?"

"But how do you—"

"Lawyers talk, Jocko." Stranahan emptied the golf balls out

of the beer stein and rolled them back across the carpet toward his brother-in-law. "I've still got a few friends in town," he said. "I'm still plugged in."

Kipper Garth leaned his putter in the corner behind his desk. "I'm suing *you* remember? Defamation, it's called."

"Don't make me laugh."

The lawyer's eyes narrowed. "Mick, I know why you're here. Chloe's been killed and you're afraid you'll take the fall. You need a lawyer, so here you are, looking for a goddamn freebie."

"I said don't make me laugh."

"Then what is it?"

"Who's getting your malpractice stuff these days?"

Kipper Garth started flicking through his Rolodex; it was the biggest Rolodex that Stranahan had even seen, the size of a pot roast. Kipper Garth said, "I've got a couple main guys, why?"

"These guys you've got, can they get state records?"

"What kind of records?"

Christ, the man was lame. "Discipline records," Stranahan explained, "from the medical board."

"Gee, I don't know."

"There's a shocker."

"What's going on, Mick?"

"This: You help me out, I'll lay off of you. Permanently."

Kipper Garth snorted. "I'm supposed to be grateful? Pardon me if I don't give a shit."

Naturally, thought Stranahan, it would come to this. The pertinent papers were wadded in his back pocket. He got them out, smoothed them with the heel of one hand and laid them out carefully, like solitaire cards, on Kipper Garth's desk.

The lawyer muttered, "What the hell?"

"Pay attention," Stranahan said. "This one here is the bill of sale for your spiffy new Maserati. That's a Xerox of the check—fifty-seven thousand, eight something, what a joke. Anyway, the account that check was written on is your clients' trust account, Jocko. We're talking deep shit. Forget disbarment, we're talking felony."

Kipper Garth's upper lip developed an odd tic.

"I'm paying it back," he said hoarsely.

"Doesn't matter," Mick Stranahan said. "Now, some of this other crap—that's a hotel bill from the Grand Bay in Coconut Grove. Same weekend you told Katie you were in Boston with the ABA. Anyway, it's none of my business but you don't look like a man that could drink three bottles of Dom all by your lonesome. See, it's right there on the bill." Stranahan pointed, but Kipper Garth's eyes were focused someplace else, some place far away. By now his lip was twitching like a porch lizard.

"You," he said to Stranahan. "You jerk."

"Now what's this dinner for two, Jocko? My sister was at Grandma's with the kids that night, if memory serves. Dinner for two at Max's Place, what exactly was that? Probably just a client, no?"

Kipper Garth collected himself and said, "All right, Mick."

"You understand the situation."

"Yes."

"It was easier than you think," Stranahan said. "See, once you're plugged in, it's hard to get unplugged. I mean, once you know this stuff is out there, it's real easy to find." A half-dozen phone calls was all it took.

Kipper Garth began folding the papers, creasing each one with a great deal of force.

Stranahan said, "What scares you more, Jocko, the Florida Bar, the county jail, or an expensive divorce?"

Wearily, Kipper Garth said, "Did you mean what you said before, about the disbarment and all that?"

"You're asking because you know I don't have to deal, isn't that right? Maybe that's true—maybe you'd do me this favor for nothing. But fair is fair, and you ought to get something in return. So, yeah, I'll lay off. Just like I promised."

Kipper Garth said, "Then I'll talk to my guys about getting the damn state files. Give me a name, please."

"Graveline," said Stranahan. "Dr. Rudy Graveline."

Kipper Garth winced. "Jeez, I've heard that name. I think he's in my yacht club."

Mick Stranahan clapped his hands. "Yo ho ho," he said.

* * *

Later, on the way to see her plastic surgeon, Tina asked Mick: "Why didn't you make love to me last night?"

"I thought you enjoyed yourself."

"It was sweet, but why'd you stop?"

Stranahan said: "Because I've got this terrible habit of falling in love."

Tina rolled her eyes. "After one night?"

"True story," Stranahan said. "All five of the women I married, I proposed to them the first night we went to bed."

"Before or after?" Tina asked.

"After," he said. "It's like a disease. The scary part is, they tend to say yes."

"Not me."

"I couldn't take that chance."

"You're nuts," Tina said. "Does this mean we're never gonna do it?"

Stranahan sighed, feeling old and out of it. His ex-wife just gets murdered, some asshole doctor's trying to kill him, a TV crew is lurking around his house—all this, and Tina wants to know about getting laid, wants a time and date. Why didn't she believe him about the others?

He stopped at a self-service Shell station and filled three plastic Farm Stores jugs with regular unleaded. When he went up to pay, nobody said a word. He put the gallon jugs in the trunk of the Imperial and covered them with a bunch of boat rags.

Back in the car, Tina gave him a look. "You didn't answer my question."

"You've got a boyfriend," Stranahan said, wishing he could've come up with something better, more original.

"Richie? Richie's history," said Tina. *'No problema.'*

It always amazed Stranahan how they could make boyfriends disappear, snap, just like that.

"So," Tina said, "how about tonight?"

"How about I call you," he said, "when things cool off?"

"Yeah," Tina muttered. "Sure."

Stranahan was glad when they got to the doctor's office. It

was a two-story peach stucco building in Coral Gables, a refurbished old house. The plastic surgeon's name was Dicer. Craig E. Dicer; a nice young fellow, too nice to say anything nasty about Rudy Graveline at first. Stranahan badged him and tried again. Dr. Dicer took a good hard look at the gold State Attorney's investigator shield before he said: "Is this off the record?"

"Sure," said Stranahan, wondering: Where do these guys learn to talk like this?

"Graveline's a butcher," Dr. Dicer said. "A hacker. Everybody in town's mopped up after him, one time or another. Fortunately, he doesn't do much surgery himself anymore. He got wise, hired a bunch of young sharpies, all board certified. It's like a damn factory up there."

"Whispering Palms?"

"You've seen it?" Dr. Dicer asked.

Stranahan said no, but it was his next stop. "If everybody in Miami knows that Graveline's a butcher, how does he get any patients?"

Dr. Dicer laughed caustically. "Hell, man, the patients don't know. You think some housewife wants her tits poofed goes downtown to the courthouse and looks up the lawsuits? No way. Rudy Graveline's got a big rep because he's socially connected. He did the mayor's niece's chin, this I know for a fact. And old Congressman Carberry? Graveline did his girlfriend's eyelids. Or somebody at Whispering Palms did; Rudy always takes the credit."

Tina, who hadn't been saying much since the car, finally cut in. "Talk to models and actresses," she said. "Whispering Palms is in. Like tofu."

"Jesus," said Stranahan.

Dr. Dicer said, "Can I ask why you're interested?"

"Really, you don't want to know," Stranahan said.

"I guess not."

"*I* want to know," Tina said.

Stranahan pretended not to hear her. He said to Dr. Dicer: "One more question, then we'll let you get back to work. This is hypothetical."

Dr. Dicer nodded, folded his hands, got very studious looking.

Stranahan said: "Is it possible to kill somebody during a nose job?"

By way of an answer, Dr. Dicer took out a pink neoprene replica of a bisected human head, a bronze Crane mallet, and a small Cottle chisel. Then he demonstrated precisely how you could kill somebody during a nose job.

When Chemo got to the Gay Bidet, a punk band called the Chicken Chokers had just finished wringing their sweaty jock straps into a cocktail glass and guzzling it down on stage.

"You're late," said Chemo's boss, a man named Freddie. "We already had three fights."

"Car trouble," said Chemo. "Radiator hose." Not an apology, an explanation.

Freddie pointed at the small bandage and said, "What happened to your chin?"

"A zit," Chemo said.

"A zit, that's a good one."

"What's that supposed to mean?"

"Nothing," Freddie said. "Don't mean nothing." He had to watch the wisecracks around Chemo. The man made him nervous as a gerbil. Freaking seven-foot cadaver, other clubs would kill for a bouncer like that.

Freddie said, "Here, you got a message."

Chemo said thank you, went outside to a pay phone on Collins and called Dr. Rudy Graveline's beeper. At the tone, Chemo pushed in the number of the pay phone, hung up, and waited. All the way out here, he could hear the next band cranking up. The Crotch Rockets, it sounded like. Their big hit was *Lube-Job Lover*. Chemo found it somewhat derivative.

The telephone rang. Chemo waited for the third time before picking up.

"We have got a problem." said Rudy Graveline, raspy, borderline terrified.

Chemo said, "Aren't you going to ask about my chin?"

"No!"

"Well, it stings like hell."

Dr. Graveline said, "I told you it would."

Chemo said, "How long've I gotta wear the Band-Aid?"

"Till it starts to heal, for Chrissakes. Look, I've got a major situation here and if you don't fix it, the only person's going to care about your complexion is the goddamn undertaker. One square inch of perfect chin, maybe you're thinking how gorgeous you look. Well, think open casket. How's that for gorgeous?"

Chemo absently touched his new bandage. "Why're you so upset?"

"Mick Stranahan's alive."

Chemo thought: The bitch in the sailor suit, she got the wrong house.

"By the way," Rudy Graveline said angrily, "I'd like to thank you for not telling me how you drowned the man's wife in the middle of Biscayne Bay. From what was on TV, I'm just assuming it was you. Had your subtle touch." When Chemo didn't respond for several moments, the doctor said: "Well?"

Chemo asked, "Is that a siren at your end?"

"Yes," Rudy said archly, "yes, that would be a siren. Now, aren't you going to ask how I know that Stranahan's still alive?"

"All right," Chemo said, "how do you know?"

"Because," the doctor said, "the bastard just blew up my Jag."

11

Christina Marks knocked twice, and when no one answered she walked in. The man in the hospital bed had a plastic oxygen mask over his mouth. Lying there he looked as small as a child. The covers were pulled up to the folds of his neck. His face was mottled and drawn. When Christina approached the bed, the man's blue eyes opened slowly and he waved. When he lifted the oxygen mask away from his mouth, she saw that he was smiling.

"Detective Gavigan?"

"The one and only."

"I'm Christina Marks." She told him why she had come, what she wanted. When she mentioned Vicky Barletta, Timmy Gavigan made a zipper motion across his lips.

"What's the matter?" Christina asked.

"That's an open case, lady. I can't talk about it." Timmy Gavigan's voice was hollow, like it was coming up a pipe from his dead lungs. "We got regulations about talking to the media," he said.

"Do you know Mick Stranahan?" Christina said.

"Sure I know Mick," Timmy Gavigan said. "Mick came to see me a while back."

"About this case?"

"Mick's in my scrapbook," Timmy Gavigan said, looking away.

Christina said, "He's in some trouble."

"He didn't get married again, the dumb bastard?"

"Not that kind of trouble," Christina said. "This time it was the Barletta case."

"Mick's a big boy," said Timmy Gavigan. "My guess is, he can handle it." He was smiling again. "Honey, you sure are pretty."

"Thank you," said Christina.

"Can you believe, six months ago I'd be trying to charm you right into the sack. Now I can't even get up to take a whizz. Here a gorgeous woman comes to my room and I can't raise my goddamn head, much less anything else."

She said, "I'm sorry."

"I know what you're thinking—a dying man, he's likely to say anything. But I mean it, you're something special. I got high standards, always did. I mean, hell, I might be dead, but I ain't blind."

Christina laughed softly. Timmy Gavigan reached for the oxygen mask, took a couple of deep breaths, put it down again. "Give me your hand," he said to Christina Marks. "Please, it's all right. What I got, you can't catch."

Timmy Gavigan's skin was cold and papery. Christina gave a little squeeze and tried to pull away, but he held on. She noticed his eyes had a sparkle.

"You've been to the file?"

She nodded.

"I took a statement from that doctor, Rudy Something."

Christina said, "Yes, I read it."

"Help me out," said Timmy Gavigan, squinting in concentration. "What the hell did he say again?"

"He said it was a routine procedure, nothing out of the ordinary."

"Yeah, I remember now," Timmy Gavigan said. "He was a precious thing, too, all business. Said he'd done five thousand nose jobs and this was no different from the others. And I said maybe not, but this time your patient vanished from the face of the earth. And he said she was fine last time he saw her. Walked out of the office all by herself. And I said yeah, walked straight into the fucking twilight zone. Pardon my French."

Christina Marks said, "You've got a good memory."

"Too bad I can't breathe with it." Timmy Gavigan took another hit of oxygen. "Fact is, we had no reason to think the doctor was involved. Besides, the nurse backed him up. What the hell was his name again?"

"Graveline."

Timmy Gavigan nodded. "Struck me as a little snot. If only you could arrest people for that." He coughed, or maybe it was a chuckle. "Did I mention I was dying?"

Christina said yes, she knew.

"Did you say you were on TV?"

"No, I'm just a producer."

"Well, you're pretty enough to be on TV."

"Thank you."

"I'm not being very much help, I know," said Timmy Gavigan. "They got me loaded up on morphine. But I'm trying to think if there was something I left out."

"It's all right, you've been helpful."

She could tell that each breath was torture.

He said, "Your idea is that the doctor did it, is that right? See, that's a new angle—let me think here."

Christina said, "It's just a theory."

Timmy Gavigan shifted under the covers and turned slightly to face her. "He had a brother, was that in the file?"

No, Christina said. Nothing about a brother.

"Probably not," Timmy Gavigan said. "It didn't seem important at the time. I mean, the doc wasn't even a suspect."

"I understand."

"But he did have a brother, I talked to him maybe ten minutes. Wasn't worth typing it up." Timmy Gavigan motioned for a cup of water and Christina held it to his lips.

"Jesus, I must be a sight," he said. "Anyway, the reason I mention it—let's say the doctor croaked Vicky. Don't know why, but let's say he did. What to do about the body? That's a big problem. Bodies are damn tough to get rid of, Jimmy Hoffa being the exception."

"What does the doctor's brother do?"

Timmy Gavigan grinned, and color flashed to his cheeks. "That's my point, honey. The brother was a tree trimmer."

Christina tried to look pleased at this new information, but mostly she looked puzzled.

"You don't know much about tree trimming, do you?" Timmy Gavigan said in a teasing tone. Then he gulped more oxygen.

She said, "Why did you go see the doctor's brother?"

"I didn't. Didn't have to. I met him right outside the clinic— I forget the damn name."

"The Durkos Medical Center."

"Sounds right." Timmy Gavigan paused, and his free hand moved to his throat. When the pain passed, he continued. "Outside the clinic, I saw this guy hacking on the black olive trees. Asked him if he was there the day Vicky disappeared, if he saw anything unusual. Naturally he says no. After, I ask his name and he tells me George Graveline. So like the genius I am, I say: You related to the doctor? He says, yeah, and that's about it."

"George Graveline." Christina Marks wrote the name down.

Timmy Gavigan lifted his head and eyed the notebook. "Tree trimmer," he said, "Make sure you put that down."

"Tell me what it means, please."

"No, you ask Mick."

She said, "What makes you so sure I'll see him?"

"Wild hunch."

Then Timmy Gavigan said something that Christina Marks couldn't quite hear. She leaned over and asked him, in a whisper, to repeat it.

"I said, you sure are beautiful." He winked once, then closed his eyes slowly.

"Thanks for holding my hand," he said.

And then he let go.

Whenever there was a bombing in Dade County, somebody in the Central Office would call Sergeant Al García for help, mainly because García was Cuban and it was automatically assumed that the bombing was in some way related to exile politics. García had left orders that he was not to be bothered about bombings unless somebody actually died, since a dead body was the customary prerequisite of homicide investigation. He also sent detailed memoranda explaining that Cubans were not the only ones who tried to bomb each other in South Florida, and he listed all the mob and labor and otherwise non-Cuban bombings over the last ten years. Nobody at the Central Office paid much attention to García's pleadings, and they still summoned him over the most chickenshit of explosions.

This is what happened when Dr. Rudy Graveline's black Jaguar sedan blew up. García was about to tell the dispatcher to piss off, until he heard the name of the complainant. Then, fifteen minutes behind the fire trucks, he drove straight to Whispering Palms.

What had happened was: Rudy had gone to the airport to pick up a potentially important patient, a world-famous actress who had awakened one morning in her Bel Air mansion, glanced at herself naked in the mirror, and burst into tears. She got Dr. Graveline's name from a friend of a friend of Pernell Roberts's poolboy, and called to tell the surgeon that she was flying to Miami for an emergency consultation. Because of the actress's fame and wealth (most of it accumulated during a messy divorce from one of the Los Angeles Dodgers), Rudy agreed to meet the woman at the airport and give a personal tour of Whispering Palms. He was double-parked in front of the Pan Am terminal when he first noticed the beat-up old Chrysler pull in behind him, its rear end sticking into traffic. Rudy noticed the car again on his way back to the beach—the actress yammering away about the practical joke she once played on Richard Chamberlain while they were shooting some miniseries; Rudy with a worried eye on the rearview, because the Imperial was right there, on his bumper.

The other car disappeared somewhere on Alton Road, and Rudy didn't think about it again until he and the actress walked out of Whispering Palms; Rudy with a friendly hand on her elbow, she with a fistful of glossy surgery brochures. The Imperial was parked right across from Rudy's special reserved slot. The same big man was behind the wheel. The actress didn't know anything was wrong until the man got out of the Chrysler and whistled at a Yellow Cab, which was conveniently parked under a big ficus tree at the north end of the lot. When the taxi pulled up, the man from the Imperial opened the back door and told the actress to get in. He said the cabbie would take her straight to the hotel. She said she wasn't staying in any *hotel*, that she'd rented a villa in Golden Beach where Eric Clapton once lived; the big man said fine, the cabbie knew the way.

Finally the actress got in, the taxi drove off, and it was just the stranger and Rudy Graveline alone in the parking lot. When the man introduced himself, Rudy tried very hard not to act terrified. Mick Stranahan said that he wasn't yet certain why Dr. Graveline was trying to have him killed, but that it was a very bad idea, overall. Dr. Graveline replied that he didn't know what on earth the man was talking about. Then Mick Stranahan walked across the parking lot, got in his Chrysler, turned on the ignition, placed a coconut on the accelerator, got out of the car, reached through the driver's window and slipped it into Drive. Then he jumped out of the way and watched the Imperial plow directly into the rear of Dr. Rudy Graveline's black Jaguar sedan. The impact, plus the three jugs of gasoline that Mick Stranahan had strategically positioned in the Jaguar's trunk, caused the automobile to explode in a most spectacular way.

When Rudy Graveline recounted this story to Detective Sergeant Al García, he left out two details—the name of the man who did it, and the reason.

"He never said why?" said Al García, all eyebrows.

"Not a word," lied Dr. Graveline. "He just destroyed my car and walked away. The man was obviously deranged."

García grunted and folded his arms. Smoke was still rising from the Jag, which was covered with foam from the firetrucks. Rudy acted forlorn about the car, but García knew the truth. The only reason the asshole even bothered with the police was for the insurance company.

The detective said, "You don't know the guy who did this?"

"Never saw him before."

"That's not what I asked."

Rudy said, "Sergeant, I don't know what you mean."

García was tempted to come out and ask the surgeon if it were true that he was trying to bump off Mick Stranahan, like Stranahan had said. That was a fun question, the kind García loved to ask, but the timing wasn't right. For now, he wanted Rudy Graveline to think of a him as a big, dumb cop, not a threat.

"A purely random attack," García mused.

"It would appear so," Rudy said.

"And you say the man was short and wiry?"

"Yes," Rudy said.

"How short?"

"Maybe five one," Rudy said. "And he was black."

"How black?"

"Very black," the doctor said. "Black as my tires."

Al García dropped to a crouch and shone his flashlight on the front hub of the molten Jag. "Michelins," he noted. "The man was as black as Michelins."

"Yes, and he spoke no English."

"Really. What language was it?"

"Creole," Rudy Graveline said. "I'm pretty sure."

García rubbed his chin. "So what we've got in the way of an arsonist," he said, "is a malnourished Haitian midget."

Rudy frowned. "No," he said seriously, "he was taller than that."

García said the man apparently had picked the trunk lock in order to put the containers of gasoline inside the doctor's car. "That shows some thinking," the detective said.

"Could still be crazy," Rudy said. "Crazy people can surprise you."

One tow truck driver put the hooks on what was left of Rudy's black Jaguar. Another contemplated the remains of the Chrysler Imperial, which García kept referring to as "that ugly piece of elephant shit." His hatred for Chryslers went back to his patrol days.

Lennie Goldberg, a detective from Intelligence, came up and said, "So, what do you think, Al? Think it was Cubans?"

"No, Lennie, I think it was the Shining Path. Or maybe the freaking Red Brigade." It took Lennie Goldberg a couple of beats to catch on. Irritably García said, "Would you stop this shit about the Cubans? This was a routine car bomb, okay? No politics, no Castro, no CIA. No fucking Cubans, got it?"

"Jeez, Al, I was just asking." Lennie thought García was getting very touchy on the subject.

"Use your head, Lennie." García pointed at the wreck. "This look like an act of international terrorism? Or does it look like some dirtball in a junker went nuts?"

Lennie said, "Could be either, Al. With bombings, sometimes you got to look closely for the symbolism. Maybe there's a message in this. Aren't Jaguars manufactured in Britain? Maybe this is the IRA."

García groaned. A message, for Christ's sake. And symbolism! This is what happens when you put a moron in the intelligence unit: he gets even dumber.

A uniformed cop handed Rudy Graveline a copy of the police report. The doctor folded it carefully with three creases, like a letter, and placed it in the inside pocket of his jacket.

Al García turned his back on Lennie Goldberg and said to Rudy, "Don't worry, we'll find the guy."

"You will?"

"No sweat," said García, noticing how uncomfortable Rudy seemed. "We'll run the V.I.N. number on the Chrysler and come up with our Haitian dwarf, or whatever."

"Probably a stolen vehicle," Rudy remarked.

"Probably not," said Al García. *Vehicle?* Now the guy was doing Jack Webb. García said: "No, sir, this definitely was a premeditated act, the act of a violent and unstable perpetrator. We'll do our best to solve it, Doctor, you've got my word."

"Really, it's not that big a deal."

"Oh, it is to us," García said. "It is indeed a big deal."

"Well, I know you're awfully busy."

"Oh, not too busy for something like this," García said in

the heartiest of tones. "The firebombing of a prominent physician—are you kidding? Starting now, Dr. Graveline, your case is priority one."

García was having a ball, acting so damn gung ho; the doctor looked wan and dyspeptic.

The detective said, "You'll be hearing back from me real soon."

"I will?" said Rudy Graveline.

Reynaldo Flemm had been in a dark funk since his clandestine visit to Whispering Palms. Dr. Graveline had lanced his ego; this, without knowing Reynaldo's true identity or the magnitude of his fame. Three days had passed, and Flemm had scarcely been able to peek out the door of his Key Biscayne hotel room. He had virtually stopped eating most solid food, resorting to a diet of protein cereal and lemon Gatorade. Every time Christina Marks knocked, Reynaldo would call out that he was in the bathroom, sick to his stomach, which was almost true. He couldn't tear himself away from the mirror. The surgeon's dire assessment of Reynaldo's nose—"two sizes too large for your face"—was savage by itself, but the casual criticism of his weight was paralyzing.

Flemm was examining himself naked in the mirror when Christina came to the door again.

"I'm sick," he called out.

"Ray, this is stupid," Christina scolded from the hallway. She didn't know about his trip to the clinic. "We've got to talk about Maggie," she said.

There was the sound of drawers being opened and closed, and maybe a closet. For a moment Christina thought he might be getting ready to emerge.

"Ray?"

"What about Maggie?" he said. Now it sounded like he was inches from the door. "Didn't you straighten out that shit about 20/20?"

Christina said, "That's what we have to talk about. Fifteen thousand is ludicrous. Let me in, Ray."

"I'm not well."

"Open the damn door or I'm calling New York."

"No, Chris, I'm not at my best."

"Ray, I've seen you at your best, and it's not all that great. Let me in, or I start kicking." And she did. Reynaldo Flemm couldn't believe it, the damn door was jumping off its hinges.

"Hey, stop!" he cried, and opened it just a crack.

Christina saw that he wore a towel around his waist, and nothing else. A bright green pair of elastic cyclist shorts lay on the floor.

"Hawaii?" Christina said. "You told that bimbette we'd send her to Hawaii."

Reynaldo said, "What choice did I have? You want to lose this story?"

"Yes," Christina said, "this story is serious trouble, Ray. I want to pack up and go home."

"And give it to ABC? Are you nuts?" He opened the door a little more. "We're getting so close."

Christina tried to bait him. "How about we fly up to Spartanburg tomorrow? Do the biker segment, like we planned?"

Reynaldo loved to do motorcycle gangs, since they almost always attacked him while the tape was rolling. The Spartanburg story had a sex-slavery angle as well, but Flemm still didn't bite.

"That'll wait," he said.

Christina checked both ways to make sure no one was coming down the hall. "You heard about Chloe Simpkins?"

Reynaldo Flemm shook his head. "I haven't seen the news," he admitted, "in a couple of days."

"Well, she's dead," Christina said. "Murdered."

"Oh, God."

"Out by the stilt houses."

"No shit? What an opener."

"Forget it, Ray, it's a mess." She shouldered her way into his room. He sat down on the bed, his knees pressed together under the towel. A tape measure was coiled in his left hand. "What's that for?" Christina asked, pointing.

"Nothing," Flemm said. He wasn't about to tell her that he had been measuring his nose in the mirror. In fact, he had been taking the precise dimensions of all his facial features, to compare proportions.

He said, "When is Chloe's funeral? Let's get Willie and shoot the stand-up there."

"Forget it." She explained how the cops would probably be looking for them anyway, to ask about the five hundred dollars. In its worst light, somebody might say that they contributed to Chloe's death, put her up to something dangerous.

"But we didn't," Reynaldo Flemm whined. "All we got from her was Stranahan's location, and barely that. A house in the bay, she said. A house with a windmill. Easiest five bills that woman ever made."

Christina said, "Like I said, it's a big mess. It's time to pull out. Tell Maggie to go fly her kite for Hugh Downs."

"Let's wait a couple more days." He couldn't stand the idea of giving up; he hadn't gotten beat up once on this whole assignment.

"Wait for what?" Christina said testily.

"So I can think. I can't think when I'm sick."

She resisted the temptation to state the obvious. "What exactly is the matter?" she asked.

"Nothing I care to talk about," Flemm said.

"Ah, one of those male-type problems."

"Fuck you."

As she was leaving, Christina asked when he would be coming out of his hotel room to face the real world. "When I'm good and ready," Flemm replied defensively.

"Take your time, Ray. Tomorrow's interview is off."

"You canceled it—why?"

"It canceled itself. The man died."

Flemm gasped. "Another murder!"

"No Ray, it wasn't murder." Christina waved good-bye. "Sorry to disappoint you."

"That's okay," he said, sounding like a man on the mend, "we can always fudge it."

12

After Timmy Gavigan's funeral, García offered Mick Stranahan a ride back to the marina.

"I noticed you came by cab," the detective said.

"Al, you got eyes like a hawk."

"So where's your car?"

Stranahan said, "I guess somebody stole it."

It was a nice funeral, although Timmy Gavigan would have made fun of it. The chief stood up and said some things, and afterwards some cops young enough to be Timmy's grandchildren shot off a twenty-one gun salute and accidently hit a power transformer, leaving half of Coconut Grove with no electricity. Stranahan had worn a pressed pair of jeans, a charcoal sports jacket, brown loafers and no socks. It was the best outfit he owned; he'd thrown out all his neckties when he moved to the stilt house. Stranahan caught himself sniffling a little toward the end of the service. He made a mental note to clip the obit from the newspaper and glue it in Timmy Gavigan's scrapbook, the way he promised. Then he would mail the scrapbook up to Boston, where Timmy's daughters lived.

Driving back out the Rickenbacker Causeway, García was saying, "Didn't you have an old Chrysler? Funny thing, we got one of those shitheaps in a fire the other night. Somebody filed off the V.I.N. numbers, so we can't trace the damn thing—maybe it's yours, huh?"

"Maybe," said Mick Stranahan, "but you keep it. The block was cracked. I was ready to junk it anyway."

García drummed his fingers on the steering wheel, which meant he was running out of patience.

"Hey, Mick?"

"What?"

"Did you blow up that asshole's Jag?"

Stranahan stared out at the bay and said, "Who?"

"The doctor. The one who wants to kill you."

"Oh."

Something was not right with this guy, García thought. Maybe the funeral had put him in a mood, maybe it was something else.

"We're getting into an area," the detective said, "that makes me very nervous. You listening, *chico*?"

Stranahan pretended to be watching some topless girl on a sailboard.

García said, "You want to play Charlie Bronson, okay, but let me tell you how serious this is getting. Forget the doctor for a second."

"Yeah, how? He's trying to kill me."

"Well, chill on that for a minute and think about this: Murdock and Salazar got assigned to Chloe's murder. Do I have to spell it out, or you want me to stop the car so you can go ahead and puke?"

"Jesus," said Mick Stranahan.

Detectives John Murdock and Joe Salazar had been tight with the late Judge Raleigh Goomer, the one Stranahan had shot. Murdock and Salazar had been in on the bond fixings, part of the A-team. They were not Mick Stranahan's biggest fans.

"How the hell did they get the case?"

"Luck of the draw," García said. "Nothing I could do without making it worse."

Stranahan slammed a fist on the dashboard. He was damn tired of all this bad news.

García said, "So they come out here to do a canvass, right? Talk to people at the boat ramp, the restaurant, anyone who might have seen your ex on the night she croaked. They come back with statements from two waitresses and a gas attendant, and guess who they say was with Chloe? You, Blue Eyes.''

"That's a goddamn lie, Al.''

"You're right. I know it's a lie because I drive out here the next day on my lunch hour and talked to these same people myself. On my lunch hour! Show them two mugs, including yours, and strike out. Oh for ten. So Frick and Frack are lying. I don't know what I can do about it yet—it's a tricky situation, them sticking together on their story.'' García took a cigar from his breast pocket. Wrapper and all, he jammed it in the corner of his mouth. "I'm telling you this so you know how goddamn serious it's getting, and maybe you'll quit this crazy car-bombing shit and give me a chance to do my job. How about it?''

Absently, Stranahan said, "This is the worst year of my life, and it's only the seventeenth of January.''

García chewed the cellophane off the cigar. "I don't know why I even bother to tell you anything,'' he grumbled. "You're acting like a damn zombie.''

The detective made the turn into the marina with a screech of the tires. Stranahan pointed toward the slip where his aluminum skiff was tied up, and García parked right across from it. He kept the engine running. Stranahan tried to open the door, but García had it locked with a button on the driver's side.

The detective punched the lighter knob in the dashboard and said, "Don't you have anything else you want to ask? Think real hard, Mick.''

Stranahan reached across and earnestly shook García's hand. "Thanks for everything, Al. I mean it.''

"Hey, are we having the same conversation? What the fuck is the matter with you?''

Stranahan said, "It's been a depressing week.''

"Don't you even want to know what the waitress and the pump jockey really said? About the guy with Chloe?''

"What guy?''

García clapped his hands. "Good, I got your attention. Excellent!'' He pulled the lighter from the dash and fired up the cigar.

"What guy?" Stranahan asked again.

Making the most of the moment, García took his notebook from his jacket and read aloud: "White male, early thirties, approximately seven feet tall, two hundred fifty pounds, freckled, balding—"

"Holy shit."

"—appeared to be wearing fright makeup, or possibly some type of Halloween mask. The waitresses couldn't agree on what, but they all said basically the same thing about the face. Said it looked like somebody dragged it across a cheese grater."

Mick Stranahan couldn't recall putting anybody in jail who matched that remarkable description. He asked García if he had any leads.

"We're busy calling the circuses to see who's escaped lately," the detective said sarcastically. "I swear, I don't know why I tell you anything."

He pushed the button to unlock the doors. "We'll be in touch," he said to Stranahan, waving him out of the police car. "And stay away from the damn doctor, okay?"

"You bet," said Mick Stranahan. All he could think of was: *Seven feet tall.* Poor Chloe.

Dr. Rudy Graveline now accepted the possibility that his world was imploding, and that he must prepare for the worst. Bitterly he thought of all the crises he had survived, all the professional setbacks, the lawsuits, the peer review hearings, the hospital expulsions, the hasty relocations from one jurisdiction to another. There was the time he augmented the breasts of a two-hundred-pound woman who had wanted a reduction instead; the time he nearly liposuctioned a man's gall bladder right out of his abdomen; the time he mistakenly severed a construction worker's left ear while removing a dime-sized cyst—Rudy Graveline had survived all these. He believed he'd found safe haven in South Florida; having figured out the system, and how to beat it, he was sure he had it made. And suddenly a botched nose job had come back to spoil it all. It didn't seem fair.

Rudy sat at his desk and leafed dispiritedly through the most recent bank statements. The Whispering Palms surgical complex was raking in money, but the overhead was high and the mortgage was a killer. Rudy had not been able to siphon off nearly as much as he had hoped. Once his secret plan had been to retire in four years with six million put away; it now seemed likely that he would be forced to get out much sooner, and with much less. Having already been banned from practicing medicine in California and New York—by far the most lucrative markets for a plastic surgeon—Rudy Graveline's thoughts now turned to the cosmopolitan cities of South America, a new frontier of vanity, sun-baked and ripe with wrinkles; a place where a Harvard medical degree still counted for something. Riffling through his CDs, he wondered if it was too late to weasel out of the Old Cypress Towers project: get liquid and get gone.

He was studying a map of Brazil when Heather Chappell, the famous actress, came into the office. She wore the pink terry-cloth robe and bath slippers that Whispering Palms provided to all its VIP guests. Heather's lipstick was candy apple, her skin had a caramel tan, and her frosted blond hair was thick and freshly brushed. She was a perfectly beautiful thirty-year-old woman who, for reasons unfathomable, despised her own body. A dream patient, as far as Rudy Graveline was concerned.

She sat in a low-backed leather chair and said, "I've had it with the spa. Let's talk about my operation."

Rudy said, "I wanted you to unwind for a couple of days, that's all."

"It's been a couple days."

"But aren't you more relaxed?"

"Not really," Heather said. "Your masseur, what's his name—"

"Niles?"

"Yeah, Niles. He tried to cornhole me yesterday. Aside from that, I've been bored to tears."

Rudy smiled with practiced politeness. "But you've had a chance to think about the different procedures."

"I didn't need to think about anything, Dr. Graveline. I was ready the first night off the plane. Have you been dodging me?"

"Of course not."

"I heard your car got blown up." She said it in a schoolgirl's voice, like it was gossip she'd picked up in study hall.

Rudy tried to neutralize his inflection. "There was an accident," he said. "Very minor."

"The night I came, wasn't it? That hunk in the parking lot, the guy who put me in the taxi. What's going on with him?"

Rudy ignored the question. "I can schedule the surgery for tomorrow," he said.

"Fine, but I want you to do it," Heather said. "You personally."

"Of course," Rudy said. He'd stay in the O.R. until they put her under, then he'd head for the back nine at Doral. Let one of the young hotshots do the knife work.

"What did you decide?" he asked her.

Heather stood up and stepped out of the slippers. Then she let the robe drop to the carpet. "You tell me," she said.

Rudy's mouth went dry at the sight of her.

"Well," he said. "Let's see." The problem was, she didn't need any surgery. Her figure, like her face, was sensational. Her tan breasts were firm and large, not the least bit droopy. Her tummy was tight and flat as an iron. There wasn't an ounce of fat, a trace of a stretch mark, the slenderest serpentine shadow of a spider vein—not on her thighs, her legs, not anywhere. Nothing was out of proportion. Naked, Heather looked like an "after," not a "before."

Rudy was really going to have to scramble on this one. He put on his glasses and said, "Come over here, Miss Chappell, let me take a closer look."

She walked over and, to his stupefaction, climbed up on the onyx desk, her bare feet squeaking on the slick black surface. Standing, she vamped a movie pose—one hand on her hip, the other fluffing her hair. As Rudy's eyes traveled up those long legs, he nearly toppled over backwards in his chair.

"The nose, obviously," Heather said.

"Yes," said Rudy, thinking: She has a great straight nose. What the hell am I going to do?

"And the breasts," Heather said, taking one in each hand and studying them. Like she was in the produce section, checking out the grapefruits.

Bravely Rudy asked, "Would you like them larger or smaller?"

Heather glared at him. "Bigger, of course! And brand-new nipples."

Jesus, Rudy muttered under his breath. "Miss Chappell," he said, "I wouldn't advise new nipples. There could be serious complications and, really, it isn't necessary." Little pink rosebuds, that's what her nipples looked like. Why, Rudy wondered, would she ever want new ones?

In a pouty voice, Heather said all right, leave the nipples. Then she pivoted on the desktop and patted her right thigh. "I want two inches off here."

"That much?" Rudy was sweating. He didn't see it, plain and simple. Two inches of what?

"Stand up," Heather told him. "Look here."

He did, he looked hard. His chin was about three inches from her pubic bone. "Two inches," Heather repeated, turning to show him the other thigh, "from both sides."

"As you wish," the doctor said. What the hell, he'd be on the golf course anyway. Let the whiz kids figure it out.

Heather dropped to her knees on the desk, so the two of them were nearly face to face. "And I want my eyelids done," she said, pointing with a long cranberry fingernail, "and my neck, too. You said no scars, remember?"

"Don't worry," Rudy assured her.

"Good," Heather said. "Anything else?"

"Not that I can see."

"How about my butt?" She spun around on the desk, showing it to Rudy; looking over one shoulder, waiting for his professional opinion.

"Well," said Rudy, running his fingers along the soft round curves.

"Hey," said Heather, "easy there." She squirmed around to face him. "Are you getting worked up?"

Rudy Graveline said, "Of course not." But he was. He couldn't figure it out, either; all the thousands of female bodies he got to see and feel. This was no ordinary lust, this was something fresh and wonderous. Maybe it was the way she bossed him around.

"I saw you in *Fevers of the Heart*," Rudy said, idiotically. He had rented the cassette for a pool party. "You were quite good, especially the scene on the horse."

"Sit down," Heather told him, and he did. She was bare-assed on the desk, legs swinging mischievously on either side of him. He put a clammy hand on each knee. "Maybe now's a good time to talk about money," she said.

For Rudy Graveline, the ultimate test of sobriety. In his entire career he had never traded sex for his surgical services, never even discounted. Money was money, pussy was pussy—a credo he drilled into his sure-handed young assistants. Some things in life you don't give away."

To Heather Chappell, he said, "I'm afraid it's going to be expensive."

"Is it?" She swung one leg up and propped her foot on his right shoulder.

"All these procedures at once, yes, I'm afraid so."

"How much, Dr. Graveline?"

Up came the other leg, and Rudy was scissored.

"Come here a second," Heather said.

Rudy Graveline was torn between the thing he loved the most and the thing he needed most: Sex and money. The warm feel of Heather's bare heels on his shoulders was like the weight of the world. And heaven, too.

Her toes tickled his ears. "I said, come here."

"Where?" Rudy peeped, reaching out.

"God, are you blind?"

Chemo bought an Ingram submachine gun to go with his .22 pistol. He got it from a man who had come to the club one night with a bunch of Jamaicans. The man himself was not a Jamaican; he was from Colombia. Chemo found this out when he stopped him at the door and told him he couldn't come inside the Gay Bidet with a machine gun.

"But this is Miami," the man had said with a Spanish accent.

"I've got my orders," Chemo said.

The man agreed to let Chemo take the gun while he and his pals went inside, which turned out to be a smart thing. As the band was playing a song called *Suck Till You're Sore*, a local skinhead gang went into a slam-dancing frenzy, and fights broke out all over the place. The Jamaicans took off, but the Colombian stayed behind to do battle. At one point he produced a pocket knife and tried to surgically remove the swastika tattoo off the proud but hairless chest of a teenaged skinhead. The band took a much-needed break while the Beach police rushed in for the arrests. Later, when Chemo spotted the Colombian in the back of the squad car, he tapped on the window and asked about the Ingram. The Colombian said keep it and Chemo said thanks, and slipped a twenty-dollar bill through the crack of the window.

The thing Chemo liked best about the Ingram was the shoulder strap. He put it on and showed it to his boss, Freddie, who said, "Get the fuck outta here with that thing!"

The next day, the eighteenth of January, Chemo got up early and drove out to Key Biscayne. He knew it would be unwise to go to the same marina where he had taken Chloe, so he looked around for another boat place. He found one near the Marine Stadium, where they race the big Budweiser speedboats. At first a kid with badly bleached hair tried to rent him a twenty-foot Dusky for a hundred ten dollars a day, plus a hundred fifty security deposit. Chemo didn't have that kind of money.

"Got a credit card?" the kid asked.

"No," said Chemo. "What about that thing over there?"

"That's a jet ski," the kid said.

It was designed like a waterbug with handlebars. You drove it like a motorcycle, only standing up. This one was yellow, with the word *Kawasaki* on the front.

"You don't want to try it," the kid with yellow hair said.

"Why not?"

"Because," the kid said, laughing, "you're too tall, man. Hit a wake, it'll snap your spine."

Chemo figured the guy was just trying to talk him into renting something bigger, something he didn't need.

"How much is the jet ski?" he said.

"Twenty an hour, but you got to sign a waiver." The kid was thinking that, as tall as this guy is, he doesn't look healthy enough to ride a jet ski; he looks kind of tapped-out and sickly, like he's been hanging from the wall of some dungeon for a couple months. The kid was thinking maybe he ought to ask if the guy knew how to swim, just in case.

Chemo handed him two twenties.

The kid said, "I'll still need a deposit."

Chemo said he didn't have any more money. The kid said he'd take Chemo's wristwatch, but Chemo said no, he didn't want to give it up. It was a Heuer diving watch, silver and gold links, made in Switzerland. Chemo had swiped it off a young architect who was overdosing in the men's room at the club. While the jerk was lying there in the stall, trying to swallow his tongue, Chemo grabbed his wrist and replaced the Heuer with his own thirty-dollar Seiko with the fake alligator band.

"No jet ski without a deposit," said the kid with yellow hair.

"How about a gun?" Chemo said.

"What kind?"

Chemo showed him the .22 and the kid said okay, since it was a Beretta he'd hang onto it. He stuck it in the front of his chinos and led Chemo to the jet ski. He showed Chemo how the choke and the throttle worked, and tossed him a bright red life vest.

"You can change in the shed," the kid said.

"Change?"

"You got a swimsuit, right?" The kid hopped back on the dock and gave Chemo the keys. "Man, you don't want to ride these things in heavy pants."

"I guess not," said Chemo, unbuckling his trousers.

* * *

A shrimper named Joey agreed to take Christina Marks anywhere she wanted. When she gave him a hundred-dollar bill, Joey looked at it and said, "Where you going, Havana?"

"Stiltsville," Christina said, climbing into the pungent shrimp boat. "And I need a favor."

"You bet," said Joey, tossing off the ropes.

"After you drop me off, I need you to stay close. Just in case."

Joey aimed the bow down the canal, toward the mouth of Norris Cut. "In case what?" he asked.

"In case the man I'm going to see doesn't want me to stay."

Joey grinned and said, "I can't imagine that. Here, you want a beer?"

He motored down the ocean side of Key Biscayne in amiable silence. Christina stood next to him at the wheel, guardedly watching the swarm of hungry seagulls that wailed and dove behind the stern. When the shrimp boat passed the Cape Florida lighthouse at the tip of the island, Christina saw the stilt houses to the south.

"Which one?" Joey shouted over the engines. When Christina pointed, Joey smiled and gave her a crusty wink.

"What's that mean?"

"Him," Joey said. "Why didn't you say so?"

They were maybe two hundred yards off the radio towers and making the wide turn into the channel when Joey nudged Christina Marks and pointed with his chin. Up ahead, something swift and yellow was crossing one of the tidal flats, bouncing severely in the choppy water. It was an odd, gumdrop-shaped craft, and a tall pale figure appeared to be standing in the middle, holding on with both arms.

Joey eased back on the throttle to give way.

"I hate those fool things," he said. "Damn tourists don't know where the hell they're going."

They watched it cross from the starboard side, no more than thirty yards ahead of them. Joey frowned and said, "I'll be goddamned." He snatched a rag from his tool box and wiped the salty film from the shrimp boat's windshield.

"Look," he said to Christina. "Now you've seen it all."

The tall pale man driving the jet ski was nude except for his soggy Jockey shorts.

And black sunglasses.

And a gleaming wristwatch.

And an Ingram .45 submachine gun strapped on his bare shoulder.

Christina Marks was astonished. "What do you suppose he's doing out here with *that*?"

"Whatever the hell he wants," said Joey the shrimper.

13

Earlier that day, Tina and two of her girlfriends had appeared at the stilt house in a borrowed Bayliner Capri. They saw Mick Stranahan sleeping on the roof beneath the windmill, the Remington shotgun at his side.

Tina's friends were alarmed. They voted to stay in the boat while Tina went up on the dock and approached the house.

"Richie wants me back," she called to Stranahan.

He sat up and rubbed his eyes. "What?"

"I said, Richie wants me back. I wanted you to be the first to know."

"Why?" Stranahan said, his voice thick.

"So you could change my mind."

Stranahan noticed that a seagull had crapped all over the shotgun while he was asleep. "Damn," he said under his breath. He took a black bandanna from the pocket of his jeans and wiped the shotgun.

"Well?" came Tina's voice from below. "You going to change my mind or not?"

"How?"

"Sleep with me."

"I already did," Stranahan said.

"You know what I mean."

"Go back to Richie," Stranahan advised. "If he hits you again, file charges."

"Why are you so afraid?"

Stranahan slid butt-first down the grainy slope of the roof, to a spot from which Tina was visible in her tiny tangerine thong swimsuit.

"We've been over this," Stranahan said to her.

"But I don't want to marry you," she said. "I promise. Even if you ask me afterwards, I'll say no—no matter how great it was. Besides, I'm not a waitress. You said all the others were waitresses."

He groaned and said, "Tina, I'm sorry. It just won't work."

Now she looked angry. One of the other girls in the Bayliner turned on the radio and Tina snapped at her, told her to shut off the damn music. "How do you know it won't work?" she said to Stranahan.

"I'm too old."

"Bullshit."

"And you're too young."

"Double bullshit."

"Okay," he said. "Then name the Beatles."

"What?" Tina forced a caustic laugh. "Are you serious?"

"Dead serious," Stranahan said, addressing her from the edge of the roof. "If you can name all the Beatles, I'll make love to you right now."

"I don't believe this," Tina said. "The fucking Beatles."

Stranahan had done the math in his head: She was nineteen, which meant she had been born the same year the band broke up.

"Well, there's Paul," Tina said.

"Last name?"

"Come on!"

"Let's hear it."

"McCartney, okay? I don't believe this."

Stranahan said, "Go on, you're doing fine."

"Ringo," Tina said. "Ringo Starr. The drummer with the nose."

"Good."

"And then there's the guy who died. Lennon."

"First name?"

"I know his son is Julian."

"His son doesn't count."

Tina said, "Yeah, well, you're an asshole. It's *John*. John Lennon."

Stranahan nodded appreciatively. "Three down, one to go. You're doing great."

Tina folded her arms and tried to think of the last Beatle. Her lips were pursed in a most appealing way, but Stranahan stayed on the roof. "I'll give you a hint," he said to Tina. "Lead guitar."

She looked up at him, triumph shining in her gray eyes. "Harrison," she declared. "Keith Harrison!"

Muttering, Stranahan crabbed back up to his vantage beneath the legs of the windmill. Tina said some sharp things, all of which he deserved, and then got on the boat with her friends and headed back across the bay toward Dinner Key and, presumably, Richie.

Joey the shrimper spit over the transom and said, "Well, there's your boy."

Christina Marks frowned. Mick Stranahan lay naked in the shape of a T on the roof of the house. His tan legs were straight, and each arm was extended. He had a bandanna pulled down over his eyes to shield them from the white rays of the sun. Christina Marks thought he looked like the victim of a Turkish firing squad.

"He looks like Christ," said Joey. "Don't you think he looks like Christ? Christ without a beard, I mean."

"Take me up to the house," Christina said. "Do you have a horn on this thing?"

"Hell, he knows we're here."

"He's sleeping."

"No, ma'am," Joey said. "You're wrong." But he sounded the horn anyway. Mick Stranahan didn't stir.

Joey idled the shrimp boat closer. The tide was up plenty high, rushing sibilantly under the pilings of the house. Clutching a brown grocery bag, Christina stepped up on the dock and waved the shrimper away.

"Thanks very much."

Joey said, "You be sure to tell him what we saw. About the big freak on the water scooter."

She nodded.

"Tell him first thing," Joey said. He pulled back on the throttle and the old diesel moaned into reverse. The engine farted an odious cloud of blue smoke that enveloped Christina Marks. She coughed all the way up the stairs.

When she got to the main deck, Stranahan was sitting on the edge of the roof, legs dangling.

"What's in the bag?"

"Cold cuts, wine, cheese. I thought you might be hungry."

"This how they do it in New York?"

The sack was heavy, but Christina didn't put it down. She held it like a baby, with both arms, but not too tightly. She didn't want him to think it was a chore. "What are you talking about?" she asked.

"The wine and cheese," Stranahan said. "There's a sense of ceremony about it. Maybe it's necessary where you come from, but not here."

"Fuck you," said Christina Marks. "I'm on expense account, hotshot."

Stranahan smiled. "I forgot." He hopped off the roof and landed like a cat. She followed him into the house and watched him slip into blue jean cutoffs, no underwear. She put the bag on the kitchen counter and he went to work, fixing lunch. From the refrigerator he got some pickles and a half pound of big winter shrimp, still in the shell.

As he opened the wine, he said, "Let's get right to it: You've heard something."

"Yes," Christina said. "But first: You won't believe what we just saw. A man with a machine gun, on one of those water-jet things."

"Where?"

She motioned with her chin. "Not even a mile from here."

"What did he look like?"

Christina described him. Stranahan popped the cork.

"I guess we better eat fast," he said. He was glad he'd brought the shotgun down from the roof after Tina and her friends had left, when he went to find a fresh bandanna. Subconsciously he glanced at the Remington, propped barrel-up in the corner of the same wall with the stuffed marlin head.

Christina peeled a shrimp, dipped it tail-first into a plastic thimble of cocktail sauce. "Are you going to tell me who he is, the man in the underwear?"

"I don't know," Stranahan said. "I honestly don't. Now tell me what else."

This would be the most difficult part. She said, "I went to see your friend Tim Gavigan at the hospital."

"Oh."

"I was there when he died."

Stranahan cut himself three fat slices of cheddar. "Extreme unction," he said. "Too bad you're not a priest."

"He wanted me to tell you something. Something he remembered about the Vicky Barletta case."

With a mouthful of cheese, Stranahan said, "Tell me you didn't take that asshole up to the VA. Flemm—you didn't let him have a crack at Timmy in that condition, did you?"

"Of course not," she said sharply. "Now listen: Tim Gavigan remembered that the plastic surgeon has a brother. George Graveline. He saw him working outside the clinic."

"Doing what?" Stranahan asked.

"This is what Tim wanted me to tell you: The guy is a tree trimmer. He said you'd know what that means. He was going on about Hoffa and dead bodies."

Stranahan laughed. "Yeah, he's right. It's perfect."

Impatiently Christina said, "You want to fill me in?"

Stranahan chomped on a pickle. "You know what a wood chipper is? It's like a king-sized sideways Cuisinart, except they use it to shred wood. Tree companies tow them around like a U-Haul. Throw the biggest branches down this steel chute and they come out sawdust and barbecue chips."

"Now I get it," Christina said.

"Something can pulverize a mahogany tree, think of what it could do to a human body."

"I'd rather not."

"There was a famous murder case in New Jersey, they had everything but the corpse. The corpse was ground up in a wood chipper so basically all they found was splinters of human bone— not enough for a good forensic I.D. Finally somebody found a molar, and the tooth had a gold filling. That's how they made the case."

Christina was still thinking about bone splinters.

"At any rate," Stranahan said, "it's a helluva good lead. Hurry now, finish up." He wedged the cork into the half-empty wine bottle and started wrapping the leftover cold cuts and cheese in wax paper. Christina was reaching for one last shrimp when he snatched the dish away and put it in the refrigerator.

"Hey!"

"I said hurry."

She noticed how deliberately he was moving, and it struck her that something was happening. "What is it, Mick?"

"You mean you don't hear it?"

Christina said no.

"Just listen," he said, and before she knew it the stilt house was shuttered, and the door closed, and the two of them were alone in the corner of the bedroom, sitting on the wooden floor. At first the only sound Christina Marks heard was the two of them breathing, and then came some scratching noises that Stranahan said were seagulls up on the roof. Finally, when she leaned her head against the plywood wall, she detected a far-away hum. The longer she listened, the more distinct it became.

The pitch of the motor was too weak to be an airplane and too high to be much of a boat.

"Jesus, it's him," she said with a tremble.

Stranahan acknowledged the fact with a frown. "You know," he said, "this used to be a pretty good neighborhood."

Chemo wondered about the Ingram, about the effects of salt spray on the firing mechanism. He didn't know much about machine guns, but he suspected that it was best not to get them wet. The ride out to Stiltsville had been wetter than he'd planned.

He parked the jet ski beneath one of the other stilt houses to wait for the shrimp boat to leave Mick Stranahan's place. He saw a good-looking woman in a white cottony top and tan safari shorts hop off the shrimp boat and go upstairs, so Chemo began to work her into the scenario. He didn't know if she was a wife or a girlfriend or what, but it didn't matter. She was there, and she had to die. End of story.

Chemo pried open a toolshed and found a rag for the Ingram. Carefully he wiped off the moisture and salt. The gun looked fine, but there was only one way to be sure. He took an aluminum mop handle from the shed and busted the padlock off the door of the house. Once, inside he quickly found a target: an old convertible sofa, its flowered fabric showing traces of mold and mildew. Chemo shut the door to trap the noise. Then he knelt in front of the sofa, put the Ingram to his shoulder and squeezed off three rounds. Dainty puffs of white fuzz and dust rose with the impact of each bullet. Chemo lowered the gun and carefully examined the .45 caliber holes in the cushions.

Now he was ready. He slung the gun strap over his shoulder and pulled his soggy Jockey shorts up snugly on his waist. He was about to go when he thought of something. Quickly he moved through the house, opening doors until he found a bathroom.

At the sink Chemo took off his sunglasses and put his face to the mirror. With a forefinger he tested the tiny pink patch of flesh that Dr. Rudy Graveline had dermabraded. The patch no longer stung; in fact, it seemed to be coming along nicely.

Chemo was extremely pleased, and ventured forth in bright spirits.

Someplace, maybe it was *Reader's Digest*, he had read where salt water actually expedited the healing process.

"Don't move," Mick Stranahan whispered.

"I wasn't planning on it."

"Unless I tell you."

From the hum of the engine, Christina Marks guessed that the jet ski was very close; no more than thirty yards.

Stranahan held the shotgun across his knees. She looked at his hands and noticed they were steady. Hers were shaking like an old drunk's.

"Do you have a plan?" she asked.

"Basically, my plan is to stay alive."

"Are you going to shoot him?"

Stranahan looked at her as if she were five years old. "Now what do you think? *Of course* I'm going to shoot him. I intend to blow the motherfucker's head off, unless you've got some objection."

"Just asking," Christina said.

Chemo was thinking: Damn Japanese.

Whoever designed these jet skis must have been a frigging dwarf.

His back was killing him; he had to hunch over like a washerwoman to reach the handlebars. Every time he hit a wave, the gun strap slipped off his bony shoulder. A couple times he thought for sure he'd lost the Ingram, or at least broken it. Damn Japanese.

As he approached Stranahan's stilt house, Chemo started thinking something else. He had already factored the girl into the scenario, figured he'd shoot her first and get it over with. But then he realized he had another problem: Surely she had seen him ski past the shrimp boat, probably noticed the machine gun, probably told Stranahan.

Who had probably put it together.

So Chemo anticipated a fight. Screw the element of surprise; the damn jet scooter was as loud as a Harley. Stranahan could hear him coming two miles away.

But where was he?

Chemo circled the stilt house slowly, eventually riding the curl of his own wake. The windows were down, the door shut. No sign of life, except for a pair of ratty looking gulls on the roof.

A thin smile of understanding came to his lips. Of course—the man was waiting inside. A little ambush action.

Chemo coasted the jet ski up to the dock and stepped off lightly. He took the Ingram off his shoulder and held it in front of him as he went up the stairs, thinking: Where's the logical place for Stranahan to be waiting? In a corner, of course.

He was pleased to find that the wooden deck went around Stranahan's entire house. Walking cautiously on storklike legs, Chemo approached the southwest corner first. Calmly he fired one shot, waist level, through the wall. He repeated the same procedure at each of the other corners, then sat on the rail of the deck and waited. When nothing happened after three minutes, he walked up to the front door and fired twice more.

Then he went in.

Christina Marks was not aware that Stranahan had been hit until she felt something warm on her bare arm. She opened her mouth to scream but Stranahan covered it with his hand and motioned for her to be quiet. She saw that his eyes were watering from the pain of the bullet wound. He removed his hand from her mouth and pointed at his left shoulder. Christina nodded but didn't look.

They heard three more gunshots, each in a different part of the house. Then came a silence that lasted a few agonizing minutes. Finally Stranahan rose to his feet with the shotgun cradled in his right arm. The left side of his body was numb and wet with blood; in the twilight of the shuttered house, he looked two-tone.

From the floor Christina watched him move. He pressed his

back to the wall and edged toward the front of the house. The next shots made Christina shut her eyes. When she opened them, she saw two perfect holes through the front door; twin sunbeams, sharp as lasers, perforated the shadows. Beneath the light shafts, Mick Stranahan lay prone on his belly, elbows braced on the wooden floor. He was aiming at the front door when Chemo opened it.

Stranahan's shotgun was a Remington 1100, a semi-automatic twelve-gauge, an excellent bird gun that holds up to five shells. Later, when Stranahan measured the distance from the door to where he had lain, he would marvel at how any human being with two good eyes could miss a seven-foot target at a distance of only nineteen feet four inches. The fact that Stranahan was bleeding to death at the time was not, in his view, a mitigating excuse.

In truth, it was the shock of the intruder's appearance that had caused Stranahan to hesitate—the sight of this gaunt, pellucid, frizzle-haired freak with a moonscape face that could stop a freight train.

So Stranahan had stared for a nanosecond when he should have squeezed the trigger. For someone who looked so sickly, Chemo moved deceptively fast. As he dove out of the doorway, the first blast from the Remington sprinkled its rain of birdshot into the bay.

"Shit," Stranahan said, struggling to his feet. On his way toward the door he slipped on his own blood and went down again, his right cheek slamming hard on the floor; this, just as Chemo craned around the corner and fired a messy burst from the Ingram. Rolling in a sticky mess, Stranahan shot back.

Chemo slammed the door from the outside, plunging the house into darkness once more.

Stranahan heard the man running on the outside deck, following the apron around the house. Stranahan took aim through the walls. He imagined that the man was a rising quail, and he led accordingly. The first blast tore a softball-sized hole in the wall of the living room. The second punched out the shutter in the kitchen. The third and final shot was followed by a grunt and a splash outside.

"Christina!" Stranahan shouted. "Quick, help me up."

But when she got there, biting back tears, crawling on bare knees, he had already passed out.

Chemo landed on his back in the water. He kicked his legs just to make sure he wasn't paralyzed; other than a few splinters in his scalp, he seemed to be fine. He figured that the birdshot must have missed him, that the concussion so close to his head was what threw him off balance.

Instinctively he held the Ingram high out of the water with his right hand, and paddled furiously with his left. He knew he had to make it under cover of the house before Stranahan came out; otherwise he'd be a sitting duck. Chemo saw that the machine gun was dripping, so he figured it must have gotten dunked in the fall. Would it still fire? And how many rounds were left? He had lost count.

These were his concerns as he made for the pilings beneath the stilt house. Progress was maddeningly slow; by paddling with only one hand, Chemo tended to move himself in a frothy circle. In frustration he paddled more frenetically, a tactic that decreased the perimeter of his route but brought him no closer to safety. He expected at any second to see Stranahan burst onto the deck with the shotgun.

Beneath Chemo there appeared in the water a long gray-blue shadow, which hung there as if frozen in glass. It was Stranahan's silent companion, Liza, awakened from its afternoon siesta by the wild commotion.

A barracuda this age is a creature of sublime instinct and flawless precision, an eating machine more calculating and efficient than any shark in the ocean. Over time the great barracuda had come to associate human activity with feeding; its impulses had been tuned by Stranahan's evening pinfish ritual. As Chemo struggled in the shadows, the barracuda was on full alert, its cold eyes trained upward in anticipation. The blue-veined legs that kicked impotently at its head, the spastic thrashing—these posed no threat.

Something else had caught its attention: the familiar rhythmic glint of stunned prey on the water's surface. The barracuda struck with primitive abandon, streaking up from the deep, slashing, then boring back toward the pilings.

There, beneath the house, the great fish flared its crimson gills in a darkening sulk. What it had mistaken for an easy meal of silver pinfish turned out to be no such thing, and the barracuda spit ignominiously through its fangs.

It was a testimony to sturdy Swiss craftsmanship that the Heuer diving watch was still ticking when it came to rest on the bottom. Its stainless silver and gold links glistened against Chemo's pale severed hand, which reached up from the turtle grass like some lost piece of mannequin.

14

On Washington Avenue there was a small shop that sold artificial limbs. Dr. Rudy Graveline went there on his lunch hour and purchased four different models of prosthetic hands. He paid cash and made sure to get a receipt.

Later, back at Whispering Palms, he arranged the artificial hands in an attractive row on the top of his onyx desk.

"What about this one?" he asked Chemo.

"It's a beaut," Chemo said trenchantly, "except I've already got one on *that* arm."

"Sorry." Rudy Graveline picked up another. "Then look here—state-of-the-art technology. Four weeks of therapy, you can deal blackjack with this baby."

"Wrong color," Chemo remarked.

Rudy glanced at the artificial hand and thought: Of course it's the wrong color, they're *all* the wrong damn color. "It's a tough match," the doctor said. "I looked for the palest one they had."

"I hate them all," Chemo said. "Why does it have to be a hand, anyway?"

"You didn't like the mechanical hooks," Rudy Graveline reminded him. "Talk about advanced, you could load a gun, even type with those things. But you said no."

"Damn right I said no."

Rudy put down the prosthesis and said: "I wish you wouldn't take that tone with me. I'm doing the best I can."

"Oh, yeah."

"Look, didn't I advise you to see a specialist?"

"And didn't I advise you, you're crazy? The cops'll be hunting all over."

"All right," Rudy said in a calming voice. "Let's not argue."

It had been three weeks since Chemo had shown up behind Whispering Palms on a blood-streaked water scooter—a vision that Dr. Rudy Graveline would carry with him for the rest of his life. It had happened during an afternoon consult with Mrs. Carla Crumworthy, heiress to the Crumworthy panty-shield fortune. She had come to complain about the collagen injections that Rudy Graveline had administered to give her full, sensual lips, which is just what every rheumatoid seventy-one-year-old woman needs. Mrs. Crumworthy had lamented that the results were nothing like she had hoped, that she now resembled one of those Ubangi tribal women from the *National Geographic*, the ones with the ceramic platters in their mouths. And, in truth, Dr. Rudy Graveline was concerned about what had happened because Mrs. Crumworthy's lips had indeed grown bulbous and unwieldy and hard as cobblestones. As he examined her (keeping his doubts to himself), Rudy wondered if maybe he had injected too much collagen, or not enough, or if maybe he'd zapped it into the wrong spots. Whatever the cause, the result was undeniable: Mrs. Carla Crumworthy looked like a duck wearing mauve lipstick. A malpractice jury could have a ball with this one.

Dr. Graveline had been whisking through his trusty Rolodex, searching for a kind-hearted colleague, when Mrs. Crumworthy suddenly rose to her feet and shrieked. Pointing out the picture window toward Biscayne Bay, the old woman had blubbered in terror, her huge misshapen lips slapping together in wet percussion. Rudy had no idea what she was trying to say.

He spun around and looked out the window.

The yellow jet ski lay on its side, adrift in the bay. Somehow Chemo had dragged himself, soaking wet and stark naked, over the ledge of the seawall behind the clinic. He didn't look well enough to be dead. His gray shoulders shivered violently in the sunshine, and his eyes flickered vaguely through puffy purple slits. Chemo swung the bloody stump to show Dr. Graveline what had happened to his left hand. He pointed gamely at the elastic wrist tourniquet that he had fashioned from his Jockey shorts, and Rudy would later concede that it had probably saved his life.

Mrs. Carla Crumworthy was quickly ushered to a private recovery suite and oversedated, while Rudy and two young assistant surgeons led Chemo to an operating room. The assistants argued that he belonged at a real trauma center in a real hospital, but Chemo adamantly refused. This left the doctors with no choice but to operate or let him bleed to death.

Gently discouraged from participating in the surgery, Rudy had been content to let the young fellows work unimpeded. He spent the time making idle conversation with the woozy Chemo, who had rejected a general anesthetic in favor of an old-fashioned intravenous jolt of Demerol.

Since that evening, Chemo's post-op recovery had progressed swiftly and in relative luxury, with the entire staff of Whispering Palms instructed to accommodate his every wish. Rudy Graveline himself was exceedingly attentive, as he needed Chemo's loyalty now more than ever. He had hoped that the killer's spirits would improve at the prospect of reconstructing his abbreviated left arm.

"A new hand," Rudy said, "would be a major step back to a normal life."

"I never had a normal life," Chemo pointed out. Sure, he would miss the hand, but he was more pissed off about losing the expensive wristwatch.

"What are my other options?" Chemo asked.

"What do you mean?"

"I mean, besides these things." He waved his stump contemptuously at the artificial hands.

"Well," Rudy said, "frankly, I'm out of ideas." He gathered the prostheses from his desk and put them back in the box. "I told you this isn't my field," he said to Chemo.

"You keep trying to dump me off on some other surgeon, but it won't work. It's you or nobody."

"I appreciate your confidence," Rudy said. He leaned forward in his chair and put on his glasses. "Can I ask, what's that on your face?"

Chemo said, "It's Wite-Out."

After a careful pause, Dr. Graveline said, "Can I ask—"

"I might go out to the club later. I wanted to cover up these darn patches."

Out of pity Rudy had agreed to dermabrade several more one-inch squares along Chemo's chin.

"You covered them with Wite-Out?"

Chemo said, "Your secretary loaned me a bottle. The color's just right."

Rudy cleared his throat. "It's not so good for your skin. Please, let me prescribe a mild cosmetic ointment."

"Forget it," said Chemo. "This'll do fine. Now what about a new thing for my arm?" With his right hand he gestured at the bandaged limb.

Rudy folded his hands in his lap, a relaxed gesture that damn near exuded professional confidence. "As I said before, we've gone over most of the conventional options."

Chemo said, "I don't like therapy. I want something easy to use, something practical."

"I see," said Rudy Graveline.

"And durable, too."

"Of course."

"Also, I don't want people to stare."

Rudy thought: Beautiful. A seven-foot, one-handed geek with Wite-Out painted on his face, and he's worried about people staring.

"So what do you think?" Chemo pressed.

"I think," said Rudy Graveline, "we've got to use our imaginations."

Detective John Murdock bent his squat, porky frame over the rail of the hospital bed and said, "Wake up, fuckwad."

Which was pretty much his standard greeting.

Mick Stranahan did not open his eyes.

"Get out of here," said Christina Marks.

Detective Joe Salazar lit a Camel and said, "You don't look like a nurse. Since when do nurses wear blue jeans?"

"Good point," said John Murdock. "I think you're the one should get out of here."

"Yeah," said Joe Salazar. "We got official business with this man." Salazar was as short as his partner, only built like a stop sign. Fat, florid face stuck on a pipestem body.

"Now I know who you are," Christina said. "You must be Murdock and Salazar, the crooked cops."

Stranahan nearly busted out laughing, but he pressed his eyes closed, trying to look asleep.

"I see what we got here," said Murdock. "What we got here is some kinda Lily Tomlin."

"Sure," said Joe Salazar, though he didn't know who his partner was talking about. He assumed it was somebody they'd arrested together. "Sure," he chimed in, "a regular Lily Thomas."

Christina Marks said, "The man's asleep, so why don't you come back another time?"

"And why don't you go change your tampon or something?" snapped John Murdock. "We've got business here."

"We got questions," Joe Salazar added. When he took the

Camel cigarette out of his mouth, Christina noticed, the end was all soggy and mulched.

She said, "I was there when it happened, if you want to ask me about it."

Salazar had brought a Xerox of the marine patrol incident report. He took it out of his jacket, unfolded it, ran a sticky brown finger down the page until he came to the box marked Witnesses. "So you're Initial C. Marks?"

"Yes," Christina said.

"We've been looking all over Dade County for you. Two, three weeks we've been looking."

"I changed hotels," she said. She had moved from Key Biscayne over to the Grove, to be closer to Mercy Hospital.

John Murdock, the senior of the two detectives, took a chair from the corner, twirled it around, and sat down straddling it.

"Just like in the movies," Christina said. "You think better, sitting with your legs like that?"

Murdock glowered. "What suppose we just throw your tight little ass in the women's annex for a night or two, would you enjoy that? Just you and all the hookers, maybe a lesbo or two."

"Teach you some manners," Joe Salazar said, "and that's not all."

Christina smiled coolly. "And here I thought you boys wanted a friendly chat. Maybe I'll just call hospital security and tell them what's going on up here. After that, maybe I'll call the newspapers."

Mick Stranahan was thinking: She'd better be careful. These guys aren't nearly as dumb as they look.

Murdock said, "One time we booked a big lesbo looked just like Kris Kristofferson. I'm not kidding, we're talking major facial hair. And mean as a bobcat."

"Resisting with violence, two counts," Salazar recalled. "On top of the murder."

"Manslaughter," John Murdock cut in. "Actually, womanslaughter, if there is such a thing. Jesus, what a mess. I can't even think about it, so close to lunch."

"Involved a fire hose," Salazar said.

"I said enough," Murdock protested. "Anyhow, I think she's still in the annex. The one who looks like Kristofferson. I think she runs the drama group."

Salazar said, "You like the theater, Miss Marks?"

"Sure," Christina said, "but mainly I like television. You guys ever been on TV? Maybe you've heard of the Reynaldo Flemm show."

"Yeah," Joe Salazar said, excitedly. "One time I saw him get his ass pounded by a bunch of Teamsters. In slow motion, too."

"*That* asshole," Murdock muttered.

"We finally agree," Christina said. "Unfortunately, he happens to be my boss. We're in town taping a big story."

The two detectives glanced at one another, trying to decide on a plan without saying it. Salazar stalled by lighting up another Camel.

Lying in bed listening, Mick Stranahan figured they'd back off now, just to be safe. Neither of these jokers wanted to see his own face on prime-time TV.

Murdock said, "So tell us what happened." Salazar stood in the empty corner, resting his fat head against the wall.

Christina said, "You've got photographic memories, or maybe you'd prefer to take some notes?" Murdock motioned to his partner, who angrily stubbed out his cigarette and dug a worn spiral notebook from his jacket.

She began with what she had seen from the wheelhouse of Joey's shrimp boat—the tall man toting a machine gun on the jet scooter. She told the detectives about how Stranahan had battened down the stilt house, and how the man had started shooting into the corners. She told them how Stranahan had been wounded in the shoulder, and how he had fired back with a shotgun until he passed out. She told them she had heard a splash outside, then a terrible cry; ten, maybe fifteen minutes later she'd heard somebody rev up the jet ski, but she was too scared to go to a window. Only when the engine was a faint whine in the distance did she peer through the bullet holes in the front door to see if the gunman had gone. She told the detectives how she had half-carried Stranahan down the stairs to where his skiff was docked, and how she had hand-cranked the outboard by herself. She told them how he had groggily pointed across the bay and said there was a big hospital on the mainland, and by the time they got to Mercy there was so much blood in the bottom of the skiff that she was bailing with a coffee mug.

After Christina had finished, Detective John Murdock said, "That's quite a story. I bet *Argosy* magazine would go for a story like that."

Joe Salazar leafed through his notebook and said, "I think I missed something, lady. I think I missed the part where you explained why you're at Stranahan's house in the first place. Maybe you could repeat it."

Murdock said, "Yeah, I missed that, too."

"I'd be happy to tell you why I was there," Christina said. "Mr. Flemm wanted Mr. Stranahan to be interviewed for an upcoming broadcast, but Mr. Stranahan declined. I went to his house in the hopes of changing his mind."

"I'll bet," Salazar said.

"Joe, be nice," said his partner. "Tell me, Miss Marks, why'd you want to interview some dweeb P.I.? I mean, he's nobody. Hasn't been with the State Attorney for years."

From his phony coma Stranahan wondered how far Christina Marks would go. Not too far, he hoped.

"The interview involved a story we were working on, and that's all I can say."

Murdock said, "Gee, I hope it didn't concern a murder."

"I really can't—"

"Because murder is our main concern. Me and Joe."

Christina Marks said, "I've cooperated as much as I can."

"And you've been an absolute peach about it," said Murdock. "Fact, I almost forgot why we came in the first place."

"Yeah," said Detective Joe Salazar, "the questions we got, you can't really answer. Thanks just the same."

Murdock slid the chair back to the corner. "See, we need to talk to Rip Van Rambo here. So I think you'd better go." He smiled for the first time. "And I apologize for that wisecrack about the Kotex. Not very professional, I admit."

"It was tampons," Joe Salazar said.

"Whatever."

Christina Marks said, "I'm not leaving this room. This man is recovering from a serious gunshot wound and you shouldn't disturb him."

"We spoke to his doctor—"

"You're lying."

"Okay, we put in a call. The guy never called back."

Salazar walked up to the hospital bed and said, "He don't look so bad. Anyway, three weeks is plenty of time. Wake him up, Johnny."

"Have it your way," Christina said. She got a legal pad from her shoulder bag, uncapped a felt-tip pen, and sat down, poised to write.

"Now what the hell are you doing?" Salazar said.

"Forget about her," Murdock said. He leaned close to Stranahan's face and sang, "Mi-ick? Mick, buddy? Rise and shine."

Stranahan growled sleepily, blowing a mouthful of stale, hot breath directly into Murdock's face.

"Holy Christ," the detective said, turning away.

Salazar said, "Johnny, I swear he's awake." He cupped his hand at Stranahan's ear and shouted: *"Hey, fuckwad, you awake?"*

"Knock it off," Christina said.

"I know how you can tell," Salazar went on. "Grab his dick. If he's asleep he won't do nothing. If he's awake he'll jump ten feet out of this frigging bed."

Murdock said, "Aw, you're crazy."

"You think he'd let one of us grab his schlong if he was wide awake? I'm telling you, Johnny, it's a sure way to find out."

"Okay, you do it."

"Nuh-uh, we flip a coin."

"Screw you, Joe. I ain't touching the man's privates. The county doesn't pay me enough."

Stranahan was lying there, thinking: Thattaboy, Johnny, stick to the book.

From the corner Christina said, "Lay a finger on him, I'll see that Mr. Stranahan sues the living hell out of both of you. When he wakes up."

"Not that old line," Salazar said with a laugh.

She said, "Beat the shit out of some jerk on the street, that's one thing. Grab a man's sexual organs while he's lying unconscious in a hospital bed—try to get the union worked up about *that*. You guys just kiss your pensions good-bye."

Murdock shot Christina Marks a bitter look. "When he wakes up, you be sure to tell him something. Tell him we know he drowned his ex-wife, so don't be surprised if we show up in Stiltsville with a waterproof warrant. Tell him he'd be smart to sell that old house, too, case a storm blows it down while he's off at Raiford."

With secretarial indifference, Christina jotted every word on the legal pad. Murdock snorted and stalked out the door. Joe Salazar followed two steps behind, pocketing his own notebook, fumbling for a fresh Camel.

"Lady," he said out of the side of his mouth, "you got to learn some respect for authority."

That weekend, a notorious punk band called the Fudge Packers was playing the Gay Bidet. Freddie didn't like them at all. There were fights every night; the skinheads, the Latin Kings, the 34th Street Players. This is what Freddie couldn't understand: Why the spooks and spics even showed up for a band like this. Usually they had better taste. The Fudge Packers were simply dreadful—four frigging bass guitars, now what the hell kind of music was that? No wonder everybody was fighting: take their minds off the noise.

Since Chemo had disappeared, Freddie had hired a new head bouncer named Eugene, guy used to play in the World Football League. Eugene was all right, big as a garbage dumpster, but he couldn't seem to get people's attention the way Chemo did. Also, he was slow. Sometimes it took him five minutes to get down off the stage and pound heads in the crowd. By comparison Chemo had moved like a cat.

Freddie also was worried about Eugene's pro-labor leanings. One week at the Gay Bidet and already he was complaining about how loud the music was, could they please turn it down? You're kidding, Freddie had said, turn it down? But Eugene said damn right, his eardrums were fucking killing him. He said if his ears kept hurting he might go deaf and have to file a workman's comp, and Freddie said what's that? Then Eugene started going on about all his football injuries and, later, some shit that had happened to him working construction down in Homestead. He told Freddie about how the unions always took care of him, about how one time he was laid up for six weeks with a serious groin pull and never missed a paycheck. Not one.

Freddie could scarcely believe such a story. To him it sounded like something out of Communist Russia. He was delighted the night Chemo came back to work.

"Eugene, you're fired," Freddie said. "Go pull your groin someplace else."

"What?" said Eugene, cocking his head and leaning closer.

"Don't pull that deaf shit with me," Freddie warned. "Now get lost."

On his way out of Freddie's office, Eugene sized up his towering replacement. "Man, what happened to you?"

"Gardening accident," Chemo replied. Eugene grimaced sympathetically and said good-bye.

Freddie turned to Chemo. "Thank God you're back. I'm afraid to ask."

"Go ahead. Ask."

"I don't think so," Freddie said. "Just tell me, you okay?"

Chemo nodded. "Fine. The new band sounds like vomit."

"Yeah, I know," Freddie said. "Geez, you should see the crowd. Be careful in there."

"I'm ready for them," Chemo said, hoisting his left arm to show Freddie the new device. He and Dr. Rudy Graveline had found it on sale at a True Value hardware store.

"Wow," said Freddie, staring.

"I got it rigged special for a six-volt battery," Chemo explained. He patted the bulge under his arm. "Strap it on with an Ace bandage. Only weighs about nine pounds."

"Neat," said Freddie, thinking: Sweet Jesus, this can't be what I think it is.

A short length of anodyzed aluminum piping protruded from the padding over Chemo's amputation. Bolted to the end of the pipe was a red saucer-sized disc made of hard plastic. Coiled tightly on a stem beneath the disc was a short length of eighty-pound monofilament fishing line.

Freddie said, "Okay, now I'm gonna ask."

"It's a Weed Whacker," Chemo said. "See?"

15

George Graveline was sun-tanned and gnarled and sinewy, with breadloaf arms and wide black Elvis sideburns. The perfect tree trimmer.

George was not at all jealous of his younger brother, the plastic surgeon. Rudy deserved all the fine things in life, George reasoned, because Rudy had gone to college for what seemed like eternity. In George's view, no amount of worldly riches was worth sitting in a stuffy classroom for years at a stretch. Besides, he loved his job as a tree trimmer. He loved the smell of sawdust and fresh sap, and he loved gassing yellow jacket nests; he loved the whole damn outdoors. Even Florida winters could get miserably hot, but a person could adjust. George Graveline had a motto by which he faithfully lived: *Always park in the shade.*

He did not often see his wealthy brother, but that was all right. Dr. Rudy was a busy man, and for that matter so was

George. In Miami a good tree trimmer always had his hands full: year-round growth, no real seasons, no time for rest. Mainly you had your black olives and your common ficus tree, but the big problem there wasn't the branches so much as the roots. A twenty-year-old ficus had a root system could swallow the New York subway. Digging out a big ficus was a bitch. Then you had your exotics: the Australian pines, the melaleucas, and those God-forsaken Brazilian pepper trees, which most people mistakenly called a holly. Things grew like fungus, but George loved them because the roots weren't so bad and a couple good men could rip one out of the ground, no sweat. His favorite, though, was when people wanted their Brazilian pepper trees trimmed. Invariably these were customers new to Florida, novice suburbanites who didn't have the heart or the brains to actually *kill* a living tree. So they'd ask George Graveline to please just trim it back a little, and George would say sure, no problem, knowing that in three months it'd shoot out even bushier than before and strangle their precious hibiscus as sure as a coathanger. No denying there was damn good money in the pepper-tree racket.

On the morning of February tenth, George Graveline and his crew were chopping a row of Australian pines off Krome Avenue to make room for a new medium-security federal prison. George and his men were not exactly busting their humps, since it was a government contract and nobody ever came by to check. George was parked in the shade, as usual, eating a roast-beef hoagie and drinking a tall Budweiser. The driver's door of the truck was open and the radio was on a country-music station, though the only time you could hear the tunes was between the grinding roars of the wood chipper, which was hooked to the bumper of George Graveline's truck. The intermittent screech of the machine didn't disturb George at all; he had grown accustomed to hearing only fragments of Merle Haggard on the radio and to letting his imagination fill in the musical gaps.

Just as he finished the sandwich, George glanced in the rearview and noticed a big blond man with one arm in a sling. The man wore blue jeans, boots, and a flannel shirt with the left sleeve cut away. He was standing next to the wood chipper, watching George's crew chief toss pine stumps into the steel maw.

George swung out of the truck and said, "Hey, not so close."

The man obligingly took a step backward. "That's some machine." He gestured at the wood chipper. "Looks brand new."

"Had her a couple years," George Graveline said. "You looking for work?"

"Naw," the man said, "not with this bum wing. Actually I was looking for the boss. George Graveline."

George wiped the hoagie juice off his hands. "That's me," he said.

The crew chief heaved another pine limb into the chipper. The visitor waited for the buzzing to stop, then he said, "George, my name is Mick Stranahan."

"Howdy, Mick." George stuck out his right hand. Stranahan shook it.

"George, we don't know each other, but I feel like I can talk to you. Man to man."

"Sure."

"It's about your little brother."

"Rudolph?" Warily George folded his big arms.

"Yes, George," Stranahan said. "See, Rudy's been trying to kill me lately."

"Huh?"

"Can you believe it? First he hires some mobster to do the hit, now he's got the world's tallest white man with the world's worst case of acne. I don't know what to tell you, but frankly it's got me a little pissed off." Stranahan looked down at his sling. "This is from a .45-caliber machine gun. Honestly, George, wouldn't you be upset, too?"

George Graveline rolled the tip of his tongue around the insides of his cheeks, like he was probing for a lost wad of Red Man. The crew chief automatically kept loading hunks of pine into the wood chipper, which spit them out the chute as splinters and sawdust. Stranahan motioned to George that they should go sit in the truck and talk privately, where it was more quiet.

Stranahan settled in on the passenger side and turned down the country music. George said, "Look, mister, I don't know who you are but—"

"I told you who I am."

"Your name is all you said."

"I'm a private investigator, George, if that helps. A few years back I worked for the State Attorney. On murder cases, mostly."

George didn't blink, just stared like a toad. Stranahan got a feeling that the man was about to punch him.

"Before you do anything incredibly stupid, George, listen for a second."

George leaned out the door of the truck and hollered for the crew chief to take lunch. The whine of the wood chipper died, and suddenly the two men were drenched in silence.

"Thank you," Stranahan said.

"So talk."

"On March 12, 1986, your brother performed an operation on a young woman named Victoria Barletta. Something terrible happened, George, and she died on the operating table."

"No way."

"Your brother Rudy panicked. He'd already been in a shitload of trouble over his state medical license—and killing a patient, well, that's totally unacceptable. Even in Florida. I think Rudy was just plain scared."

George Graveline said, "You're full of it."

"The case came through my office as an abduction-possible-homicide. Everybody assumed the girl was snatched from a bus bench in front of your brother's clinic because that's what he told us. But now, George, new information has come to light."

"What kind of information?"

"The most damaging kind," Mick Stranahan said. "And for some reason, your brother thinks that I am the one who's got it. But I'm not, George."

"So I'll tell him to leave you alone."

"That's very considerate, George, but I'm afraid it's not so simple. Things have gotten out of hand. I mean, look at my damn shoulder."

"Mmmm," said George Graveline.

Stranahan said, "Getting back to the young woman. Her body was never found, not a trace. That's highly unusual."

"It is?"

"Yes, it is."

"So?"

"So, you wouldn't happen to know anything about what happened, would you?"

George said, "You got some nerve."

"Yes, I suppose I do. But how about answering the question?"

"How about this," said George Graveline, reaching for Mick Stranahan's throat.

With his good arm Stranahan intercepted George's toad-eyed lunge. He seized one of the tree-trimmer's stubby thumbs and twisted it clean out of the socket. It made a faintly audible pop, like a bottle of flat champagne. George merely squeaked as the color flooded from his face. Stranahan let go of the limp purple thumb, and George pinched it between his knees, trying to squeeze away the pain.

"Boy, I'm really sorry," Stranahan said.

George grabbed at himself and gasped, "You get out of here!"

"Don't you want to hear the rest of my theory, the one I'm going to tell the cops? About how you tossed that poor girl's body into the wood chipper just to save your brother's butt?"

"Go on," George Graveline cried, "before I shoot you myself."

Mick Stranahan got out of George's truck, shut the door and leaned in through the open window. "I think you're overreaction," he said to the tree trimmer. "I really do."

"Eat shit," George replied, wheezing.

"Fine," Stranahan said. "I just hope you're not this rude to the police."

Christina Marks was dreading her reunion with Reynaldo Flemm. They met at twelve-thirty in the lobby of the Sonesta.

She said, "You've done something to your hair."

"I let it grow," Flemm said self-consciously. "Where've you been, anyway? What's the big secret?"

Christina couldn't get over the way he looked. She circled him twice, staring.

"Ray, nobody's hair grows that fast."

"It's been a couple weeks."

"But it's all the way to your shoulders."

"So what?"

"And it's so yellow."

"Blond, goddammit."

"And so . . . kinky."

Stiffly, Reynaldo Flemm said, "It was time for a new look."

Christina Marks fingered his locks and said, "It's a bloody wig."

"Thank you, Agatha Christie."

"Don't get sore," she said. "I kind of like it."

"Really?"

Despairing of his physical appearance since his visit to Whispering Palms, Reynaldo Flemm had flown back to New York and consulted a famous colorologist, who had advised him that blond hair would make him look ten years younger. Then a makeup man at ABC had told Reynaldo that long hair would make his nose look thinner, while *kinked* long hair would take twenty pounds off his waist on camera.

Armed with this expert advice, Reynaldo had sought out Tina Turner's wig stylist, who was booked solid but happy to recommend a promising young protégé in the SoHo district. The young stylist's name was Leo, and he pretended to recognize Reynaldo Flemm from television, which was all the salesmanship he needed. Reynaldo told Leo the basics of what he wanted, and Leo led him to a seven-hundred-dollar wig that looked freshly hacked off the scalp of Robert Plant, the rock singer. Or possibly Dyan Cannon.

Reynaldo didn't care. It was precisely the look he was after.

"I do kind of like it," Christina Marks said, "only we've got to do something about the Puerto Rican mustache."

Flemm said, "The mustache stays. I've had it since my first

local Emmy." He put his hands on her shoulders. "Now, suppose you tell me what the hell's been going on."

Christina hadn't talked to Reynaldo since the day Mick Stranahan was shot, and then she had told him next to nothing. She had called from the emergency room at Mercy Hospital, and said something serious had happened. Reynaldo had asked if she were hurt, and Christina said no. Then Reynaldo had asked what was so damn serious, and she said it would have to wait for a few weeks, that the police were involved and the whole Barletta story would blow up if they didn't lay low. She had promised to get back to him in a few days, but all she did was leave a message in Reynaldo's box at the hotel. The message had begged him to be patient, and Reynaldo had thought what the hell and gone back to Manhattan to hunt for some new hair.

"So," he said to Christina, "let's hear it."

"Over here," she said, and led him to a booth in the hotel coffee shop. She waited until he'd stuffed a biscuit in his mouth before telling him about the shooting.

"Theesus!" Flemm exclaimed, spitting crumbs. He looked as if he were about to cry, and in fact he was. "You got shot at? Really?"

Christina nodded uneasily.

"With a machine gun? Honest to God?" Plaintively he added, "Was it an Uzi?"

"I'm not sure, Ray."

Christina knew his heart was breaking; Reynaldo had been waiting his entire broadcast career for an experience like that. Once he had drunkenly confided to Christina that his secret dream was to be shot in the thigh—live on national television. Not a life-threatening wound, just enough to make him go down. "I'm tired of getting beat up," he had told Christina that night. "I want to break some new ground." In Reynaldo's secret dream, the TV camera would jiggle at the sound of gunshots, then pan dramatically to focus on his prone and bloodsplattered form sprawled on the street. In the dream, Reynaldo would be clutching his microphone, bravely continuing to broadcast while paramedics worked feverishly to save his life.

The last clip, as Reynaldo dreamed it, was a close-up of his famous face: the lantern jaw clenched in agony, a grimace showcasing his luxurious capped teeth. Then the trademark sign-off: *"This is Reynaldo Flemm, reporting In Your Face!"*—just as the ambulance doors swung shut.

"I can't believe this," Reynaldo moaned over his breakfast. "Producers aren't supposed to get shot, the talent is."

Christina Marks sipped a three-dollar orange juice. "In the first place, Ray, I wasn't the one who got shot—"

"Yeah but—"

"In the second place, you would've pissed your pants if you'd been there. This is no longer fun and games, Ray. Somebody is trying to murder Stranahan. Probably the same goon who killed his ex-wife."

Flemm was still pouting. "Why didn't you tell me you were going out to Stiltsville?"

"You were locked in your room, remember? Measuring your body parts." Christina patted his arm. "Have some more marmalade."

Worriedly, Reynaldo asked, "Does this mean you get to do the stand-up? I mean, since you eyewitnessed the shooting and not me."

"Ray, I have absolutely no interest in doing a stand-up. I don't want to be on camera."

"You mean it?" His voice dripped with relief. Pathetic, Christina thought; the man is pathetic.

Clearing his throat, Reynaldo Flemm said, "I've got some bad news of my own, Chris."

Christina dabbed her lips with the corner of the napkin. "Does it involve your trip to New York?"

Flemm nodded yes.

"And, perhaps, Maggie Gonzalez?"

"I'm afraid so," he said.

"She's missing again, isn't she, Ray?"

Flemm said, "We had a dinner set up at the Palm."

"And she never showed."

"Right," he said.

"Was this before or after you wired her the fifteen thousand?" Christina asked.

"Hey, I'm not stupid. I only sent half."

"Shit." Christina drummed her fingernails on the table.

Reynaldo Flemm sighed and turned away. Absently he ran a hand through his new golden tendrils. "I'm sorry," he said finally. "You still want to dump this story?"

"No," Christina said. "No, I don't."

Mick Stranahan looked through mug shots all morning, knowing he would never find the killer's face.

"Look anyway," said Al García.

Stranahan flipped to another page. "Is it just my imagination," he said, "or are these assholes getting uglier every year?"

"I've noticed that, too," García said.

"Speaking of which, I got a friendly visit from Murdock and Salazar at the hospital." Stranahan told García what had happened.

"I'll report it to I.A., if you want," García said.

I.A. was Internal Affairs, where detectives Murdock and Salazar probably had files as thick as the Dade County Yellow Pages.

"Don't push it," said Stranahan. "I just wanted you to know what they're up to."

"Pricks," García grunted. "I'll think of something."

"I thought you had clout."

"Clout? All I got is a ten-cent commendation and a gimp arm, same as you. Only mine came from a sawed-off."

"I'm impressed," said Mick Stranahan. He closed the mug book and pushed it across the table. "He's not in here, Al. You got one for circus freaks?"

"That bad, huh?"

Stranahan said, "Bad's not the word." It wasn't.

"Want to try a composite? Let me call one of the artists."

"No, that's all right," Stranahan said. "I wouldn't know where to start. Al, you wouldn't believe this guy."

The detective gnawed the tip off a cigar. "He's got to be the same geek who did Chloe. Thing is, I got witnesses saw them out at the marina having a drink, chatting like the best of friends. How do you figure that?''

''She always had great taste in men.'' Stranahan stood up, gingerly testing the strap of his sling.

''Where you going?''

''I'm off to do a B-and-E.''

''Now don't say shit like that.''

''It's true, Al.''

''I'm not believing this. Tell me you're bullshitting, Mick.''

''If it makes you feel better.''

''And call me,'' García said in a low voice, ''if you turn up something good.''

At half-past three, Mick Stranahan broke into Maggie Gonzalez's duplex for the second time. The first thing he did was play back the tape on the answering machine. There were messages from numerous relatives, all demanding to know why Maggie had missed her cousin Gloria's baby shower. The only message that Mick Stranahan found interesting was from the Essex House hotel in downtown New York. A nasal female clerk requested that Miss Gonzalez contact them immediately about a forty-three-dollar dry-cleaning bill, which Maggie had forgotten to pay before checking out. The Essex House clerk had efficiently left the time and date of the phone message: January twenty-eighth at ten o'clock in the morning.

The next thing Mick Stranahan did was to sift through a big stack of Maggie's mail until he found the most recent Visa card bill, which he opened and studied at her kitchen table. That Maggie was spending somebody else's money in Manhattan was obvious: She had used her personal credit card only twice. One entry was $35.50 at Ticketron, probably for a Broadway show; the other charge was from a clothing shop for $179.40, more than Maggie was probably carrying in cash at the time. The clothing store was in the Plaza Hotel; the transaction was dated February 1.

Mick Stranahan was getting ready to leave the duplex when

Maggie's telephone rang twice, then clicked over to the machine. He listened as a man came on the line. Stranahan thought he recognized the voice, but he wasn't certain. He had only spoken with the man once.

The voice on the machine said: "Maggie, it's me. I tried the Essex but they said you checked out. . . . Look, we've really got to talk. In person. Call me at the office right away, collect. Wherever you are, okay? Thanks."

As the man gave the number, Stranahan copied it in pencil on the Formica counter. After the caller hung up, Stranahan dialed 411 and asked for the listing of the Whispering Palms Spa and Surgery Center in Bal Harbour. A recording gave the main number as 555-7600. The phone number left by Maggie's male caller was 555-7602.

Rudy Graveline, Stranahan thought, calling on his office line.

The next number Stranahan dialed was 1-212-555-1212. Information for Manhattan. He got the number of the Plaza, dialed the main desk, and asked for Miss Maggie Gonzalez's room. A woman picked up on the fourth ring.

"Is this Miss Gonzalez?" Stranahan asked, trying to mimic a Brooklyn accent.

"Yes, it is."

"This is the concierge downstairs." Like there was an *upstairs* concierge. "We were just wondering if you had any dry cleaning you needed done this evening."

"What are you talking about, I'm still waiting for those three dresses I sent out Sunday," Maggie said, not pleasantly.

"Oh, I'm very sorry," Mick Stranahan said. "I'll see to it immediately."

Then he hung up, grabbed the white pages off the kitchen counter, and looked up the number for Delta Airlines.

16

On his way to Miami International, Mick Stranahan stopped at his brother-in-law's law office. Kipper Garth was on the speaker phone, piecing out a slip-and-fall to one of the Brickell Avenue buzzards.

Mick Stranahan walked in and said, "The files?"

Kipper Garth motioned to a wine-colored chair and put a finger to his waxy lips. "So, Chuckie," he said to the speaker phone, "what're you thinking?"

"Thinking maybe two hundred if we settle," said the voice on the other end.

"Two hundred!" Kipper exclaimed. "Chuckie, you're nuts. The woman tripped over her own damn dachshund."

"Kip, they'll settle," the other lawyer said. "It's the biggest grocery chain in Florida, they always settle. Besides, the dog croaked—that's fifty grand right there for mental anguish."

"But dogs aren't even allowed in the store, Chuckie. If it was somebody else's dachshund she tripped on, then we'd really have something. But this was her own fault."

Sardonic laughter crackled over the speaker box. "Kip, buddy, you're not thinking like a litigator," the voice said. "I went to the supermarket myself and guess what: No signs!"

"What do you mean?"

"I mean no No Dogs Allowed–type signs. Not a one posted in Spanish. So how was our poor Consuelo to know?"

"Chuckie, you're beautiful," said Kipper Garth. "If that ain't negligence—"

"Two hundred thou," Chuckie said, "that's my guess. We'll split sixty-forty."

"Nope," Kipper Garth said, staring coldly at the speaker box. "Half-and-half. Same as always."

"Excuse me." It was Mick Stranahan. Kipper Garth frowned and shook his head; not now, not when he was closing the deal.

The voice on the phone said: "Kip, who's that? You got somebody there?"

"Relax, Chuckie, it's just me," Stranahan said to the box. "You know—Kipper's heroin connection? I just dropped by with my briefcase full of Mexican brown. Can I pencil you in for a kilo?"

Frantically Kipper Garth jabbed two fingers at the phone buttons. The line went dead and the speaker box hummed the dial tone. "You're fucking crazy," he said to Mick Stranahan.

"I've got a plane to catch, Jocko. Where are the Graveline files?"

"You're crazy," Kipper Garth said again, trying to stay calm. He buzzed for a secretary, who lugged in three thick brown office folders.

"There's a conference room where you can read this shit in private."

Mick Stranahan said, "No, this is fine." With Kipper Garth stewing, Stranahan skimmed quickly through the files on Rudy Graveline. It was worse than he thought—or better, depending on one's point of view.

"Seventeen complaints to the state board," Stranahan marveled.

"Yeah, but no action," Kipper Garth noted. "Not even a reprimand."

Stranahan looked up, lifting one of the files. "Jocko, this is a gold mine."

"Well, Mick, I'm glad I could help. Now, if you don't mind, it's getting late and I've got a few calls to make."

Stranahan said, "You don't understand, I wanted this stuff for you, not me."

Peevishly Kipper Garth glanced at his wristwatch. "You're

right, Mick, I *don't* understand. What the hell do I want with Graveline's files?''

''Names, Jocko.'' Stranahan opened the top folder and riffled the pages dramatically. ''You got seventeen names, seventeen leads on a silver platter. You got Mrs. Susan Jacoby and her boobs that don't match. You got Mr. Robert Mears with his left eye that won't close and his right eye that won't open. You got, let's see, Julia Kelly with a shnoz that looks like a Phillips screwdriver—Jesus, you see the Polaroid of that thing? What else? Oh, you got Ken Martinez and his lopsided scrotum. . . .''

Kipper Garth waved his arms. ''Mick, that's enough! What would I want with all this crap?''

''I figured you'll need it, Jocko.''

''For what?''

''For suing Doctor Rudy Graveline.''

''Very funny,'' Kipper Garth said. ''I told you, the man's in my yacht club. Besides, he's been sued before.''

''Sue him again,'' Mick Stranahan said. ''Sue the mother like he's never been sued before.''

''He'd settle out. Doctors always settle.''

''Don't let him. Don't settle for anything. Not for ten million dollars. Sign up one of these poor misfortunate souls and go to the frigging wall.''

Kipper Garth stood up and adjusted his necktie, suddenly on his way to some important meeting. ''I can't help you, Mick. Get yourself another lawyer.''

''You don't do this favor for me,'' said Stranahan, ''and I'll go tell Katie about your trip to Steamboat next month with Inga or Olga or whatever the hell her name is, I got it written down here somewhere. And for future reference, Jocko, don't ever put your ski bunny's plane tickets on American Express. I know it's convenient and all, but it's very, very risky. I mean, with the computers they got these days, I can pull out your goddamned seat assignments—5A and 5B, I think it is.''

All Kipper Garth could say was: ''How'd you do that?''

''I told you before, I'm still plugged in.'' A travel agent in

Coral Gables who owed him one. It was so damn easy Stranahan couldn't bear to tell his brother-in-law.

"What's the point of all this?" Kipper Garth asked.

"Never mind, just do it. Sue the asshole."

The lawyer lifted his pinstriped coat off the back of the chair and checked it for wrinkles. "Mick, let me shop this around and get back to you."

"No, Jocko. No referrals. You do this one all by yourself."

The lawyer sagged as if struck by a brick.

"You heard me right," Stranahan said.

"Mick, please." It was a pitiable peep. "Mick, I don't do this sort of thing."

"Sure you do. I see the billboards all over town."

Kipper Garth nibbled on a thumbnail to mask the spastic twitching of his upper lip. The thought of actually going to court had pitched him into a cold sweat. A fresh droplet made a shiny trail from the furrow of his forehead to the tip of his well-tanned nose.

"I don't know," he said, "it's been so long."

"Aw, it's easy," Stranahan said. "One of your paralegals can draw up the complaint. That'll get the ball rolling." With a thud he stacked the Graveline files on Kipper Garth's desk; the lawyer eyed the file as if it were nitroglycerine.

"A gold mine," Stranahan said encouragingly. "I'll check back in a few days."

"Mick?"

"Relax. All you've got to do is go down to the courthouse and sue."

Wanly, Kipper Garth said, "I don't have to win, do I?"

"Of course not," Stranahan said, patting his arm. "It'll never get that far."

Dr. Rudy Graveline lived in a palatial three-story house on northern Biscayne Bay. The house had Doric pillars, two spiral staircases, and more imported marble than the entire downtown art museum. The house had absolutely no business being on Miami Beach, but in fairness it looked no more silly or out of place than any of the other garish mansions. The house was on the same palm-lined avenue where two of the Bee Gees lived, which meant that Rudy had been forced to pay about a hundred thousand more than the property was worth. For the first few years the women whom Rudy dated were impressed to be in the Bee Gees' neighborhood, but lately the star value had worn off and Rudy had quit mentioning it.

It was Heather Chappell, the actress, who brought it up first.

"I think Barry lives around here," she said as they were driving back to Rudy's house after dinner at the Forge.

"Barry who?" Rudy asked, his mind off somewhere.

"Barry Gibb. The singer. *Staying alive, staying alive, ooh, ooh, ooh.*"

As much as he loved Heather, Rudy wished she wouldn't try to sing.

"You know Barry personally?" he asked.

"Oh sure. All the guys."

"That's Barry's place there," Rudy Graveline said, pointing. "And Robin lives right here."

"Let's stop over," Heather said, touching his knee. "It'll be fun."

Rudy said no, he didn't know the guys all that well. Besides, he never really liked their music, especially that disco shit. Immediately Heather sank into a deep pout, which she heroically maintained all the way back to Rudy's house, up the stairs, all the way to his bedroom. There she peeled off her dress and panties and lay facedown on the king-sized bed. Every few minutes she would raise her cheek off the satin pillow and sigh disconsolately, until Rudy couldn't stand it anymore.

"Are you mad at me?" he asked. He was in his boxer shorts, standing in the closet where he had hung his suit. "Heather, are you angry?"

"No."

"Yes, you are. Did I say something wrong? If I did, I'm sorry." He was blubbering like a jerk, all because he wanted to get laid in the worst way. The sight of Heather's perfect bare bottom—the one she wanted contoured—was driving him mad.

In a tiny voice she said, "I love the Bee Gees."

"I'm sorry," Rudy said. He sat on the corner of the bed and stroked her peachlike rump. "I liked their early stuff, I really did."

Heather said, "I loved the disco, Rudy. It just about killed me when disco died."

"I'm sorry I said anything."

"You ever made love to disco music?"

Rudy thought: What is happening to my life?

"Do you have any Village People tapes?" Heather asked, giving him a quick saucy look over the shoulder. "There's a song on their first album, I swear, I could fuck all night to it."

Rudy Graveline was nothing if not resourceful. He found the Village People tape in the discount bin of an all-night record store across from the University of Miami campus in Coral Gables. He sped home, popped the cassette into the modular sound system, cranked up the woofers, and jogged up the spiral staircase to the bedroom.

Heather said, "Not here." She took him by the hand and led him downstairs. "The fireplace," she whispered.

"It's seventy-eight degrees," Rudy remarked, kicking off his underwear.

"It's not the fire," Heather said, "it's the marble."

One of the selling points of the big house was an oversized fireplace constructed of polished Italian marble. Fireplaces were considered a cozy novelty in South Florida, but Rudy had never used his, since he was afraid the expensive black marble would blister in the heat.

Heather crawled in and got on her back. She had the most amazing smile on her face. "Oh, Rudy, it's so cold." She lifted her buttocks off the marble and slapped them down; the squeak made her giggle.

Rudy stood there, naked and limp, staring like an idiot. "We could get hurt," he said. He was thinking of what the marble would do to his elbows and kneecaps.

"Don't be such a geezer," Heather said, hoisting her hips and wiggling them in his face. She rolled over and pointed to the twin smudges of condensation on the black stone. "Look," she said. "Just like fingerprints."

"Sort of," Rudy Graveline mumbled.

She said, "I must be hot, huh?"

"I guess so," Rudy said. His skull was ready to split; the voices of the Village People reverberated in the fireplace like mortar fire.

"Oh, God," Heather moaned.

"What is it?" Rudy asked.

"The song. That's my song." She squeaked to her knees and seized him ferociously around the waist. "Come on down here," she said. "Let's dance."

In order to prolong his tumescence, Dr. Rudy Graveline had trained himself to think of anything but sex while he was having sex. Most times he concentrated on his unit trusts and tax shelters, which were complicated enough to keep orgasm at bay for a good ten to fifteen minutes. Tonight, though, he concentrated on something different. Rudy Graveline was thinking of his daunting predicament—of Victoria Barletta and the upcoming television documentary about her death; of Mick Stranahan, still alive and menacing; of Maggie Gonzalez, spending his money somewhere in New York.

More often than not, Rudy found he could ruminate with startling clarity during the throes of sexual intercourse. He had arrived at many crucial life decisions in such moments—the clutter of the day and the pressure from his patients seemed to vanish in a crystal vacuum, a mystic physical void that permitted Rudy to concentrate on his problems in a new light and from a new angle.

And so it was that—even with Heather Chappell clawing his shoulders and screaming disco drivel into his ear, even with the flue vent clanging in the chimney above his head, and even with his knees grinding mercilessly on the cold Italian marble—Rudy was able to focus on the most important crisis of his life. Both pain and pleasure dissipated; it was as if he were alone, alert and sensitized, in a cool dark chamber. Rudy thought about everything that had happened so far, and then about what he must do now. It wasn't a bad plan. There was, however, one loose end.

Rudy snapped out of his cognitive trance when Heather cried, "Enough already!"

"What?"

"I said you can stop now, okay? This isn't a damn rodeo." She was all out of breath. Her chest was slick with sweat.

Rudy quit moving.

"What were you thinking of?" Heather asked.

"Nothing."

"Did you come?"

"Sure," Rudy lied.

"You were thinking of some other girl, weren't you?"

"No, I wasn't." Another lie.

He had been thinking of Maggie Gonzalez, and how he should have killed her two months ago.

The next day at noon, George Graveline arrived at the Whispering Palms surgery clinic and demanded to see his brother, said it was an emergency. When Rudy heard the story, he agreed.

The two men were talking in hushed, worried tones when Chemo showed up an hour later.

"So what's the big rush?" he said.

"Sit down," Rudy Graveline told him.

Chemo was dressed in a tan safari outfit, the kind Jim Fowler wore on the *Wild Kingdom* television show.

Rudy said, "George, this is a friend of mine. He's working for me on this matter."

Chemo raised his eyebrows. "Happened to your thumb?" he said to George.

"Car door." Rudy's brother did not wish to share that painful detail of his encounter with Mick Stranahan.

George Graveline had a few questions of his own for the tall stranger, but he held them. Valiantly he tried not to stare at Chemo's complexion, which George assessed as some tragic human strain of Dutch elm disease. What finally drew the tree trimmer's attention away from Chemo's face was the colorful Macy's shopping bag in which Chemo concealed his newly extended left arm.

"Had an accident," Chemo explained. "I'm only wearing this until I get a customized cover." He pulled the shopping bag off the Weed Whacker. George Graveline recognized it immediately—the lightweight household model.

"Hey, that thing work?"

"You bet," Chemo said. He probed under his arm until he found the toggle switch that jolted the Weed Whacker to life. It sounded like a blender without the top on.

George grinned and clapped his hands.

"That's enough," Rudy said sharply.

"No, watch," said Chemo. He ambled to the corner of the office where Rudy kept a beautiful potted rubber plant.

"Oh no," the doctor said, but it was too late. Gleefully Chemo chopped the rubber plant into slaw.

"Yeah!" said George Graveline.

Rudy leaned over and whispered, "Don't encourage him. He's a dangerous fellow."

Basking in the attention, Chemo left the Weed Whacker unsheathed. He sat down next to the two men and said, "Let's hear the big news."

"Mick Stranahan visited George yesterday," Rudy said. "Apparently the bastard's not giving up."

"What'd he say?"

"All kinds of crazy shit," George said.

Rudy had warned his brother not to tell Chemo about Victoria Barletta or the wood chipper or Stranahan's specific accusation about what had happened to the body.

Rudy twirled his eyeglasses and said: "I don't understand why Stranahan is so damn hard to kill."

"Least we know he's out of the hospital," Chemo said brightly. "I'll get right on it."

"Not just yet," Rudy said. He turned to his brother. "George, could I speak to him alone, please?"

George Graveline nodded amiably at Chemo on his way out

the door. "Listen, you ever need work," he said, "I could use you and that, uh . . ."

"Prosthesis," Chemo said. "Thanks, but I don't think so."

When they were alone, Rudy opened the top drawer of his desk and handed Chemo a large brown envelope. Inside the envelope were an eight-by-ten photograph, two thousand dollars in traveler's checks, and an airline ticket. The person in the picture was a handsome, sharp-featured woman with brown eyes and brown hair; her name was printed in block letters on the back of the photograph. The plane ticket was round-trip, Miami to La Guardia and back.

Chemo said, "Is this what I think it is?"

"Another job," Dr. Rudy Graveline said.

"It'll cost you."

"I'm prepared for that."

"Same as the Stranahan deal," Chemo said.

"Twenty treatments? You don't *need* twenty more treatments. Your face'll be done in two months."

"I'm not talking about dermabrasion," Chemo said. "I'm talking about my ears."

Rudy thought: Dear God, will it never end? "Your ears," he said to Chemo, "are the last things that need surgical attention."

"The hell is that supposed to mean?"

"Nothing, nothing. All I'm saying is, once we finish the dermabrasions you'll look as good as new. I honestly don't believe you'll want to touch a thing, that's how good your face is going to look."

Chemo said, "My ears stick out too far and you know it. You want me to do this hit, you'll fix the damn things."

"Fine," Rudy Graveline sighed, "fine." There was nothing wrong with the man's ears, only what was between them.

Chemo tucked the envelope into his armpit and bagged up the Weed Whacker. "Oh yeah, one more thing. I'm out of that stuff for my face."

"What stuff?"

"You know," Chemo said, "the Wite-Out."

Rudy Graveline found a small bottle in his desk and tossed it to Chemo, who slipped it into the breast pocket of his Jim Fowler safari jacket. "Call you from New York," he said.

"Yes," said Rudy wearily. "By all means."

17

Christina Marks slipped out of the first-class cabin while Reynaldo Flemm was autographing a cocktail napkin for a flight attendant. The flight attendant had mistaken the newly bewigged Reynaldo for David Lee Roth, the rock singer. The Puerto Rican mustache looked odd with all that blond hair, but the flight attendant assumed it was meant as a humorous disguise.

Mick Stranahan was sitting in coach, a stack of outdoors magazines on the seat next to him. He saw Christina coming down the aisle and smiled. "My shadow."

"I'm not following you," she said.

"Yes, you are. But that's all right." He moved the magazines and motioned her to sit down.

"You look very nice." It was the first time he had seen her in a dress. "Some coincidence, that you and the anchorman got the same flight as I did."

Christina said, "He's not an anchorman. And no, it's not a coincidence that we're on the same plane. Ray thinks it is, but it's not."

"Ray thinks it is, huh? So this was your idea, following me."

"Relax," Christina said. Ever since the shooting she had stayed close; at first she rationalized it as a journalist's instinct—the Barletta story kept coming back to Stranahan, didn't it? But then she had found herself sleeping some nights at the hospital, where nothing newsworthy was likely to happen; sitting in the corner and watching him in the hospital bed, long after it was obvious he would make a full recovery. Christina couldn't deny she was attracted to him, and worried about him. She also had a feeling he was moderately crazy.

Stranahan said, "So you guys are going to trail me all around New York. A regular tag team, you and Ray."

"Ray will be busy," Christina said, "on other projects."

The jetliner dipped slightly, and a shaft of sunlight caught the side of her face, forcing her to look away. For the first time Stranahan noticed a sprinkling of light freckles on her nose and cheeks: cinnamon freckles, the kind that children have.

"Did I ever thank you for saving my life?" he asked.

"Yes, you did."

"Well, thanks again." He poured some honey-roasted peanuts into the palm of her hand. "Why are you following me?"

"I'm not," she said.

"If it's only to juice up your damn TV show, then I'm going to get angry."

Christina said, "It's not that."

"You want to keep an eye on me."

"You're an interesting man. You make things happen."

Stranahan popped a peanut and said. "That's a good one."

Christina Marks softened her tone. "I'll help you find her."

"Find who?"

"Maggie Gonzalez."

"Who said she was lost? Besides, you got her on tape, right? The whole sordid story."

"Not yet," Christina admitted.

Stranahan laughed caustically. "Oh brother," he said.

"Listen, I got a trail of bills she's been sending up to the office. Between the two of us, we could find her in a day. Besides, I think she'll talk to me. The whole sordid story, on tape—like you said."

Stranahan didn't mention that he already knew where Maggie

Gonzalez was staying, and that he was totally confident that he could persuade her to talk.

"You're the most helpful woman I ever met," he said to Christina Marks. "So unselfish, too. If I didn't know better, I'd think maybe you were hunting for Maggie because she beat you and the anchorman out of some serious dough."

Christina said, "I liked you better unconscious."

Stranahan chuckled and took her hand. He didn't let go like she thought he would, he just held it. Once, when the plane hit some turbulence, Christina jumped nervously. Without looking up from his *Field & Stream*, Stranahan gave her hand a squeeze. It was more comforting than suggestive, but it made Christina flush.

She retreated to the role of professional interviewer. "So," she said, "tell me about yourself."

"You first," Stranahan said; a brief smile, then back to the magazine.

Oddly, she found herself talking—talking so openly that she sounded like one of those video-dating tapes: Let's see. I'm thirty-four years old, divorced, born in Richmond, went to the University of Missouri journalism school, lettered on the swim team, graduated magna, got my first decent news job with the ABC affiliate in St. Louis, then three years at WBBM in Chicago until I met Ray at the Gacy trial and he offered me an assistant producer's job, and here I am. Now it's your turn, Mick."

"Pardon?"

"Your turn," Christina Marks said. "That's my life story, now let's hear yours."

Stranahan closed the magazine and centered it on his lap. He said, "My life story is this: I've killed five men, and I've been married five times."

Christina slowly pulled her hand away.

"Which scares you more?" Mick Stranahan said.

When Dade County Commissioner Roberto Pepsical broke the news to The Others (that is, the other crooked commissioners), they all had the same reaction: Nope, sorry, too late.

Dr. Rudy Graveline had offered major bucks to rezone prime green space for the Old Cypress Towers project, and the commissioners had gone ahead and done it. They couldn't very well put it back on the agenda and reverse the vote—not without arousing the interest of those goddamned newspaper reporters. Besides, a deal was a deal. Furthermore, The Others wanted to know about the promised twenty-five thousand dollar bribe: specifically, where was it? Was Rudy holding out? One commissioner even suggested that a new vote to rescind the zoning and scrap the project could be obtained only by doubling the original payoff.

Roberto Pepsical was fairly sure that Dr. Rudy Graveline would not pay twice for essentially the same act of corruption. In addition, Roberto didn't feel like explaining to the doctor that if Old Cypress Towers were to expire on the drawing board, so would a plethora of other hidden gratuities that would have winged their way into the commissioners' secret accounts. From downtown bankers to the zoning lawyers to the code inspectors, payoffs traditionally trickled upward to the commissioners. The ripple effect of killing a project as large as Rudy's was calamitous, bribery-wise.

Roberto hated being the middleman when the stakes got this high. By nature he was slow, inattentive, and somewhat easily confused. He hadn't taken notes during Rudy's late-night phone call, and maybe he should have. This much he remembered clearly: The doctor had said that he'd changed his mind about Old Cypress Towers, that he'd decided to move his money out of the country instead. When Roberto protested, the doctor told him there'd been all kinds of trouble, serious trouble— specifically, that hinky old surgical case he'd mentioned that day at lunch. The proverbial doo-doo was getting ready to hit the proverbial fan, Rudy had said; somebody was out to ruin him. He told Roberto Pepsical to pass along his most profound apologies to The Others, but there was no other course for the doctor to take. Since his problem wasn't going away, Old Cypress Towers would.

The solution was so obvious that even Roberto grasped it immediately. The apartment project could be rescued, and so could the commissioners' bribes. Once Roberto learned that Dr. Rudy Graveline's problem had a name, he began checking with his connections at the Metro-Dade Police Department.

Which led him straight to detectives John Murdock and Joe Salazar.

Roberto considered the mission of such significance that he took the radical step of skipping his normal two-hour lunch to stop by the police station for a personal visit. He found both detectives at their desks. They were eating hot Cuban sandwiches and cleaning their revolvers. It was the first time Roberto had ever seen Gulden's mustard on a .357.

"You're sure," said the commissioner, "that this man is a murder suspect?"

"Yep," said John Murdock.

"Number one suspect," added Joe Salazar.

Roberto said, "So you're going to arrest him?"

"Of course," Salazar said.

"Eventually," said Murdock.

"The sooner the better," Roberto said.

John Murdock glanced at Joe Salazar. Then he looked at Roberto and said, "Commissioner, if you've got any information about this man . . ."

"He's been giving a friend of mine a hard time, that's all. A good friend of mine." Roberto knew better than to mention Rudy Graveline's name, and John Murdock knew better than to ask.

Joe Salazar said, "It's a crime to threaten a person. Did Stranahan make a threat?"

"Nothing you could prove," Roberto said. "Look, I'd appreciate it if you guys would keep me posted."

"Absolutely," John Murdock promised. He wiped the food off his gun and shoved it back in the shoulder holster.

"This is very important," Roberto Pepsical said. "Extremely important."

Murdock said, "Don't worry, we'll nail the fuckwad."

"Yeah," said Joe Salazar. "It's only a matter of time."

"Not much time, I hope."

"We'll do what we can, Commissioner."

"There might even be a promotion in it."

"Oh boy, a promotion," said John Murdock. "Joey, you hear that? A promotion!" The detective burped at the commissioner and said, "How about some green instead?"

Roberto Pepsical winced as if a hornet had buzzed into his ear. "Jesus, are you saying—"

"Money," said Joe Salazar, chomping a pickle. "He means money."

"Let me get this straight: You guys want a bribe for solving a murder?"

"No," Murdock said, "just for making the arrest."

"I can't believe this."

"Sure you can," Joe Salazar said. "Your friend wants Stranahan out of the way, right? The county jail, that's fucking out of the way."

Roberto buried his rubbery chin in his hands. "Money," he murmured.

"I don't know what you guys call it over at Government Center, but around here we call it a bonus." John Murdock grinned at the county commissioner. "What *do* you guys call it?"

To Roberto it seemed reckless to be discussing a payoff in the middle of the detective squad room. He felt like passing gas.

In a low voice he said to John Murdock, "All right, we'll work something out."

"Good."

The commissioner stood up. He was about to reach out and shake their hands, but he changed his mind. "Look, we never had this meeting," he said to the two detectives.

"Of course not," John Murdock agreed.

Joe Salazar said, "Hey, you can trust us."

About as far as I can spit, thought Roberto Pepsical.

* * *

Three days before Mick Stranahan, Christina Marks, and Reynaldo Flemm arrived in Manhattan, and four days before the man called Chemo showed up, Maggie Gonzalez walked into a video-rental shop on West 52nd Street and asked to make a tape. She gave the shop clerk seventy-five dollars cash, and he led her to "the studio," a narrow backroom paneled with cheap brown cork. The studio reeked of Lysol. On the floor was a stained gray mattress and a bright clump of used Kleenex, which, at Maggie's insistence, the clerk removed. A Sony video camera was mounted on an aluminum tripod at one end of the room; behind it, on another stem, was a small bank of lights. The clerk opened a metal folding chair and placed it eight feet in front of the lens.

Maggie sat down, opened her purse and unfolded some notes she had printed on Plaza stationery. While she read them to herself, the clerk was making impatient chewing-gum noises in his cheeks, like he had better things to do. Finally Maggie told him to start the tape, and a tiny red light twinkled over the Sony's cold black eye.

Maggie was all set to begin when she noticed the clerk hovering motionless in the darkest corner, a cockroach trying to blend into the cork. She told the guy to get lost, waited until the door slammed, then took a breath and addressed the camera.

"My name is Maggie Orestes Gonzalez," she said. "On the twelfth of March, 1986, I was a witness to the killing of a young woman named Victoria Barletta . . ."

The taping took fourteen minutes. Afterwards Maggie got two extra copies made at twenty dollars each. On the way back to the hotel she stopped at a branch of the Merchant Bank and rented a safe-deposit box, where she left the two extra videotapes. She took the original up to her room at the Plaza, and placed it in the nightstand, under the room-service menu.

The very next day Maggie Gonzalez took a cab to the office of Dr. Leonard Leaper on the corner of 50th Street and Lexington. Dr. Leaper was a nationally renowned and internationally published plastic surgeon; Maggie had read up on him in the journals. "You have a decent reputation," she told Dr. Leaper. "I hope it's not just hype." Her experiences in Dr. Rudy Graveline's surgical suite had taught her to be exceedingly careful when choosing a physician.

Neutrally Dr. Leaper said, "What can I do for you, young lady?"

"The works," Maggie replied.

"The works?"

"I want a bleph, a lift, and I want the hump taken out of this nose. Also, I want you to trim the septum so it looks like this." With a finger she repositioned the tip of her nose at a perky, Sandy Duncan–type angle. "See?"

Dr. Leaper nodded.

"I'm a nurse," Maggie said. "I used to work for a plastic surgeon."

"I figured something like that," Dr. Leaper said. "Why do you want these operations?"

"None of your business."

Dr. Leaper said, "Miss Gonzalez, if indeed you worked for a surgeon then you understand I've got to ask some personal questions. There are good reasons for elective cosmetic surgery and bad reasons, good candidates and poor candidates. Some patients believe it will solve all their problems, and of course it won't—"

"Cut the crap," Maggie said, "and take my word: Surgery will definitely solve my problem."

"Which is?"

"None of your business."

Dr. Leaper stood up. "Then I'm afraid I can't help."

"You guys are all alike," Maggie complained.

"No, we're not," Dr. Leaper said. "That's why you're here. You wanted somebody good."

His composure was maddening. Maggie said, "All right— will you do the surgery if I tell you the reason?"

"If it's a good one," the doctor replied.

She said, "I need a new face."

"Why?"

"Because I am about to . . . testify against someone."

Dr. Leaper said, "Can you tell me more?"

"It's a serious matter, and I expect he'll send someone to find me before it's over. I don't want to be found."

Dr. Leaper said, "But surgery can only do so much—"

"Look, I've seen hundreds of cases, and I know good results from bad results. I also know the limitations of the procedures. You just do the nose, the neck, the eyes, maybe a plastic implant in the chin . . . and let me and Lady Clairol do the rest. I guarantee the bastard won't recognize me."

Dr. Leaper locked his hands. In a grave voice he said, "Let me understand: You're a witness in a criminal matter?"

"Undoubtedly," Maggie said. "A homicide, to be exact."

"Oh, dear."

"And I must testify, Doctor." The word *testify* was a stretch, but it wasn't far from the truth. "It's the right thing for me to do," Maggie asserted.

"Yes," said Dr. Leaper, without conviction.

"So, you see why I need your help."

The surgeon sighed. "Why should I believe you?"

Maggie said, "Why should I lie? If it weren't an emergency, don't you think I would have had this done a long time ago, when I could've got a deal on the fees?"

"I suppose so."

"Please, Doctor. It's not vanity, it's survival. Do my face, you'll be saving a life."

Dr. Leaper opened his schedule book. "I've got a lipo tomorrow at two, but I'm going to bump him for you. Don't eat or drink anything after midnight—"

"I know the routine," Maggie Gonzalez said ebulliently. "Thank you very much."

"It's all right."

"One more thing."

"Yes?" said Dr. Leaper, cocking one gray eyebrow.

"I was wondering if there's any chance of a professional discount? I mean, since I *am* a nurse."

* * *

Mick Stranahan stood on the curb outside La Guardia Airport and watched Reynaldo Flemm climb into a long black limousine. The limo driver, holding the door, eyed Reynaldo's new hair and looked to Christina Marks for a clue. She said something quietly to the driver, then waved good-bye to Reynaldo in the backseat. Through the smoked gray window Stranahan thought he saw Flemm shoot him a bitter look as the limo pulled away.

"I don't like this place," Stranahan muttered, his breath frosty.

"What places *do* you like?" Christina asked.

"Old Rhodes Key. That's one place you won't see frozen spit on the sidewalk. Fact, you won't even see a sidewalk."

"You old curmudgeon." Christina said it much too sarcastically for Stranahan. "Come on, let's get a cab."

Her apartment was off 72nd Street on the Upper East Side. Third floor, one bedroom with a small kitchen and a garden patio scarcely big enough for a Norway rat. The furniture was low and modern: glass, chrome, and sharp angles. One of those sofas you put together like a jigsaw puzzle. Potted plants occupied three of the four corners in the living room. On the main wall hung a vast and frenetic abstract painting.

Stranahan took a step back and studied it. "Boy, I don't know," he said.

From the bedroom came Christina's voice. "You like it?"

"Not really," Stranahan said.

When Christina walked out, he saw that she had changed to blue jeans and a navy pullover sweater. She stood next to him in front of the painting and said, "It's supposed to be springtime. Spring in the city."

"Looks like an Amoco station on fire."

"Thank you," Christina said. "Such a sensitive man."

Stranahan shrugged. "Let's go. I gotta check in."

"Why don't you stay here?" She gave it a beat. "On the sectional."

"The sectional? I don't think so."

"It's safer than a hotel, Mick."

"I'm not so sure."

Christina said, "Don't flatter yourself."

"It's not me I was thinking of. Believe it or not."

"Sorry. Please stay."

"The Great Reynaldo will not be pleased."

"All the more reason," Christina said.

They ate a late lunch at a small Italian restaurant three blocks from Christina's apartment. She ordered a pasta salad and Perrier, while Stranahan had spaghetti and meatballs and two beers. Then they took a taxi to the Plaza Hotel.

"She's here?" Christina asked, once in the lobby and again in the elevator.

Stranahan knocked repeatedly on the door to Maggie Gonzalez's room, but no one answered. Maggie was in bed, coasting through a codeine dreamland with a brand-new face that she had not yet seen. The sound of Mick Stranahan's knocking was but a muffled drumbeat in her delicious pharmaceutical fog, and Maggie paid it no attention. It would be hours before the drumming returned, and by then she would be conscious enough to stumble toward the door.

Her big mistake had been to call Dr. Rudy Graveline four days earlier when she had gotten the message on her machine in Miami. Curiosity had triumphed over common sense; Maggie had been dying for an update on the Stranahan situation. She needed to stay close to Rudy, but not too close. It was a dicey act. She wanted the doctor to believe that they were on the same side, his side. She also wanted to keep the expense money coming.

The phone call, though, had been peculiar. At first Dr. Graveline had seemed relieved to hear her voice. But the more questions Maggie had asked—about Stranahan, the TV people, the money situation—the more remote the doctor had become, his voice getting tighter and colder on the other end. Finally Rudy had said that something had come up in the office, could he call her right back? Certainly, Maggie had said and—stupidly, it turned out—had given Rudy the phone number at the hotel. Days later the doctor still had not called back, and Maggie wondered why in the hell he had tried to reach her in the first place.

The answer was simple.

On the thirteenth of February, the man known as Chemo got off a Pan Am flight from Miami to New York. He wore a dusty broad-brimmed hat pulled down tightly to shadow his igneous face, a calfskin golf-bag cover snapped over his left arm to conceal the prosthesis, a pea-green woolen overcoat to protect against the winter wind, and heavy rubber-soled shoes to combat the famous New York City slush. He also had in his possession a Rapala fishing knife, the phone number of a man in Queens who would sell him a gun, and a slip of prescription paper on which were written these words in Dr. Rudy Graveline's spastic scrawl: "Plaza Hotel, Rm. 966."

18

When they returned from the Plaza to the apartment, Mick Stranahan said to Christina Marks: "Sure you want a killer sleeping on the sectional?"

"Do you snore?"

"I'm serious."

"Me, too." From a closet she got a flannel sheet, a blanket, and two pillows. "I've got a space heater that works, sometimes," she said.

"No, this is fine." Stranahan pulled off his shoes, turned on Letterman and stretched out on the sofa, which he had rearranged to contain his legs. He heard the shower running in the bathroom. After a few minutes Christina came out in a cloud of steam and sat down at the kitchen table. Her cheeks were flushed from the hot water. She wore a short blue robe, and her hair was wet. Stranahan could tell she'd brushed it out.

"We'll try again first thing in the morning," he said.

"What?"

"Maggie's room at the hotel."

"Oh, right." She looked distracted.

He sat up and said, "Come sit here."

"I don't think so," Christina said.

Stranahan could tell she had the radar up. He said, "I must've scared you on the plane."

"No, you didn't." She wanted to ask about everything, his life; he was trying to make it easier and not doing so well.

"You didn't scare me," Christina said again. "If you did, I wouldn't let you stay." But he had, and she did. That worried her even more.

Stranahan picked up the remote control and turned off the television. He heard sirens passing on the street outside and wished he were home, asleep on the bay.

When Christina spoke again, she didn't sound like a seasoned professional interviewer. She said, "Five men?"

Stranahan was glad she'd started with the killings. The marriages would be harder to justify.

"Are we off the record?"

She hesitated, then said yes.

"The men I killed," he began, "would have killed me first. You'll just have to take my word." Deep down, he wasn't sure about Thomas Henry Thomas, the fried-chicken robber. That one was a toss-up.

"What was it like?" Christina asked.

"Horrible."

She waited for the details; often men like Stranahan wanted to tell about it. Or needed to.

But all he said was: "Horrible, really. No fun at all."

She said, "You regret any of them?"

"Nope."

She had one elbow propped on the table, knuckles pressed to

her cheek. The only sound was the hissing of the radiator pipes, warming up. Stranahan peeled off his T-shirt and put it in a neat pile with his other clothes.

"I'll get a hotel room tomorrow."

"No, you won't," she said. "I'm not frightened."

"You haven't heard about my wives."

She laughed softly. "Five already at your age. You must be going for the record."

Stranahan lay back, hands locked behind his head. "I fall in love with waitresses. I can't help it."

"You're kidding."

"Don't be a snob. They were all smarter than I was. Even Chloe."

Christina said, "If you don't mind me saying so, she seemed like a very cold woman."

He groaned at the memory.

"What about the others, what were they like?"

"I loved them all, for a time. Then one day I didn't."

Christina said, "Doesn't sound like love."

"Boy, are you wrong." He smiled to himself.

"Mick, you regret any of them?"

"Nope."

The radiator popped. The warmth of it made Stranahan sleepy, and he yawned.

"What about lovers?" Christina asked—a question sure to jolt him awake. "All waitresses, no exceptions?"

"Oh, I've made some exceptions." He scratched his head and pretended there were so many he had to add them up. "Let's see, there was a lady probate lawyer. And an architect . . . make that two architects. Separately, of course. And an engineer for Pratt Whitney up in West Palm. An honest-to-God rocket scientist."

"Really?"

"Yeah, really. And they were all dumber than I was." Stranahan pulled the blanket up to his neck and closed his eyes. "Good night, Christina."

"Good night, Mick." She turned off the lights, returned to

the kitchen table, and sat in the gray darkness for an hour, watching him sleep.

When Maggie Gonzalez heard the knocking again, she got out of bed and weaved toward the noise. With outstretched arms she staved off menacing walls, doorknobs, and lampshades, but barely. She navigated through a wet gauze, her vision fuzzed by painkillers. When she opened the door, she found herself staring at the breast of a pea-green woolen overcoat. She tilted her throbbing head, one notch at a time, until she found the man's face.

"Uh," she said.

"Jesus H. Christ," said Chemo, shoving her back in the room, kicking the door shut behind him, savagely cursing his own rotten luck. The woman was wrapped from forehead to throat in white surgical tape—a fucking mummy! He took the photograph from his overcoat and handed it to Maggie Gonzalez.

"Is that you?" he demanded.

"No." The answer came from parchment lips, whispering through a slit in the bandages. "No, it's not me."

Chemo could tell that the woman was woozy. He told her to sit down before she fell down.

"It's you, isn't it? You're Maggie Gonzalez."

She said, "You're making a big mistake."

"Shut up." He took off his broad-brimmed hat and threw it on the bed. Through the peepholes in the bandage, Maggie was able to get a good look at the man's remarkable face.

She said, "My God, what happened to you?"

"Shut the fuck up."

Chemo unbuttoned his overcoat, heaved it over a chair, and paced. The trip was turning into a debacle. First the man in Queens had sold him a rusty Colt .38 with only two bullets. Later, on the subway, he had been forced to flee a group of elderly Amish in the fear that they might recognize him from his previous life. And now this—confusion. While Chemo was reasonably sure that the bandaged woman was Maggie Gonzalez, he didn't want to screw up and kill the wrong person. Dr. Graveline would never understand.

"Who are you?" Maggie said thickly. "Who sent you?"

"You ask too many questions."

"Please, I don't feel very well."

Chemo took the Colt from the waistband of his pants and pointed it at the bandaged tip of her new nose. "Your name's Maggie Gonzalez, isn't it?"

At the sight of the pistol, she leaned forward and vomited all over Chemo's rubber-soled winter shoes.

"Jesus H. Christ," he moaned and bolted for the bathroom.

"I'm sorry," Maggie called after him. "You scared me, that's all."

When Chemo came back, the shoes were off his feet and the gun was back in his pants. He was wiping his mouth with the corner of the towel.

"I'm really sorry," Maggie said again.

Chemo shook his head disgustedly. He sat down on the corner of the bed. To Maggie his legs seemed as long as circus stilts.

"You're supposed to kill me?"

"Yep," Chemo said. With the towel he wiped a fleck of puke off her nightgown.

Blearily she studied him and said, "You've had some dermabrasion."

"So?"

"So how come just little patches—why not more?"

"My doctor said that would be risky."

"Your doctor's full of it," Maggie said.

"And I guess you're an expert or something."

"I'm a nurse, but you probably know that."

Chemo said, "No, I didn't." Dr. Graveline hadn't told him a thing.

Maggie went on, "I used to work for a plastic surgeon in Miami. A butcher with a capital B."

Subconsciously Chemo's fingers felt for the tender spots on his chin. He was almost afraid to ask.

"This surgeon," he said to Maggie, "what was his name?"

"Graveline," she said. "Rudy Graveline. Personally, I wouldn't let him trim a hangnail."

Lugubriously Chemo closed his bulbous red eyes. Through the codeine, Maggie thought he resembled a giant nuclear-radiated salamander, straight from a monster movie.

"How about this," he said. "I'll tell you what happened to my face if you tell me what happened to yours."

It was Chemo's idea to have breakfast in Central Park. He figured there'd be so many other freaks that no one would notice them. As it turned out, Maggie's Tut-like facial shell drew more than a few stares. Chemo tugged his hat down tightly and said, "You should've worn a scarf."

They were sitting near Columbus Circle on a bench. Chemo had bought a box of raisin bagels with cream cheese. Maggie said her stomach felt much better but, because of the surgical tape, she was able to fit only small pieces of bagel into her mouth. It was a sloppy process, but two fat squirrels showed up to claim the crumbs.

Chemo was saying, "Your nose, your chin, your eyelids—Christ, no wonder you hurt." He took out her picture and looked at it appraisingly. "Too bad," he said.

"What's that supposed to mean?"

"I mean, you were a pretty lady."

"Maybe I still am," Maggie said. "Maybe prettier."

Chemo put the photograph back in his coat. "Maybe," he said.

"You're going to make me cry and then everything'll sting." He said, "Knock it off."

"Don't you think I feel bad enough?" Maggie said. "I get a whole new face—and for what! A month from now and you'd never have recognized me. I could've sat in your lap on the subway and you wouldn't know who I was."

Chemo thought he heard sniffling behind the bandages. "Don't fucking cry," he said. "Don't be a baby."

"I don't understand why Rudy sent you," Maggie whined.

"To kill you, what else?"

"But why now? Nothing's happened yet."

Chemo frowned and said, "Keep it down." The pink patches on his chin tingled in the cold air and made him think about Rudy Graveline. Butcher with a capital B, Maggie had said. Chemo wanted to know more.

A thin young Moonie in worn corduroys came up to the park bench and held out a bundle of red and white carnations. "Be happy," the kid said to Maggie. "Five dollars."

"Get lost," Chemo said.

"Four dollars,' said the Moonie. "Be happy."

Chemo pulled the calfskin cover off his Weed Whacker and flicked the underarm toggle for the battery pack. The Moonie gaped as Chemo calmly chopped the bright carnations to confetti.

"Be gone, Hop-sing," Chemo said, and the Moonie ran away. Chemo recloaked the Weed Whacker and turned to Maggie. "Tell me why the doctor wants you dead."

It took her several moments to recover from what she had seen. Finally she said, "Well, it's a long story."

"I got all day," Chemo said. "Unless you got tickets to *Phantom* or something."

"Can we go for a walk?"

"No," Chemo said sharply. "Remember?" He had thrown his vomit-covered shoes and socks out the ninth-floor window of Maggie's room at the Plaza. Now he was sitting in bare feet in Central Park on a forty-degree February morning. He wiggled his long bluish toes and said to Maggie Gonzalez: "So talk."

She did. She told Chemo all about the death of Victoria Barletta. It was a slightly shorter recital than she'd put on the videotape, but it was no less shocking.

"You're making this up," Chemo said.

"I'm not either."

"He killed this girl with a nose job?"

Maggie nodded. "I was there."

"Jesus H. Christ."

"It was an accident."

"That's even worse," Chemo said. He tore off his hat and threw it on the sidewalk, spooking the squirrels. "This is the same maniac who's working on my face. I can't fucking stand it!"

By way of consolation, Maggie said: "Dermabrasion is a much simpler procedure."

"Yeah, tell me about simple procedures." Chemo couldn't believe the lousy luck he had with doctors. He said, "So what does all this have to do with him wanting you dead?"

Maggie told Chemo about Reynaldo Flemm's TV investigation (without mentioning that she had been the tipster), told how she had warned Rudy about Mick Stranahan, the investigator. She was careful to make it sound as if Stranahan was the whistle-blower.

"Now it's starting to make sense," Chemo said. "Graveline wants me to kill *him*, too." He held up the arm-mounted Weed Whacker. "He's the prick that cost me this hand."

"Rudy can't afford any witnesses," Maggie explained, "or any publicity. Not only would they yank his medical license, he'd go to jail. Now do you understand?"

Do I ever, thought Chemo.

The white mask that was Maggie's face asked: "Are you still going to kill me?"

"We'll see," Chemo replied. "I'm sorting things out."

"How much is that cheap bastard paying you?"

Chemo plucked his rumpled hat off the sidewalk. "I'd rather not say," he muttered, clearly embarrassed. No way would he let that butcher fuck with his ears. Not now.

Christina Marks and Mick Stranahan got to the Plaza Hotel shortly before ten. From the lobby Stranahan called Maggie's room and got no answer. Christina followed him into the elevator and, as they rode to the ninth floor, she watched him remove a small serrated blade from his wallet.

"Master key," he said.

"Mick, no. I could get fired."

"Then wait downstairs."

But she didn't. She watched him pick the lock on Maggie's

door, then slipped into the room behind him. She said nothing and scarcely moved while he checked the bathroom and the closets to see if they were alone.

"Mick, come here."

On the bedstand were two prescription bottles, a plastic bedpan, and a pink-splotched surgical compress. Stranahan glanced at the pills: Tylenol No. 3 and Darvocet. The bottle of Darvocets had not yet been opened. A professional business card lay next to the telephone on Maggie's nightstand. Stranahan chuckled drily when he read what was on the card:

LEONARD R. LEAPER, M.D.
Certified by the American Board of Plastic Surgery
Office: 555-6600   Nights and Emergencies: 555-6677

"How nice," Christina remarked. "She took our money and got a face-lift."

Stranahan said, "Something's not right. She ought to be in bed."

"Maybe she went for brunch at the Four Seasons."

He shook his head. "These scrips are only two days old, so that's when she had the surgery. She's still got to be swollen up like a mango. Would you go out in public looking like that?"

"Depends on how much dope I ate."

"No," Stranahan said, scanning the room, "Something's not right. She ought to be here."

"What do you want to do?"

Stranahan said they should go downstairs and wait in the lobby; in her condition, Maggie shouldn't be hard to spot. "But first," he said, "let's really go through this place."

Christina went to the dresser. Under a pile of Maggie's bras and panties she found three new flowered bikinis, the price tags from the Plaza Shops still attached. Maggie was definitely getting ready for Maui.

"Oh, Miss Marks," Stranahan sang out. "Lookie here."

It was a video cassette in a brown plastic sleeve. The sleeve was marked with a sticker from Midtown Studio Productions.

Stranahan tossed Christina the tape. She tossed it back.

"We can't take that, it's larceny."

He said, "It's not larceny to take something you already own."

"What do you mean?"

"If this is what I think it is, you've paid for it already. The Barletta story, remember?"

"We don't know that. Could be anything—home movies, maybe."

Stranahan smiled and stuffed the cassette into his coat. "Only one way to find out."

"No," Christina said.

"Look, you got a VCR at your place. Let's go watch the tape. If I'm wrong, then I'll bring it back myself."

"Oh, I see. Just sneak in, put it back where you got it, tidy up the place."

"Yeah, if I'm wrong. If it turns out to be Jane Fonda or something. But I don't think so."

Christina Marks knew better; it was madness, of course. She could lose her job, blow a perfectly good career if they were caught. But, then again, this hadn't turned out to be the typical Reynaldo Flemm exposé. She had damn near gotten machine-gunned over this one, so what the hell.

Grudgingly she said, "Is it Beta or VHS?"

Stranahan gave her a hug.

Then they heard the key in the door.

The two couples said nothing for the first few seconds, just stared. Mick Stranahan and Christina Marks had the most to contemplate: a woman wrapped in tape, and a beanpole assassin with one arm down to his knees.

Maggie Gonzalez was the first to speak: "It's him."

"Who?" Chemo asked. He had never seen Stranahan up close, not even at the stilt house.

"Him," Maggie repeated through the bandages. "What're you doing in my room?"

"Hello, Maggie," Stranahan said, "assuming it's you under there. It's sure been a long time."

"And you!" Maggie grunted, pointing at Christina Marks.

"Hi, again," said Christina. "I thought you'd be in Hawaii by now."

Chemo said, "I guess everybody's old pals except me." He pulled the .38 out of his overcoat. "Nobody move."

"Another one who watches too much TV," Stranahan whispered to Christina.

Chemo blinked angrily. "I don't like you one bit."

"I assumed as much from the fact you keep trying to kill me." Stranahan had seen some bizarros in his day, but this one took the cake. He looked like Fred Munster with bulimia. One eye on the gun, Stranahan asked, "Do you have a name?"

"No," Chemo said.

"Good. Makes for a cheaper tombstone."

Chemo told Maggie to close the door, but Maggie didn't move. The sight of the pistol had made her nauseated all over again, and she was desperately trying to keep down her breakfast bagels.

"What's the matter now?" Chemo snapped.

"She doesn't look so hot," Christina said.

"And who the fuck are you, Florence Nightingale?"

"What happened to your arm?" Christina asked him. A cool customer she was; Stranahan admired her poise.

Chemo got the impression that he was losing control, which made no sense, since he was the one with the pistol. "Shut up, all of you," he said, "while I kill Mr. Stranahan here. *Finally.*"

At these words, Maggie Gonzalez upchucked gloriously all over Chemo's gun arm. Given his general translucence, it was impossible to tell if Chemo blanched. He did, however, wobble perceptibly.

Mick Stranahan stepped forward and punched him ferociously in the Adam's apple. The man went down like a seven-foot Tinkertoy, but did not release his grip on the gun. Maggie backed up and screamed, a primal wail that poured from the hole in her bandage and filled the hallway. Stranahan decided there was no time to finish the job. He pushed Christina Marks through the doorway and told her to go for the elevator. Gagging and spitting blood, Chemo rolled out of his fetal curl and took a wild shot at Christina as she ran down the hall. The bullet twanged impotently off a fire extinguisher and was ultimately stopped by the opulent Plaza wallpaper.

Before Chemo could fire again, Stranahan stomped on his wrist, still slippery from Maggie's used bagels. Chemo would not let go of the gun. With a growl he swung his refurbished left arm like a fungo bat across his body. It caught Stranahan in the soft crease behind the knee and brought him down. The two men wrestled for the pistol while Maggie howled and clawed chimp-like at her swaddled head.

It was a clumsy fight. Tangled in the killer's gangliness, Stranahan could not shield himself from a clubbing by Chemo's oversized left arm. Whatever it was—and it wasn't a human fist— it hurt like hell. His skull chiming, Stranahan tried to break free.

Suddenly he felt the dull barrel of the .38 against his throat. He flinched when he heard the click, but nothing else followed. No flash, no explosion, no smell. The bullet, Chemo's second and only remaining round, was a dud. Chemo couldn't believe it—that asshole in Queens had screwed him royal.

Stranahan squirmed loose, stood up, and saw that they had attracted an audience. All along the corridor, doors were cracked open, some more than others. Under Maggie's keening he could hear excited voices. Somebody was calling the police.

Stranahan groped at his coat to make sure that the videotape was still in his pocket, kicked Chemo once in the groin (or where he estimated that the giant's groin might be), then jogged down the hallway.

Christina Marks was considerate enough to hold the elevator.

19

Dr. Rudy Graveline was a fellow who distrusted chance and prided himself on preparation, but he had not planned a love affair with a Hollywood star. Heather Chappell was a distraction—a fragrant, gorgeous, elusive, spoiled, sulky bitch of a distraction. He couldn't get enough of her. Rudy had come to crave the tunnel of clear thinking that enveloped him while making love to Heather; it was like a sharp cool drug. She screwed him absolutely numb, left him aching and drained and utterly in focus with his predicament.

For a while he kept cooking up lame excuses for postponing Heather's elaborate cosmetic surgery—knowing it would put her out of action for weeks. Sex with Heather had become a crucial component of Rudy Graveline's daily regimen; like a long-distance runner, he had fallen into a physical rhythm that he could not afford to break. TV people were after him, his medical career was in jeopardy, a homicide rap was on the horizon—and salvation depended on a crooked halfwit politician and a one-armed, seven-foot hit man. Rudy needed to stay razor-sharp until the crisis was over, and Heather had become vital to his clarity.

He treated her like a queen and it seemed to work. Heather's initial urgency to schedule the surgery had subsided during the day-long shopping sprees, the four-star meals, the midnight yacht cruises up and down the Intracoastal. In recent days, though, she again had begun to press Rudy not only about the date for the operations, but the cost. She was dropping broad hints to the effect that for all her bedroom labors she deserved a special discount, and Rudy found himself weakening on the subject. Finally, one night, she waited until he was inside her to bring up the money again, and Rudy breathlessly agreed to knock forty percent off the usual fee. Afterwards he was furious at himself, and blamed his moment of weakness on stress and mental fatigue.

Deep down, the doctor knew better: He was trapped. While he dreaded the prospect of Heather Chappell's surgery, he feared that she would leave him if he didn't agree to do it. He probably would have done it for free. He had become addicted to her body—a radiantly perfect body that she now wanted him to *improve*. The task would have posed a career challenge for the most skillful of plastic surgeons; for a hack like Rudy Graveline, it was flat-out impossible. Naturally he planned to let his assistants do it.

Until Heather dropped another surprise.

"My agent says I should tape the operation, love."

Rudy said, "You're kidding."

"Just to be on the safe side."

"What, you don't trust me?"

"Sure I do," Heather said. "It's my damn agent, is all. She says since my looks are everything, my whole career, I should be careful, legal-wise. I guess she wants to make sure nothing goes wrong—"

Rudy sprung out of bed, hands on his hips. "Look, I told you these operations are not necessary at all."

"And I told you, I'm sick of doing sitcoms and *Hollywood Squares*. I need to get back in the movies, hon, and that means I need a new look. That's why I came down here."

Rudy Graveline had never tried to talk anyone out of surgery before, so he was forced to improvise. By and large it was not such a terrible speech. He said, "God was very good to you, Heather. I have patients who'd give fifty grand to look half as beautiful as you look: teenagers who'd kill for that nose you want me to chisel, housewives who'd trade their firstborn child for tits like yours—"

"Rudolph," Heather said, "save it."

He tried to pull up his underwear but the elastic snagged on heavily bandaged kneecaps, the product of the disco tryst in the fireplace.

"I am appalled," Rudy was huffing, "at the idea of video-taping in my surgical suite." In truth he wasn't appalled so much as afraid: A video camera meant he couldn't hand off to the other surgeons and duck out to the golf course. He'd have to perform every procedure himself, just as Heather had demanded. You couldn't drug a damn camera; it wouldn't miss a stitch.

"This just isn't done," Rudy protested.

"Oh, it is, too," Heather said. "I see stuff like that on PBS all the time. Once I saw them put a baboon heart inside a human baby. They showed the whole thing."

"It isn't done *here*," Rudy said.

Heather sat up, making sure that the bedsheets slipped off the slope of her breasts. "Fine, Rudolph," she said. "If that's the way you want it, I'll fly back to California tonight. There's only about a dozen first-rate surgeons in Beverly Hills that would give anything to do me."

The ice in her voice surprised him, though it shouldn't have. "All right," he said, pulling on his robe, "we'll video the surgery. Maybe Robin Leach can use a clip on his show."

Heather let the wisecrack pass; she was focused on business. She asked Rudy Graveline for a date they could begin.

"A week," he said. He had to clear his mind a few more times. In another week he also would have heard something definite from Chemo, or maybe Roberto Pepsical.

"And we're not doing all this at once," he added. "You've got the liposuction, the breast augmentation, the rhinoplasty, the eyelids, and the rhytidectomy—that's a lot of surgery, Heather."

"Yes, Rudolph." She had won and she knew it.

"I think we'll start with the nose and see how you do."

"Or how *you* do," Heather said.

Rudy had a queasy feeling that she wasn't kidding.

* * *

The executive producer of *In Your Face* was a man known to Reynaldo Flemm only as Mr. Dover. Mr. Dover was in charge of the budget. Upon Reynaldo's return to New York, he found a message taped to his office door. Mr. Dover wanted to see him right away.

Immediately Reynaldo called the apartment of Christina Marks, but hung up when Mick Stranahan answered the phone. Reynaldo was fiercely jealous; beyond that, he didn't think it was fair that he should have to face Mr. Dover alone. Christina was the producer, she knew where all the money went. Reynaldo was merely the talent, and the talent never knew anything.

When he arrived at Mr. Dover's office, the secretary did not recognize him. "The music division is on the third floor," she said, scarcely making eye contact.

Reynaldo riffled his new hair and said, "It's me."

"Oh, hi, Ray."

"What do you think?"

The secretary said, "It's a dynamite disguise."

"It's not a disguise."

"Oh."

"I wanted a new look," he explained.

"Why?" asked the secretary.

Reynaldo couldn't tell her the truth—that a rude plastic surgeon told him he had a fat waist and a big honker—so he said: "Demographics"

The secretary looked at him blankly.

"Market surveys," he went on. "We're going for some younger viewers."

"Oh, I see," the secretary said.

"Long hair is making quite a comeback."

"I didn't know," she said, trying to be polite. "Is that real, Ray?"

"Well, no. Not yet."

"I'll tell Mr. Dover you're here."

Mr. Dover was a short man with an accountant's pinched demeanor, a fishbelly complexion, tiny black eyes, and the slick, sloping forehead of a killer whale. Mr. Dover wore expensive dark suits and yuppie suspenders that, Reynaldo suspected, needed adjustment.

"Ray, what can you tell me about this Florida project?" Mr. Dover never wasted time with small talk.

"It's heavy," Reynaldo replied.

"Heavy."

"Very heavy." Reynaldo noticed his expense vouchers stacked in a neat pile on the corner of Mr. Dover's desk. This worried him, so he said, "My producer was almost murdered."

"I see."

"With a machine gun," Reynaldo added.

Mr. Dover pursed his lips. "Why?"

"Because we're getting close to cracking this story."

"You're getting close to cracking my budget, Ray."

"This is an important project."

Mr. Dover said, "A network wouldn't blink twice, Ray, but we're not one of the networks. My job is to watch the bottom line."

Indignantly Reynaldo thought: *I eat twits like you for breakfast.* He was good at thinking tough thoughts.

"Investigations cost money," he said tersely.

With shiny pink fingernails Mr. Dover leafed through the receipts on his desk until he found the one he wanted. "Jambala's House of Hair," he said. "Seven hundred and seventeen dollars."

Reynaldo blushed and ground his caps. Christina should be here for this; she'd know how to handle this jerk.

Mr. Dover continued: "I don't intend to interfere, nor do I intend to let these extravagances go on forever. As I understand it, the program is due to air next month."

"All the spots have been sold," Reynaldo said. "They've been sold for six months." He couldn't resist.

"Yes, well I suggest you try not to spend all that advertising revenue before the broadcast date—just in case it doesn't work out."

"And when hasn't it worked out?"

Reynaldo regretted his words almost instantly, for Mr. Dover was only too happy to refresh his memory. There was the time Flemm claimed to have discovered the wreckage of Amelia Earhart's airplane (it turned out to be a crop duster in New Zealand); the time he claimed to have an exclusive interview with the second gunman from Dealey Plaza (who, it later turned out, was barely seven years old on the day of the Kennedy assassination); the time he uncovered a Congressional call-girl ring (only to be caught boffing two of the ladies in a mop closet at the Rayburn Building). These fiascos each resulted in a canceled broadcast, snide blurbs in the press, and great sums of lost revenue, which Mr. Dover could recall to the penny.

"Ancient history," Reynaldo Flemm said defensively.

Unspoken was the fact that no such embarrassments had happened since Christina Marks had been hired. Every show had been finished on time, on budget. Reynaldo did not appreciate the connection, but Mr. Dover did.

"You understand my concern," he said. "How much longer do you anticipate being down in Miami?"

"Two weeks. We'll be editing." Sounded good, anyway.

"So, shall we say, one more trip?"

"That ought to do it," Reynaldo agreed.

"Excellent." Mr. Dover straightened the stack of Reynaldo's expense receipts, lining up all the little corners in perfect angles. "By the way, Miss Marks wasn't harmed, was she?"

"No, just scared shitless. She's not used to getting shot at." As if he was.

"Did they catch this person?"

"Nope," Reynaldo said, hard-bitten, like he wasn't too surprised.

"My," said Mr. Dover. He hoped that Christina Marks was paid up on her medical plan and death benefits.

"I told you it was heavy," Reynaldo said, rising. "But it'll be worth it, I promise."

"Good," said Mr. Dover. "I can't wait."

Reynaldo was three steps toward the door when Mr. Dover said, "Ray?"

"Yeah."

"Forgive me, but I was just noticing."

"That's all right." He'd been wondering how long it would take the twerp to mention something about the hair.

But from behind the desk Mr. Dover smiled wickedly and patted his midsection. "You've put on a pound or three, haven't you, Ray?"

In the elevator Reynaldo angrily tore off his seven-hundred-dollar wig and hurled it into a corner, where it lay like a dead Pekingese. He took the limo back to his apartment, stripped off his clothes, and stood naked for a long time in front of the bedroom mirror.

Reynaldo decided that Mr. Graveline was right: His nose was too large. And his belly had thickened.

He pivoted to the left, then to the right, then back to the left. He sucked in his breath. He flexed. He locked his knuckles behind his head and tightened his stomach muscles, but his belly did not disappear.

In the mirror Reynaldo saw a body that was neither flabby nor lean: an average body for an average forty-year-old man. He saw a face that was neither dashing nor weak: small darting eyes balanced by a strong, heavy jaw, with a nose to match. He concluded that his instincts about preserving the mustache were sound: When Reynaldo covered his hairy upper lip with a bare finger, his nose assumed even greater prominence.

Of course, something radical had to be done. Confidence was the essence of Reynaldo's camera presence, the core of his masculine appeal. If he were unhappy with himself or insecure about his appearance, it would show up on his face like a bad rash. The whole country would see it.

Standing alone at the mirror, Reynaldo hatched a plan that would solve his personal dilemma and wrap up the Barletta story simultaneously. It was a bold plan because it would not include Christina Marks. Reynaldo Flemm would serve as his own producer and would tell Christina nothing, just as she had told him nothing for two entire weeks after the shooting in Stiltsville.

The shooting. Still it galled him, the sour irony that *she* would be the one to get the glory—after all his years on the streets. To have his producer nearly assassinated while he dozed on the massage table at the Sonesta was the lowest moment in Reynaldo's professional career. He had to atone.

In the past he had always counted on Christina to worry about the actual nuts-and-bolts journalism of the program. It was Christina who did the reporting, blocked out the interviews, arranged for the climactic confrontations—she even wrote the scripts. Reynaldo Flemm was hopelessly bored by detail, research, and the rigors of fact checking. He was an action guy, and he saved his energy for when the tape was rolling. Whereas Christina had filled three legal pads with notes, ideas, and questions about Victoria Barletta's death, Reynaldo cared about one thing only: Who could they get on tape? Rudy Graveline was the big enchilada, and certainly Victoria's still-grieving mother was a solid bet. Mick Stranahan had been another obvious choice—the embarrassed investigator, admitting four years later that he had overlooked the prime suspect, the doctor himself.

But the Stranahan move had backfired, and nearly made a news-industry martyr of Christina Marks. Fine, thought Reynaldo, go ahead and have your fling. Meanwhile Willie and I will be kicking some serious quack ass.

Every time Dr. Rudy Graveline got a phone call from New York or New Jersey, he assumed it was the mob. The mob had generously put him through Harvard Medical School, and in return Rudy occasionally extended his professional courtesies to mob guys, their friends or family. It was Rudy himself who had redone the face of Tony (The Eel) Traviola, the hit man who later washed up dead on Cape Florida beach with a marlin hole through his sternum. Fortunately for Rudy, most mob fugitives were squeamish about surgery, so he wound up doing mainly their wives, daughters, and mistresses. Noses, mostly, with the occasional face-lift.

That's the kind of call Rudy expected when his secretary told him that New York was on the line.

"Yes?"

"Hello, Doctor Graveline."

The voice did not belong to Curly Eyebrows or any of his cousins.

"Who is this?"

"Johnny LeTigre, remember me?"

"Of course." The hinky male stripper. Rudy said, "What are you doing in New York?"

"I had a gig in the Village, but I'm on my way back to Miami." This was Reynaldo Flemm's idea of being fast on his feet. He said, "Look, I've been thinking about what you said that day at the clinic."

Rudy Graveline could not remember exactly what he had said. "Yes?"

"About my nose and my abdomen."

Then it came back to Rudy. "Your nose and abdomen, yes, I remember."

"You were right," Reynaldo went on. "We don't always see ourselves the way other people do."

Rudy was thinking: Get to the damn point.

"I'd like for you to do my nose," Reynaldo declared.

"All right."

"And my middle—what's that operation called?"

"Suction-assisted lipectomy," Rudy said.

"Yeah, that's it. How much'd that set me back?"

Rudy recalled that this was a man who offered ten grand to have a mole removed from his buttocks.

"Fifteen thousand," Rudy said.

"Geez!" said the voice from New York.

"But that's if I perform the procedures myself," Rudy explained. "Keep in mind, I've got several very competent associates who could handle your case for, oh, half as much."

The way that Rudy backed off on the word *competent* was no accident, but Reynaldo Flemm didn't need a sell job. Quickly he said, "No, I definitely want you. Fifteen it is. But I need the work done this week."

"Out of the question." Rudy would be immersed in preparation for the Heather Chappell marathon.

"Next week at the latest," Reynaldo pressed.

"Let me see what I can do. By the way, Mr. LeTigre, what is the status of your mole?"

Reynaldo had almost forgotten about the ruse that originally had gained his entry to Whispering Palms. Again he had to wing it. "You won't believe this," he said to Dr. Rudy Graveline, "but the damn thing fell off."

"Are you certain?"

"Swear to God, one morning I'm standing in the shower and I turn around and it's gone. Gone! I found it lying there in the bed. Just fell off, like an acorn or something."

"Hmmm," Rudy said. The guy was a flake, but who cared. "I threw it away, is that okay?"

"The mole?"

"Yeah, I thought about saving it in the freezer, maybe having some tests run. But then I figured what the hell and I tossed it in the trash."

"It was probably quite harmless," Rudy Graveline said, dying to hang up.

"So I'll call you when I get back to Miami."

"Fine," said the doctor. "Have a safe trip, Mr. LeTigre."

Reynaldo Flemm was beaming when he put down the phone. This would be something. Maybe even better than getting shot on the air.

20

Maggie Gonzalez said: "Tell me about your hand."

"Shut up," Chemo grumbled. He was driving around Queens, trying to find the sonofabitch who had sold him the bad bullets.

"Please," Maggie said. "I am a nurse."

"Too bad you're not a magician, because that's what it's gonna take to make my hand come back. A fish got it."

At a stop light he rolled down the window and called to a group of black teenagers. He asked where he could locate a man named Donnie Blue, and the teenagers told Chemo to go blow himself. "Shit," he said, stomping on the accelerator.

Maggie asked, "Was it a shark that did it?"

"Do I look like Jacques Cousteau? I don't know what the hell it was—some big fish. The subject is closed."

By now Maggie was reasonably confident that he wasn't going to kill her. He would have done it already, most conveniently during the scuffle back at the Plaza. Instead he had grabbed her waist and hustled her down the fire exit, taking four steps at a time. Considering the mayhem on the ninth floor, it was a miracle they got out of the place without being stopped. The lobby was full of uniformed cops waiting for elevators, but nobody looked twice at the Fun Couple of the Year.

As Chemo drove, Maggie said, "What about your face?"

"Look who's talking."

"Really, what happened?"

Chemo said, "You always this shy with strangers? Jesus H. Christ."

212

"I'm sorry," she said. "Professional curiosity, I guess. Besides, you promised to tell me."

"Do the words *none of your fucking business* mean anything?"

From behind the bandages a chilly voice said, "You don't have to be crude. Swearing doesn't impress me."

Chemo found the street corner where he had purchased the rusty Colt .38 and the dead bullets, but there was no sign of Donnie Blue. Every inquiry was met by open derision, and Chemo's hopes for a refund began to fade.

As he circled the neighborhood Maggie said, "You're so quiet."

"I'm thinking."

"Me, too."

"I'm thinking I was seriously gypped by your doctor pal." Chemo didn't want to admit that he had agreed to murder two people in exchange for a discount on minor plastic surgery.

"If I had known about this dead girl—"

"Vicky Barletta."

"Right," Chemo said. "If I had known that, I would have jacked my price. Jacked it way the hell up."

"And who could blame you," Maggie said.

"Graveline never told me he killed a girl."

They were heading out the highway toward La Guardia. Maggie assumed there were travel plans.

She said, "Rudy's a very wealthy man."

"Sure, he's a doctor."

"I can ruin him. That's why he wanted me dead."

"Sure, you're a witness," Chemo said.

Something dismissive in his tone alarmed her once again. She said, "Killing me won't solve anything now."

Chemo's forehead crinkled where an eyebrow should have been. "It won't?"

Maggie shook her head from side to side in dramatic emphasis. "I made my own tape. A videotape, at a place in Manhattan. Everything's on it, everything I saw that day."

Chemo wasn't as rattled as she thought he might be; in fact, his mouth curled into a dry smile. His lips looked like two pink snails crawling up a sidewalk.

"A video," he mused.

Maggie teased it along. "You have any idea what that bastard would pay for it?"

"Yes," Chemo said. "Yes, I think I do."

At the airport, Maggie told Chemo she had to make a phone call. To eavesdrop he squeezed inside the same booth, his chin digging into the top of her head. She dialed the number of Dr. Leonard Leaper and informed the service that she had to leave town for a while, but that the doctor should not be concerned.

"I already told him I was a witness in a murder," Maggie explained to Chemo. "If what happened at the hotel turns up in the newspapers, he'll think I was kidnapped."

"But you were," Chemo pointed out.

"Oh, not really."

"Yes, *really*." Chemo didn't care for her casual attitude; just who did she take him for?

Maggie said, "Know what I think? I think we could be partners."

They got on line at the Pan Am counter, surrounded by a typical Miami-bound contingent—old geezers with tubas for sinuses; shiny young hustlers in thin gold chains; huge hollow-eyed families that looked like they'd staggered out of a Sally Struthers telethon. Chemo and Maggie fit right in.

He told her, "I only got one plane ticket."

She smiled and stroked her handbag, which had not left her arm since their breakfast in Central Park. "I've got a Visa card," she said brightly. "Where we headed?"

"Me, I'm going back to Florida."

"Not like that, you're not. They've got rules against bare feet, I'm sure."

"Hell," Chemo said, and loped off to locate some cheap shoes. He came back wearing fuzzy brown bathroom slippers, size 14, purchased at one of the airport gift shops. Maggie was saving him a spot at the ticket counter. She had already arranged for him to get an aisle seat (because of his long legs), and she would be next to him.

Later, waiting in the boarding area, Maggie asked Chemo if his name was Rogelio Luz Sanchez.

"Oh sure."

"That's what it says on your ticket."

"Well, there you are," Chemo said. He couldn't even *pronounce* Rogelio Luz Sanchez—some alias cooked up by Rudy Graveline, the dumb shit. Chemo looked about as Hispanic as Larry Bird.

After they took their seats on the airplane, Maggie leaned close and asked, "So, can I call you Rogelio? I mean, I've got to call you *something*."

Chemo's hooded lids blinked twice very slowly. "The more you talk, the more I want to spackle the holes in that fucking mask."

Maggie emitted a reedy, birdlike noise.

"I think we can do business," Chemo said, "but only on two conditions. One, don't ask any more personal questions, is that clear? Two, don't ever puke on me again."

"I said I was sorry."

The plane had started to taxi and Chemo raised his voice to be heard over the engines. "Once I get some decent bullets I'll be using that gun, and God help you if you toss your cookies when I do."

Maggie said, "I'll do better next time."

One of the flight attendants came by and asked Maggie if she needed a special meal because of her medical condition, and Maggie remarked that she wasn't feeling particularly well. She said the coach section was so crowded and stuffy that she was having trouble breathing. The next thing Chemo knew, they were sitting up in first class and sipping red wine. Having noticed his disability, the friendly flight attendant was carefully cutting Chemo's surf-and-turf into bite-sized pieces. Chemo glanced at Maggie and felt guilty about coming down so hard.

"That was a slick move," he said, the closest he would come to a compliment. "I never rode up here before."

Maggie exhibited no surprise at this bit of news. Her eyes looked sad and moist behind the white husk.

Chemo said, "You still want to be partners?"

She nodded. Carefully she aimed a forkful of lobster for the damp hole beneath her nostrils in the surgical bandage.

"Graveline's gonna scream when he learns about your video-tape," Chemo said with a chuckle. "Where is it, anyway?"

When Maggie finished chewing, she said, "I've got three copies."

"Good thinking."

"Two of them are locked up at a bank. The third one, the original tape, that's for Rudy. That's how we get his attention."

Chemo smiled a yellow smile. "I like it."

"You won't like this part," Maggie said. "Stranahan swiped the tape from the hotel room. We can't show it to Rudy until we get it back."

"Hell," Chemo said. This was terrible—Mick Stranahan and that TV bitch loose with the blackmail goodies. Just terrible. He said, "I've got to get to them before they get to Graveline, otherwise we're blown out of the water. He'll be on the first flight to Panama and we'll be holding our weenies."

From Maggie came a muffled, disapproving noise.

"It's just an expression," Chemo said. "Lighten up, for Chrissakes."

After the flight attendants removed the meal trays, Chemo lowered the seat back and stretched his endless legs. Almost to himself, he said, "I don't like this Stranahan guy one bit. When we get to Miami, we hit the ground running."

"Yes," Maggie agreed, easing into the partnership, "we've got to get the tape."

"That, too," said Chemo, tugging his hat down over his eyes.

The news of gunshots and a possible kidnapping at the Plaza Hotel rated five paragraphs in the *Daily News*, a page of photos in the *Post* and nothing in the *Times*. That morning New York detectives queried a teletype to the Metro-Date Police Department stating that the victim of the abduction was believed to be a Miami woman named Margaret Orestes Gonzalez, a guest at the hotel. The police teletype described her assailant as a white male, age unknown, with possible burn scars on his face and a height of either six foot four or eight foot two, depending on which witness you believed. The teletype further noted that a Rapala fishing knife found on the carpet outside the victim's room was traced to a shipment that recently had been sold to a retail establishment known as Bubba's Bait and Cold Beer, on Dixie Highway in South Miami. Most significantly, a partial thumb-print lifted from the blade of the knife was identified as belonging to one Blondell Wayne Tatum, age thirty-eight, six foot nine, one hundred eighty-one pounds. Mr. Tatum, it seemed, was wanted in the state of Pennsylvania for the robbery-at-pitchfork of a Chemical Bank, and for the first-degree murder of Dr. Gunther MacLeish, an elderly dermatologist. Tatum was to be considered armed and dangerous. Under AKAs, the police bulletin listed one: Chemo.

"Chemo?" Sergeant Al García read the teletype again, then pulled it off the bulletin board and took it to the Xerox machine. By the time he got back, a new teletype had been posted in its place.

This one was even more interesting, and García's cigar bobbed excitedly as he read it.

The new teletype advised Metro-Dade police to disregard the kidnap query. Miss Margaret Gonzalez had phoned the New York authorities to assure them that she was in no danger, and to explain that the disturbance at the Plaza Hotel was merely a dispute between herself and a male companion she had met in a bar.

Maggie had hung up before detectives could ask if the male companion was Mr. Blondell Wayne Tatum.

Commissioner Roberto Pepsical arranged to meet the two crooked detectives at a strip joint off LeJeune Road, not far from the airport. Roberto got there early and drank three strong vodka tonics to give him the courage to say what he'd been told to say.

He figured he was so far over his head that being drunk couldn't make it any worse.

Dutifully the commissioner had carried Detective Murdock's proposal to Dr. Rudy Graveline, and now he had returned with the doctor's reply. It occurred to Roberto, even as a naked woman with gold teeth delivered a fourth vodka, that the role of an elected public servant was no longer a distinguished one. He found himself surrounded by ruthless and untrustworthy people—nobody played a straight game anymore. In Miami, corruption had become a sport of the masses. Roberto had been doing it for years, of course, but jerks like Salazar and Murdock and even Graveline—they were nothing but dilettantes. Moochers. They didn't know when to back off. The word *enough* was not in their vocabulary. Roberto hated the idea that his future depended on such men.

The crooked cops showed up just as the nude Amazonian mud-wrestling match began on stage. "Very nice place," Detective John Murdock said to the commissioner. "Is that your daughter up there?"

Joe Salazar said, "The one on the right, she even looks like you. Except I think you got bigger knockers."

Roberto Pepsical flushed. He was sensitive about his weight. "You're really funny," he said to the detectives. "Both of you should've been comedians instead of cops. You should've been Lawrence and Hardy."

Murdock smirked. "Lawrence and Hardy, huh? I think the commissioner has been drinking."

Salazar said, "Maybe we hurt his feelings."

The vodka was supposed to make Roberto Pepsical cool and brave; instead it was making him hot and dizzy. He started to tell the detectives what Rudy Graveline had said, but he couldn't hear himself speak over the exhortations of the wrestling fans. Finally Murdock seized him by the arm and led him to the restroom. Joe Salazar followed them in and locked the door.

"What's all this for?" Roberto said, belching in woozy fear. He thought the detectives were going to beat him up.

Murdock took him by the shoulders and pinned him to the

condom machine. He said, "Joe and I don't like this joint. It's noisy, it's dirty, it's a shitty fucking joint to hold a serious conversation. We are offended, Commissioner, by what we see taking place on the stage out there—naked young females with wet mud all over their twats. You shouldn't have invited us here."

Joe Salazar said, "That's right. Just so you know, I'm a devoted Catholic."

"I'm sorry," said Roberto Pepsical. "It was the darkest place I could think of on short notice. Next time we'll meet at St. Mary's."

Someone knocked on the restroom door and Murdock told him to go away if he valued his testicles. Then he said to Roberto: "What is it you wanted to tell us?"

"It's a message from my friend. The one with the problem I told you about—"

"The problem named Stranahan?"

"Yes. He says five thousand each."

"Fine," said John Murdock.

"Really?"

"Long as it's cash."

Salazar added, "Not in sequence. And not bank-wrapped."

"Certainly," Roberto Pepsical said. Now came the part that made his throat go dry.

"There's one part of the plan that my friend wants to change," he said. "He says it's no good just arresting this man and putting him in jail. He says this fellow has a big mouth and a vivid imagination." Those were Rudy's exact words; Roberto was proud of himself for remembering.

Joe Salazar idly tested the knobs on the condom machine and said, "So you got a better idea, right?"

"Well . . . ," Roberto said.

Murdock loosened his grip on the commissioner and straightened his jacket. "You're not the idea man, are you? I mean, it was your idea to meet at this pussy parlor." He walked over to the urinal and unzipped his trousers. "Joe and I will think of something. We're idea-type guys."

Salazar said, "For instance, suppose we get a warrant to arrest the suspect for the murder of his former wife. Supposing we proceed to his residence and duly identify ourselves as sworn police officers. And supposing the suspect attempts to flee."

"Or resists with violence," Murdock hypothesized.

"Yeah, the manual is clear," Salazar said.

Murdock shook himself off and zipped up. "In a circumstance such as that, we could use deadly force."

"I imagine you could," said Roberto Pepsical, sober as a choirboy.

The three of them stood there in the restroom, sweating under the hot bare bulb. Salazar examined a package of flamingo-pink rubbers that he had shaken loose from the vending machine.

Finally Murdock said, "Tell your friend it sounds fine, except for the price. Make it ten apiece, not five."

"Ten," Roberto repeated, though he was not at all surprised. To close the deal, he sighed audibly.

"Come on," said Joe Salazar, unlocking the door. "We're missing the fingerpaint contest."

Over the whine of the outboard Luis Córdova shouted: "There's no point in stopping."

Mick Stranahan nodded. Under ceramic skies, Biscayne Bay unfolded in a dozen shifting hues of blue. It was a fine, cloudless morning: seventy degrees, and a northern breeze at their backs. Luis Córdova slowed the patrol boat a few hundred yards from the stilt house. He leaned down and said: "They tore the place up pretty bad, Mick."

"You sure it was cops?"

"Yeah, two of them. Not uniformed guys, though. And they had one of the sheriff boats."

Stranahan knew who it was: Murdock and Salazar.

"Those goons from the hospital," said Christina Marks. She stood next to Luis Córdova at the steering console, behind the Plexiglas windshield. She wore a red windbreaker, baggy knit pants, and high-top tennis shoes.

From a distance Stranahan could see that the door to his house had been left open, which meant it had probably been looted and vandalized. What the kids didn't wreck, the seagulls would. Stranahan stared for a few moments, then said: "Let's go, Luis."

The trip to Old Rhodes Key took thirty-five minutes in a light, nudging sea. Christina got excited when they passed a school of porpoises off Elliott Key, but Stranahan showed no interest. He was thinking about the videotape they had watched at Christina's apartment—Maggie Gonzalez, describing the death of Vicky Barletta. Twice they had watched it. It made him mad but he wasn't sure why. He had heard of worse things, seen worse things. Yet there was something about a doctor doing it, getting away with it, that made Stranahan furious.

When they reached the island, Luis Córdova dropped them at a sagging dock that belonged to an old Bahamian conch fisherman named Cartwright. Cartwright had been told they were coming.

"I got the place ready," he told Mick Stranahan. "By the way, it's good to see you, my friend."

Stranahan gave him a hug. Cartwright was eighty years old. His hair was like cotton fuzz and his skin was the color of hot tar. He had Old Rhodes Key largely to himself and seldom entertained, but he had happily made an exception for his old friend. Years ago Stranahan had done Cartwright a considerable favor.

"White man tried to burn me out," he told Christina Marks. "Mick took care of things."

Stranahan hoisted the duffel bags over his shoulders and trudged toward the house. He said, "Some asshole developer wanted Cartwright's land but Cartwright didn't want to sell. Things got sticky."

The conch fisherman cut in: "I tell the story better. The man offered me one hunnert towsind dollars to move off the island and when I says no thanks, brother, he had some peoples pour gasoline all on my house. Luckily it rain like hell. Mick got this man arrested and dey put him in the big jail up Miami. That's the God's truth."

"Good for Mick," Christina said. Naturally she had assumed that Stranahan had killed the man.

"Asshole got six years and did fifteen months. He's out already." Stranahan laughed acidly.

"That I didn't know," Cartwright said thoughtfully.

"Don't worry, he won't ever come back to this place."

"You don't tink so?"

"No, Cartwright, I promise he won't. I had a long talk with the man. I believe he moved to California."

"Very fine," Cartwright said with obvious relief.

House was a charitable description for where the old fisherman lived: bare cinderblock walls on a concrete foundation; no doors in the doorways, no glass in the windows; a roof woven from dried palm fronds.

"Dry as a bone," Cartwright said to Christina. "I know it don't look like much, but you be dry inside here."

Gamely she said, "I'll be fine."

Stranahan winked at Cartwright. "City girl," he said.

Christina jabbed Stranahan in the ribs. "And you're Daniel Boone, I suppose. Well, fuck you both. I can handle myself."

Cartwright's eyes grew wide.

"Sorry," Christina said.

"Don't be," Cartwright said with a booming laugh. "I love it. I love the sound of a womanly voice out here."

For lunch he fixed fresh lobster in a conch salad. Afterwards he gathered some clothes in a plastic garbage bag, told Mick good-bye and headed slowly down to the dock.

Christina said, "Where's he going?"

"To the mainland," Stranahan replied. "He's got a grandson in Florida City he hasn't seen in a while."

From where they sat, they could see Cartwright's wooden skiff motoring westward across the bay; the old man had one hand on the stem of the throttle, the other shielding his eyes from the low winter sun.

Christina turned to Stranahan. "You arranged it this way."

"He's a nice guy. He doesn't deserve any trouble."

"You really think they'll find us all the way out here?"

"Yep," Stranahan said. He was counting on it.

21

The clerical staff of Kipper Garth's law office was abuzz: Clients—real live clients—were coming in for a meeting. Most of the secretaries had never seen any of Kipper Garth's clients because he generally did not allow them to visit. Normally all contact took place over the telephone, since Kipper Garth's practice was built exclusively on referrals to other lawyers. The rumor this day (and an incredible one, at that) was that Kipper Garth was going to handle a malpractice case all by himself; one of the senior paralegals had been vaguely instructed to prepare a complaint for civil court. The women who worked Kipper Garth's phone bank figured that it must be a spectacularly egregious case if their boss would tackle it solo, for his fear of going to court was well known. Kipper Garth's staff couldn't wait to get a look at the new clients.

They arrived at eleven sharp, a man and a woman. The clerks, secretaries, and paralegals were startled: It was an unremarkable couple in their mid-thirties. The man was medium-build and ordinary looking, the woman had long ash-blond hair and a nice figure. Neither displayed any obvious scars, mutilations, or crippling deformities. Kipper Garth's staff was baffled—the hushed wagering shifted back and forth between psychiatric aberration and sexual dysfunction.

Both guesses were wrong. The problem of John and Marie Nordstrom was far more peculiar.

Kipper Garth greeted them crisply at the door and led them

to two high-backed easy chairs positioned in front of his desk. The lawyer was extremely nervous and hoped it didn't show. He hoped he would ask the right questions.

"Mr. Nordstrom," he began, "I'd like to review some of the material in the state files."

Nordstrom looked around the elegant office and said: "Are we the only ones?"

"What do you mean?"

"Are we the only ones to sue? Over the phone you said a whole bunch of his patients were suing."

Kipper Garth tugged restlessly at the sleeves of his coat. "Well, we've been talking to several others with strong cases. I'm sure they'll come around. Meanwhile you and your wife expressed an interest—"

"But not alone," John Nordstrom said. "We don't want to be the only ones." His wife reached across and touched his arm. "Let's listen to him," she said. "It can't hurt."

Kipper Garth waited for the moment of tension to pass. It didn't. He motioned toward the walnut credenza behind his desk. "See all those files, Mr. Nordstrom? Patients of Dr. Rudy Graveline. Most of them have suffered more than you and your wife. Much more."

Nordstrom said, "So what's your point?"

"The point is, Mr. Nordstrom, a monster is loose. Graveline is still in business. On a good day his clinic takes in a hundred grand in surgical fees. One hundred grand! And every patient walks in there thinking that Dr. Graveline is one brilliant surgeon, and some of them find out the hard way that he's not. He's a putz."

Mrs. Nordstrom said: "You don't have to tell us."

Kipper Garth leaned forward and, ministerially, folded his hands. "For me, this case isn't about money." He sounded so damn earnest that he almost believed himself. "It isn't about money, it's about morality. And conscience. And concern for one's fellow man. I don't know about you folks, but my stomach churns when I think how a beast like Rudolph Graveline is allowed to continue to destroy the lives of innocent, trusting people." Kipper Garth swiveled his chair slowly and gestured again at the stacks of files. "Look at all these victims—men and women just like yourselves. And to think that the state of Florida has done nothing to stop this beast. It makes me nauseous."

"Me, too," said Mrs. Nordstrom.

"My mission," continued Kipper Garth, "is to find someone with the courage to go after this man. Shut him down. Bring to light his incompetence so that no one else will have to suffer. The place to do that is the courtroom."

John Nordstrom sniffed. "Don't tell me the sonofabitch's never been sued before."

Kipper Garth smiled. "Oh yes. Yes, indeed, Dr. Graveline has been sued before. But he's always escaped the glare of publicity and the scrutiny of his peers. How? By settling the cases out of court. He buys his way out, never goes to trial. This time he won't get off so lightly, Mr. Nordstrom. This time, with your permission, I want to take him to the wall. I want to go all the way. I'm talking about a trial."

It was a damn mellifluous speech for a man accustomed to bellowing at a speaker box. If not moved, the Nordstroms were at least impressed. A self-satisfied Kipper Garth wondered if he could ever be so smooth in front of a jury.

Marie Nordstrom said: "In person you look much younger than on your billboards."

The lawyer acknowledged the remark with a slight bow.

Mrs. Nordstrom nudged her husband. "Go ahead, tell him what happened."

"It's all in the file," John Nordstrom said.

"I'd like to hear it again," Kipper Garth said, "in your own words." He pressed a button on the telephone console, and a stenographer with a portable machine entered the office. She was followed by a somber-looking paralegal wielding a long yellow pad. Mutely they took positions on either side of Kipper Garth. Nordstrom scanned the trio warily.

His wife said: "It's a little embarrassing for us, that's all."

"I understand," Kipper Garth said. "We'll take our time."

Nordstrom shot a narrow look at his wife. "You start," he said.

Calmly she straightened in the chair and cleared her throat. "Two years ago, I went to Dr. Graveline for a routine breast augmentation. He came highly recommended."

"Your manicurist," John Nordstrom interjected, "a real expert."

Kipper Garth raised a tanned hand. "Please."

Marie Nordstrom continued: "I insisted that Dr. Graveline himself do the surgery. Looking back on it, I would've been better off with one of the other fellows at the clinic—anyway, the surgery was performed on a Thursday. Within a week it was obvious that something was very wrong."

Kipper Garth said, "How did you know?"

"Well, the new breasts were quite . . . hard."

"Try concrete," John Nordstrom said.

His wife went on: "They were extremely round and tight. Too tight. I mean, they didn't even bounce."

A true professional, Kipper Garth never let his eyes wander below Mrs. Nordstrom's neckline.

She said: "When I saw Dr. Graveline again, he assured me that this was normal for cases like mine. He had a name for it and everything."

"Capsular contracture," said the paralegal, without looking up from her notes.

"That's it," Mrs. Nordstrom said. "Dr. Graveline told me everything would be fine in a month or two. He said they'd be soft as little pillows."

"And?"

"And we waited, just like he told us. In the meantime, of course, John kept wanting to try them out."

"Hey," Nordstrom said, "I paid for the damn things."

"I understand," said Kipper Garth. "So you made love to your wife?"

Nordstrom's cheeks reddened. "You know the rest."

With his chin Kipper Garth pointed toward the stenographer and the paralegal, both absorbed in transcribing the incident.

Nordstrom sighed and said, "Yeah, I made love to my wife. Or tried to."

"That's when the accident happened between John and my breasts," continued Mrs. Nordstrom. "I'm not sure if it was the left one or the right one that got him."

Nordstrom muttered, "I'm not sure, either. It was a big hard boob, that's all I know."

Kipper Garth said, "And it actually put your eye out?"

John Nordstrom nodded darkly.

His wife said: "Technically they called it a detached retina. We didn't know it was so serious right away. John's eye got swollen and then there was some bleeding. When his vision didn't come back after a few days, we went to a specialist . . . but it was already too late."

Gently Kipper Garth said, "I noticed that you told the ophthalmic surgeon a slightly different story. You told him you were poked by a Christmas tree branch."

Nordstrom glared, with his good eye, at the lawyer. "What the hell would *you* have told him—that you were blinded by a tit?"

"It must have been difficult," Kipper Garth said, his voice rich with sympathy. "And this was your right eye, according to the file."

"Yeah," said Nordstrom, pointing.

"They gave him a glass one," his wife added. "You can hardly tell."

"*I* can sure as hell tell," Nordstrom said.

Kipper Garth asked: "Did it affect your work?"

"Are you kidding? I lost my job."

"Really?" The lawyer suppressed a grin of delight, but mentally tacked a couple more zeros to the pain-and-suffering demand.

Mrs. Nordstrom said: "John was an air-traffic controller. You can well imagine the problems."

"Yeah, and the jokes," Nordstrom said bitterly.

Kipper Garth leaned back and locked his hands across his vest. "Folks, how does ten million sound?"

Nordstrom snorted. "Come off it."

"We get the right jury, we can probably do twelve."

"Twelve million dollars—no shit?"

"No shit," said Kipper Garth. "Mrs. Nordstrom, I need to ask you something. Did this, uh, condition with your breasts ever improve?"

She glanced down at her chest. "Not much."

"Not much is right," said her husband. "Take my word, they're like goddamn bocci balls."

The guy would be poison as a witness, Kipper Garth decided; the jury would hate his guts. No wonder other lawyers had balked at taking the case. Kipper Garth thanked the Nordstroms for their time and showed them to the door. He promised to get back to them in a few days with some important papers to review.

After the couple had gone, Kipper Garth ordered the stenographer to transcribe the interview and make a half-dozen copies. Then he told the paralegal to type up a malpractice complaint against Dr. Rudy Graveline and the Whispering Palms Spa and Surgery Center.

"Can you handle that?" Kipper Garth asked.

"I think so," the paralegal said, coolly.

"And afterwards go down to the courthouse and do . . . whatever it is needs to be done."

"We'll go together," the paralegal said. "You might as well learn your way around."

Kipper Garth agreed pensively. If only his ski bunny knew what their dalliance had cost him. That his blackmailer was his own frigging brother-in-law compounded the humiliation. "One more question," Kipper Garth said to his paralegal. "After we file the lawsuit, then what?"

"We wait," she replied.

The lawyer giggled with relief. "That's all?"

"Sure, we wait and see what happens," the paralegal said. "It's just like dropping a bomb."

"I see," said Kipper Garth. Just what he needed in his life. A bomb.

* * *

Freddie was napping in his office at the Gay Bidet when one of the ticket girls stuck her head in the doorway and said there was a man wanted to see him. Right away Freddie didn't like the looks of the guy, and would have taken him for a cop except that cops don't dress so good. The other thing Freddie didn't like about the guy was the way he kept looking around the place with his nose twitching up in the air like a swamp rabbit, like there was something about the place that really stunk. Freddie didn't appreciate that.

"This isn't what I expected," the man said.

"The fuck you expect, Regine's?" Boldly Freddie took the offensive.

"This isn't a gay bar?" the man asked, "I assumed from the name . . ."

Freddie said, "I didn't name the place, pal. All I know is, it rhymes. That doesn't automatically make it no fruit bar. Now state your business or beat it."

"I need to see one of your bouncers."

"What for?"

The man said, "I'm his doctor."

"He sick?"

"I don't know until I see him," said Rudy Graveline.

Freddie was skeptical. Maybe the guy was a doctor, maybe not; these days everybody was wearing white silk suits.

"Which of my security personnel you want to see?" asked Freddie.

"He's quite a big man."

"They're all big, mister. I don't hire no munchkins."

"This one is extremely tall and thin. His face is heavily scarred, and he's missing his left hand."

"Don't know him," Freddie said, playing it safe. In case the guy was a clever bail bondsman or an undercover cop with a wardrobe budget.

Rudy said: "But he told me he works here."

Freddie shook his head and made sucking sounds through his front teeth. "I have a large staff, mister, and turnover to match.

Not everybody can take the noise.'' He jerked a brown thumb toward the fiberboard wall, which was vibrating from the music on the other side.

"Sounds like an excellent band," Rudy said lamely.

"Cathy and the Catheters," Freddie reported with a shrug. "Queen of slut rock, all the way from London." He pushed himself to his feet and stretched. "Sorry I can't help you, mister—"

At that instant the ticket girl flung open the door and told Freddie that a terrible fight had broken out and he better come quick. Rudy Graveline was huffing at Freddie's heels by the time a path had been cleared to the front of the stage. There a gang of anorexic Nazi skinheads had taken on a gang of flabby redneck bikers in a dispute over tattoos—specifically, whose was the baddest. The battle had been joined by a cadre of heavyset bouncers, each sporting a pink Gay Bidet T-shirt with the word SECURITY stenciled on the back. The vicious fighting seemed only to inspire more volume from the band and more random slam-dancing from the other punkers.

Towering above the melee was Chemo himself, his T-shirt ragged and bloody, and a look of baleful concentration on his face. Even through the blinding strobes, Rudy Graveline could see that the Weed Whacker attached to Chemo's stub was unsheathed and fully operative; the monofilament cutter was spinning so rapidly that it appeared transparent and harmless, like a hologram. In horror Rudy watched Chemo lower the buzzing device into the tangle of humanity—the ensuing screams rose plangently over the music. As if by prearrangement, the other bouncers backed off and let Chemo work, while Freddie supervised from atop an overturned amplifier.

The fighting subsided quickly. Splints and bandages were handed out to fallen bikers and skinheads alike, while the band took a break. An expression of fatherly admiration in his shoe-button eyes. Freddie patted Chemo on the shoulder, then disappeared backstage. Rudy Graveline worked his way through the sweaty crowd, stepping over the wounded and semiconscious until he reached Chemo's side.

"Well, that was amazing," Rudy said.

Chemo glanced down at him and scowled. "Fucking battery died. I hope that's it for the night."

The surgeon said, "We really need to talk."

"Yes," Chemo agreed. "We sure do."

As soon as Chemo and Rudy went backstage, they ran into Freddie, Cathy, and two of the Catheters sharing some hash in a glass pipe. Through a puff of blue smoke Freddie said to Chemo: "This jerkoff claimed he's your doctor."

"Was," Chemo said. "Can we use the dressing room?"

"Anything you want," Freddie said.

"Watch out for my python," Cathy cautioned.

The dressing room was not what Rudy had expected. There was a folding card table, an old-fashioned coat rack, a blue velour sofa, a jagged triangle of broken mirror on the wall and, in one corner, an Igloo cooler full of Heinekens. On the naked floor was a low flat cage made from plywood and chicken wire in which resided a nine-foot Burmese python, the signature of Cathy's big encore.

Rudy Graveline took a chair at the card table while Chemo stretched out on the whorehouse sofa.

Rudy said: "I was worried when you didn't call from New York. What happened?"

Chemo ran a whitish tongue across his lip. "Aren't you even going to ask about my face, how it's healing?"

The doctor seemed impatient. "It looks fine from here. It looks like the dermabrasion is taking nicely."

"As if you'd know."

Rudy's mouth twitched. "Now what is that supposed to mean?"

"It means you're a fucking menace to society. I'm getting myself another doctor—Maggie's picking one out for me."

Rudy Graveline felt the back of his neck go damp. It wasn't as if he had not expected problems with Chemo—that was the reason for choosing Roberto Pepsical and his crooked cops as a contingency. But it was merely failure, not betrayal, that Rudy had anticipated from his homicidal stork.

"Maggie?" the doctor said. "Maggie Gonzalez?"

"Yeah, that's the one. We had a long talk, she told me some things."

"Talking to her wasn't the plan," Rudy said.

"Yeah, well, the plan has been changed." Chemo reached into the Igloo cooler and got a beer. He twisted off the cap, tilted the bottle to his lips, and glowered at the doctor the whole time he gulped it down. Then he belched once and said: "You tried to gyp me."

Rudy said, "That's simply not true."

"You didn't tell me the stakes. You didn't tell me about the Barletta girl."

The color washed from Rudy's face. Stonily he stared into his own lap. Suddenly his silk Armani seemed as hot and heavy as an army blanket.

Chemo rolled the empty Heineken bottle across the bare terrazzo floor until it clanked to rest against the snake cage. The sleek green python flicked its tongue once, then went back to sleep.

Chemo said, "And all this time, I thought you knew what the fuck you were doing. I trusted you with my own face." He laughed harshly and burped again. "Jesus H. Christ, I bet your own family won't let you carve the bird on Thanksgiving, am I right?"

In a thin abraded voice, Rudy Graveline said: "So Maggie is still alive."

"Yeah, and she's going to stay that way as long as I say so." Chemo swung his spidery legs off the sofa and sat up, straight as a lodgepole. "Because if anything should happen to her, you are going to be instantly famous. I'm talking TV, Dr. Frankenstein."

By now Rudy was having difficulty catching his breath.

Chemo went on. "Your nurse is a smart girl. She made three videotapes for insurance. Two of them are locked up safe and sound in New York. The other . . . well, you'd better pray that I find it before it finds you."

"Go do it." Rudy's voice was toneless and weak.

"Naturally this will be very expensive."

"Whatever you need," the doctor croaked. This was a scenario he had never foreseen, something beyond his worst screaming nightmares.

"I didn't realize plastic surgeons made so much dough," Chemo remarked. "Maggie was telling me."

"The overhead," Rudy said, fumbling, "is sky-high."

"Well, yours just got higher by seven feet." Chemo produced a small aerosol can of WD-40 and began lubricating the rotor mechanism of the Weed Whacker. Without glancing up from his chore, he said, "By the way, Frankenstein, you're getting off easy. Last time a doctor screwed me over, I broke his frigging neck."

In his mental catacomb Rudy clearly heard the snap of the old dermatologist's spine, watched as the electrolysis needle fell from the old man's lifeless hand and clattered on the office floor.

As soon as he regained his composure, Rudy asked, "Who's got the missing tape?"

"Oh, take a wild guess." There was amusement in Chemo's dry tone.

"Shit," said Rudy Graveline.

"My sentiments exactly."

22

Reynaldo Flemm hadn't even finished explaining the plan before Willie, the cameraman, interrupted. "What about Christina?" he asked. "What does she say?"

"Christina is tied up on another project."

Willie eyed him skeptically. "What project?"

"That's not important."

Willie didn't give up; he was accustomed to Reynaldo treating him like hired help. "She in New York?"

Reynaldo said, "She could be in New Delhi for all I care. Point is, I'm producing the Barletta segment. Get used to it, buddy."

Willie settled back to sip his planter's punch and enjoy the rosy tropical dusk. They had a deck table facing the ocean at an outdoor bar, not far from the Sonesta on Key Biscayne. Reynaldo Flemm was nursing a Perrier, so Willie was confident of having the upper hand. Reynaldo was the only person he knew who blabbed more when he was sober than when he was drunk. Right now Reynaldo was blabbing about his secret plan to force Dr. Rudy Graveline to confess in front of the television camera. It was the most ludicrous scheme that Willie had ever heard, the sort of thing he'd love to watch, not shoot.

After a decent interval, Willie put his rum drink on the table and said: "Who's blocking out the interview?"

"Me."

"The questions, too?"

Reynaldo Flemm reddened.

Willie said, "Shouldn't we run this puppy by the lawyers? I think we got serious trespass problems."

"Ha," Reynaldo scoffed.

Sure, Willie thought sourly, go ahead and laugh. I'm the one who always gets tossed in the squad car. I'm the one gets blamed when the cops bang up the camera.

Reynaldo Flemm said, "Let me worry about the legalities, Willie. The question is: Can you do it?"

"Sure, I can do it."

"You won't need extra lights?"

Willie shook his head. "Plenty of light," he said. "Getting the sound is where I see the problem."

"I was wondering about that, too. I can't very well wear the wireless."

Willie chuckled in agreement. "No, not hardly."

Reynaldo said, "You'll think of something, you always do. Actually, I prefer the hand-held."

"I know," Willie said. Reynaldo disliked the tiny cordless clip-on microphones; he favored the old baton-style mikes that you held in your hand—the kind you could thrust in some crooked politician's face and make him pee his pants. Christina Marks called it Reynaldo's "phallic attachment." She postulated that, in Reynaldo's mind, the microphone had become a substitute for his penis.

As Willie recalled, Reynaldo didn't think much of Christina's theory.

He said to Willie: "This'll be hairy, but we've done it before. We're a good team."

"Yeah," said Willie, half-heartedly draining his glass. Some team. The basic plan never changed: Get Reynaldo beat up. *Now remember*, he used to tell Willie, *we got to live up to the name of the show. Stick it right in his motherloving face, really piss him off.* Willie had it down to an art: He'd poke the TV camera directly at the subject's nose, the guy would push the camera away and tear off in a fury after Reynaldo Flemm. *Now remember*, Reynaldo would coach, *when he shoves you, jiggle the camera like you were really shaken up. Make the picture super jerky looking, the way they do on* Sixty Minutes. If by chance the interview subject lunged after Willie instead of Reynaldo, Willie had standing orders to halt taping, shield the camera and defend himself—in that order. Invariably the person doing the pummeling got tired of banging his fists on a bulky, galvanized Sony and redirected his antagonism toward the arrogant puss of Reynaldo Flemm. *It's me they're tuning in to see*, Reynaldo would say, *I'm the talent here.* But if the beating became too severe or if Reynaldo got outnumbered, Willie's job then was to stow the camera (carefully) and start swinging away. Many times he had felt like a rodeo clown, diverting Reynaldo's enraged attackers until Reynaldo could escape, usually by locking himself in the camera van. The van was where, at Reynaldo's insistence, Christina Marks waited during ambush interviews. Reynaldo maintained that this was for her own safety, but in reality he worried that if something happened to her, it might end up on tape and steal his thunder.

Reflecting upon all this, Willie ordered another planter's punch. This time he asked the waitress for more dark rum on the top. He said to Reynaldo, "What makes you think this doctor guy'll break?"

"I've met him. He's weak."

"That's what you said about Larkey McBuffum."

Larkey McBuffum was a crooked Chicago pharmacist who had been selling steroid pills to junior high school football players. When Reynaldo and Willie had burst into Larkey's drug store to confront him, the old man had maced Willie square in the eyes with an aerosol can of spermicidal birth-control foam.

"I'm telling you, the surgeon's a wimp," Reynaldo was saying. "Put a mike in his face and he'll crack like a fucking Triscuit."

"I'll stay close on him," Willie said.

"Not too close," Reynaldo Flemm cautioned. "You gotta be ready to pull back and get us both in the shot, right before it happens."

Willie stirred the dark rum with his finger. "You mean, when he slugs you?"

"Of course," Reynaldo said curtly. "Christ, you ought to know the drill by now. *Of course* when he slugs me."

"Will that be," Willie asked playfully, "before or after the big confession?"

Reynaldo gnawed on this one a few seconds before giving up. "Just get it, that's all," he said stiffly. "Whenever it happens, get every bloody second on tape. Understand?"

Willie nodded. Sometimes he wished he were still freelancing for the networks. A coup in Haiti was a picnic compared to this.

The Pennsylvania State Police were happy to wire a photograph of Blondell Wayne Tatum to Sergeant Al García at the Metro-Dade Police Department. García was disappointed, for the photograph was practically useless. It had been taken more than twenty years earlier by a feature photographer for a small rural newspaper. At the time, the paper was running a five-part series on how the Amish sect was coping with the social pressures of the twentieth century. Blondell Wayne Tatum was one of several teenaged Amish youths who were photographed while playing catch with a small pumpkin. Of the group, Blondell Wayne Tatum was the only one wearing a brand-new Rawlings outfielder's mitt.

For purposes of criminal identification, the facsimile of the newspaper picture was insufficient. García knew that the man named Chemo no longer wore a scraggly pubescent beard, and that he since had suffered devastating facial trauma as a result of a freak dermatology accident. Armed with these revisions, García enlisted the help of a police artist named Paula Downs. He tacked the newspaper picture on Paula's easel and said: "Third one from the left."

Paula slipped on her eyeglasses, but that wasn't enough. She took a photographer's loupe and peered closely at the picture. "Stringbean," she said. "Sixteen, maybe seventeen years old."

García said: "Make him thirty-eight now. Six foot nine, one hundred eighty pounds."

"No sweat," Paula said.

"And lose the beard."

"Let's hope so. Yuk."

With an unwrapped cigar, García tapped on the photograph. "Here's the hard part, babe. A few years ago this turkey had a bad accident, got his face all fried up."

"Burns?"

"Yup."

"What kind—gas or chemical?"

"Electrolysis."

Paula peered at the detective over the rim of her spectacles and said, "That's very humorous, Al."

"I swear. Got it straight from the Pennsylvania cops."

"Hmmmm." Paula chewed on the eraser of her pencil as she contemplated the photograph.

Al García described Chemo's face to Paula the way that Mick

Stranahan had described it to him. As García spoke, the artist began to draw a freehand composite. She held the pencil at a mild angle and swept it in light clean ovals across the onionskin paper. First came the high forehead, the sharp chin, then the cheekbones and the puffy blowfish eyes and the thin cruel lips. Before long, the gangly young Amish kid with the baseball mitt became a serious-looking felon.

Paula got up and said, "Be right back." Moments later she returned with a salt shaker from the cafeteria. She lifted the onionskin and copiously sprinkled salt on the drawing pad. With the heel of her left hand she spread the grains evenly. After replacing the onionskin that bore Chemo's likeness, Paula selected a stubby fat pencil with a soft gray lead. She held it flat to the paper, as if it were a hunk of charcoal, and began a gentle tracing motion across the drawing. Instantly the underlying salt crystals came into relief. García smiled: The effect was perfect. It gave Chemo's portrait a harsh granular complexion, just as Mick Stranahan had described.

"You're a genius," García told Paula Downs.

She handed him the finished composite. "You get some winners, Al."

He went to the Xerox room and made a half-dozen copies of the sketch. He stuck one in John Murdock's mailbox. On the back of Murdock's copy García had printed the name Blondell Wayne Tatum, the AKA, and the date of birth. Then García had written: "This is your guy for the Simpkins case!!!!"

Murdock, he knew, would not appreciate the help.

García spent the rest of the afternoon on Key Biscayne, showing Chemo's composite to dock boys, bartenders, and cocktail waitresses at Sunday's-on-the-Bay. By four o'clock the detective had three positive I.D.'s saying that the man in the drawing was the same one who had been drinking with Chloe Simpkins Stranahan on the evening she died.

Now Al García was a happy man. When he got back to police headquarters, he called a florist and ordered a dozen long-stemmed roses for Paula Downs. While he was on the phone, he noticed a small UPS parcel on his desk. García tore it open with his free hand.

Inside was a videotape in a plastic sleeve. On the sleeve was a scrap of paper, attached with Scotch tape. A note.

"I told you so. Regards, Mick."

García took the videotape to the police audio room, where a couple of the vice guys were screening the very latest in bestiality *vérité*. García told them to beat it and plugged Stranahan's tape into a VHS recorder. He watched it twice. The second time, he stubbed out his cigar and took notes.

Then he went searching for Murdock and Salazar.

In the detective room, nobody seemed to know where they were. García didn't like the looks of things.

The copy of Paula's sketch of Blondell Wayne Tatum lay crumpled next to an empty Doritos bag on John Murdock's desk. "Asshole," García hissed. He didn't care who heard him. He pawed through the rest of Murdock's debris until he found a pink message slip. The message was from the secretary of Circuit Judge Cassie B. Ireland.

García groaned. Cassie Ireland had been a devoted golfing partner of the late and terminally crooked Judge Raleigh Goomer. Cassie himself was known to have serious problems with drinking and long weekends in Law Vegas. The problems were in the area of chronic inability to afford either vice.

The message to Detective John Murdock from Judge Cassie Ireland's secretary said: "Warrant's ready."

Al García used Murdock's desk phone to call the judge's chambers. He told the secretary who he was. Not surprisingly, the judge was gone for the day. Gone straight to the tiki bar at the Airport Hilton, García thought.

To the judge's secretary he said, "There's been a little mixup down here. Did Detective Murdock ask Judge Ireland to sign a warrant?"

"Sure did," chirped the secretary. "I've still got the paper-work right here. John and his partner came by and picked it up yesterday morning."

Al García figured he might as well ask, just to make sure. "Can you tell me the name on the warrant?"

"Mick Stranahan," the secretary replied. "First-degree murder."

Christina Marks found the darkness exciting. As she floated naked on her back, the warm water touched her everyplace. Sometimes she stood up and curled her toes in the cool, rough sand, to see how deep it was. A few yards away, Mick Stranahan broke the surface with a swoosh, a glistening blond sea creature. He sounded like a porpoise when he blew the air from his lungs.

"This is nice," Christina called to him.

"No hot showers on the key," he said. "No shower, period. Cartwright is a no-frills guy."

"I said it's nice. I mean it."

Stranahan swam closer and rose to his feet. The water came up to his navel. In the light from a quarter moon Christina could make out the fresh bullet scar on his shoulder; it looked like a smear of pink grease. She found herself staring—he was different out here on the water. Not the same man whom she had seen in the hospital or at her apartment. On the island he seemed larger and more feral, yet also more serene.

"It's so peaceful," Christina said. They were swimming on a marly bonefish flat, forty yards from Cartwright's dock.

"I'm glad you can relax," Stranahan said. "Most women would be jittery, having been shot at twice by a total stranger."

Christina laughed easily, closed her eyes and let the wavelets tickle her neck. Mick was right; she ought to be a nervous wreck by now. But she wasn't.

"Maybe I'm losing my mind," she said to the stars. She heard a soft splash as he went under again. Seconds later something cool brushed against her ankle, and she smiled. "All right, mister, no funny business."

From a surprising distance came his voice: "Sorry to disappoint you, but that wasn't me."

"Oh, no." Christina rolled over and kicked hard for the deep channel, but she didn't get far. Like a torpedo he came up beneath her and slid one arm under her hips, the other around her chest. As he lifted her briskly out of the water, she let out a small cry.

"Easy," Stranahan said, laughing. "It was only a baby bonnet shark—I saw it."

He was standing waist-deep on the flat, holding her like an armful of firewood. "Relax," he said. "They don't eat bigshot TV producers."

Christina turned in his arms and held him around the neck. "Is it gone?" she asked.

"It's gone. Want me to put you down?"

"Not really, no."

In the moonlight he could see enough of her eyes to know what she was thinking. He kissed her on the mouth.

She thought: This is crazy. I love it.

Stranahan kissed her again, longer than the first time.

"A little salty," she said, "but otherwise very nice."

Christina let her hands wander. "Say there, what happened to your jeans?"

"I guess they came off in the undertow."

"What undertow?" She started kissing him up and down the neck; giggling, nipping, using the tip of her tongue. She could feel the goose flesh rise on his shoulders.

"There really *was* a shark," he said.

"I believe you. Now take me back to the island. Immediately."

Stranahan said, "Not right this minute."

"You mean we're going to do it out here?"

"Why not?"

"Standing up?"

"Why not?"

"Because of the sharks. You said so yourself."

Stranahan said. "You'll be safe, just put your legs around me."

"Nice try."

He kissed her again. This was a good one. Christina wrapped her legs around his naked hips.

Stranahan stopped kissing long enough to catch his breath and say, "I almost forgot. Can you name the Beatles?"

"Not right this minute."

"Yes, now. Please."

"You're a damn lunatic."

"I know," he said.

Christina pressed so close and so hard that water sluiced up between her breasts and splashed him on the chin. "That's what you get," she said. Then, nose to nose: "John, Paul, George, and Ringo."

"You're terrific."

"And don't forget Pete Best."

"I think I love you," Stranahan said.

Later he caught a small grouper from the dock, and fried it for dinner over an open fire. They ate on the ocean side of the island, under a stand of young palms. Stranahan used a pair of old lobster traps for tables. The temperature had dropped into the low seventies with a sturdy breeze. Christina wore a tartan flannel shirt, baggy workout trousers, and running shoes. Stranahan wore jeans, sneakers, and a University of Miami sweatshirt. Tucked in the waist of his jeans was a Smith .38 he had borrowed from Luis Córdova. Stranahan was reasonably certain that he would not have to fire it.

Christina was on her second cup of coffee when she said, "I've been a pretty good sport about all this, don't you agree?"

"Sure." He had his eyes on the faraway lights of a tramp freighter plowing south in the Gulf Stream.

Christina said, "I know I've asked before, but I'm going to try again: What the hell are we doing out here?"

"I thought you liked this place."

"I love it, Mick, but I still don't understand."

"We can't go back to the stilt house. Not yet, anyway."

"But why come here?" She was nearly out of patience with the mystery.

"Because I needed a place where something could happen, and no one would see it. Or hear it."

"Mick—"

"There's no other way." He stood up and poured out the cold dregs of his coffee, which splattered against the bare serrated coral. He noticed that the tide was slipping out. "There's no other way to deal with people like this," he said.

Christina turned to him. "You don't understand. I can't do this, I can't be a part of this."

"You wanted to come along."

"To observe. To report. To get the story."

Stranahan's laugh carried all the way to Hawk Channel. "Story?"

She knew how silly it sounded, and was. Willie had the television cameras, and Reynaldo Flemm had Willie. Reynaldo . . . another macho head case. He had sounded so odd when she had phoned from the mainland; his voice terse and icy, his laugh thin and ironic. He was cooking up something, although he denied it to Christina. Even when she told him about the wild incident at the Plaza, about how she had almost been shot *again*, Reynaldo's reaction was strangely muted and unreadable. When she had called again two hours later from a pay booth at the marina, the secretary in New York told Christina that Reynaldo had already left for the airport. The secretary went on to report, in a snitchy tone, that Reynaldo had withdrawn fifteen thousand dollars from the emergency weekend travel account—the account normally reserved for commercial airline disasters, killer earthquakes, political assassinations, and other breaking news events. Christina Marks could not imagine what Reynaldo intended to do with fifteen grand, but she assumed it would be a memorable folly.

And there she was in Florida: no camera, no crew, no star. So she had boarded the marine patrol boat with Mick Stranahan and Luis Córdova.

Standing in the moonglow, watching the tide lick the coral under her feet, Christina said again: "I can't be a part of this."

Stranahan put an arm around her. It reminded Christina of the hugs her father sometimes gave her when she was a child and something sad had made her cry. A gesture that said he was sorry, but nothing could be done; sometimes the world was not such a good place.

"Mick, let's just go to the police."

"These *are* the police. Remember?"

She looked at his face, searching the shadows for his expression. "So that's who you're waiting for."

"Sure. Who'd you think?"

Christina pretended to slap herself on the forehead. "Oh, silly me—I thought it might be that huge skinny freak who keeps trying to shoot us."

Stranahan shook his head. "Him, we don't wait for."

"Mick, this still isn't right."

But the hug was finished, and so was the discussion. "There's a lantern back at the house," he told her. "I want you to take a walk around the island. A long walk, okay?"

23

Joe Salazar said, "You got to steer yesterday."

"For Christ's sake," mumbled Murdock.

"Come on, Johnny, it's my turn."

They were gassing up the boat at Crandon Marina on Key Biscayne. It was the sheriff's department's boat, a nineteen-foot Aquasport with a forest-green police stripe down the front. It was the same boat that the two detectives had borrowed the day before. The sergeant in charge of the marine division had not wanted to loan the boat to Murdock or Salazar because it was obvious that neither knew how to navigate. The sergeant wondered if they even knew how to swim. Both men were wearing new khaki deck shorts that revealed pale legs, chubby legs that had seldom been touched by salt or sunlight: landlubber's legs. The sergeant had surrendered the Aquasport only when John Murdock flashed the murder warrant and said the suspect had been spotted on a house way out in Stiltsville. The sergeant had asked why they weren't taking any backups along, since there was room on the boat, but Murdock hadn't seemed to hear the question.

When the two detectives had returned to the dock a few hours later, the sergeant had been pleasantly surprised to find no major structural damage to the Aquasport or its drive shaft. But when Murdock and Salazar in their stupid khakis showed up again the following afternoon, the sergeant wondered how long their luck would hold out on the water.

"Go ahead and drive," Murdock grumped at the gas dock. "I don't give a shit."

Joe Salazar took a stance behind the steering console. He tried not to gloat. Then it occurred to him: "Where do we look now?"

The day before, Stranahan's stilt house had been empty. They had torn the rooms apart for clues to his whereabouts, found none, and departed in frustration. The whole way back, Murdock had complained about how the shoulder holster was chafing through his mesh tank top. Twice they had run the boat aground on bonefish flats, and both times Murdock had forced Salazar to hop out in the mud and push. For this, if for nothing else, Salazar figured that he deserved to be the captain today.

Murdock said: "I tell you where we look. We look in every goddamn stilt house on the bay."

"Yeah, like a regular canvass."

"Door to door, except by boat. You know the fuckwad's out there somewhere."

Joe Salazar felt better now that they had a plan. He paid the dock attendant for the gasoline, cranked up the big Evinrude on the back of the Aquasport, and aimed the bow toward Bear Cut. Or tried. The boat didn't want to move.

The dock attendant snickered. "Helps to untie it," he said, pointing with one of his bright white sneakers.

Sheepishly Joe Salazar unhitched the lines off the bow and stern and shoved off. John Murdock said, "What a wiseass that guy was. Didn't he see we had guns?"

"Sure he did," Salazar replied, steering tentatively toward the channel.

"This town is gone to shit," Murdock said, spitting over the gunwale, "when a guy with a gun has to put up with that kind of bull."

"Everybody's a wiseass," Joe Salazar agreed. Nervously he was watching a gray outboard coming in the other direction along the opposite side of the channel. The boat had a blue police light mounted in the center. A young Latin man in a gray uniform stood behind the windshield. He waved to them: the world-weary wave of one cop to another.

"What do I do?" Salazar asked.

"Try waving back," said Murdock.

Salazar did. The man in the gray boat changed his course and idled toward them.

"Grouper trooper," John Murdock whispered. Salazar nodded as if he knew what his partner was talking about. He didn't. He also didn't know how to stop the Aquasport. Every time he pulled down on the throttle, the engine jolted into reverse. When he pushed the lever the other way, the boat would shudder and shoot forward. Backward, forward, backward again. The big Evinrude sounded like it was about to blow up. Joe Salazar could tell that Murdock was seething.

"Try neutral," the young marine patrolman called. "Move the throttle sideways till it clicks."

Salazar did as he was told, and it worked.

"Thanks!" he called back.

Under his breath, Murdock said: "Yeah, thanks for making us look like a couple of jerkoffs."

The marine patrol boat coasted up on the port side of the Aquasport. The young officer introduced himself as Luis Córdova. He asked where the two detectives were headed, and if he could help. Joe Salazar told him they were going to Stiltsville to serve a murder warrant.

"Only one guy lives out there that I know of," Luis Córdova said.

Murdock said: "That's the guy we want."

"Mick Stranahan?"

"You know him?"

"I know where he lives," said Luis Córdova, "but he's not there now. I saw him only yesterday."

"Where?" blurted Joe Salazar. "Was he alone?"

"Yeah, he was alone. Sitting on the conch dock down at Old Rhodes Key."

Murdock said, "Where the hell's that?"

"South of Elliott."

"Where the hell's Elliott?"

The marine patrolman said, "Why don't you guys just wait a few hours and follow me down? The tide won't be right until dusk. Besides, you might need some extra muscle with this guy."

"No. Thanks anyway." John Murdock's tone left no chance for discussion. "But we could use a map, if you got one."

Luis Córdova disappeared briefly behind the steering console. When he stood up again, he was smiling. "Just happened to have an extra," he said.

A half hour out of the marina, Joe Salazar said to his partner: "Maybe we should've asked what he meant about the tides."

The Aquasport was stuck hard on another mud flat, this one a mile south of Soldier Key. John Murdock cracked open his third can of beer and said: "You're the one wanted to drive."

Salazar leaned over the side of the boat and studied the situation. He decided there was no point in getting out to push. "It's only six inches deep," he said, a childlike marvel in his voice. "On the map it sure looked like plenty of water, didn't it?"

Murdock said, "If you're a starfish, it's plenty of water. If you're a boat, it's a goddamn beach. Another thing: I told you to get three bags of ice. Look how fast this shit is melting." He kicked angrily at the cooler.

Joe Salazar continued to stare at the shallow gin-clear water. "I think the tide's coming in," he said hopefully.

"Swell," said Murdock. "That means it's only what?—another four, five hours in the mud. Fanfuckingtastic. By then it'll be good and dark, too."

Salazar pointed out that the police boat was equipped with excellent lights. "Once we get off the flat, it's a clean shot down to the island. Deep water the whole trip."

He had never seen his partner so jumpy and short-tempered. Normally John Murdock was the picture of a cool tough cop, but Salazar had watched a change come over him beginning the night they took the down payment from Commissioner Roberto Pepsical. Five thousand cash, each. Five more when it was done. To persuade the detectives that he was not the booze-swilling lech that he had appeared to be at the nudie joint, the commissioner had arranged the payoff meeting to take place in one of the empty confessionals at St. Mary's Catholic Church in Little Havana. The confessional was dimly lit and no bigger than a broom closet; the three conspirators had to stand sidewise to fit. It had been a dozen years since Joe Salazar had stepped inside a confessional and not much had changed. The place reeked of damp linen and guilt, just as he remembered. He and Murdock stuffed the cash in their jackets and bolted out the door together, nearly trampling a quartet of slow-footed nuns. Commissioner Roberto Pepsical stayed alone in the confessional and recited three Hail Marys. He figured it couldn't hurt.

Back in the car, John Murdock had not displayed the crude and cocky ebullience that usually followed the taking of a hefty bribe; rather, his mood had been taciturn and apprehensive. It had stayed that way for two days.

Now, with the boat stuck fast on the bonefish flat, Murdock sulked alone in the stern, glaring at the slow crawl of the incoming tide. Joe Salazar lit a Camel and settled in for a long, tense afternoon. He didn't feel so well himself, but at least he knew why. This was the biggest job they'd ever done, and the dirtiest. By a mile.

* * *

In fact, the tides would not have mattered if either of the two detectives had known how to read a marine chart. Even at dead low, there was plenty of water from Cape Florida all the way to Old Rhodes Key. All you had to do was follow the channels, which were plainly marked on Luis Córdova's map.

Mick Stranahan knew that Murdock and Salazar would run the boat aground. He also knew that it would be nighttime before they could float free, and that they would make the rest of the trip at a snail's pace, fearful of repeating the mishap.

He and Luis Córdova had talked this part out. Together they had calculated that the two detectives would reach the island between nine and midnight, provided they didn't hit the shoal off Boca Chita and shear the prop off the Evinrude. Luis had offered to tail the Aquasport at a discreet distance, but Stranahan told him no. He didn't want the marine patrolman anywhere near Old Rhodes Key when it happened. If Luis was there, he'd want to do it by the book. Wait for the assholes to make their move, then try to arrest them. Stranahan knew it would never work that way—they'd try to kill Luis, too. And even if Luis was as sharp as Stranahan thought, it would be a mess for him afterwards. An automatic suspension, a grand jury, his name all over the newspapers. No way, Stranahan told him, no hero stuff. Just give them the map and get lost.

Besides, Stranahan already had his hands full with Christina Marks on the island.

"I don't want to go for a walk," she said. "Grandmothers and widows go for walks. I'm staying here with you."

"So you can take notes, or what?" He handed her a Coleman lantern. The jumpy white light made their shadows clash on the cinderblock walls. Stranahan said, "You're not a reporter anymore, you're a goddamn witness."

She said, "Is this your idea of pillow talk? Half an hour ago we were making love, and now I'm a 'goddamn witness.' You ever thought of writing poetry, Mick?"

He was down on one knee, pulling items from one of the duffel bags. Without looking up, he said, "You said you couldn't be a part of this, I'm trying to accommodate you. As for the afterglow, you want to waltz in the moonlight, we'll do that later. Right now there's a pair of bad cops on their way out here to shoot me.''

"You don't know that.''

"Yeah, you're right,'' Stranahan said. "They're probably just collecting Toys for Tots. Now go.''

He stood up. In the lantern light, Christina saw that his arms were full: binoculars, a poplin windbreaker, a pair of corduroys, an Orioles cap, a fishing knife, and a round spool of some kind.

She said, "It's not for the damn TV show that I want to stay. I'm scared for you. I don't know why—since you're being such a prick—but I'm worried about you, I admit it.''

When Stranahan spoke again, the acid was gone from his voice. "Look, if you stay . . . if you were to see something, they'd make you testify. Forget reporter's privilege and First Amendment—doesn't count for a damn thing in a situation like this. If you witness a crime, Chris, they put you under oath. You don't want that.''

"Neither do you.''

He smiled drily. She had him on that one. It was true: He didn't want any witnesses. "You've had enough excitement,'' he told her. "Twice I've nearly gotten you killed. If I were you, I'd take that as a hint.''

Christina said, "What if you're wrong about them, Mick? What if they only want to ask more questions? Even if they're coming to arrest you, you can't just—''

"Go,'' he said. Later he would explain that these cops were buddies of the late Judge Raleigh Goomer, and that what they wanted from Mick Stranahan was payback. Asking questions was not at all what they had in mind. "Take the path I showed you. Follow the shoreline about halfway down the island and you'll come to a clearing. You'll see some plastic milk crates, an empty oil drum, an old campfire hole. Wait there for me.''

Christina gave him a frozen look, but he didn't feel it. His mind was in overdrive, long gone.

"There's some fruit and candy bars in the Tupperware,'' he said. "But don't feed the raccoons, they bite like hell.''

She was twenty yards down the path when she heard him call, "Hey, Chris, you forgot the bug spray."

She shook her head and kept walking.

Fifteen minutes later, when Stranahan was sure she was gone, he carried his things down to Cartwright's dock. There he lit another lantern and hung it on a nail in one of the pilings. Then he pulled off his sneakers, kicked out of his jeans, and slid naked into the cool flowing tides.

For Joe Salazar, it was a moment of quiet triumph at the helm. "By God, we did it."

John Murdock made a snide chuckle. "Yeah, we found it," he said. "The Atlantic fucking Ocean. A regular needle in a haystack, Joe. And all it took was three hours of dry humping these islands."

Salazar didn't let the sarcasm dampen his newfound confidence. The passage through Sand Cut had been hairy; even at a slow speed, navigating the swift serpentine channel at night was an accomplishment worth savoring. Murdock knew it, too; not once had he tried to take the wheel.

"So this is the famous Elliott Key." Murdock scratched his sunburned cheeks. The Aquasport idled half a mile offshore, rocking in a brisk chop. The beer was long gone, the ice melted. In the cool breeze Murdock had slipped into a tan leather jacket, the one he always wore to work; it looked ridiculous over his khaki shorts. Dismally he slapped at his pink shins, where a horsefly was eating supper.

Joe Salazar held the chart on his lap, a flashlight in his right hand. With the other hand he pointed: "Like I said, Johnny, from here it's a straight nine-mile run to Rhodes. Twelve feet of water the whole way."

Murdock said, "So let's go, Señor Columbus. Maybe we can make it before Christmas." He readjusted his shoulder holster for the umpteenth time.

Salazar hesitated. "Once we get there, what exactly is the plan?"

"Get that goddamn flashlight out of my face." Murdock's

eyelids were swollen and purple. Too much sun, too much beer. It worried Salazar; he wanted his partner to be sharp.

"The plan is simple," Murdock said. "We arrive with bells on—sirens, lights, the works. We yell for Stranahan to come out with his hands up. Go ahead with the whole bit—serve the warrant, do the Miranda, all that shit. Then we shoot him like he was trying to get away."

"Do we cuff him first?"

"Now, how would that look? No, we don't cuff him first. Jesus Christ." Murdock spit into the water. He'd been spitting all afternoon. Salazar hoped this wasn't a new habit.

Murdock said, "See, Joe, we shoot him in the back. That way it looks like he's running away. Then we get on this boat radio, if one of us can figure out how to use the goddamn thing, and call for air rescue."

"Which'll take forever to get here."

"Exactly. But then we're covered, procedure-wise."

It sounded like a solid plan, with only one serious variable. Joe Salazar decided to put the variable out of his mind. He stowed the flashlight, reclaimed his post at the wheel of the police boat and steered a true course for Old Rhodes Key.

A straight line through open seas. No sweat.

The channel that leads from the ocean to the cut of Old Rhodes Key is called Caesar Creek. It is deep and fairly broad, and well charted with lighted markers. For this Joe Salazar was profoundly thankful. Having mastered the balky throttle, he guided the Aquasport in at half-speed, with John Murdock standing (or trying to) in the bow. Murdock cupped his hands around his eyes to block the peripheral light; he was peering at the island, searching for signs of Mick Stranahan. Two hundred yards from the mouth of the cut, Salazar killed the engine and joined his chubby partner on the front of the boat.

"There he is!" Murdock's breathing was raspy, excited.

Salazar squinted into the night. "Yeah, Johnny, sitting under that light on the dock."

They could see the lantern and, in its white penumbra, the

figure of a man with his legs hanging over the planks. The figure wore a baseball cap, a tan jacket, and long pants. From the angle of the cap, the man's head appeared to be down, chin resting on his chest.

"Dumb fuckwad's asleep." Murdock's laugh was high and brittle. He already had his pistol out.

"Then I guess we better do it," Salazar said.

"By all means." Murdock dropped to a crouch.

They had tested the blue lights and siren on the way down, so Salazar knew where the switches were. He flipped them simultaneously, then turned the ignition key. As the Evinrude growled to life, Salazar put all his weight to the throttle.

Gun in hand, John Murdock clung awkwardly to the bow rail as the Aquasport planed off and raced toward the narrow inlet. The wind spiked Murdock's hair and flattened his cheeks. His teeth were bared in a wolfish expression that might have passed for a grin.

As the boat got closer, Joe Salazar expected Mick Stranahan to wake up at any moment and look in their direction—but the man didn't move.

A half mile away, sitting on a milk crate under some trees, Christina Marks heard the police siren. With a shiver she closed her eyes and waited for the sound of gunfire.

They could have come one of several ways. The most likely was the oceanside route, following Caesar Creek into the slender fork between tiny Hurricane Key and Old Rhodes. This was the easiest way to Cartwright's dock.

But a westward approach, out of Biscayne Bay, would leave more options and offer more cover. They could come around Adams Key, or circle the Rubicons and sneak through the grassy flats behind Totten. But that would be a tricky and perilous passage, almost unthinkable for someone who had never made the trip.

Not at night, Stranahan decided, not these guys.

He had gambled that they would come by the ocean.

In the water he had carried only the knife and the spool. Four times he made the swim between Old Rhodes and Hurricane Key; not a long swim, but enervating against a strong outbound current. After pulling himself up on Cartwright's dock for the last time, Stranahan had rubbed the cold ache from his legs and arms. It had taken a long time to catch his breath.

Then he pulled on some dry clothes, got the .38 that Luis Córdova had loaned him, and sat down to wait.

The spool in Stranahan's duffel had contained five hundred yards of a thin plastic monofilament. The line was calibrated to a tensile strength of one hundred twenty pounds, for it was designed to withstand the deep-water surges of giant marlin and bluefin tuna. It was the strongest fishing line manufactured in the world, tournament quality. For further advantage it was lightly tinted a charcoal gray, which made it practically invisible underwater.

Even out of the water, the line was sometimes impossible to see.

At night, for instance. Stretched across a mangrove creek.

Undoubtedly John Murdock never saw it.

He was squatting toadlike on the front of the boat, training his .357 at the figure on the dock as they made their approach. Under Joe Salazar's hand, the Aquasport was moving at exactly forty-two miles per hour.

Mick Stranahan had strung three taut vectors between the islands. The lines were fastened to the trunks of trees and crossed the water at varying heights. The lowest of the lines was snapped immediately by the bow of the speeding police boat. The other two garroted John Murdock in the belly and the neck, respectively.

Joe Salazar, in the bewildering final millisecond of his life, watched his partner thrown backwards, bug-eyed and gurgling, smashed to the deck by unseen hands. Then the same spectral claw seized Salazar by the throat, chopped him off his feet, bounced his overripe skull off the howling Evinrude and twanged him directly into the creek.

The noise made by the fishing line when it snapped on Joe Salazar's neck was very much like that of a gunshot.

Christina Marks ran all the way back to Cartwright's dock. Along the way she dropped the Coleman lantern, hissing, on some rocks. But she kept running. When she got there, Caesar Creek was black and calm. She saw no boat, no sign of intruders.

On the dock, the familiar figure of a man in a baseball cap slouched beneath another lantern, this one glowing brightly.

"Mick, what happened?"

Then Christina realized that it wasn't a man at all, but a scarecrow wearing Stranahan's poplin jacket and long corduroys. The body of the scarecrow was stuffed with palm leaves and dried seaweed. The head was a green coconut. The baseball cap fit like a charm.

24

The Aquasport wedged itself deep in the mangroves on Totten Key. The engine was dead, but the prop was still twirling when Mick Stranahan got there. Barefoot, he monkeyed through the slick rubbery branches until he could see over the side of the battered boat. In his right hand he held Luis Córdova's .38.

He didn't need it. Detective John Murdock wasn't dead, but he would be soon. He lay motionless on the deck, his knees drawn up in pain. Blackish blood oozed from his nose. Only one eye was open, rhythmically illuminated by the strobing blue police light. Cracked but still flashing, the light dangled from a nest of loose wires on the console. It looked like a fancy electric Christmas ornament.

Stranahan felt his stomach shrink to a knot. He put the pistol in his jeans and swung his legs over the gunwale. "John?"

Murdock's eye blinked, and he grunted weakly.

Stranahan said, "Try to take it easy." Like the guy had a choice. "One quick question, I've got to ask. You fellows were going to kill me, weren't you?"

"Damn right," rasped the dying detective.

"Yeah, that's what I thought. I can't believe you're still sore about Judge Goomer."

Murdock managed a bloody grin and said, "You dumb fuckwad."

Stranahan leaned forward and brushed a horsefly off Murdock's forehead. "But if it wasn't revenge for the judge, then why pull something like this?" Silence gave him the answer. "Don't tell me somebody paid you."

Murdock nodded, or tried. His neck wasn't working so well; it looked about twice as long as it was supposed to be.

"Stranahan said, "You took money for this? From who?"

"Eat me," Murdock replied.

"It was probably the doctor," Stranahan speculated. "Or a go-between. That would make more sense."

Murdock's reply came out as a dank rattle. Mick Stranahan sighed. Queasiness at the sight of Murdock had given way to emotional exhaustion.

"John, it's some kind of city, isn't it? All I wanted out here was some peace and solitude. I was through with all this crap."

Murdock gave a hateful moan, but Stranahan needed to talk. "Here I'm minding my own business, feeding the fish, not bothering a soul, when some guy shows up to murder me. At my very own house, John, in the middle of the bay! All because some goddamn doctor thinks I'm going to break open a case that's so old it's mildewed."

The dying Murdock seemed hypnotized by the flashing blue light. It was ticking much faster than his own heart. One of the detective's hands began to crawl like an addled blue crab, tracking circles on the blood-slickened deck.

Stranahan said, "I know it hurts, John, but there's nothing I can do."

In a slack voice Murdock said, "Fuck you, shithead." Then his eye closed for the last time.

Mick Stranahan and Christina Marks were waiting when Luis Córdova pulled up to the dock at nine sharp the next morning.

"Where to?" he asked Stranahan.

"I'd like to go back to my house, Luis."

"Not me," said Christina Marks. "Take me to Key Biscayne. The marina is fine."

Stranahan said, "I guess that means you still don't want to marry me."

"Not in a million years," Christina said. "Not in your wildest dreams."

Stranahan turned to Luis Córdova. "She didn't get much sleep. The accommodations were a bit too . . . rustic."

"I understand," said the marine patrolman. "But, otherwise, a quiet night?"

"Fairly quiet," Stranahan said.

The morning was sunny and cool. The bay had a light washboard ripple that made the patrol boat seem to fly. As they passed the Ragged Keys, Stranahan nudged Luis Córdova and pointed to the white-blue sky. "Choppers!" he shouted over the engine noise. Christina Marks saw them, too: three Coast Guard rescue helicopters, chugging south at a thousand feet.

Without glancing from the wheel, Luis Córdova said, "There's a boat overdue from Crandon. Two cops."

"No shit?"

"They found a body this morning floating off Broad Creek. Homicide man named Salazar."

"What happened?"

"Drowned," yelled Luis Córdova. "Who knows how."

Christina Marks listened to the two men going back and forth. She wasn't sure how much Luis Córdova knew, but it was more than Stranahan would ever tell her. She felt angry and insulted and left out.

When they arrived at the stilt house, Stranahan took out the Smith .38 and returned it to Luis. The marine patrolman was relieved to see that it had not been fired.

Stranahan hoisted two of the duffel bags and hopped off the patrol boat.

From the dock he said, "Take care, Chris." He wanted to say more, but it was the wrong time. She was still fuming about last night, furious because he wouldn't tell her what had happened. She had kicked the coconut head off the scarecrow, that's how mad she had gotten. It was at that moment he'd asked her to marry him. Her reply had been succinct, to say the least.

Now she turned away coldly and said to Luis Córdova: "Can we get going, please."

Stranahan waved them off and trudged up the steps to inspect the looted house. The first thing he saw on the floor was the big marlin head; the tape on the fractured bill had been torn off in the fall. Stranahan stepped over the stuffed fish and went to the bedroom to check for the shotgun. It was still wedged up in the box spring where he had hidden it.

The whole place was a mess all right, depressing but not irreparable. Stranahan was glad, in a way, to have such a large chore ahead of him. Take his mind off Murdock and Salazar and Old Rhodes Key. And Christina Marks, too.

She was the first woman he had loved who had ever said no to marriage. It was quite a feeling.

Luis Córdova came back to the stilt house as Mick Stranahan was finishing lunch. There was a burly new passenger on the boat: Sergeant Al García.

Stranahan greeted them at the door and said, "Two Cubans with guns is never good news."

Luis Córdova said, "Al is working the dead cops."

"Cops plural?" Stranahan's eyebrows arched.

García sat down heavily on one of the barstools. "Yeah, we found Johnny Murdock inside the boat. The boat was up in a frigging tree."

"Where?" Stranahan asked impassively.

"Not far from where you and your lady friend went camping last night." García patted his pockets and cursed. He was out of cigars. He took out a pack of Camels and lit one half-heartedly. He glanced up at the beakless marlin hanging from a new nail on the wall.

Luis Córdova said, "I told Al about how I gave you a lift down to the island after your house got trashed."

Stranahan wasn't upset. If asked, Luis would tell the truth about what he saw, what he knew for a fact. Most likely he had already told García about loaning the two detectives a map of the bay. Nothing strange about that.

"You hear anything funny last night?" Al García asked. "By the way, where's the girl?"

"I don't know," Stranahan said.

"What about last night?"

"A boat went by about eleven. Maybe a little later. Sounded like an outboard. What the hell happened, Al—somebody do these guys?"

García was puffing hard on the cigarette, and blowing circles of smoke, like he did with his stogies. "Way it looks," he said, "they were going wide open. Missed the channel completely."

"You said the boat was in a tree."

"That's how fast the bozos were going. Way it looks, Salazar got thrown, hit his head. He drowned right away but the tide took him south."

"Broad Creek," Luis Córdova said. "A mullet man found the body."

García went on: "Murdock stayed in the boat, but it didn't save him. We're talking major head trauma. The medical examiner thinks a mangrove branch or something snapped his neck. Same with Salazar. Figures it happened when they hit the trees."

"Wide open?"

Luis Córdova said, "The throttle was all the way down. You got to be nuts to run that creek wide open at night."

"Or amazingly stupid," Stranahan said. "Let me guess who they were looking for."

García nodded. "You're on some roll, Mick. A regular arch-angel of death, you are. First your ex, now Murdock and Sala-zar. I'm noticing that bad things happen to people who fuck with you. Seems to be a pattern going way back."

Stranahan said, "I can't help it these jerks don't know how to drive a boat."

Luis Córdova said, "It was an accident, that's all."

"I just find it interesting," said Al García. "Maybe the word is ironic, I don't know. Anyway, you're right, Mick. The two boys were coming to pay you a visit. They kept it real quiet around the shop, too. I can only guess why." He reached in his jacket and took out a soggy white piece of paper. The paper was folded three times, pamphlet sized.

García showed it to Stranahan. "We found this in Salazar's back pocket."

Stranahan knew what it was. He'd seen a thousand just like it. The word *warrant* was still legible in the standard judicial calligraphy. As he handed it back to García, Stranahan wondered whether he was about to be arrested.

"What is this?" he asked.

"Garbage," García replied. He crumpled the sodden docu-ment in his right hand and lobbed it out a window into the water.

Stranahan smiled. "You liked the videotape."

"Obviously," said the detective.

At the Holiday Inn where they got a room, Maggie Gonzalez was going through the yellow pages column by column, telling Chemo which plastic surgeons were good enough to finish the dermabrasion treatments on his face; some of the names were new to her, but others she remembered from her nursing days. Chemo was stooped in front of the bathroom mirror, picking laconically at the patches left on his chin by Dr. Rudy Graveline.

Out of the side of his mouth, Chemo said, "Fucker's not returning my calls."

"It's early," Maggie said. "Rudy sleeps late on his day off."

"I want to see some cash. Today."

"Don't worry."

"The sooner I get the money, the sooner I can take care of this." Meaning his skin. In the mirror, Chemo could see Maggie's expression—at least, as much of it as the bandages revealed—and something that resembled genuine sympathy in her eyes. Not pity, sympathy.

She was the first woman who had ever looked at him that way. Certainly she seemed sincere about helping him find a new plastic surgeon. Chemo thought: She's either a truly devoted nurse or a sneaky little actress.

Maggie ripped a page of physicians from the phone book and said offhandedly, "How much are we hitting him for?"

"A million dollars," Chemo said. His sluglike lips quivered into a smile. "You said he's loaded."

"Yeah, he's also cheap."

"A minute ago you said don't worry."

"Oh, he'll pay. Rudy's cheap, but he's also a coward. All I'm saying is, he'll try to play coy at first. That's his style."

"Coy?" Chemo thought: What in the fuck is she talking about? "I wouldn't know about coy," he said. "I got a Weed Whacker strapped to my arm."

Maggie said, "Hey, I'm on your side. I'm just telling you, he can be stubborn when he wants."

"You know what I think? I think you're in this for more than the money. I think you want to see a show."

Maggie's brown eyes narrowed above the gauze. "Don't be ridiculous."

"Yeah," Chemo said, "I think you'd enjoy it if the boys got nasty with each other. I think you've got your heart set on blood."

He was beaming as if he had just discovered the secret of the universe.

Dr. Rudy Graveline stared at the vaulted ceiling and contemplated his pitiable existence. Chemo had turned blackmailer. Maggie Gonzalez, the bitch, was still alive. So was Mick Stranahan. And somewhere out there a television crew was lurking, waiting to grill him about Victoria Barletta.

Aside from that, life was peachy.

When the phone rang, Rudy pulled the bedsheet up to his chin. He had a feeling it was more bad news.

"Answer it." Heather Chappell's muffled command came from beneath a pillow. "Answer the damn thing."

Rudy reached out from the covers and seized the receiver fiercely, as if it were the neck of a cobra. The grim gassy voice on the other end of the line belonged to Commissioner Roberto Pepsical.

"You see the news on TV?"

"No," Rudy said. "But I got the paper here somewhere."

"There's a story about two policemen who died."

"Yeah, so?"

"In a boat accident," Roberto said.

"Cut to the punch line, Bobby."

"Those were the guys."

"What guys?" asked Rudy. Next to him, Heather mumbled irritably and wrapped the pillow tightly around her ears.

"The guys I told you about. *My* guys."

"Shit," said Rudy.

Heather looked up raggedly and said: "Do you mind? I'm trying to sleep."

Rudy told Roberto that he would call him right back from another phone. He put on a robe and hurried down the hall to his den, where he shut the door. Numbly he dialed Roberto's private number, the one reserved for bagmen and lobbyists.

"Let me make sure I understand," Rudy said. "You were using police officers as hit men?"

"They promised it would be a cinch."

"And now they're dead." Rudy was well beyond the normal threshold of surprise. He had become conditioned to expect the worst. He said, "What about the money—can I get it back?"

Roberto Pepsical couldn't believe the nerve of this cheapskate. "No, you can't get it back. I paid them. They're dead. You want the money back, go ask their widows."

The commissioner's tone had become impatient and firm. It

made Rudy nervous; the fat pig should have been apologizing all over himself.

Rudy said, "All right, then, can you get somebody else to do it?"

"Do what?"

"Do Stranahan. The offer's still open."

Roberto laughed scornfully on the other end; Rudy was baffled by this change of attitude.

"Listen to me," the commissioner said. "The deal's off, forever. Two dead cops is major trouble, Doctor, and you just better hope nobody finds out what they were up to."

Rudy Graveline wanted to drop the subject and crawl back to bed. "Fine, Bobby," he said. "From now on, we never even met. Good-bye."

"Not so fast."

Oh brother, Rudy thought, here we go.

Roberto said, "I talked to The Others. They still want the original twenty-five."

"That's absurd. Cypress Towers is history, Bobby. I'm through with it. Tell your pals they get zippo."

"But you got your zoning."

"I don't need the damn zoning," Rudy protested. "They can have it back, understand? Peddle it to some other dupe."

Roberto's voice carried no trace of understanding, no patience for a compromise. "Twenty-five was the price of each vote. You agreed. Now The Others want their money."

"Don't you ever get sick of being an errand boy?"

"It's my money, too," Roberto said soberly. "But yeah, I do get sick of being an errand boy. I get sick a dealing with cheap scuzzbuckets like you. When it comes to paying up, doctors are the fucking worst."

"Hey," Rudy said, "it doesn't grow on trees."

"A deal is a deal."

In a way, Roberto was glad that Dr. Graveline was being such a prick. It felt good to be the one to drop the hammer for a change. He said, "You got two business days to cover me and The Others."

"What?" Rudy bleated.

"Two days, I'm calling my banker in the Caymans and having him read me the balance in my account. If it's not heavier by twenty-five, you're toast."

Rudy thought: This can't be the same man, not the way he's talking to me.

Roberto Pepsical went on, detached, businesslike: "Me and The Others got this idea that we—meaning the county—should start certifying all private clinics. Have our own testing, license hearings, bi-monthly inspections, that sort of thing. It's our feeling that the general public needs to be protected."

"Protected?" Rudy said feebly.

"From quacks and such. Don't you agree?"

Rudy thought: The whole world has turned upside down.

"Most clinics won't have anything to worry about," Roberto said brightly, "once they're brought up to county standards."

"Bobby, you're a bastard."

After Rudy Graveline slammed down the phone, his hand was shaking. It wouldn't stop.

At the breakfast table, Heather stared at Rudy's trembling fingers and said, "I sure don't like the looks of that."

"Muscle spasms," he said. "It'll go away."

"My surgery is tomorrow," Heather said.

"I'm aware of that, darling."

They had spent the better part of the morning discussing breast implants. Heather had collected testimonials from all her Hollywood actress friends who ever had boob jobs. Some of them favored the Porex line of soft silicone implants, others liked the McGhan Biocell 100, and still others swore by the Replicon. Heather herself was leaning toward the Silastic II Teardrop model, because they came with a five-year written warranty.

"Maybe I better check with my agent," she said.

"Why?" Rudy asked peevishly.

"This is my body we're talking about. My career."

"All right," Rudy said. "Call your agent. What do I know? I'm just the surgeon." He took the newspaper to the bathroom and sat down on the john. Ten minutes later, Heather knocked lightly on the door.

"It's too early on the coast," she said. "Melody's not in the office."

"Thanks for the bulletin."

"But a man called for you."

Rudy folded the newspaper across his lap and braced his chin in his hands. "Who was it, Heather?"

"He didn't give his name. Just said he was a patient."

"That certainly narrows it down."

"He said he came up with a number. I think he was talking about money."

Crazy Chemo. It had to be. "What did you tell him?" Rudy asked through the door.

"I told him you were unavailable at the moment. He didn't sound like he believed me."

"Gee, I can't imagine," said Rudy.

"He said he'll come by the clinic later."

"Splendid." He could hear her breathing at the door. "Heather, is there something else?"

"Yes, there was a man out front. A process server from the courthouse."

Rudy felt himself pucker at both ends.

Heather said, "He rang the bell about a dozen times, but I wouldn't open the door. Finally he went away."

"Good girl," Rudy said. He sprang off the toilet, elated. He flung open the bathroom door, carried Heather into the shower, and turned on the water, steamy hot. Then he got down on his bare knees and began kissing her silky, perfect thighs.

"This is our last day," she said in a whisper, "before the operation."

Rudy stopped kissing and looked up, the shower stream hitting him squarely in the nostrils. Through the droplets he could see the woman of his dreams squeezing her perfect breasts in her perfect hands. With a playful laugh, she said, "Say so long to these little guys."

God, Rudy thought, what am I doing? The irony was wicked.

All the rich geezers and chunky bimbos he had conned into plastic surgery, patients with no chance of transforming their looks or improving their lives—now he finds one with a body and face that are absolutely flawless, perfect, classic, and she's begging for the knife.

A crime against nature, Rudy thought; and he, the instrument of that crime.

He stood up and made reckless love to Heather right there in the shower. She braced one foot on the bath faucet, the other on the soap dish, but Rudy was too lost in his own locomotions to appreciate the artistry of her balance.

The faster he went, the easier it was to concentrate. His mind emptied of Chemo and Roberto and Stranahan and Maggie. Before long Rudy Graveline was able to focus without distraction on his immediate crisis: the blond angel under the shower, and what she had planned for the next day.

Before long, an idea came to Rudy. It came to him with such brilliant ferocity that he mistook it for an orgasm.

Heather Chappell didn't particularly care what it was, as long as it was over. The hot water had run out, and she was freezing the orbs of her perfect bottom against the clammy bathroom tiles.

25

Mick Stranahan asked Al García to wait in the car while he went to see Kipper Garth. The law office was a chorus of beeping telephones as Stranahan made his way through the labyrinth of modular desks. The secretaries didn't bother to try to stop him. They could tell he wasn't a client.

Inside his personal sanctum, Kipper Garth sat in a familiar pose, waiting for an important call. He was tapping a Number 2 pencil and scowling at the speaker box. "I did exactly what you wanted," he said to Stranahan. "See for yourself."

The Nordstroms' malpractice complaint was clipped in a thin brown file on the corner of Kipper Garth's desk. He had been waiting all day for the moment to show his brother-in-law how well he had done. He handed Stranahan the file and said, "Go ahead, it's all there."

Stranahan remained standing while he read the lawsuit. "This is very impressive," he said, halfway down the second page. "Maybe Katie's right, maybe you do have some genuine talent."

Kipper Garth accepted the compliment with a cocky no-sweat shrug. Stranahan resisted the impulse to inquire which bright young paralegal had composed the document, since the author could not possibly be his brother-in-law.

"This really happened?" Stranahan asked. "The man lost an eye to a . . ."

"Hooter," Kipper Garth said. "His wife's hooter, fortunately. Means we can automatically double the pain-and-suffering."

Stranahan was trying to imagine a jury's reaction to such a mishap. The case would never get that far, but it was still fun to think about.

"Has Dr. Graveline been served?"

"Not yet," Kipper Garth reported. "He's ducked us so far, but that's fine. We've got a guy staking out the medical clinic, he'll grab him on the way in or out. The lawsuit's bad enough, but your man will go ape when he finds out we've got a depo scheduled already."

"Excellent," Stranahan said.

"He'll get it postponed, of course."

"It doesn't matter. The whole idea is to keep the heat on. That's why I brought this." Stranahan handed Kipper Garth a page of nine names, neatly typed.

"The witness list," Stranahan explained. "I want you to file it with the court as soon as possible."

Skimming it, Kipper Garth said, "This is highly unusual."

"How would you know?"

"It *is*, dammit. Nobody gives up their witnesses so early in the case."

"You do," said Mick Stranahan. "As of now."

"I don't get it."

"Heat, Jocko, remember? Send one of the clerks down to the courthouse and put this list in the Nordstrom file. You might even courier a copy over to Graveline's place, just for laughs."

Kipper Garth noticed that all but one of the names on the witness list belonged to other doctors—specifically, plastic and reconstructive surgeons: experts who would presumably testify to Rudy Graveline's shocking incompetence in the post-op treatment of Mrs. Nordstrom's encapsulated breast implants.

"Not bad," said Kipper Garth, "but who's this one?" With a glossy fingernail he tapped the last name on the list.

"That's a former nurse," Stranahan said.

"Disgruntled?"

"You might say that."

"And about what," said Kipper Garth, "is she prepared to testify?"

"The defendant's competence," Stranahan replied, "or lack thereof."

Kipper Garth stroked a chromium sideburn. "Witness-wise, I think we're better off sticking with these hotshot surgeons."

"Graveline won't give a shit about them. The nurse's name is what will get his attention. Trust me."

With feigned authority, the lawyer remarked that testimony from an embittered ex-employee wouldn't carry much weight in court.

"We're not going to court," Stranahan reminded him. "Not for malpractice, anyway. Maybe for a murder."

"You're losing me again," Kipper Garth admitted.

"Stay lost," said Stranahan.

* * *

George Graveline's tree-trimming truck was parked off Crandon Boulevard in a lush tropical hammock. Buttonwoods, gumbo limbo, and mahogany trees—plenty of shade for George Graveline's truck. The county had hired him to rip out the old trees to make space for some tennis courts. Before long a restaurant would spring up next to the tennis courts and, after that, a major resort hotel. The people who would run the restaurant and the hotel would receive the use of the public property for practically nothing, thanks to their pals on the county commission. In return, the commissioners would receive a certain secret percentage of the refreshment concessions. And the voters would have brand-new tennis courts, whether they wanted them or not.

George Graveline's role in this civic endeavor was small, but he went at it with uncharacteristic zest. In the first two hours he and his men cleared two full acres of virgin woods. Afterwards George Graveline sat down in the truck cab to rest, while his workers tossed the uprooted trees one at a time into the automatic wood chipper.

All at once the noise died away. George Graveline opened his eyes. He could hear his foreman talking to an unfamiliar voice behind the truck. George stuck his head out the window and saw a stocky Cuban guy in a brown suit. The Cuban guy had a thick mustache and a fat unlit cigar in one corner of his mouth.

"What can I do for you?" George Graveline asked.

The Cuban guy reached in his coat and pulled out a gold police badge. As he walked up to the truck, he could see George Graveline's Adam's apple sliding up and down.

Al García introduced himself and said he wanted to ask a few questions.

George Graveline said, "You got a warrant?"

The detective smiled. "I don't need a warrant, *chico*."

"You don't?"

García shook his head. "Nope. Here, take a look at this." He showed George Graveline the police composite of Blondell Wayne Tatum, the man known as Chemo. "Ever see this bird before?"

"No, sir," said the tree trimmer, but his expression gave it away. He looked away too quickly from the drawing; anyone else would have stared.

García said, "This is a friend of your brother's."

"I don't think so."

"No?" García shifted the cigar to the other side of his mouth. "Well, that's good to know. Because this man's a killer, and I can't think of one good reason why he'd be hanging out with a famous plastic surgeon."

George Graveline said, "Me neither." He turned on the radio and twirled the tuner knob back and forth, pretending to look for his favorite country station. García could sense the guy was about to wet his pants.

The detective said, "I'm not the first homicide man you ever met, am I?"

"Sure. What do you mean?"

"Hell, it was four years ago," García said. "You probably don't even remember. It was outside your brother's office, the place he had before he moved over to the beach."

With a fat brown finger George Graveline scratched his neck. He scrunched his eyebrows, as if trying to recall.

García said: "Detective's name was Timmy Gavigan. Skinny Irish guy, red hair, about so big. He stopped to chat with you for a couple minutes."

"No, I surely don't remember," George said, guardedly.

"I'll tell you exactly when it was—it was right after that college girl disappeared," García said. "Victoria Barletta was her name. Surely you remember. There must've been cops all over the place."

"Oh yeah." Slowly it was coming back to George; that's what he wanted the cop to think.

"She was one of your brother's patients, the Barletta girl."

"Right," said George Graveline, nodding. "I remember how upset Rudolph was."

"But you don't remember talking to Detective Gavigan?"

"I talked to lots of people."

García said, "The reason I mention it, Timmy remembered you."

"Yeah, so?"

"You know, he never solved that damn case. The Barletta girl, after all these years. And now he's dead, Timmy is." García stepped to the rear of the truck. Casually he put one foot on the bumper, near the hitch of the wood chipper. George Graveline opened the door of the truck and leaned out to keep an eye on the Cuban detective.

The two men were alone. George's workers had wandered off to find a cool place to eat lunch and smoke some weed; it was hard to unwind with a cop hanging around.

Curiously Al García bent over the wood chipper and peered at a decal on the engine mount. The decal was in the cartoon likeness of a friendly raccoon. "Brush Bandit—is that the name of this mother?"

"That's right," said George Graveline.

"How does it work exactly?"

George motioned sullenly. "You throw the wood into that hole and it comes out here, in the back of the truck. All grinded up."

García whistled over his cigar. "Must be some nasty blade."

"It's a big one, yessir."

García took his foot off the truck bumper. He held up the drawing of Chemo one more time. "You see this guy, I want you to call us right away."

"Surely," said George Graveline. The detective gave him a business card. The tree trimmer glanced at it, decided it was authentic, slipped it into the back pocket of his jeans.

"And warn your brother," García said. "Just in case the guy shows up."

"You betcha," said George Graveline.

Back in the unmarked county car, parked a half-mile down the boulevard at the Key Biscayne fire station, Mick Stranahan said: "So how'd it go?"

"Just like we figured," García replied. *"Nada."*

"What do you think of Timmy's theory? About how they got rid of the body?"

"If the doctor really killed her then, yeah, it's possible. That's quite a machine brother George has got himself."

Stranahan said, "Too bad brother George won't flip."

García rolled up the windows and turned on the air-conditioning to cool off. He knew what Stranahan was thinking and he was right: Brother George could blow the whole thing wide open. If Maggie were dead or gone, the videotape alone would not be enough for an indictment. They would definitely need George Graveline to talk about Vicky Barletta.

"I'm going for some fresh air," Stranahan said. "Why don't you meet me back here in about an hour?"

García said, "Where the hell you off to?"

Stranahan got out of the car. "For a walk, do you mind? Go get some coffee or flan or something."

"Mick, don't do anything stupid. It's too nice a day for being stupid."

"Hey, it's a lovely day." Stranahan slammed the car door and crossed the boulevard at a trot.

"Shit," García muttered. *"Mierda!"*

He drove down to the Oasis restaurant and ordered a cup of overpowering Cuban coffee. Then he ordered another.

George Graveline was still alone when Mick Stranahan got there. He was leaning against the truck fender, staring at his logger boots. He looked up at Stranahan, straightened, and said, "You put that damn cop on my ass."

"Good morning, George," said Stranahan. "It's certainly nice to see you again."

"Fuck you, hear?"

"Are we having a bad day? What is it—cramps?"

George Graveline was one of those big, slow guys who squint when they get angry. He was squinting now. Methodically he clenched and unclenched his fists, as if he were practicing isometrics.

Stranahan said, "George, I've still got that problem I told

you about last time. Your brother's still got some goon trying to murder me. I'm really at the end of my rope."

"You got that right."

"My guess," continued Stranahan, "is that you and Rudy had a brotherly talk after last time. My guess is that you know exactly where I can locate this goony hit man."

"Screw you," said George Graveline. He kicked the switch on the wood chipper and the motor growled to life.

Stranahan said, "Aw, what'd you do that for? How'm I supposed to hear you over all that damn racket?"

George Graveline lunged with both arms raised stiff in fury, a Frankenstein monster with Elvis jowls. He was clawing for Stranahan's neck. Stranahan ducked the grab and punched George Graveline hard under the heart. When the tree trimmer didn't fall, Stranahan punched him twice in the testicles. This time George went down.

Stranahan placed his right foot on the husky man's neck and applied the pressure slowly, shifting his weight from heel to toe. By reflex George's hands were riveted to his swollen scrotum. He was helpless to fight back. He made a noise like a tractor tire going flat.

"I can't believe you did that," Stranahan muttered. "Isn't it possible to have a civilized conversation in this town without somebody trying to kill you?"

It was a rhetorical question but George Graveline couldn't hear it over the wood chipper, anyway. Stranahan leaned over and shouted: "Where's the goon?"

George did not answer promptly, so Stranahan added more weight on the Adam's apple. George was not squinting anymore; both eyes were quite large.

"Where is he?" Stranahan repeated.

When George's lips started moving, Stranahan let up. The voice that came out of the tree trimmer's mouth had a fuzzy electronic quality. Stranahan knelt to hear it.

"Works on the beach," said George Graveline.

"Can we be more specific?"

"At a club."

"What club, George? There's lots of nightclubs on Miami Beach."

George blinked and said, "Gay Bidet." Now it was done, he thought. His brother Rudy was a goner.

"Thank you, George," said Stranahan. He removed his shoe from the tree trimmer's throat. "This is a good start. I'm very encouraged. Now let's talk about Vicky Barletta."

George Graveline lay there with his head in the moist dirt, his groin throbbing. He lay there worrying about his brother the doctor, about what horrible things would happen to him all because of George's big mouth. Rudy had confided in him, trusted him, and now George had let his brother down. Lying there dejectedly, he decided that no matter how much pain was inflicted upon him, he wasn't going to tell Mick Stranahan what had happened to that college girl. Rudy had made a mistake, everybody makes mistakes. Why, one time George himself got a work order mixed up and cut down a whole row of fifty-foot royal palms, when it was mangy old Brazilians he was supposed to chop. Still, they didn't put him in jail or anything, just made him pay a fine. Hundred bucks a tree, something like that. Why should a doctor be treated any different? As he reflected upon Rudy's turbulent medical career, George Graveline removed one of his hands from his swollen scrotum. The free hand happened to settle on a hunk of fresh-cut mahogany concealed by his left leg. The wood was heavy, the bark coarse and dry. George closed his fingers around it. It felt pretty good.

Still kneeling, Mick Stranahan nudged George Graveline's shoulder and said, "Penny for your thoughts."

And George hit him square on the back of the skull.

Stranahan didn't see the blow, and at first he thought he'd been shot. He heard a man shouting and what sounded like an ambulance. The rescue scene played vividly in his imagination. He waited to feel the paramedics' hands ripping open his shirt. He waited for the cold clap of the stethoscope on his chest, for the sting of the I.V. needle in his arm. He waited for the childlike sensation of being lifted onto the stretcher.

None of this came, yet the sound of the ambulance siren

would not go away. In his crashing sleep, Stranahan grew angry. Where were the goddamn EMTs? A man's been shot here!

Then, blessedly, he felt someone lifting him. Lifting him under the arms, someone strong. It hurt, oh, God, how it hurt, but that was all right—at least they had come. But then he was falling again, falling or dying, he couldn't be sure. And in his crashing sleep he heard the moan of the siren rise to such a pitch that he wanted to cover his ears and scream for it to stop, please God.

And it did stop.

Somebody shut off the wood chipper.

Stranahan awoke to the odd hollow silence that follows a sharp echo. His eardrums fluttered. The air smelled pungently of cordite. He found himself on his knees, weaving, a drunk waiting for communion. His shirt was damp, his pulse rabbity. He checked himself and saw he was mistaken, he hadn't been shot. There was no ambulance, either, just the tree truck.

Al García sat on the bumper. His gun was in his right hand, which hung heavily at his side. He was as pale as a flounder.

There was no sign of George Graveline anywhere.

"You all right?" Stranahan asked.

"No," said the detective.

"Where's the tree man?"

With the gun García pointed toward the bin of the tree truck, where the wood chipper had spit what bone and jelly was left of George Graveline.

After he had tried to feed Mick Stranahan into the maw.

And Al García had shot him twice in the back.

And the impact of the bullets had slammed him face-forward down the throat of the tree-eating machine.

26

Chemo got the Bonneville out of the garage and drove out to Whispering Palms, but the receptionist said that Dr. Graveline wasn't there. Noticing the dramatic topography of Chemo's face, the receptionist told him she could try the doctor at home for an emergency. Chemo said thanks, anyway.

After leaving the clinic, he walked around to the side of the building where the employees parked. Dr. Graveline's spiffy new Jaguar XJ-6 was parked in its space. This was the Jaguar that the doctor had purchased immediately after Mick Stranahan had blown up his other one. The sedan was a rich shade of red; candy apple, Chemo guessed, though the Jaguar people probably had a fancier name for it. The windows of the car were tinted gray so that you couldn't see inside. Chemo assumed that Dr. Graveline had a burglar alarm wired on the thing, so he was careful not to touch the doors or the hood.

He ambled to the rear of the clinic, by the water, and peeked through the bay window into Rudy's private office. There was the doctor, yakking on the phone. Chemo was annoyed; it was rude of Graveline to be ducking him this way. Rude, hell. It was just plain stupid.

When Chemo turned the corner of the building, he saw a short man in an ill-fitting gray suit standing next to Rudy's car. The man wore dull brown shoes and black-rimmed eyeglasses. He looked to be in his mid-fifties. Chemo walked up to him and said, "Are you looking for Graveline?"

The man in the black-rimmed glasses appraised Chemo skittishly and said, "Are you him?"

"Fuck no. But this is his car."

"They told me he wasn't here."

"They lied," Chemo said. "Hard to believe, isn't it?"

The man opened a brown billfold to reveal a cheap-looking badge. "I work for the county," he said. "I'm trying to serve some papers on the doctor. I been trying two, three days."

Chemo said, "See that side door? You wait here, he'll be out soon. It's almost five o'clock."

"Thanks," said the process server. He went over and stood, idiotically, by the side entrance to the clinic. He clutched the court papers rolled up in one hand, as if he were going to sap the doctor when he came out.

Chemo slipped the calfskin sheath off the Weed Whacker and turned his attention to Rudy's new Jaguar. He chose as his starting place the left front fender.

Initially it was slow going—those British sure knew how to paint an automobile. At first the Weed Whacker inflicted only pale stripes on the deep red enamel. Chemo tried lowering the device closer to the fender and bracing it in position with his good arm. It took fifteen minutes for the powerful lawn cutter to work its way down to the base steel of the sedan. Chemo moved its buzzing head back and forth in a sweeping motion to enlarge the scar.

From his waiting post outside the clinic door, the process server watched the odd ceremony with rapt fascination. Finally he could stand it no longer, and shouted at Chemo.

Chemo turned away from the Jaguar and looked at the man in the black-rimmed glasses. He flicked the toggle switch to turn off the Weed Whacker, then cupped his right hand to his ear.

The man said, "What are you doing with that thing?"

"Therapy," Chemo answered. "Doctor's orders."

Like many surgeons, Dr. Rudy Graveline was a compulsive man, supremely organized but hopelessly anal retentive. The day after the disturbing phone call from Commissioner Roberto Pepsical, Rudy meticulously wrote out a list of all his career-threatening problems. By virtue of the scope of his extortion, Roberto Pepsical was promoted to the number three spot, behind Mick Stranahan and Chemo. Rudy studied the list closely. In the larger context of a possible murder indictment, Roberto Pepsical was chickenshit. Expensive chickenshit, but chickenshit just the same.

Rudy Graveline dialed the number in New Jersey and waited for Curly Eyebrows to come on the line.

"Jeez, I told you not to call me here. Let me get to a better phone." The man hung up, and Rudy waited. Ten minutes later the man called back.

"Lemme guess, your problem's got worse."

"Yes," said Rudy.

"That local talent you hired, he wasn't by himself after all."

"He was," Rudy said, "but not now."

"That's pretty funny." Curly Eyebrows laughed flatulently. Somewhere in the background a car blasted its horn. The man said, "You rich guys are something else. Always trying to do it on the cheap."

"Well, I need another favor," Rudy said.

"Such as what?"

"Remember the hunting accident a few yeas ago?"

Curly Eyebrows said, "Sure. That doctor. The one was giving you a hard time."

The man in New Jersey didn't remember the name of the dead doctor, but Rudy Graveline certainly did. It was Kenneth Greer, one of his former partners at the Durkos Center. The one who figured out what had happened to Victoria Barletta. The one who was trying to blackmail him.

"That was a cinch," said Curly Eyebrows. "I wish they all could be hunters. Every deer season we could clean up the Gambinos that way. Hunting accidents."

The man in New Jersey had an itch—on the line Rudy Graveline heard the disgusting sound of fat fingers scratching hairy flesh. He tried not to think about it.

"Somebody new is giving me a hard time," the doctor said. "I don't know if you can help, but I thought I'd give it a shot."

"I'm listening."

"It's the Dade County Commission," Rudy said. "I need somebody to kill them. Can you arrange it?"

"Wait a minute—"

"All of them," Rudy said, evenly.

"Excuse me, Doc, but you're fucking crazy. Don't call me no more."

"Please," Rudy said. "Five of them are shaking me down for twenty-five grand each. The trouble is, I don't know which five. So my idea is to kill all nine."

Curly Eyebrows grunted. "You got me confused."

Patiently Rudy explained how the bribe system worked, how each commissioner arranged for four crooked colleagues to go along on each controversial vote. Rudy told the man in New Jersey about the Old Cypress Towers project, about how the commissioners were trying to pinch him for the zoning decision he no longer needed.

"Hey, a deal is a deal," Curly Eyebrows said unsympathetically. "Seems to me you got yourself in a tight situation." Now it sounded like he was picking his teeth with a comb.

Rudy said, "You won't help?"

"Won't. Can't. Wouldn't." The man coughed violently, then spit. "Much as the idea appeals to me personally—killing off an entire county commission—it'd be bad for business."

"It was just an idea," Rudy said. "I'm sorry I bothered you."

"Want some free advice?"

"Why not."

Curly Eyebrows said, "Who's the point man in this deal? You gotta know his name, at least."

"I do."

"Good. I suggest something happens to the bastard. Something awful bad. This could be a lesson to the other eight pricks, you understand?"

Rudy Graveline said yes, he understood.

"Trust me," said the man in New Jersey. "I been in this end of it for a long time. Sort of thing makes an impression, especially dealing with your mayors and aldermen and those types. These are not exactly tough guys."

"I suppose not." Rudy cleared his throat. "Listen, that's a very good idea. Just do one of them."

"That's my advice," said the man in New Jersey.

"Could you arrange it?"

"Shit, I ain't risking my boys on some lowlife county pol. No way. Talent's too hard to come by these days—you found that out yourself."

Rudy recalled the newspaper story about Tony the Eel, washed up dead on the Cape Florida beach. "I still feel bad about that fellow last month," the doctor said.

"Hey, it happens."

"But still," said Rudy morosely.

"You ought to get out of Florida," advised Curly Eyebrows. "I been telling all my friends, it's not like the old days. Fuck the pretty beaches, Doc, them Cubans are crazy. They're not like you and me. And then there's the Jews and the Haitians, Christ!"

"Times change," said Rudy.

"I was reading up on it, some article about stress. Florida is like the worst fucking place in America for stressing out, besides Vegas. I'm not making this up."

Dispiritedly, Rudy Graveline said, "It seems like everybody wants a piece of my hide."

"Ain't it the fucking truth."

"I swear, I'm not a violent person by nature."

"Costa Rica," said the man in New Jersey. "Think about it."

Commissioner Roberto Pepsical got to the church fifteen minutes early and scouted the aisles: a bag lady snoozing on the third pew, but that was it. To kill time Roberto lit a whole row of devotional candles. Afterwards he fished through his pocket change and dropped a Canadian dime in the coin box.

When the doctor arrived, Roberto waddled briskly to the back of the church. Rudy Graveline was wearing a tan sports jacket and dark, loose-fitting pants and a brown striped necktie. He looked about as calm as a rat in a snake hole. In his right hand was a black Samsonite suitcase. Wordlessly Roberto brushed past him and entered one of the dark confessionals. Rudy waited about three minutes, checked over both shoulders, opened the door, and went in.

"God," he exclaimed.

"He's here somewhere." The commissioner chuckled at his own joke.

Rudy had never been inside a confession booth before. It was smaller and gloomier than he had imagined; the only light was a tiny amber bulb plugged into a wall socket.

Roberto had planted his fat ass on the kneeling cushion with his back to the screen. Rudy checked to make sure there wasn't a priest on the other side, listening. Priests could be awful quiet when they wanted.

"Remember," the commissioner said, raising a finger. "Whisper."

Right, Rudy thought, like I was going to belt out a Gershwin tune. "Of all the screwy places to do this," he said.

"It's quiet," Roberto Pepsical said. "And very safe."

"And very small," Rudy added. "You had anchovies for dinner, didn't you?"

"There are no secrets here," said Roberto.

With difficulty, Rudy wedged himself and the Samsonite next to the commissioner on the kneeling bench. Roberto's body heat bathed both of them in a warm acrid fog, and Rudy wondered how long the oxygen would hold out. He had never heard of anyone suffocating in confession; on the other hand, that was exactly the sort of incident the Catholics would cover up.

"You ready?" Roberto asked with a wink. "What's that in your pocket?"

"Unfortunately, that's a subpoena. Some creep got me on the way out of the clinic tonight." Rudy had been in such a hurry that he hadn't even looked at the court papers; he was somewhat accustomed to getting sued.

Roberto said, "No wonder you're in such a lousy mood."

"It's not that so much as what happened to my new car. It got vandalized—actually, scoured is the word for it."

"The Jag? That's terrible."

"Oh, it's been a splendid day," Rudy said. "Absolutely splendid."

"Getting back to the money . . ."

"I've got it right here." The doctor opened the suitcase across both their laps, and the confessional was filled with the sharp scent of new money. Rudy Graveline was overwhelmed—it really did *smell*. Robert picked up a brick of hundred-dollar bills. "I thought I said twenties."

"Yeah, and I would've needed a bloody U-Haul."

Roberto Pepsical snapped off the bank wrapper and counted out ten thousand dollars on the floor between his feet. Then he added up the other bundles in the suitcase to make sure the total came to one twenty-five.

Grinning, he held up one of the loose hundreds. "I don't see many of these. Whose picture is that—Eisenhower's?"

"No," said Rudy, stonily.

"What'd the bank say? About you taking all these big bills."

"Nothing," Rudy said. "This is Miami, Bobby."

"Yeah, I guess." Ebulliently the commissioner restacked the cash bundles and packed them in the Samsonite. He scooped up the loose ten thousand dollars and shoved the thick wad into the pockets of his suit. "This was a smart thing you did."

Rudy said, "I'm not so sure."

"You know that plan I told you about . . . about licensing the medical clinics and all that? Me and The Others, we decided to drop the whole thing. We figure that doctors like you got enough rules and regulations as it is."

"Glad to hear it," said Rudy Graveline. He wished he had brought some Certs. Roberto could use a whole roll.

"How about a drink?" the commissioner asked. "We could stop at the Versailles, get a couple pitchers o' sangría."

"Yum."

"Hey, it's my treat."

"Thanks," said the doctor, "but first you know what I'd like to do? I'd like to say a prayer. I'd like to thank the Lord that this problem with Cypress Towers is finally over.''

Roberto shrugged. ''Go ahead.''

''Is it all right, Bobby? I mean, since I'm not Catholic.''

''No problem.'' The commissioner grunted to his feet, turned around in the booth and got to his knees. The cushion squeaked under his weight. ''Do like this,'' he said.

Rudy Graveline, who was slimmer, had an easier time with the turnaround maneuver. With the suitcase propped between them, the two men knelt side by side, facing the grated screen through which confessions were heard.

''So pray,'' Roberto Pepsical said. ''I'll wait till you're done. Fact, I might even do a couple Hail Marys myself, long as I'm here.''

Rudy shut his eyes, bowed his head, and pretended to say a prayer.

Roberto nudged him. ''I don't mean to tell you what to do,'' he said, ''but in here it's not proper to pray with your hands in your pockets.''

''Of course,'' said Rudy, ''I'm sorry.''

He took his right hand from his pants and placed it on Roberto's doughy shoulder. It was too dark for the commissioner to see the hypodermic syringe.

''Hail Mary,'' Roberto said, ''full of grace, the Lord is with thee. Blessed ar—ow!''

The commissioner pawed helplessly at the needle sticking from his jacket at the crook of the elbow. Considering Rudy's general clumsiness with injections, it was a minor miracle that he hit the commissioner's antecubital vein on the first try. Roberto Pepsical hugged the doctor desperately, a panting bear, but already the deadly potassium was streaming toward the valves of his fat clotty heart.

Within a minute the seizure killed him, mimicking the symptoms of a routine infarction so perfectly that the commissioner's relatives would never challenge the autopsy.

Rudy removed the spent syringe, retrieved the loose cash from Roberto's pocket, picked up the black suitcase, and slipped out of the stuffy confessional. The air in the church seemed positively alpine, and he paused to breathe it deeply.

In the back row, an elderly Cuban couple turned at the sound of his footsteps on the terrazzo. Rudy nodded solemnly. He hoped they didn't notice how badly his legs were shaking. He faced the altar and tried to smile like a man whose soul had been cleansed of all sin.

The old Cuban woman raised a bent finger to her forehead and made the sign of the cross. Rudy worried about Catholic protocol and wondered if he was expected to reply. He didn't know how to make the sign of the cross, but he put down the suitcase and gave it a gallant try. With a forefinger he touched his brow, his breast, his right shoulder, his left shoulder, his naval, then his brow again.

"Live long and prosper," he said to the old woman and walked out the doors of the church.

When he got home, Rudy Graveline went upstairs to see Heather Chappell. He sat next to the bed and took her hand. She blinked moistly over the edge of the bandages.

Rudy kissed her knuckles and said, "How are you feeling?"

"I don't know about you," Heather said, "but I'm feeling a hundred years old."

"That's to be expected. You had quite a day."

"You sure it went okay?"

"Beautifully," Rudy said.

"The nose, too?"

"A masterpiece."

"But I don't remember a thing."

The reason Heather couldn't remember the surgery was because there had been no surgery. Rudy had drugged her copiously the night before and kept her drugged the whole day. Heather had lain unconscious for seven hours, whacked out on world-class pharmaceutical narcotics. By the time she awoke, she felt like she'd been sleeping for a month. Her hips, her breasts, her neck, and her nose were all snugly and expertly bandaged, but no scalpel had touched her fine California flesh.

Rudy hoped to persuade Heather that the surgery was a glowing success; the absence of scars, a testament to his wizardry. Obviously he had weeks of bogus post-operative counseling ahead of him.

"Can I see the video?" she asked form the bed.

"Later," Rudy promised. "When you're up to snuff."

He had ordered (by FedEx) a series of surgical training cassettes from a medical school in California. Now it was simply a matter of editing the tapes into a plausible sequence. Gowned, masked, and anesthetized on the operating table, all patients looked pretty much alike to a camera. Meanwhile, all you ever saw of the surgeon was his gloved hands; Heather would never know that the doctor on the videotape was not her lover.

She said, "It's incredible, Rudolph, but I don't feel any pain."

"It's the medication," he said. "The first few days, we keep you pretty high."

Heather giggled. "Eight miles high?"

"Nine," said Rudy Graveline, "at least."

He tucked her hand beneath the sheets and picked up something from the bedstand. "Look what I've got."

She squinted through the fuzz of the drugs. "Red and blue and white," she said dreamily.

"Plane tickets," Rudy sad. "I'm taking you on a trip."

"Really?"

"To Costa Rica. The climate is ideal for your recovery."

"For how long?"

Rudy said, "A month or two, maybe longer. As long as it takes, darling."

"But I'm supposed to do a *Password* with Jack Klugman."

"Out of the question," said Rudy. "You're in no condition for that type of stress. Now get some sleep."

"What's that noise?" she asked, lifting her head.

"The doorbell, sweetheart. Lie still now."

"Costa Rica," Heather murmured. "Where's that, anyhow?"

Rudy kissed her on the forehead and told her he loved her.

"Yeah," she said. "I know."

Whoever was at the door was punching the button like it was a jukebox. Rudy hurried down the stairs and checked through the glass peephole.

Chemo signaled mirthlessly back at him.

"Shit." Rudy sighed, thought of his Jaguar, and opened the door.

"Why did you destroy my car?"

"Teach you some manners," Chemo said. Another bandaged woman stood at his side.

"Maggie?" Rudy Graveline said. "Is that you?"

Chemo led her by the hand into the big house. He found the living room and made himself comfortable in an antique rocking chair. Maggie Gonzalez sat on a white leather sofa. Her eyes, which were Rudy's only clue to her mood, seemed cold and hostile.

Chemo said, "Getting jerked around is not my favorite thing. I ought to just kill you."

"What good would that do?" Rudy said. He stepped closer to Maggie and asked, "Who did your face?"

"Leaper," she said.

"Leonard Leaper? Up in New York? I heard he's good—mind if I look?"

"Yes," she said, recoiling. "Rogelio, make him get away!"

"Rogelio?" Rudy looked quizzically at Chemo.

"It's your fucking fault," he said. "That's the name you put on the tickets. Now leave her alone." Chemo stopped rocking. He eyed Rudy Graveline as if he were a palmetto bug.

The surgeon sat near Maggie on the white leather sofa and said to Chemo, "So how're the dermabrasions healing?"

Self-consciously the killer's hand went to his chin. "All of a sudden you're concerned about my face. Now that you're afraid."

"Well, you look good," Rudy persisted. "Really, it's a thousand percent improvement."

"Jesus H. Christ."

Irritably Maggie said, "Let's get the point, okay? I want to get out of here."

"The money," Chemo said to the doctor. "We decided on one million, even."

"For what!" Rudy was trying to stay cool, but his tone was trenchant.

Chemo started rocking again. "For everything," he said. "For Maggie's videotape. For Stranahan. For stopping that TV show about the dead girl. That's worth a million dollars. In fact, the more I think about it, I'd say it's worth two."

Rudy folded his arms and said, "You do everything you just said, and I'll gladly give you a million dollars. As of now, you get nothing but expenses because you haven't done a damn thing but stir up trouble."

"That's not true," Maggie snapped.

"We've been busy," Chemo added. "We got a big surprise."

Rudy said, "I've got a big surprise, too. A malpractice suit. And guess whose name is on the witness list?"

He jerked an accusing thumb at Maggie, who said, "That's news to me."

Rudy went on, "Some fellow named Nordstrom. Lost his eye in some freak accident and now it's all my fault."

Maggie said, "I never heard of a Nordstrom."

"Well, your name is right there in the file. Witness for the plaintiff. Why should I pay you people a dime?"

"All the more reason," Chemo said. "I believe it's called hush money."

"No," said the doctor, "that's not the way it goes."

Chemo stood up from the rocker. He took two large steps across the living room and punched Rudy Graveline solidly in the gut. The doctor collapsed in a gagging heap on the Persian carpet. Chemo turned him over with one foot. Then he cranked up the Weed Whacker.

"Oh God," cried Rudy, raising his hands to shield his eyes. Quickly Maggie moved out of the way, her facial bandages crinkled in trepidation.

"I got a new battery," Chemo said. "A Die-Hard. Watch this."

He started weed-whacking Rudy's fine clothes. First he

shredded the shirt and tie, then he tried trimming the curly brown hair on Rudy's chest. The doctor yelped pitiably as nasty pink striations appeared beneath his nipples.

Chemo was working the machine toward Rudy's pubic zone when he spied something inside the tattered lining of the surgeon's tan coat. He turned off the Weed Whacker and leaned down for a closer look.

With his good hand Chemo reached into the silky entrails of Rudy's jacket and retrieved the severed corner of a one-hundred-dollar bill. Excitedly he probed around until he found more: handfuls, blessedly unshredded.

Chemo spread the money on the coffee table, beneath which Rudy thrashed and moaned impotently. The stricken surgeon observed the accounting firsthand, gazing up through the frosted glass. As the cash grew to cover the table, Rudy's face hardened into a mask of abject disbelief. On his way back from the church he had meant to stop at the clinic and return the money to the drop safe. Now it was too late.

"Count it," Chemo said to Maggie.

Excitedly she riffled through the bills. "Nine thousand two hundred," she reported. "The rest is all chopped up."

Chemo dragged Dr. Graveline from under the coffee table. "Why you carrying this much cash?" he said. "Don't tell me the Jag dealer won't take credit cards." His moist salamander eyes settled on the black Samsonite, which Rudy had stupidly left in the middle of the hallway.

Rudy sniffled miserably as he watched Chemo kick open the suitcase and crouch down to count the rest of the money. "Well, well," said the killer.

"What are you going to do with it?" the doctor asked.

"Gee, I think we'll give it to the United Way. Or maybe Jerry's kids." Chemo walked over to Rudy and poked his bare belly with the warm head of the Weed Whacker. "What the hell you think we're going to do with it? We're gonna spend it, and then we're gonna come back for more."

After they had gone, Dr. Rudy Graveline sprawled on the rumpled Persian carpet for a long time, thinking: This is what a Harvard education has gotten me—extorted, beaten, stripped, scandalized, and chopped up like an artichoke. The doctor's fingers gingerly explored the tumescent stripes that crisscrossed his chest and abdomen. If it didn't sting so much, the sight would be almost comical.

It occurred to Rudy Graveline that Chemo and Maggie had forgotten to tell him their big secret, whatever it was they had done, whatever spectacular felony they had committed to earn this first garnishment.

And it occurred to Rudy that he wasn't all that curious. In fact, he was somewhat relieved not to know.

27

The man from the medical examiner's office took one look in the back of the tree truck and said: "Mmmm, lasagna."

"That's very funny," said Al García. "You oughta go on the Carson show. Do a whole routine on stiffs."

The man from the medical examiner's office said, "Al, you gotta admit—"

"I told you what happened."

"—but you gotta admit, there's a humorous aspect."

Coroners made Al García jumpy; they always got so cheery when somebody came up with a fresh way to die.

The detective said, "If you think it's funny, fine. You're the one's gotta do the autopsy."

"First I'll need a casserole dish."

"Hilarious," said García. "Absolutely hilarious."

The man from the medical examiner's office told him to lighten up, said everybody needs a break in the monotony, no matter what line of work. "I get tired of gunshot wounds," the coroner said. "It's like a damn assembly line down there. GSW head, GSW thorax, GSW neck—it gets old, Al."

García said, "Listen, go ahead, make your jokes. But I need you to keep this one outta the papers."

"Good luck."

The detective knew it wouldn't be easy to keep the lid on George Graveline's death. Seven squad cars, an ambulance, and a body wagon—even in Miami, that'll draw a crowd. The gawkers were being held behind yellow police ribbons strung along Crandon Boulevard. Son the minicams would arrive, and the minicams could zoom in for close-ups.

"I need a day or two," García said. "No press, and no next of kin."

The man from the medical examiner shrugged. "It'll take at least that long to make the I.D., considering what's left. I figure we'll have to go dental."

"Whatever."

"I'll need to impound the truck," the coroner said. "And this fancy toothpick machine."

García said he would have them both towed downtown.

The coroner stuck his head into the maw of the wood chipper and examined the blood-smeared blades. "There ought to be bullet fragments," he said, "somewhere in this mess."

García said, "Hey, Sherlock, I told you what happened. I shot the asshole, okay? My gun, my bullets."

"Al, don't take all the fun out of it." The man from the medical examiner reached into the blades of the wood chipper and carefully plucked out an item that the untrained eye would have misidentified as a common black woolly-bear caterpillar.

The coroner held it up for Al García to see.

The detective frowned. "What, do I get a prize or something? It's a sideburn, for Chrissakes."

"Very good," said the coroner.

García flicked the soggy nub of his cigar into the bushes and went looking for George Graveline's crew of tree trimmers. There were three of them sitting somberly in the backseat of a county patrol car. Al García got in front, on the passenger side. He turned around and spoke to them through the cage. The men's clothes smelled like pot. García asked if any of them had seen what had happened, and to a one they answered no, they'd been on their lunch break. The officers from Internal Review had asked the same thing.

"If you didn't see anything," García said, "then you don't have much to tell the reporters, right?"

In unison the tree trimmers shook their heads.

"Including the name of the alleged victim, right?"

The tree trimmers agreed.

"This is damned serious," said García. "I don't believe you boys would purposely obstruct a homicide investigation, would you?"

The tree trimmers promised not to say a word to the media. Al García asked a uniformed cop to give the men a lift home, so they wouldn't have to walk past the minicams on their way to the bus stop.

By this time, the ambulance was backing out, empty. García knocked on the driver's window. "Where's the guy you were working on?"

"Blunt head wound?"

"Right. Big blond guy."

"Took off," said the ambulance driver. "Gobbled three Darvocets and said so long. Wouldn't even let us wrap him."

García cursed and bearishly swatted at a fresh-cut buttonwood branch.

The ambulance driver said, "You see him, be sure and tell him he oughta go get a skull X-ray."

"You know what you'd find?" García said. "Shit for brains, that's what."

Reynaldo Flemm picked up an attractive young woman at a nightclub called Biscayne Baby in Coconut Grove. He took her to his room at the Grand Bay Hotel and asked her to wait while he ran the water in the Roman tub. Still insecure about his impugned physique, Reynaldo didn't want the young woman to see him naked in the bright light. He lowered himself into the bath, covered the vital areas with suds, double-checked himself in the mirrors, then called for the young woman to join him. She came in the bathroom, stripped, and climbed casually into the deep tub. When Reynaldo tickled her armpits with his toes, the young woman politely pushed his legs away.

"So, what do you do?" he asked.

"I told you, I'm a legal secretary."

"Oh, yeah." When Reynaldo got semi-blitzed on screwdrivers, his short-term memory tended to vapor-lock. "You probably recognize me," he said to the young woman.

"I told you already—no."

Reynaldo said, "Normally my hair's black. I colored it this way for a reason."

He had revived the Johnny LeTigre go-go dancer disguise for his confrontation with Dr. Rudy Graveline. He had dyed his hair brown and slicked it straight back with a wet comb. He looked like a Mediterranean sponge diver.

"Imagine me with black hair," he said to the legal secretary, who flicked a soap bubble off her nose and said no, she still wouldn't recognize him.

He said, "You get TV, right? I'm Reynaldo Flemm."

"Yeah?"

"From *In Your Face*."

"Oh, sure."

"Ever seen it?"

"No," said the secretary, "but I don't watch all that much television." She was trying to be nice. "I think I've seen your commercials," she said.

Flemm shrunk lower in the tub.

"Is it, like, a game show?" the woman asked.

"No, it's a news show. I'm an investigative reporter."

"Like that guy on *Sixty Minutes*?"

Reynaldo bowed his head. Feeling guilty, the secretary slid across the tub and climbed on his lap. She said, "Hey, I believe you."

"Thanks a bunch."

She felt a little sorry for him; he seemed so small and wounded among the bubbles. She said, "You certainly look like you could be on television."

"I *am* on fucking television. I've got my own show."

The woman said, "Okay, whatever."

"I could loan you a tape—you got a VCR?"

The secretary told him to hush. She put her lips to his ear and said, "Why don't we try it right here?"

Reynaldo half-heartedly slipped one arm around her waist and began kissing her breasts. They were perfectly lovely breasts, but Reynaldo's heart wasn't in it. After a few moments the woman said, "You're not really in the mood, huh?"

"I *was*."

"I'm sorry. Here, let me do your back."

Reynaldo's buttocks squeaked as he turned around in the tub so the secretary could scrub him. He watched her in the mirror; her hands felt wondrously soothing. Eventually he closed his eyes.

"There you go," she said, kneading his shoulder blades. "My great big TV star."

Reynaldo found he was getting excited again. He touched himself, underwater, just to make sure. He was smiling until he opened his eyes and saw something new in the mirror.

A man standing in the doorway. The man with the tarpon gaff.

"Sorry to interrupt," said Mick Stranahan.

The woman squealed and dove for a towel. Reynaldo Flemm groped for floating suds to cover his withering erection.

"I was looking for Christina," Stranahan said. He walked up to the Roman tub with the gaff held under one arm, like a riding crop. "She's not in her hotel room."

"How'd you find me?" Reynaldo's voice was reedy and taut, definitely not an anchorman's voice.

"Miami is not one of the world's all-time great hotel towns," Stranahan said. "Hotshot celebrities like you always end up in the Grove. But tell me: Why's Christina still registered out at Key Biscayne?"

Nervously the secretary said, "Who's Christina?"

Stranahan said: "Ray, I asked you a question." He poked the fish gaff under the suds and scraped the point across the bottom of the tub. The steel screeched ominously against the ceramic. Reynaldo Flemm drew up his knees and sloshed protectively into a corner.

"Chris doesn't know I'm here," he said. "I ditched her."

Stranahan told the legal secretary to get dressed and go home. He waited until she was gone from the bathroom before he spoke again.

"I checked Christina's room at the Sonesta. She hasn't been there for two days."

Reynaldo said, "What're you going to do to me?" He couldn't take his eyes off the tarpon gaff. Wrapping his arms around his knees, he said, "Don't hurt me."

"For Christ's sake."

"I mean it!"

"Are you crying?" Stranahan couldn't believe it—another dumb twit overreacting. "Just tell me about Christina. Her notebooks were still in the room, and so was her purse. Any ideas?"

"Uuunnngggh." The pink of Flemm's tongue showed between his front teeth. It was a cowering, poodle-like expression, amplified by trembling lips and liquid eyes.

"Settle down," said Stranahan. His head felt like it was full of wet cement. The Darvocets had barely put a ripple in the pain. What a shitty day.

He said, "You haven't seen her?"

Violently Reynaldo shook his head no.

They heard a door slam—the secretary, making tracks. Stranahan used the gaff to pull the plug in the Roman rub. Wordlessly he watched the soapy water drain, leaving Reynaldo bare and shriveled and flecked with suds.

"What's with the hairdo?" Stranahan asked.

Reynaldo composed himself and said, "For a show."

Stranahan tossed him a towel. He said, "I know what you're

doing. You're acing Christina out of the Barletta story. I saw your notes on the table."

Flemm reddened. It had taken him three hours to come up with ten questions for Dr. Rudy Graveline. Carefully he had printed the questions on a fresh legal pad, the way Christina Marks always did. He had spent the better part of the afternoon trying to memorize them before calling it quits and heading over to Biscayne Baby for some action.

"I don't care about your show," Stranahan said, "but I care about Christina."

"Me, too."

"It looked like somebody pushed his way into her hotel room. There was a handprint on the door."

Reynaldo said, "Well, it wasn't mine."

"Stand up," Stranahan told him.

Flemm wrapped himself into the towel as he stood up in the tub. Stranahan measured him with his eyes. "I believe you," he said. He went back to the living room to wait for Reynaldo to dry off and get dressed.

When Flemm came out, wearing an absurd muscle shirt and tight jeans, Stranahan said, "When are you going to see the doctor?"

"Soon," Reynaldo replied. Then, blustery: "None of your business." He felt so much tougher with a shirt on.

Stranahan said, "If you wait, you'll have a better story."

Reynaldo rolled his eyes—how many times had he heard that one! "No way," he said. The snide pomposity had returned to his voice.

"Ray, I'm only going to warn you once. If something's happened to Christina because of you, or if you do something that brings her any harm, you're done. And I'm not talking about your precious TV career."

Flemm said, "You sound pretty tough, long as you've got that hook."

Stranahan tossed the tarpon gaff at Reynaldo and said, "There—see if it works for you, too."

Reynaldo quickly dropped it on the carpet. As a rule he didn't fight with crazy people unless cameras were rolling. Otherwise, what was the point?

"I hope you find her," Reynaldo said.

Stranahan stood to leave. "You better pray that I do."

At the Gay Bidet, Freddie didn't even bother to get up from the desk to introduce himself. "I'm gonna tell you the same as I told that Cuban cop, which is nothing. I got a policy not to talk about employees, past or present."

Stranahan said, "But you know the man I'm asking about."

"Maybe, maybe not."

"Is he here?"

"Ditto," said Freddie. "Now get the fuck gone."

"Actually, I'm going to look around."

"Oh, you are?" Freddie said. "Like hell." He punched a black buzzer under the desk. The door opened and Stranahan momentarily was drowned by the vocal stylings of the Fabulous Foreskins, performing their opening set. The man who entered Freddie's office was a short muscular Oriental. He wore a pink Gay Bidet security T-shirt, stretched to the limit.

Freddie said, "Wong, please get this dog turd out of my sight."

Stranahan waved the tarpon gaff and its sinister glint caused Wong to hesitate. Disdainfully Freddie glowered at the bouncer and said, "What happened to all that kung-fu shit?"

Wong's chest began to swell.

Stranahan said, "I've had a lousy day, and I'm really in no mood. You like having a liquor license?"

Freddie said, "What're you talkin' about, do I like it?"

"Because you oughta enjoy it tonight, while you can. If you don't answer my questions, here's what happens to you and this toilet bowl of a nightclub: First thing tomorrow, six nasty bastards from Alcohol and Beverage come by and shut your ass down. Why? Because you lied when you got your liquor license, Freddie. You got a felony record in Illinois and Georgia, and you lied about that. Also, you've been serving to minors, big time. Also, your bartender just tried to sell me two grams of Peruvian. You want, I can keep going.''

Freddie said, ''Don't bother.'' He instructed Wong to get lost. When they were alone again, he said to Stranahan, ''That rap in Atlanta was no good.''

''So you're not a pimp. Excellent. The beverage guys will be very impressed, Freddie. Be sure to tell them you're not a pimp, no matter what the FBI computer says.''

''What the fuck is it you want?''

''Just tell me where I can find my tall, cool friend. The one with the face.''

Freddie said, ''Truth is, I don't know. He took off a couple days ago. Picked up his paycheck and quit. Tried to give me back the T-shirt, the dumb fuck—like somebody else would wear the damn thing. I told him to keep it for a souvenir.''

''Did he say where he was going?'' Stranahan asked.

''Nope. He had two broads with him, you figure it out.'' Freddie flashed a mouthful of nubby yellow teeth. ''Creature from the Black Lagoon, and still he gets more poon than me.''

''What did the women look like?' Stranahan asked.

''One, I couldn't tell. Her face was all busted up, cuts and bruises and Band-Aids. He must've beat the hell out of her for something. The other was a brunette, good-looking, on the thin side. Not humongous titties but nice pointy ones.''

Stranahan couldn't decide whether it was Freddie or the music that was aggravating his headache. ''The thin one—was she wearing blue jeans?''

Freddie said he didn't remember.

''Did they say anything?''

''Nope, not a word.''

''Did he have a gun?''

Freddie laughed again. ''Man, he doesn't need a gun. He has that whirly thing on his arm.'' Freddie told Stranahan what the thing was and how the man known as Chemo would use it.

''You're kidding.''

''Like hell,'' said Freddie. ''Guy was the best goddamn bouncer I ever had.''

Stranahan handed the club owner a fifty-dollar bill and the phone number of the bait shop at the marina. "This is in case he comes back. You call me before you call the cops."

Freddie pocketed the money. Reflectively he said: "Freak like that with two broads, man, it just proves there's no God."

"We'll see," said Stranahan.

28

Chemo's first instinct was to haul ass with the doctor's cash, which was more than he would see in a couple of Amish lifetimes. Forget about the Stranahan hit, just blow town. Maggie Gonzalez told him, don't be such a small-timer, remember what we've got here: A surgeon on the hook. A money machine, for God's sake. Maggie assured him that a million, even two million, was do-able. There wasn't anything that Rudy Graveline wouldn't give to save his medical license.

Goosing the Bonneville along Biscayne Boulevard, Chemo said, "What I've got now, I could get my face patched and still have enough for a year in Barbados. Maybe even get some real hair—those plug deals they stick in your scalp. I read where that's what they did to Elton John."

"Sure," Maggie said. "I know some doctors who do hair."

She was trying to play Chemo the way she played all her men, but it wasn't easy. Beyond his desire for a clear complexion, she had yet to discover what motivated him. While Chemo appreciated money, he hardly displayed the proper lust for it. As for sex, he expressed no interest whatsoever. Maggie chose to believe that he was deterred by her bruises and bandages; once the facelift had healed, her powers of seduction would return.

Then the only obstacle would be a logistical one: What would you do with the Weed Whacker under the sheets?

As Chemo pulled up to the Holiday Inn at 125th Street, Maggie said, "If it would make you feel better, we could move to a nicer hotel."

"What would make me feel better," Chemo said, "is for you to give me the keys to the suitcase." He turned off the ignition and held out his right hand.

Maggie said, "You think I'm dumb enough to try and rip you off?"

"Yes," said Chemo, reaching for her purse. "Plenty dumb enough."

Christina Marks heard the door open and prayed it was the maid. It wasn't.

The lights came on and Chemo loomed incuriously over the bed. He checked the knots at Christina's wrists and ankles, while Maggie stalked into the bathroom and slammed the door.

After Chemo removed the towel from her mouth, Christina said, "What's the matter with her?"

"She thinks I don't trust her. She's right."

"For what it's worth," Christina said, "she already conned my boss out of a bundle."

"I'll keep that in mind." Chemo sat on the corner of the bed, counting the cash that he had taken from Dr. Rudy Graveline's pockets. Counting wasn't easy with only one hand. Christina watched inquisitively. After he was finished, Chemo put five thousand in the suitcase with the rest of the haul; forty-two hundred went down the heels of his boots. He slid the suitcase under the bed.

"How original," Christina said.

"Shut up."

"Could you untie me, please? I have to pee."

"Jesus H. Christ."

"You want me to wet the bed?" she said. "Ruin all your cash?"

Chemo got Maggie out of the bathroom and made her help

undo the knots. They had bound Christina to the bed frame with nylon clothesline. Once freed, she rubbed her wrists and sat up stiffly.

"Go do your business," Chemo said. Then, to Maggie: "Stay with her."

Christina said, "I can't pee with somebody watching."

"What?"

"She's right," Maggie said. "I'm the same way. I'll just wait outside the door."

"No, do what I told you," Chemo said.

"There's no window in there," Christina said. "What'm I going to do, escape down the toilet?"

When she came out of the bathroom, Chemo was standing by the door. He led her back to the bed, made her lie down, then tied her again—another tedious chore, one-handed.

"No gag this time," Christina requested. "I promise not to scream."

"But you'll talk," said Chemo. "That's even worse."

Since the morning he had kidnapped her from the hotel on Key Biscayne, Chemo had said practically nothing to Christina Marks. Nor had he menaced or abused her in any sense—it was as if he knew that the mere sight of him, close up, was daunting enough. Christina had spied the butt of a revolver in Chemo's baggy pants pocket, but he had never pulled it; this was a big improvement over the two previous encounters, when he had nearly shot her.

She said, "I just want to know why you're doing this, what exactly you want."

He acted as if he never heard her. Maggie handed Christina a small cup of Pepsi.

"Don't let her drink too much," Chemo cautioned. "She'll be going to the head all night."

He turned on the television set and grimaced: pro basketball—the Lakers and the Pistons. Chemo hated basketball. At six foot nine, he had spent his entire adulthood explaining to rude strangers that no, he didn't play pro basketball. Once a myopic Celtics fan had mistaken him for Kevin McHale and demanded an autograph; Chemo had savagely bitten the man on the shoulder, like a horse.

He began switching channels until he found an old *Miami Vice*. He turned up the volume and scooted his chair closer to the tube. He envied Don Johnson's three-day stubble; it looked rugged and manly. Chemo himself had not shaved, for obvious reasons, since the electrolysis accident.

He turned to Maggie and asked, "Can they do hair plugs on your chin, too?"

"Oh, I'm sure," she said, though in fact she had never heard of such a procedure.

Pinned to the bed like a butterfly, Christina said, "Before long, somebody's going to be looking for me."

Chemo snorted. "That's the general idea." Didn't these women ever shut up? Didn't they appreciate his potential for violence?

Maggie sat next to Christina and said, "We need to get a message to your boyfriend."

"Who—Stranahan? He's not my boyfriend."

"Still, I doubt if he wants to see you get hurt."

Christina appraised herself—strapped to a bed, squirming in her underwear—and imagined what Reynaldo Flemm would say if he came crashing through the door. For once she'd be happy to see the stupid sonofabitch, but she knew there was no possibility of such a rescue. If Mick couldn't find her, Ray didn't have a prayer.

"If it's that videotape you're after, I don't know where it is—"

"But surely your boyfriend does," said Maggie.

Chemo pointed at the television. "Hey, lookie there!" On the screen, Detective Sonny Crockett was chasing a drug smuggler through Stiltsville in a speedboat. This was the first time Christina had seen Chemo smile. It was a harrowing experience.

Maggie said, "So how do you get in touch with him?"

"Mick? I don't know. There's no phone out there. Anytime I wanted to see him, I rented a boat."

A commercial came on the television, and Chemo turned to the women. "Jesus, I don't want to go back to that house—enough of that shit. I want him to come see me. And he will, soon as he knows I've got you."

In her most lovelorn voice, Christina said to Maggie, "I really don't think Mick cares one way or the other."

"You better hope he does," said Chemo. He pressed the towel firmly into Christina's mouth and turned back to watch the rest of the show.

On the morning of February eighteenth, the last day of Kipper Garth's law career, he filed a motion with the Circuit Court of Dade County in the case of Nordstrom v. Graveline, Whispering Palms, *et al*.

The motion requested an emergency court order freezing all the assets of Dr. Rudy Graveline, including bank accounts, certificates of deposit, stock portfolios, municipal bonds, Keogh funds, Individual Retirement Accounts, and real estate holdings. Submitted to the judge with Kipper Garth's motion was an affidavit from the Beachcomber Travel Agency stating that, on the previous day, one Rudolph Graveline had purchased two first-class airplane tickets to San José, Costa Rica. In the plea (composed entirely by Mick Stranahan and one of the paralegals), Kipper Garth asserted that it was Dr. Graveline's intention to flee the United States permanently.

Normally, a request involving a defendant's assets would have resulted in a full-blown hearing and, most likely, a denial of the motion. But Kipper Garth's position (and thus the Nordstroms') was buttressed by a discreet phone call from Mick Stranahan to the judge, whom Stranahan had known since his days as a young prosecutor in the DUI division. After a brief reminiscence, Stranahan told the judge the true reason for his call: that Dr. Rudy Graveline was a prime suspect in an unsolved four-year-old abduction case that might or might not be a homicide. Stranahan assured his friend that, rather than face the court, the surgeon would take his dough and make a run for it.

The judge granted the emergency order shortly after nine

o'clock in the morning. Kipper Garth was astonished at his own success; he never dreamed litigation could be so damn easy. He fantasized a day when he could get out of the referral racket altogether, when he would be known and revered throughout Miami as a master trial attorney. Kipper Garth liked the bill-boards, though. However high he might soar among the eagles of Brickell Avenue, the billboards definitely had to stay. . . .

At ten forty-five, Rudy Graveline arrived at his bank in Bal Harbour and asked to make a wire transfer of $250,000 from his personal account to a new account in Panama. He also requested $60,000 in U.S. currency and traveler's cheques. The young bank officer who was assisting Rudy Graveline left his office for several minutes. When he returned, one of the bank's vice presidents stood solemnly at his side.

Rudy took the news badly.

First he wept, which was merely embarrassing. Then he became enraged and hysterical and, finally, incoherent. He staggered, keening, into the bank lobby, at which point two enormous security guards were summoned to escort the surgeon from the premises.

By the time they deposited Rudy in the parking lot, he had settled himself and stopped crying.

Until one of the bank guards had pointed at the fender of the car and said, "The hell happened to your Jag, brother?"

Perhaps it was the euphoria of the legal triumph, or perhaps it was simple prurient curiosity that impelled Kipper Garth to drop by the Nordstrom household during his lunch hour. The address was in Morningside, a pleasant old neighborhood of bleached stucco houses located a few blocks off the seediest stretch of Biscayne Boulevard.

Marie Nordstrom was surprised to see Kipper Garth, but she welcomed him warmly at the door, led him to the Florida room, and offered him a cup of coffee. She wore electric-blue Lycra body tights, and her ash-blond hair was pulled back in a girlish ponytail. Kipper couldn't take his eyes off the subject of litigation, her breasts. The exercise outfit left nothing to the imagination; these were the merriest-looking breasts that Kipper Garth had ever seen. It was difficult to think of them as weapons.

"John's not here," Mrs. Nordstrom said. "He got a job interview over at the jai-alai fronton. You take cream?"

Kipper Garth took cream. Mrs. Nordstrom placed the coffee pot on a glass tray. Kipper Garth made space for her on the sofa, but she moved to a love seat, facing him from across the coffee table.

Kipper Garth said, "I just wanted to bring you up to date on the malpractice case." Matter-of-factly he told Mrs. Nordstrom about the emergency court order to freeze Dr. Graveline's assets.

"What exactly does that mean?"

"It means his money won't be going anywhere, even if he does."

Mrs. Nordstrom was not receiving the news as exuberantly as Kipper Garth had hoped; apparently she could not appreciate the difficulty of what he had done.

"John and I were talking just last night," she said. "The idea of going to trial . . . I don't know, Mr. Garth. This has been so embarrassing for both of us."

"We're in it now, Mrs. Nordstrom. There's no turning back." Kipper Garth tried to suppress the exasperation in his voice: Here Rudy Graveline was on the ropes and suddenly the plaintiffs want to back out.

"Maybe the doctor would be willing to settle the case," ventured Mrs. Nordstrom.

Kipper Garth put down the coffee cup with a clack and folded his arms. "Oh, I'm sure he would. I'm sure he'd be delighted to settle. That's exactly why we won't hear of it. Not yet."

"But John says—"

"Trust me," the lawyer said. He paused and lowered his eyes. "Forgive me for saying so, Mrs. Nordstrom, but settling this case would be very selfish on your part."

She looked startled at the word.

Kipper Garth went on: "Think of all the patients this man has harmed. This *alleged* surgeon. If we don't stop him, nobody will. If you settle the case, Mrs. Nordstrom, the butchery will continue. You and your husband will be wealthy, yes, but Rudy Graveline's butchery will continue. At his instruction, the court file will be sealed and his reputation preserved. Again. Is that really what you want?''

Kipper Garth had listened intently to his own words, and was impressed by what he had heard; he was getting damn good at oratory.

A few awkward moments passed and Mrs. Nordstrom said, ''They've got an opening for a coach over at the jai-alai. John used to play in college, he was terrific. He even went to Spain one summer and trained with the Basques.''

Kipper Garth had never heard of a Scandinavian jai-alai coach, but his knowledge of the sport was limited. Ooozing sincerity, he told Mrs. Nordstrom that he hoped her husband got the job.

She said, ''Thing is, he can't tell anybody about his eye. They'd never hire him.''

''Why not?''

''Too dangerous,'' Mrs. Nordstrom said. ''The ball they use is like a rock. A *pelota* it's called. John says it goes like a hundred and sixty miles an hour off those walls.''

Kipper Garth finished his coffee. ''I've never been to a jai-alai game.'' He hoped she would take the hint and change the conversation.

''If you're playing, it helps to have two good eyes,'' Mrs. Nordstrom explained. ''For depth perception.''

''I think I understand.''

''John says they won't let him coach if they find out about the accident.''

Now Kipper Garth got the picture. ''That's why you want to settle the lawsuit, isn't it?''

Mrs. Nordstrom said yes, they were worried about publicity. ''John says the papers and TV will go crazy with a story like this.''

Kipper thought: John is absolutely right.

''But you're a victim, Mrs. Nordstrom. You have the right to be compensated for this terrible event in your life. It says so in the Constitution.''

''John says they let cameras in the courtrooms. Is that true?''

''Yes, but let's not get carried away—''

''If it were your wife, would you want the whole world to see her tits on the six o'clock news?'' Her tone was prideful and indignant.

''I'll speak to the judge, Mrs. Nordstrom. Please don't be upset. I know you've been through hell already.'' But Kipper Garth was excited by the idea of TV cameras in the courtroom— it would be better than billboards!

Marie Nordstrom was trying not to cry and doing stolidly. She said, ''I blame that damn Reagan. He hadn't busted up the union, John'd still have his job in the flight tower.''

Kipper Garth said, ''Leave it to me and the two of you will be set for life. John won't need a job.''

Mrs. Nordstrom wistfully gazed at the two sturdy, silicon-enhanced, Lycra-covered cones on her chest. ''They say contractures are easy to fix, but I don't know.''

Kipper Garth circled the coffee table and joined her on the love seat. He put an unpracticed arm around her shoulders. ''For what it's worth,'' he said, ''they *look* spectacular.''

''Thank you,'' she whispered, ''but you just don't know— how could you?''

Kipper Garth removed the silk handkerchief from his breast pocket and gave it to Mrs. Nordstrom, who sounded like the SS Norway when she blew her nose.

''Know what I think?'' said Kipper Garth. ''I think you should let me feel them.''

Mrs. Nordstrom straightened and gave a stern sniffle.

The lawyer said: ''The only way I can begin to understand, the only way I can convey the magnitude of this tragedy to a jury, is if I can experience it myself.''

''Wait a minute—you want to feel my boobs?''

''I'm your lawyer, Mrs. Nordstrom.''

She eyed him doubtfully.

"If it were a burn case, I'd have to see the scar. Dismemberment, paraplegia, same goes."

"Looking is one thing, Mr. Garth. Touching is something else."

"With all respect, Mrs. Nordstrom, your husband is going to make a lousy witness in this case. He's going to come across as a selfish prick. Remember what he said that day in my office? Bocci balls, Mrs. Nordstrom. He said your breasts were as hard as bocci balls. This is not the testimony of a sensitive, caring spouse."

She said, "You'd be bitter, too, if it was your eye that got poked out."

"Granted. But let me try to come up with a more gentle description of your condition. Please, Mrs. Nordstrom."

"All right, but I won't take my clothes off."

"Of course not!"

She slid a little closer on the love seat. "Give me your hands," she said. "There you go."

"Wow," said Kipper Garth.

"What'd I tell you?"

"I had no idea."

"You can let go now," Mrs. Nordstrom said.

"Just a second."

But one second turned into ten seconds, and ten seconds turned into thirty, which was plenty of time for John Nordstrom to enter the house and size up the scene. Without a word he loaded up the wicker *cesta* and hurled a goatskin jai-alai ball at the slimy lawyer who was feeling up his wife. The first shot sailed wide to the left and shattered a jalousie window. The second shot dimpled the arm of the love seat with a flat *thunk*. It was then that Kipper Garth released his grip on Marie Nordstrom's astoundingly stalwart breasts and made a vain break for the back door. Whether the lawyer fully comprehended his ethical crisis or fled on sheer animal instinct would never be known. John Nordstrom's third and final jai-alai shot struck the occipital seam of Kipper Garth's skull. He was unconscious by the time his silvery head smacked the floor.

"Ha!" Nordstrom exclaimed.

"I take it you got the job," said his wife.

Willie the cameraman said they had two ways to go: they could crash the place or sneak one in.

Reynaldo Flemmm said: "Crash it."

"Think of the timing," Willie said. "The timing's got to be flawless. We've never tried anything like this." Willie was leaning toward trying a hidden camera.

Reynaldo said: "Crash it. There's no security, it's a goddamn medical clinic. Who's gonna stop you, the nurse?"

Willie said he didn't like the plan; too many holes. "What if the guy makes a run for it? What if he calls the police?"

Reynaldo said: "Where's he gonna go, Willie? That's the beauty of this thing. The sonofabitch can't run away, and he knows it. Not with the tape rolling. They got laws."

"Jesus," Willie said, "I don't like it. We've got to have a signal, you and me."

"Don't worry," Reynaldo said, "we'll have a signal."

"But what about the interview?" Willie asked. It was another way of bringing up Christina Marks.

"I wrote my own questions," Reynaldo said sharply. "Ball busters, too. You just wait."

"Okay," Willie said. "I'll be ready."

"Seven sharp," Reynaldo said. "I can't believe you're so nervous—this isn't the Crips and Bloods, man, it's a candyass doctor. He'll go to pieces, I guarantee it. True confessions, you just wait."

"Seven sharp," Willie said. "See you then."

After the cameraman had gone, Reynaldo Flemm called the Whispering Palms Spa and Surgery Center to confirm the appointment for Johnny LeTigre. To his surprise, the secretary put him through directly to Dr. Graveline.

"We still on for tomorrow morning?"

"Certainly," the surgeon said. He sounded distracted, subdued. "Remember: Nothing to eat or drink after midnight."

"Right."

"I thought we'd start with the rhinoplasty and go on to the liposuction."

"Fine by me," said Reynaldo Flemm. That's exactly how he had planned it, the nose job first.

"Mr. LeTigre, I had a question regarding the fee . . ."

"Fifteen thousand is what we agreed on."

"Correct," said Rudy Graveline, "but I just wanted to make sure—you said something about cash?"

"Yeah, that's right. I got cash."

"And you'll have it with you tomorrow?"

"You bet." Reynaldo couldn't believe this jerk. Probably grosses two million a year, and here he is drooling over a lousy fifteen grand. It was true what they said about doctors being such cheap bastards.

"Anything else I need to remember?"

"Just take plenty of fluids," Rudy said mechanically, "but nothing after midnight."

"I'll be a good boy," Reynaldo Flemm promised. "See you tomorrow."

29

The wind kicked up overnight, whistled through the planks of the house, slapped the shutters against the walls. Mick Stranahan climbed naked to the roof and lay down with the shotgun at his right side. The bay was noisy and black, hissing through the pilings beneath the house. Above, the clouds rolled past in churning gray clots, celestial dust devils tumbling across a low sky. As always, Stranahan lay facing away from the city, where the halogen crime lights stained an otherwise lovely horizon.

On nights such as this, Stranahan regarded the city as a malignancy and its sickly orange aura as a vast misty bubble of pustular gas. The downtown skyline, which had seemed to sprout overnight in a burst of civic priapism, struck Stranahan as a crass but impressive prop, an elaborate movie set. Half the new Miami skyscrapers had been built with coke money and existed largely as an inside joke, a mirage to please the banks and the Internal Revenue Service and the chamber of commerce. Everyone liked to say that the skyline was a monument to local prosperity, but Stranahan recognized it as a tribute to the anonymous genius of Latin American money launderers. In any case, it was nothing he wished to contemplate from the top of his stilt house. Nor was the view south of downtown any kinder, a throbbing congealment from Coconut Grove to the Gables to South Miami and beyond. Looking westward on a clearer evening, Stranahan would have fixed on the newest coastal landmark: a sheer ten-story cliff of refuse known as Mount Trashmore. Having run out of rural locations in which to conceal its waste, Dade County had erected a towering fetid landfill along the shore of Biscayne Bay. Stranahan could not decide which sight was more offensive, the city skyline or the mountain of garbage. The turkey buzzards, equally ambivalent, commuted regularly from one site to the other.

Stranahan was always grateful for a clean ocean breeze. He sprawled on the eastern slope of the roof, facing the Atlantic. A DC-10 took off from Miami International and passed over Stiltsville, rattling the windmill on Stranahan's house. He wondered what it would be like to wake up and find the city vaporized, the skies clear and silent, the shoreline lush and virginal! He would have loved to live here at the turn of the century, when nature owned the upper hand.

The cool wind tickled the hair on his chest and legs. Stranahan tasted salt on his lips and closed his eyes. One of his ex-wives, he couldn't remember which, had told him he ought to move to Alaska and become a hermit. You're such an old grump, she had said, not even the grizzly bears'd put up with you. Now Stranahan recalled which wife had said this: Donna, his second.

She had eventually grown tired of all his negativity. Every big city has crime, she had said. Every big city has corruption. Look at New York, she had said. Look at Chicago. Those are great goddamn cities, Mick, you gotta admit. Like so many cocktail waitresses, Donna steadfastly refused to give up on humanity. She believed that the good people of the world outnumbered the bad, and she got the tips to prove it. After the divorce, she had enrolled in night school and earned her Florida real estate license; Stranahan had heard she'd moved to Jacksonville and was going great guns in the waterfront condo market. Bleakly it occurred to him that all his former wives (even Chloe, who had nailed a CPA for a husband) had gone on to greater achievements after the divorce. It was as if being married to Stranahan had made each of them realize how much of the real world they were missing.

He thought of Christina Marks. How did he get mixed up with such a serious woman? Unlike the others he had loved and married, Christina avidly pursued that which was evil and squalid and polluted. Her job was to expose it. There was not a wisp of true innocence about her, not a trace of cheery waitress-type optimism . . . yet something powerful attracted him. Maybe because she slogged through the same moral swamps. Crooked cops, crooked lawyers, crooked doctors, crooked ex-wives, even crooked tree trimmers—these were the spawn of the city bog.

Stranahan's fingers found the stock of the shotgun, and he moved it closer. Soon he fell asleep, and he dreamed that Victoria Barletta was alive. He dreamed that he met her one night in the Rathskellar on the University of Miami campus. She was working behind the bar, wearing a pink butterfly bandage across the bridge of her nose. Stranahan ordered a beer and a cheeseburger medium, and asked her if she wanted to get married. She said sure.

The boat woke him up. It was a familiar yellow skiff with a big outboard. Stranahan saw it a mile away, trimmed up, running the flats. He smiled—the bonefish guide, his friend. With all the low dirty clouds it was difficult to estimate the time, but Stranahan figured the sun had been up no more than two hours. He dropped from the roof, stowed the Remington inside the house, and pulled on a pair of jeans so as not to startle the guide's customers, who were quite a pair. The man was sixty-five, maybe older, obese and gray, with skin like rice parchment; the woman was twenty-five tops, tall, dark blond, wearing bright coral lip gloss and a gold choker necklace.

The guide climbed up to the stilt house and said, "Mick, take a good look. Fucking lipstick on a day like this."

From the skiff, tied up below, Stranahan could hear the couple arguing about the weather. The woman wanted to go back, since there wasn't any sun for a decent tan. The old man said no, he'd paid his money and by God they would fish.

Stranahan said to his friend, "You've got the patience of Job."

The guide shook his head. "A killer mortgage is what I've got. Here, this is for you."

It was an envelope with Stranahan's name printed in block letters on the outside. "Woman with two black eyes told me to give it to you," the guide said. "Cuban girl, not bad looking, either. She offered me a hundred bucks."

"Hope you took it."

"I held out for two," the guide said.

Stranahan folded the envelope in half and tucked it in the back pocket of his jeans.

The guide said, "You in some trouble?"

"Just business."

"Mick, you don't have a business."

Stranahan grinned darkly. "True enough." He knew what his friend was thinking: Single guy, cozy house on the water, a good boat for fishing, a monthly disability check from the state—how could anybody fuck up a sweet deal like that?

"I heard some asshole shot hell out of the place."

"Yeah." Stranahan pointed to a sheet of fresh plywood on the door. The plywood covered two of Chemo's bullet holes. "I've got to get some red paint," Stranahan said.

The guide said, "Forget the house, what about your shoulder?"

"It's fine," Stranahan said.

"Don't worry, it was Luis who told me."

"No problem. You want some coffee?"

"Naw." The bonefish guide jerked a thumb in the direction of his skiff. "This old fart, he's on the board of some steel company up north. That's his secretary."

"God bless him."

The guide said, "Last time they went fishing, I swear, she strips off the bottom of her bathing suit. Not the top, Mick, the bottom part. All day long, flashing her bush in my face. Said she was trying to bleach out her hair. Here I'm poling like a maniac after these goddamn fish, and she's turning somersaults in front of the boat, trying to keep her bush in the sun."

Stranahan said, "I don't know how you put up with it."

"So today there's no sunshine and of course she's throwin' a fit. Meanwhile the old fart says all he wants is a world-record bonefish on fly. That's all. Mick, I'm too old for this shit." The guide pulled on his cap so tightly that it crimped the tops of his ears. Lugubriously he descended the stairs to the dock.

"Good luck," Stranahan said. Under the circumstances, it sounded ridiculous.

The guide untied the yellow skiff and hopped in. Before starting the engine, he looked up at Stranahan and said, "I'll be out here tomorrow, even if the weather's bad. The next day, too."

Stranahan nodded; it was good to know. "Thanks, Captain," he said.

After the skiff was gone, Stranahan returned to the top of the house and took the envelope out of his pocket. He opened it calmly because he knew what it was and who it was from. He'd been waiting for it.

The message said: "We've got your girlfriend. No cops!"

And it gave a telephone number.

Mick Stranahan memorized the number, crumpled the paper, and tossed it off the roof into the milky waves. "Somebody's been watching too much television," he said.

* * *

That afternoon, Mick Stranahan received another disturbing message. It was delivered by Luis Córdova, the young marine patrol officer. He gave Stranahan a lift by boat from Stiltsville to the Crandon Marina, where Stranahan got a cab to his sister Kate's house in Gables-by-the-Sea.

Sergeant Al García was fidgeting on the front terrace. Over his J. C. Penney suit he was wearing what appeared to be an authentic London Fog trenchcoat. Stranahan knew that García was upset because he was smoking those damn Camels again. Even before Stranahan could finish paying the cabbie, García was charging down the driveway, blue smoke streaming from his nostrils like one of those cartoon bulls.

"So," the detective said, "Luis fill you in?"

Stranahan said yes, he knew that Kipper Garth had been gravely injured in a domestic dispute.

García blocked his path up the drive. "By a client, Mick. Imagine that."

"I didn't know the client, Al."

"Name of Nordstrom, John Nordstrom." García was working the sodden nub of the Camel the same way he worked the cigars, from one side of his mouth to the other. Stranahan found it extremely distracting.

"According to the wife," García said, "the assailant returned home unexpectedly and found your brother-in-law, the almost deceased—"

"Thank you, Al."

"—found the almost deceased fondling his wife. Whereupon, the assailant attempted to strike the almost deceased at least three times with *pelotas*. That's a jai-alai ball, Mick. The third shot struck your brother-in-law at the base of the skull, rendering him unconscious."

"The dumb shit. How's Kate?"

"Puzzled," García said. "But then, aren't we all?"

"I want to see her." Stranahan sidestepped the detective and made for the front door. His sister was standing by the bay window of the Florida room and staring out at Kipper Garth's sailboat, the *Pain-and-Suffering*, which was rocking placidly at the dock behind the house. Stranahan gave Kate a hug and kissed her on the forehead.

She sniffled and said, "Did they tell you?"

"Yes, Kate."

"That he was groping a client—did they tell you?"

Stranahan said, "That's the woman's story."

Kate gave a bitter chuckle. "And you don't believe it? Come on, Mick, *I* believe it. Kipper was a pig, let's face it. You were right, I was wrong."

Stranahan didn't know what to say. "He had some good qualities." Jesus, how stupid. "*Has* some good qualities, I mean."

"The doctors say it's fifty-fifty, but I'm ready for the worst. Kipper's not a fighter."

"He might surprise you," Stranahan said without conviction.

"Mick, just so you know—I was aware of what he was up to. Some of the excuses, God, you should have heard them. Late nights, weekends, trips to God knows where. I pretended to believe him because . . . because I liked this life, Mick. The house . . . this great yard. I mean, it sounds selfish, but it felt *good* here. Safe. This is a wonderful neighborhood."

"Katie, I'm sorry."

"Neighborhoods like this are hard to find, Mick. You know, we've only been burglarized twice in four years. That's not bad for Miami."

"Not at all," Stranahan said.

"See, I had to weigh these things every time I thought about leaving." Kate put a hand on his arm and said, "You knew about all his fooling around."

"Not everything."

"Thanks for not mentioning it." She was sincere.

Stranahan felt like a complete shit, which he was. "This is my fault," he said. "I told Kipper to take this case. I *made* him take it."

"How?" she asked. "And why?"

"Whatever you're thinking, it's even worse. I can't tell you all the details, Kate, because there's going to be trouble and I want you clear of it. But you ought to know that I'm the one who got Kipper involved."

"But you're not the one who played grab-the-tittie with your client. *He* did." She turned back to the big window and folded her arms. "It's so . . . tacky."

"Yes," Stranahan agreed. "Tacky's the word."

When he came out of the house, García was waiting.

"Wasn't that courteous of me, not barging in and making a big Cuban scene in front of your sister?"

"Al, you're a fucking prince among men."

"Know why I'm wearing this trenchcoat? It's brand-new, by the way. I hadda go to another funeral: Bobby Pepsical, the county commissioner. Dropped dead in confession."

"Good place for it. He was a stone crook."

"Course he was, Mick. But I got a feeling he didn't get his penance."

"Why not?"

"Because there wasn't a priest in there. Bobby's confessing to an empty closet—that's pretty weird, huh? Anyway, they make a bunch of us go to the fucking funeral, because of who he was. That's why I've got the new coat. It was raining."

Stranahan said, "How was it? Did they screw him into the ground? That's about how crooked he was."

"I know but, Christ, have some respect for the dead." García rubbed his temples like he was massaging a cramp. "See, this is what's got me so agitated, Mick. Ever since I got into this thing with you and the doctor, so many people are dying. Dying weird, too. There's your ex, and Murdock and Salazar—another funeral! Then the business with that goddamn homicidal tree man. So after all that, here I am standing in the rain, watching them plant some scuzzbucket politician who croaks on his knees in an empty confessional, and my frigging beeper goes off. Lieutenant says some big-shot lawyer got beaned by a jai-alai ball and could be a homicide any second. A jai-alai ball! On top of which the big-shot lawyer turns out to be *your* brother-in-law. It's like a nightmare of weirdness!"

"It's been a bad month," Stranahan conceded.

"Yeah, it sure has. So what about these Nordstroms?"

"I didn't know them, I told you."

García lit up another cigarette and Stranahan made a face. "Know why I'm smoking these things? Because I'm agitated. I get agitated whenever I get jerked around, and I hate to waste a good cigar on agitation."

Stranahan said, "Can you please not blow it in my face? That's all I ask."

The detective took the cigarette out of his mouth and held it behind his back. "There, you happy? Now help me out, Mick. The assailant's wife, she says Kipper Garth phones her out of the blue and asks if she wants to sue—guess who—Rudy Graveline! Since he's the quack who gave her the encapsulated whatchamacallits."

"If that's what she says, fine."

"But lawyers aren't supposed to solicit."

"Al, this is Miami."

García took a quick drag and hid the Camel again. "My theory is you somehow got your sleazy, almost-deceased brother-in-law to sue Graveline, just to bust his balls. Shake things up. Maybe flush the giant Mr. Blondell Tatum out of his fugitive gutter. I don't expect you to open up your heart, Mick, but just tell me this: Did it work? Because if it did, you're a fucking genius and I apologize for all the shitty things I've been saying about you in my sleep."

"Did what work?"

García grinned venomously. "I thought we were buddies."

"Al, I'm not going to shut you out," Stranahan said. "For God's sake, you saved my life."

"Aw, shucks, you remembered."

Stranahan said: "Which one do you want, Al? The freaky hit man or the doctor?"

"Both."

"No, I'm sorry."

"Hey, I could arrest your ass right now. Obstruction, tampering, I'd think of something."

"And I'd be out in an hour."

García's jaw tightened for a moment and he turned away, stewing. When he turned back, he seemed more amused than angry.

"The problem is, Mick, you're too smart. You know the system too damn well. You know there's only so much I can get away with."

"Believe me, we're on the same side."

"I know, *chico*, that's what scares me."

"So, which of these bastards do you want for yourself—the surgeon or the geek?"

"Don't rush me, Mick."

30

Early on the morning of February nineteenth, Reynaldo Flemm, the famous Shock Television journalist, arrived at the Whispering Palms Spa and Surgery Center for the most sensational interview of his sensational career. A sleepy receptionist collected the $15,000 cash and counted it twice; if she was surprised by the size of the surgeon's fee, she didn't show it. The receptionist handed Reynaldo Flemm two photocopied consent forms, one for a rhinoplasty and one for a suction-assisted lipectomy. Reynaldo skimmed the paperwork and extravagantly signed as "Johnny LeTigre."

Then he sat down to wait for his moment. On a buff-colored wall hung a laminated carving of one of Rudy Graveline's pet sayings: TO IMPROVE ONE'S SELF, IMPROVE ONE'S FACE. That wasn't Reynaldo's favorite Rudyism. His favorite was framed in quilted Norman Rockwell–style letters above the water fountain:

VANITY IS BEAUTIFUL. That's the one Reynaldo had told Willie about. Be sure to get a quick shot on your way in, he had told him. What for? Willie had asked. For the irony, Reynaldo Flemm had exclaimed. For the irony! Reynaldo was proud of himself for thinking up that camera shot; usually Christina Marks was in charge of finding irony.

Soon an indifferent young nurse summoned Reynaldo to a chilly examining room and instructed him to empty his bladder, a tedious endeavor that took fifteen minutes and produced scarcely an ounce. Reynaldo Flemm was a very nervous man. In his professional life he had been beaten by Teamsters, goosed by white supremacists, clubbed by Mafia torpedoes, pistol-whipped by Bandito bikers, and kicked in the groin by the Pro-Life Posse. But he had never undergone surgery. Not even a wart removal.

Flemm stiffly removed his clothes and pulled off his hightop Air Jordans. He changed into a baby-blue paper gown that hung to his knees. The nurse gave him a silly paper cap to cover his silly dyed hair, and paper shoe covers for his bare feet.

A nurse anesthetist came out of nowhere, brusquely flipped up the tail of Reynaldo's gown and stuck a needle in his hip. The hypodermic contained a drug called Robinul, which dries up the mouth by inhibiting oral secretions. Next the nurse seized Reynaldo's left arm, swabbed it, and stuck it cleanly with an I.V. needle that dripped into his veins a lactated solution of five percent dextrose and, later, assorted powerful sedatives.

The anesthetist then led Reynaldo Flemm and his I.V. apparatus into Suite F, one of four ultramodern surgical theaters at Whispering Palms. She asked him to lie on his back and, as he stretched out on the icy steel, Reynaldo frantically tried to remember the ten searing questions he had prepared for the ambush of Dr. Rudy Graveline.

One, did you kill Victoria Barletta on March 12, 1986?

Two, why would one of your former nurses say that you did?

Three, isn't it true that you've repeatedly gotten into trouble for careless and incompetent surgery?

Four, how do you explain . . .

Explain?

Explain this strap on my fucking legs!

"Please quiet down, Mr. LeTigre."

And my arms! What've you done to my arms! I can't move my goddamn arms!

"Try to relax. Think pleasant thoughts."

Wait, wait, wait, wait, wait!

"You ought to be feeling a little drowsy."

This is wrong. This is not right. I read up on this. I got a fucking pamphlet. You're supposed to tape my eyes, not my arms. What are you smiling at, you dumb twat? Lemme talk to the doctor! Where's the doctor? Jesus Christ, that's cold. What are you *doing* down there!

"Good morning, Mr. LeTigre."

Doctor, thank God you're here! Listen good now: These Nazi nurse bitches are making a terrible mistake. I don't wanna general, I wanna a local. Just pull the I.V., okay? I'll be fine, just pull the tubes before I pass out.

"John, we're having a little trouble understanding you."

No shit, Sherlock, my tongue's so dry you could light a match on it. Please yank the needles, I can't think with these damn needles. And make 'em quit fooling around with me down there. Christ, it's cold! What're they doing!

"I assumed they told you—there's been a change of plans. I've decided to do the lipectomy first, then the rhinoplasty. It'll be easier that way."

No no no, you gotta do the nose first. Do the fucking nose.

"You should try to relax, John. Here, hold still, we're going to give you another injection."

No no no no no no no.

"That didn't hurt a bit, did it?"

I wanna ask I gotta ask right now . . .

"Go ahead, push the Sublimaze."

Did you kill . . . ?

"What did he say?"

Is it true you killed . . . ?

"This guy looks sort of familiar."

Did you . . . kill Victoria . . . Principal?

"Victoria Principal! Boy, is he whacked out."

Well did you?

"Where's the mask? Start the Forane. Give him the mask."

Willie hadn't slept much, fretting about Reynaldo's big plan. He had tried to call Christina Marks in New York, but the office said she was in Miami. But where? Reynaldo's plan was the craziest thing Willie had ever heard, starting with the signal. Willie needed a signal to know when to come crashing into the operating room with the camera. The best that Reynaldo could come up with was a scream. Willie would be in the waiting room, Reynaldo would scream.

"What exactly will you scream?" Willie had asked.

"I'll scream: WILLIE!"

Willie thought Reynaldo was joking. He wasn't.

"What about the other patients in the waiting room? I mean, here I am with a TV camera and a sound pack—what do I tell these people?"

"Tell 'em you're from PBS," Reynaldo had said. "Nobody hassles PBS."

The shot that Reynaldo Flemm most fervently wanted was this: Himself prone, prepped, cloaked in blue, preferably in the early stages of rhinoplasty and preferably bloody. That was the good thing about a nose job, you could ask for a local. Most plastic surgeons want their rhinoplasty patients to be all the way zonked, but you could get it done with a local and a mild I.V. if you could stand a little pain. Reynaldo Flemm had no doubt he could stand it.

Willie would burst like a fullback into the operating room, tape rolling, toss the baton mike to Reynaldo on the table, Reynaldo would poke it in Rudy Graveline's face and pop the questions. Bam bam bam. The nurses and scrub techs would drop whatever they were doing and run, leaving the hapless surgeon to dissolve, alone, before the camera's eye.

Wait'll he realizes who I am, Reynaldo had chortled. Be sure you go extra tight on his face.

Willie had said he needed a soundman, but Reynaldo said no, out of the question; this was to be a streamlined attack.

Willie had said all right, then we need a better signal. Just screaming isn't good enough, he had said. What if somebody else starts screaming first, some other patient?

"Who else would scream your name?" Reynaldo had asked in a caustic tone. "Listen to what I'm saying."

The plan was bold and outrageous, Willie had to admit. No doubt it would cause a national sensation, stir up all the TV critics, not to mention Johnny Carson's gag writers. There would be a large amount of cynical speculation among Ray's colleagues that what he really wanted out of this caper was a free nose job—a theory that occurred even to Willie as he listened to Reynaldo map out the big ambush. The possibility of coast-to-coast media ridicule was no deterrent; the man seemed to relish being maligned as a hack and a clown and a shameless egomaniac. He said they were jealous, that's what they were. What other broadcast journalist in America had the guts to go under the knife just to get an interview? Mike Wallace? Not in a million years, the arrogant old prune. Bill Moyers? That liberal pussy would faint if he got a hangnail!

Yeah, Willie had said, it's quite a plan.

Brilliant, Reynaldo had crowed. Try brilliant.

However inspired, the plan's success depended on several crucial factors, not the least of which was the premise that Reynaldo Flemm would be conscious for the interview.

Although the surgical procedure known as liposuction, or fat sucking, was developed in France, it has achieved its greatest mass-market popularity in the United States. It is now the most common cosmetic procedure performed by plastic surgeons in this country, with more than 100,000 operations a year. The mortality rate for suction-assisted lipectomy is relatively low, about one death for every 10,000 patients. The odds of complications—which include blood clots, fat embolisms, chronic numbness, and severe bruising—increase considerably if the surgeon performing the liposuction has had little or no training in the procedure. Rudy Graveline fell decisively into this category—a doctor who had taken up liposuction for the simple reason that it was exceedingly lucrative. No state law or licensing board or medical review committee required Rudy to study liposuction first, or become proficient, or even be tested on his surgical competence before trying it. The same libertarian standards applied to rhinoplasties or hemorrhoidectomies or even brain surgery: Rudy Graveline was a licensed physician, and legally that meant he could try any damn thing he wanted.

He did not give two hoots about certification by the American Board of Plastic Surgery, or the American Academy of Facial Plastic and Reconstructive Surgery, or the American Society of Plastic and Reconstructive Surgeons. What were a couple more snotty plaques on the wall? His patients could care less. They were rich and vain and impatient. In some exclusive South Florida circles, Rudy's name carried the glossy imprimatur of a Gucci or a de La Renta. The lacquered old crones at La Gorce or the Biltmore would point at each other's shiny chins and taut necks and sculpted eyelids and ask, not in a whisper but a haughty bray, "Is that a Graveline?"

Rudy was a designer surgeon. To have *him* suck your fat was an honor, a social plum, a mark (literally) of status. Only a boor, white trash or worse, would ever question the man's techniques or complain about the results.

Ironically, most of the surgeons who worked for Rudy Graveline at Whispering Palms were completely qualified to do suction lipectomies; they had actually trained for it—studied, observed, practiced. While Rudy admired their dedication, he thought they were overdoing things—after all, how difficult could such an operation really be? The fat itself was abundantly easy to find. Suck it out, close 'em up, next case! Big deal.

To be on the safe side, Rudy read two journal articles about liposuction and ordered an instructional video cassette for $26.95 from a medical-supply firm in Chicago. The journal articles turned out to be dense and fairly boring, but the video was an inspiration. Rudy came away convinced that any fool doctor with half a brain could vacuum fat with no problem.

The typical lipectomy patient was not a grotesque hypertensive blimp, but—like Johnny LeTigre—a healthy person of relatively normal stature and weight. The object of their complaint was medically mundane—bumper-car hips, droopy buttocks, gelatinous thighs, or old-fashioned "love handles" at the waist. Properly performed, liposuction would remove localized pockets of excess fat to improve and smooth the body's natural contour. Improperly performed, the surgery would leave a patient lumpy and lopsided and looking for a lawyer.

On the morning of Reynaldo Flemm's undercover mission, nothing as sinister as a premonition caused Rudy Graveline to change his mind about doing the nose job first. What changed the doctor's mind, as usual, was money. Because a lipectomy usually required general anesthesia, it was more labor-intensive (and costly) than a simple rhinoplasty. Rudy figured the sooner he could get done with the heavy stuff, the sooner he could get the anesthetist and her gas machine off the clock. He could do the rhino later with intravenous sedation, which was much cheaper.

That Rudy Graveline could still worry about overhead at this point, with his career crumbling, was a tribute both to his power of concentration and his ingrained devotion to profit.

He grabbed a gloveful of Reynaldo Flemm's belly roll and gave a little squeeze. Paydirt. Fat city.

Rudy selected a Number 15 blade and made a one-quarter inch incision in Reynaldo's navel. Through this convenient aperture Rudy inserted the cannula, a long tubular instrument that resembled in structure the nose of an anteater. Rudy rammed the blunt snout of the cannula into the soft meat of Reynaldo's abdomen, then scraped the instrument back and forth to break up the tissue. With his right foot the surgeon tapped a floor pedal that activated a suction machine, which vacuumed the fat particles through small holes in the tip of the cannula, down a long clear plastic tube to a glass bottle.

Within moments, the first yellow glops appeared.

Johnny LeTigre's spare tire!

Soon he would be a new man.

* * *

In the waiting room, Willie got to talking with some of the other patients. There was a charter-boat captain with a skin cancer the size of a toad on his forehead. There was a dancer from the Miami ballet who was getting her buttocks suctioned for the second time in as many years. There was a silver-haired Nicaraguan man whom Willie had often seen on television—one of the *contra* leaders—who was getting his eyelids done for eighteen hundred dollars. He said the CIA was picking up the tab.

The one Willie liked best was a red-haired stripper from the Solid Gold club up in Lauderdale. She was getting new boobs, of course, but she was also having a tattoo removed from her left thigh. When the stripper heard that Willie was from PBS, she asked if she could be in his documentary and hiked up her corduroy miniskirt to show off the tattoo. The tattoo depicted a green reticulated snake eating itself. Willie said, in a complimentary way, that he had never seen anything like it. He made sure to get the stripper's phone number so that he could call her about the imaginary program.

The hour passed without a peep from Reynaldo Flemm, and Willie began to get jittery. Reynaldo had said give it to nine o'clock before you freak, and now it was nine o'clock. The halls of Whispering Palms were quiet enough that Willie was certain he would have heard a scream. He asked the ballet dancer, who had been here before, how far it was from the waiting area to the operating room.

"Which operating room?" she replied. "They've got four."

"Shit," said Willie. "Four?"

This was shocking news. Reynaldo Flemm had made it sound like there was only one operating room, and that he would be easy to find. More worried than ever, Willie decided to make his move. He hoisted the Betacam to his shoulder, checked the mike and the cables and the belt pack and the battery levels, turned on the Frezzi light (which caused the other patients to mutter and shield their eyes), and went prowling through the corridors in search of Reynaldo Flemm.

* * *

When the telephone on the wall started tweeting, Dr. Rudy Graveline glanced up from Johnny LeTigre's gut and said: "Whoever it is, I'm not here."

The circulating nurse picked up the phone, listened for several moments, then turned to the doctor. "It's Ginny at the front desk. There's a man with a minicam running all over the place."

Rudy's surgical mask puckered. "Tell her to call the police. . . . No! Wait—" Oh Jesus. Stay calm. Stay extremely calm.

"He just crashed in on Dr. Kloppner in Suite D."

Rudy grunted unhappily. "What does he want? Did he say what he wants?"

"He's looking for you. Should I tell Ginny to call the cops or what?"

The nurse-anesthetist interrupted: "Let's not do anything until we finish up here. Let's close up this patient and get him off the table."

"She's right," Rudy said. "She's absolutely right. We're almost done here."

"Take your time," the anesthetist said with an edge of concern. Under optimum conditions, Rudy Graveline scared the daylights out of her. Under stress, there was no telling how dangerous he could be.

He said, "What're we looking at here?"

"One more pocket, maybe two hundred cc's."

"Let's do it, okay?"

The wall phone started tweeting again.

"Screw it," said Rudy. "Let it go."

He gripped the cannula like a carving knife, scraping frentically at the last stubborn colony of fat inside Reynaldo's midriff. The suction machine hummed contentedly as it filled the glass jar with gobs of unwanted pudge.

"One more minute and we're done," Rudy said.

Then the doors opened and an awesome white light bathed the operating room. The beam was brighter and hotter than the surgical lights, and it shone from the top of a camera, which sat like a second head on the shoulder of a man. A man who had no business in Rudy Graveline's operating room.

The man with the camera cried out: "Ray!"

Rudy said, "Get out of here this minute."

"Are you Dr. Graveline?"

Rudy's hand continued to work on Reynaldo Flemm's belly. "Yes, I'm Dr. Graveline. But there's nobody named Ray here. Now get out before I phone the police."

But the man with the camera on his shoulder shuffled closer, scorching the operating team with his fierce, hot light. The anesthetist, the scrub nurse, the circulating nurse, even Rudy flinched from the glare. The camera-headed man approached the table and zoomed in on the sleeping patient's face, which was partially concealed by a plastic oxygen mask. The voice behind the camera said, "Yeah, that's him!"

"Who?" Rudy said, rattled. "That's Ray?"

"Reynaldo Flemm!"

The scrub nurse said: "I told you he looked familiar."

Again Rudy asked: "Who? Reynaldo who?"

"That guy from the TV."

"This has gone far enough," Rudy declared, fighting panic. "You better . . . just get the hell out of my operating room."

Willie pushed forward. "Ray, wake up! It's me!"

"He can't wake up, you asshole. He's gassed to the gills. Now turn off that spotlight and get lost."

The scope of the journalistic emergency struck Willie at once. Reynaldo was unconscious. Christina was gone. The tape was rolling. The batteries were running out.

Willie thought: It's up to me now.

The baton microphone, Ray's favorite, the one Willie was supposed to toss to him at the moment of ambush, was tucked in Willie's left armpit. Grunting, contorting, shifting the weight of the Betacam on his shoulder, Willie was able to retrieve the mike with his right hand. In an uncanny imitation of Reynaldo Flemm, Willie thrust it toward the face of the surgeon.

Above the surgical mask, Rudy Graveline's eyes grew wide and fearful. He stared at the microphone as if it were the barrel of a Mauser. From behind the metallic hulk of the minicam, the voice asked: "Did you kill Victoria Barletta?"

A bullet could not have struck Rudy Graveline as savagely as those words.

His spine became rigid.

The pupils of his eyes shrunk to pinpricks.

His muscles cramped, one by one, starting in his toes. His right hand, the one that the held the cannula, the one buried deep in the livid folds of Reynaldo Flemm's freshly vacuumed tummy—his right hand twisted into a spastic nerveless talon.

With panic welling in her voice, the anesthetist said: "All right, that's it!"

"Almost done," the surgeon said hoarsely.

"No, that's enough!"

But Dr. Rudy Graveline was determined to finish the operation. To quit would be an admission of . . . *something*. Composure—that's what they taught you at Harvard. Above all, a physician must be composed. In times of crisis, patients and staff relied on a surgeon to be cool, calm, and composed. Even if the man lying on the operating table turned out to be . . . Reynaldo Flemm, the notorious undercover TV reporter! That would explain the woozy babbling while he was going under—the jerkoff wasn't talking about Victoria Principal, the actress. He was talking about Victoria Barletta, she of the fateful nose job.

The pain of the muscle cramps was so fierce that it brought viscous tears to Rudy Graveline's eyes. He forced himself to continue. He lowered his right shoulder into the rhythm of the liposuction, back and forth in a lumberjack motion, harder and harder.

Again, the faceless voice from behind the TV camera: "Did you kill that girl?"

The black eye of the beast peered closer, revolving clockwise in its socket—Willie, remembering Ray's instructions to zoom tight on Rudy's face. The surgeon stomped on the suction pedal as if he were squashing a centipede. The motor thrummed. The tube twitched. The glass jar filled.

Time to stop.

Time to stop!

But Dr. Rudy Graveline did not stop.

He kept on poking and sucking . . . the long hungry snout of the mechanical anteater slurping through the pit of Reynaldo's abdomen . . . down, down, down through the fascia and the muscle . . . snorkeling past the intestines, nipping at the transverse colon . . . down, down, down the magic anteater burrowed.

Until it glomped the aorta.

And the plastic tube coming out of Reynaldo's naval suddenly turned bright red.

The jar at the other end turned red.

Even the doctor's arm turned red.

Willie watched it all through the camera's eye. The whole place, turning red.

31

The first thing Chemo bought with Rudy's money was a portable phone for the Bonneville. No sooner was it out of the box than Maggie Gonzalez remarked, "This stupid toy is worth more than the car."

Chemo said, "I need a private line. You'll see."

They were driving back to the Holiday Inn after spending the morning at the office of Dr. George Ginger, the plastic surgeon. Maggie knew Dr. Ginger from the early days as one of Rudy's more competent underlings at the Durkos Center. She trusted George's skill and his discretion. He could be maddeningly slow, and he had terrible breath, but technically he was about as good as cosmetic surgeons come.

Chemo had prefaced the visit to Dr. Ginger with this warning to Maggie: "If he messes up my face, I'll kill him on the spot. And then I'll kill you."

The second thing that Chemo had bought with Rudy's money was a box of bullets for the rusty colt .38. Brand-new rounds, Federals. The good stuff.

Maggie had said, "You're going into this with the wrong attitude."

Chemo frowned. "I've had rotten luck with doctors."

"I know, I know."

"I don't even like this guy's name, George Ginger. Sounds like a fag name to me." Then he had checked the chambers on the Colt and slipped it into his pants.

"You're hopeless," Maggie had said. "I don't know why I even bother."

"Because otherwise I'll shoot you."

Fortunately the dermabrasion went smoothly. Dr. George Ginger had never seen a burn case quite like Chemo's, but he wisely refrained from inquiry. Once, when Chemo wasn't looking, the surgeon snuck a peek at the cumbersome prosthesis attached to the patient's left arm. An avid gardener, Dr. Ginger recognized the Weed Whacker instantly, but resisted the impulse to pry.

The sanding procedure took about two hours, and Chemo endured stoically, without so much as a whimper. When it was over, he no longer looked as if someone had glued Rice Krispies all over his face. Rather, he looked as if he had been dragged for five miles behind a speeding dump truck.

His forehead, his cheeks, his nose, his chin all glowed with a raw, pink, oozing sheen. The spackled damage of the errant electrolysis needle had been scraped away forever, but now it was up to Chemo to grow a new skin. While he might never enjoy the radiant peachy complexion of, say, a Christie Brinkley, at least he would be able to stroll through an airport or a supermarket or a public park without causing small children to cringe behind their mothers' skirts. Chemo conceded that this alone would be a vast improvement, socially.

Before leaving the office, Maggie Gonzalez had asked Dr. George Ginger to remove her sutures and inspect the progress of her New York facelift. He reported—with toxic breath—that everything was healing nicely, and gave Maggie a makeup mirror to look for herself. She was pleased by what she saw: The angry purple bruises were fading shadows under the eyes, and the incision scars had shrunk to tender rosy lines. She was especially delighted with her perky new nose.

Dr. Ginger studied the still-swollen promontory from several angles and nodded knowingly. "The Sandy Duncan."

Maggie smiled. "Exactly!"

Popping a codeine Tylenol, Chemo said, "Who the fuck is Sandy Duncan?"

In the Bonneville, on the way back to the motel, Chemo remarked, "Three grand seems like a lot for what he did."

"All he did was make you look human again," Maggie said. "Three grand was a bargain, if you ask me. Besides, he even gave a professional discount—fifteen percent off because I'm a nurse."

As he steered, Chemo kept leaning toward the middle of the seat to check himself in the rearview. It was difficult to judge the result of the dermabrasion, since his face was slathered in a glue-colored ointment. "I don't know," he said. "It's still pretty broken out."

Maggie thought: Broken out? It's seeping, for God's sake. "You heard what the doctor said. Give it a couple weeks to heal." With that she leaned over and commandeered the rearview to examine her own refurbished features.

A beep-beep noise came chirping out of the dashboard; the car phone. With a simian arm Chemo reached into the glove compartment and snatched it on the second ring.

With well-acted nonchalance, he wedged the receiver between his ear and his left shoulder. Maggie thought it looked ridiculous to be riding in a junker like this and talking on a fancy car phone. Embarrassed, she scooted lower in the seat.

"Hullo," Chemo said into the phone.

"Hello, Funny Face." It was Mick Stranahan. "I got your message."

"Yeah?"

"Yeah."

"And?"

"And you said to call, so I am."

Chemo was puzzled at Stranahan's insulting tone of voice. The man ought to be scared. Desperate. Begging. At least polite.

Chemo said, "I got your lady friend."

"Yeah, yeah, I read the note."

"So, you're waiting to hear my demands."

"No," said Stranahan, "I waiting to hear you sing the fucking aria from *Madame Butterfly* . . . *Of course* I want to hear your demands."

"Christ, you're in a shitty mood."

"I can barely hear you," Stanahan complained. "Don't tell me you got one of those yuppie Mattel car phones."

"It's a Panasonic," Chemo said, sharply.

Maggie looked over at him with an impatient expression, as if to say: Get on with it.

As he braked for a stop light, the phone slipped from Chemo's ear. He took his good hand off the wheel to grab for it.

"Hell!" The receiver was gooey with the antibiotic ointment from his cheeks.

Stranahan's voice cracked through the static. "Now what's the matter?"

"Nothing. Not a damn thing." Chemo carefully propped the receiver on his shoulder. "Look, here's the deal. You want to see your lady friend alive, meet me at the marina at midnight tonight."

"Fuck you."

"Huh?"

"That means no, Funny Face. No marina. I know what you want and you can have it. Me for her, right?"

"Right." Chemo figured there was no sense trying to bullshit this guy.

"It's a deal," Stranahan said, "but I'm not going anywhere. You come to me."

"Where are you now?"

"I'm at a pay phone on Bayshore Drive, but I won't be here long."

Impatiently Chemo said, "So where's the meet?"

"My place."

"That house? No fucking way."

" 'Fraid so."

The car phone started sliding again. Chemo groped frantically for it, and the Bonneville began to weave off the road. Maggie reached over and steadied the wheel.

Chemo got a grip on the receiver and snarled into it: "You hear what I said? No way am I going back to that damn stilt house."

"Yes, you are. You'll be getting another call with more information."

"Tell me now!"

"I can't," Stranahan said.

"I'll kill the Marks girl, I swear."

"You're not quite that stupid, are you?"

The hot flush of anger made Chemo's face sting even worse. He said, "We'll talk about this later. What time you gonna call?"

"Oh, not me," Mick Stranahan said. "I won't be the one calling back."

"Then who?" Chemo demanded.

But the line had gone dead.

Willie played the videotape for his friend at WTVJ, the NBC affiliate in Miami. Willie's friend was sufficiently impressed by the blood on his shirt to let him use one of the editing rooms. "You gotta see this," Willie said.

He punched the tape into the machine and sat back to chew on his knuckles. He felt like an orphan. No Christina, no Reynaldo. He knew he should call New York, but he didn't know what to say or who to tell.

Willie's friend, who was a local news producer, pointed to the monitor. "Where's that?" he asked.

"Surgery clinic over in Bal Harbour. That's the waiting room."

The friend said. "You were portable?"

"Right. Solo the whole way."

"So where's Flemm? That doesn't look like him."

"No, that's somebody else." The monitor showed an operating room where a tall bald doctor was hunched over a chubby female patient. The bald doctor was gesticulating angrily at the camera and barking for a nurse to call the authorities. "I don't know who that was," Willie said. "Wrong room."

"Now you're back in the hallway, walking. People are yelling, covering their faces."

"Yeah, but here it comes," Willie said, leaning forward. "Bingo. That's Ray on the table."

"Jeez, what're they doing?"

"I don't know."

"It looks like a goddamn Caesarean."

Willie said, "Yeah, but it was supposed to be a nose job."

"Go on!"

The audio portion of the tape grew louder.

"Yeah, that's him!"

"Who? That's Ray?"

"Reynaldo Flemm."

"I told you he looked familiar."

"Who? Reynaldo who?"

"That guy from from the TV."

"This has gone far enough. . . ."

When the frame filled with Reynaldo Flemm's gaping muzzled face, Willie's friend hit the Pause button and said, "Fucker never looked better."

"You know him?"

"I knew him back from Philadelphia. Back when he was still Ray Fleming."

"You're kidding," Willie said.

"No, man, that's his real name. Raymond Fleming. Then he got on this bi-ethnic kick . . . 'Reynaldo Flemm'—half Latin, half Eastern bloc. Told everybody in the business that his mother was a Cuban refugee and his father was with the Yugoslavian resistance. Shit, I laugh about it but that's when his career really took off."

Willie said, "Romania. What he told me, his old man was with the Romanian underground."

"His old man sold Whirlpools in Larchmont, I know for a fact. Let's see the rest."

Willie pressed the Fast Forward and squeaked the tape past the part when he confronted Dr. Rudy Graveline about Victoria Barletta; he didn't want his producer friend to hear the dead woman's name, on the offchance that the story could be salvaged. Willie slowed the tape to normal speed just as he zoomed in on the doctor's quavering eyes.

"Boris Karloff," said Willie's friend.

"Watch."

The camera angle widened to show Rudy Graveline feverishly toiling over Reynaldo's belly. Then came a mist of blood, and one of the nurses began shouting for the surgeon to stop.

"Geez," said Willie's friend, looking slightly queasy. "What's happening?"

The doctor abruptly wheeled from the operating table to confront the camera directly. In his bloody right hand was a wicked-looking instrument connected to a long plastic tube. The device was making an audible slurp-slurp noise.

"Your turn, fat boy!"

Willie's friend gestured at the monitor and said: "He called you fat boy?"

"Watch!"

On the screen, the surgeon lunged forward with the pointy slurp-slurping device. There was a cry, a dull clunk. Then the picture got jerky and went gray.

Willie pressed the Stop button. "I hauled ass," he explained to his friend. "He came at me with that sucking . . . *thing*, so I took off."

"Don't blame you, man. But what about Ray?"

Willie took the videotape out of the editing console. "That's what's got me scared. I get in the van and take off, right? Stop at the nearest phone booth and call this clinic. Whispering Palms is the name."

"Yeah, I've heard of it."

"So I call. Don't say who I am. I ask about Reynaldo Flemm. I say he's my brother. I'm s'posed to pick him up after the operation. Ask can I come by and get him. Nurse gets on the line and wants to know what's going on. She wants to know how come Ray was using a phony name when he checks in at the place. Johnny Tiger, some shit like that. I tell her I haven't got the faintest—maybe he was embarrassed, didn't want his nose job to turn up in the gossip columns. Then she says, well, he's not here. She says the doctor, this Rudy Graveline, the nurse says he drove Ray to Mount Sinai. She says she's not allowed to say anything more on the phone. So I haul ass over to Emergency at Sinai and guess what? No Ray anywhere. Fact there's nothing but strokes and heart attacks. No Reynaldo Flemm!"

Willie's friend said, "This is too fucking weird. Even for Miami."

"Best part is, now I gotta call New York and break the news."

"Oh, man."

Willie said, "Maybe I'll ship the tape first."

"Might as well," agreed the producer. "What about Ray? Think he's all right?"

"No," said Willie. "You want the truth, I'd be fucking amazed if he was all right."

The nurses had wanted to call 911, but Rudy Graveline had said no, there wasn't time. I'll take him myself, Rudy had said. He had run to the parking lot (stopping only at the front desk to pick up Reynaldo's $15,000), got the Jag and pulled up at the staff entrance.

Back in the operating suite, the anesthetist had said: "Everything's going flat."

"Then hurry, goddammit!"

They had gotten Reynaldo on a gurney and wheeled him to Rudy's car and bundled him in the passenger seat. The scrub nurse even tried to hook up the safety belt.

"Oh, forget it," Rudy had said.

"But it's a law."

"Go back to work!" Rudy had commanded. The Jaguar had peeled rubber on its way out.

Naturally he had no intention of driving to Mount Sinai Hospital. What was the point? Rudy glanced at the man in the passenger seat and still did not recognize him from television. True, Reynaldo Flemm was not at his telegenic best. His eyes were half-closed, his mouth was half-open, and his skin was the color of bad veal.

He was also exsanguinating all over Rudy's fine leather seats and burled walnut door panels. "Great," Rudy muttered. "What else." As the surgeon sped south on Alton Road, he took out the portable telephone and called his brother's tree company.

"George Graveline, please. It's an emergency."

"Uh, he's not here."

"This is his brother. Where's he working today?"

The line clicked. Rudy thought he had been cut off. Then a lady from an answering service came on and asked him to leave his number. Rudy hollered, but she wouldn't budge. Finally he surrendered the number and hung up.

He thought: I must find George and his wood-chipping machine. This is very dicey, driving around Miami Beach in a $47,000 sedan with a dead TV star in the front seat. *Bleeding* on the front seat.

The car phone beeped and Rudy grabbed at it in frantic optimism. "George!"

"No, Dr. Graveline."

"Who's this?"

"Sergeant García, Metro Homicide. You probably don't remember, but we met that night the mysterious midget Haitian blew up your car.''

Rudy's heart was pounding. Should he hang up? Did the cops know about Flemm already? But how—the nurses? Maybe that moron with the minicam!

Al García said: ''I got some bad news about your brother George.''

Rudy's mind was racing. The detective's words didn't register. ''What—could you give me that again?''

''I said I got bad news about George. He's dead.''

Rudy's foot came off the accelerator. He was coasting now, trying to think. Which way? Where?

García went on: ''He tried to kill a man and I had to shoot him. Internal Review has the full report, so I suggest you talk to them.''

Nothing.

''Doctor? You there?''

''Yuh.''

No questions, nothing.

''The way it went down, I had no choice.''

Rudy said dully, ''I understand.'' He was thinking: It's awful about George, yes, but what am I going to do with this dead person in my Jaguar?

García could sense that something strange was going on at the end of the line. He said, ''Look, I know it's a bad time, but we've got to talk about a homicide. A homicide that may involve you and your brother. I'd like to come over to the clinic as soon as possible.''

''Make it tomorrow,'' Rudy said.

''It's about Victoria Barletta.''

''I'm eager to help in any way I can. Come see me tomorrow.'' The surgeon sounded like a zombie. A heavily sedated zombie. If there was a realm beyond sheer panic, Rudy Graveline had entered it.

''Doctor, it really can't wait—''

''For heaven's sake, Sergeant, give me some time. I just found out my brother's dead, I need to make the arrangements.''

"To be blunt," García said, "as far as George goes, there's not a whole lot left to arrange."

"Call me tomorrow," Rudy Graveline said curtly. Then he threw the car phone out the window.

When the phone rang again in the Bonneville, Chemo gloated at Maggie Gonzalez. "I told you this would come in handy."

"Quit picking at your face."

"It itches like hell."

"Leave it be!" Maggie scolded. "You want it to get infected? Do you?"

On the other end of the phone was Rudy Graveline. He sounded worse than suicidal.

Chemo said, "Hey, Doc, you in your car? I'm in mine."

He felt like the king of the universe.

"No, I'm home," Rudy said. "We have a major problem."

"What's this *we* stuff? I don't have a problem. I got a hundred-twenty-odd grand, a brand-new face, a brand-new car phone. Life's looking better every day."

Rudy said, "I'm delighted for you, I really am."

"You don't sound too damn delighted."

"He got Heather." The doctor choked out the words.

"Who's Heather?" Chemo said.

"My . . . I can't believe . . . when I got home, she was gone. He took her away."

Maggie asked who was on the line and Chemo whispered the doctor's name. "All right," he said to Rudy, "you better tell me what's up."

Suddenly Rudy Graveline remembered what Curly Eyebrows had warned him about cellular phones, about how private conversations sometimes could be picked up on outside frequencies. In his quickening state of emotional deterioration, Rudy clearly envisioned—as if it were real—some nosy Coral Gables housewife overhearing his felonious litany on her Amana toaster oven.

"Come to my house," he instructed Chemo.

"I can't, I'm waiting on a call."

"This is it."

"What? You mean this is the phone call he—"

"Yes," Rudy said. "Get out here as fast as you can. We're going on a boat ride."

"Jesus H. Christ."

32

Maggie and Chemo left Christina Marks tied up in the trunk of the Bonneville, which was parked in Rudy Graveline's flagstone driveway. Miserable as she was, Christina didn't worry about suffocating inside the car; there were so many rust holes, she could actually feel a breeze.

For an hour Maggie and Chemo sat on the white leather sofa in Rudy's living room and listened to the doleful story of how he had come home to find his lover, his baby doll, his sweetie pie, his Venus, his sugar bunny, his punkin, his blond California sunbeam missing from the bedroom.

They took turns studying the kidnap note, which said:

"Ahoy! You're Invited to a Party!"

On the front of the note was a cartoon pelican in a sailor's cap. On the inside was a hand-drawn chart of Stiltsville. Chemo and Rudy grimly agreed that something had to be done permanently about Mick Stranahan.

Chemo asked about the fresh dark drops on the foyer, and Rudy said that it wasn't Heather's blood but someone else's. In chokes and sighs he told them about the mishap at the clinic with Reynaldo Flemm. Maggie Gonzalez listened to the gruesome account with amazement; she had never dreamed her modest extortion scheme would come to this.

"So, where is he?" she asked.

"In there," Rudy replied. "The Sub-Zero."

Chemo said, "The what? What're you talking about?"

Rudy led them to the kitchen and pointed at the cabinet-sized refrigerator. "The Sub-Zero," he said.

Maggie noticed that the aluminum freezer trays had been stacked on the counter, along with a half-dozen Lean Cuisines and three pints of chocolate Häagen-Dazs.

Chemo said, "That's a big fridge, all right." He opened the door and there was Reynaldo Flemm, upright and frosty as a Jell-O pop.

"It was the only way he could fit," explained Rudy. "See, I had to tear out the damn ice maker."

Chemo said, "He sure looks different on TV." Chemo propped open the refrigerator door with one knee; the cold air made his face feel better.

Maggie said nothing. This wasn't part of the plan. She was trying to think of a way to sneak out of Rudy's house and run. Go back to the motel room, grab the black Samsonite, and disappear for about five years.

Chemo closed the freezer door. He pointed to more brownish spots on the bone-colored tile and said, "If you got a mop, she can clean that up."

"Wait a second," Maggie said. "Do I look like a maid?"

"You're gonna look like a cabbage if you don't do what I say." Balefully Chemo brandished the Weed Whacker.

Maggie recalled the savage thrashing of Rudy Graveline and said, "All right, put that stupid thing away."

While Maggie mopped, Rudy moped. He seemed shattered, listless, inconsolable. He needed to think; he needed the soothing rhythm of athletic copulation, the sweet crystal tunnel of clarity that only Heather's loins could give him.

The day had begun with such promise!

Up before dawn to pack their bags. And the airline tickets—he had placed them in Heather's purse while she slept. He would drive to the clinic, perform the operation on the male go-go dancer, collect the fifteen grand, and come home for Heather.

Then it was off to the airport! Fifteen thousand was plenty for starters—a month or two in Costa Rica in a nice apartment. Time enough for Rudy's Panamanian lawyer to liquidate the offshore trusts. After that, Rudy and Heather could breathe again. Get themselves some land up in the mountains. Split-level ranch house on the side of a hill. A stable, too; she loved to ride. Rudy envisioned himself opening a new surgery clinic; he had even packed his laminated Harvard diploma, pillowing it tenderly in the suitcase among his silk socks and designer underwear. San José was crawling with wealthy expatriates and aspiring international jet-setters. An American plastic surgeon would be welcomed vivaciously.

Now, disaster. Heather—fair, nubile, perfectly apportioned Heather—had been snatched from her sickbed.

"We need a boat," Rudy Graveline croaked. "For tonight."

Chemo said, "Yeah, a big one. If I'm going back to that damn house I want to stay dry. See if you can find us a Scarab thirty-eight."

"Are you nuts?"

"Just like they had on *Miami Vice.*"

"You *are* nuts. Who's going to drive it?" Rudy stared pointedly at the unwieldy garden tool attached to Chemo's left arm. "You?"

"Yeah, me. Just get on the phone, see what you can do. We've gotta move before the cops show up."

Rudy looked stricken by the mention of police.

"Well, Jesus," Chemo said, "you got a dead man in your fridge. This is a problem."

Maggie was rinsing the mop in the kitchen sink. She said, "I've got an idea about that. You might not like it, but it's worth a try."

Rudy shrugged wearily. "Let's hear it."

"I used to work for a surgeon who knew this guy . . . this guy who would buy certain things."

"Surely you're not suggesting—"

"It's up to you," Maggie said. "I mean, Dr. Graveline, you've got yourself a situation here."

"Yeah," said Chemo. "Your ice cream is melting."

* * *

The man's name was Kimbler, and his office was in Miami's hospital district; a storefront operation on 12th Street, a purse-snatcher's jog from Jackson Hospital or the Medical Examiner's Office. The magnetic sign on the door of the office said: "International Bio-Medical Exports, Inc." The storefront window was tinted dark blue and was obscured by galvanized burglar mesh.

Kimbler was waiting for them when they arrived—Rudy, Chemo, Maggie, and Christina. Chemo had the Colt .38 in his pants pocket, pointed at Christina the whole time. He had wanted to leave her in the trunk of the Pontiac, but there was not enough room.

Kimbler was a rangy thin-haired man with tortoise-shell glasses and a buzzard's-beak nose. The office was lighted like a stockroom, with cheap egg-carton overheads. Rows of gray steel shelves covered both walls. The shelves were lined with old-fashioned Mason jars, and preserved in the Mason jars were assorted human body parts: ears, eyeballs, feet, hands, fingers, toes, small organs, large organs.

Chemo looked around and, under his breath, said, "What the fuck."

Kimbler gazed with equal wonderment at Chemo, who was truly a sight—his freshly sanded face glistening with Neosporin ointment, his extenuated left arm cloaked with its calfskin golf-bag cover, his radish-patch scalp, his handsome Jim Fowler safari jacket. Kimbler examined Chemo as if he were a prized future specimen.

"This is some hobby you got," Chemo said, picking up a jar of gall bladders. "This is better than baseball cards."

Kimbler said, "I've got the proper permits, I assure you."

Maggie explained that Kimbler sold human tissue to foreign medical schools. She said it was perfectly legal.

"The items come from legitimate sources," Kimbler added. "Hospitals. Pathology labs."

Items. Christina was nauseated at the concept. Or maybe it was just the sweet dead smell of the place.

Kimbler said, "It may sound ghoulish, but I provide a much-needed service. These items, discarded organs and such, they would otherwise go to waste. Be thrown away. Flushed. Incinerated. Overseas medical schools are in great need of clinical teaching aids—the students are extremely grateful. You should see some of the letters."

"No thanks," Chemo said. "What's a schlong go for these days?"

"Pardon me?"

Maggie cut in: "Mr. Kimbler, we appreciate you seeing us on short notice. We have an unusual problem."

Kimbler peered theatrically over the tops of his glasses. A slight smile came to his lips. "I assumed as much."

Maggie went on, "What we have is an entire . . . *item*."

"I see."

"It's a pauper-type situation. Very sad—no family, no funds for a decent burial. We're not even sure who he is."

Christina could scarcely contain herself. She had gotten a quick glimpse of a body as they angled it into trunk of the Bonneville. A young man; that much she could tell.

Kimbler said to Maggie: "What can you tell me of the circumstances? The manner of death, for instance."

She said, "An indigent case, like I told you. Emergency surgery for appendicitis." She pointed at Rudy. "Ask him, he's the doctor."

Rudy Graveline was stupefied. He scrambled to catch up with Maggie's yarn. "I was doing . . . he had a chronic heart condition. Bad arrhythmia. He should've said something before the operation, but he didn't."

Kimbler pursed his lips. "You're a surgeon?"

"Yes." Rudy wasn't dressed like a surgeon. He was wearing Topsiders, tan cotton pants, and a Bean crewneck pullover. He was dressed for a boat ride. "Here, wait." He took out his wallet and showed Kimbler an I.D. card from the Dade County Medical Society. Kimbler seemed satisfied.

"I realize this is out of the ordinary," Maggie said.

"Yes, well, let's have a look."

Chemo pinched Christina by the elbow and said, "We'll wait here." He handed Maggie the keys to the Bonneville. She and Rudy led the man named Kimbler to the car, which was parked in a city lot two blocks away.

When Maggie opened the trunk, Rudy turned away. Kimbler adjusted his glasses and craned over the corpse as if he were studying the brush strokes on a fine painting. "Hmmmmm," he said. "Hmmmmmm."

Rudy edged closer to block the view of the trunk, in case any pedestrians got curious. His concern was groundless, for no one gave the trio a second look; half the people in Miami did their business out of car trunks.

Kimbler seemed impressed by what he saw. "I don't get many whole cadavers," he remarked. "Certainly not of this quality."

"We tried to locate a next of kin," Rudy said, "but for some reason the patient had given us a phony name."

Kimbler chuckled. "Probably had a very good reason. Probably a criminal of some type."

"Every place we called was a dead end," Rudy said, lamely embellishing the lie.

Maggie stepped in to help. "We were going to turn him over to the county, but it seemed like such a waste."

"Oh, yes," said Kimbler. "The shortage of good cadavers . . . by good, I mean white and well-nourished. Most of the schools I deal with—for instance, one place in the Dominican, they had only two cadavers for a class of sixty medical students. Tell me how those kids are ever going to learn gross anatomy."

Rudy started to say something but thought better of it. The whole deal was illegal as hell, no doubt about it. But what choice did he have? For the first time in his anal-retentive, hyper-compulsive professional life he had lost control of events. He had surrendered himself to the squalid street instincts of Chemo and Maggie Gonzalez.

Kimbler was saying, "Two measly cadavers, both dysenteries. Weighed about ninety pounds each. For sixty students! And this is not so unusual in some of these poor countries. There's a med school on Guadeloupe, the best they could do was monkey skeletons. To help out I shipped down two hearts and maybe a half-dozen lungs, but it's not the same as having whole human bodies.''

Shrewd haggler that she was, Maggie had heard enough. Slowly she closed, but did not lock, the rusty trunk of the Bonneville; Reynaldo Flemm had begun to thaw.

"So," she said, "you're obviously interested."

"Yes," said Kimbler. "How does eight hundred sound?"

"Make it nine," said Maggie.

Kimbler frowned irritably. "Eight-fifty is pushing it."

"Eight seventy-five. Cash."

Kimbler still wore a frown, but he was nodding. "All right. Eight seventy-five it is."

Rudy Graveline was confused. "You're paying *us*?"

"Of course," Kimbler replied. He studied Rudy doubtfully. "Just so there's no question later, you *are* a medical doctor? I mean, your state license is current. Not that you need to sign anything, but it's good to know."

"Yes," Rudy sighed. "Yes, I'm a doctor. My license is up to date." As if it mattered. If all went as planned, he'd be gone from the country by this time tomorrow. He and Heather, together on a mountaintop in Costa Rica.

The man named Kimbler tapped cheerfully on the trunk of the Bonneville. "All right, then. Why don't you pull around back of the office. Let's get this item on ice straightaway."

Mick Stranahan brought Heather Chappell a mug of hot chocolate. She pulled the blanket snugly around her shoulders and said, "Thanks. I'm so damn cold."

He asked how she was feeling.

"Beat up," she replied. "Especially after that boat ride."

"Sorry," Stranahan said. "I know it's rough as hell—there's a front moving through so we got a big westerly tonight."

Heather sipped tentatively at the chocolate. The kidnapper, whoever he was, watched her impassively from a wicker barstool. He wore blue jeans, deck shoes, a pale yellow cotton shirt and a poplin windbreaker. To Heather the man looked strong, but not particularly mean.

In the middle of the living room was a card table, covered by an oilskin cloth. On the table was a red Sears Craftsman toolbox. The kidnapper had been carrying it when he broke into Dr. Graveline's house.

Heather nodded toward the toolbox and said, "What's in there?"

"Just some stuff I borrowed from Rudy."

The furniture looked like it came from the Salvation Army, but still there was a spartan coziness about the place, especially with the soft sounds of moving water. Heather said, "I like your house."

"The neighborhood's not what it used to be."

"What kind of fish is that on the wall?"

"It's a blue marlin. The bill broke off, I've got to get it fixed."

Heather said, "Did you catch it yourself?"

"No." Stranahan smiled. "I'm no Hemingway."

"I read for *Islands in the Stream*. With George C. Scott—did you see it?"

Stranahan said no, he hadn't.

"I didn't get the part, anyway," said Heather. "I forget now who played the wife. George C. Scott was Hemingway, and there was lots of fishing."

The beakless marlin stared down from the wall. Stranahan said, "It used to be paradise out here."

Heather nodded; she could picture it. "What're you going to do with me?"

"Not much," said Stranahan.

"I remember you," she said. "From the surgery clinic. That night in the parking lot, you put me in the cab. The night Rudolph's car caught fire."

"My name is Mick."

Being a famous actress, Heather didn't customarily introduce herself. This time she felt like she had to.

Stranahan said, "The reason I asked how you're feeling is

this.'' He held up three pill bottles and gave them a rattle. ''These were on the nightstand by your bed. Young Dr. Rudy was keeping you loaded.''

''Painkillers, probably. See, I just had surgery.''

''Not painkillers,'' Stranahan said. ''Seconal 100s. Industrial-strength, enough to put down an elephant.''

''What . . . why would he do that?''

Stranahan got off the barstool and walked over to Heather Chappell. In his right hand was a small pair of scissors. He knelt down in front of her and told her not to move.

''Oh, God,'' she said.

''Be still.''

Carefully he clipped the bandages off her face. Heather expected the salty cool air to sting the incisions, but she felt nothing but an itchy sensation.

Stranahan said, ''I want to show you something.'' He went to the bathroom and came back with a hand mirror. Heather studied herself for several moments.

In a puzzled voice she said, ''There's no marks.''

''Nope. No scars, no bruises, no swelling.''

''Rudolph said . . . See, he mentioned something about microsurgery. Lasers, I think he said. He said the scars would be so small—''

''Bullshit.'' Stranahan handed her the scissors. She gripped them in her right hand like a pistol.

''I'm going in the other room for a little while,'' he said. ''Call me when you're done and I'll explain as much as I can.''

Ten minutes later Heather was pounding on the bedroom door. She had cut off the remaining bandages and phony surgical dressings. She was standing there naked, striped with gummy adhesive, and crying softly. Stranahan bundled her in the blanket and sat her on the bed.

''He was s'posed to do my boobs,'' she said. ''And my hips. My nose, eyelids . . . everything.''

''Well, he lied,'' said Stranahan.

''Please, I wanna go back to L.A.''

''Maybe tomorrow.''

"What's going on?" Heather cried. "Can I use your phone, I've got to call my manager. Please?"

"Sorry," said Stranahan. "No telephone. No ship-to-shore. No fax. The weather's turned to shit, so we're stuck for the night."

"But I'm s'posed to do a *Password* with Jack Klugman. God, what day is it?"

Stranahan said: "Can I ask you something? You're a beautiful girl—you get points for that, okay—but how could you be so fucking dumb?"

Heather stopped crying instantly, gulped down her sobs. No man had ever talked to her this way. Well, wait; Patrick Duffy had, once. She was playing a debutante on *Dallas* and she forgot one lousy line. One out of seventeen! But later at least Patrick Duffy had said he was sorry for blowing his stack.

Mick Stranahan said, "To trust yourself to a hack like Graveline, Jesus, it's pathetic. And for what? Half an inch off your hips. A polyurethane dimple in your chin. Plastic bags inside your breasts. Think about it: A hundred years from now, your coffin cracks open and there's nothing inside but two little bags of silicone. No flesh, no bones, everything's turned to ashes except for your boobs. They're bionic. Eternal!"

In a small voice Heather said, "But everybody does it."

Stranahan tore off the blanket, and for the first time Heather was truly afraid. He told her to stand up.

"Look at yourself."

Diffidently she lowered her eyes.

"There's not a thing wrong with you," Stranahan said. "Tell me what's wrong with you."

The wind shook the shutters, and shafts of cold air sliced the room. Heather shivered, sat down, and put her hands over her nipples. Stranahan folded his arms as if he were awaiting something: an explanation.

"You're a man, I don't expect you to understand." She wondered if he would try to touch her in some way.

"Vanity I understand," Stranahan said. "Men are experts on the subject." He picked the blanket off the floor. Indifferently he draped it across her lap. "I think there's some warm clothes in one of the drawers."

He found a gray sweatsuit with a hood and a pair of men's woolen socks. Hurriedly Heather got dressed. "Just tell me," she said, still trembling, "why did Rudolph lie about this? I can't get over it—why didn't he do the operation?"

"I guess he was scared. In case you didn't notice, he's crazy about you. He probably couldn't bear the thought of something going wrong in surgery. It's been known to happen."

"But I paid him," Heather said. "I wrote the bastard a personal check."

"Stop it, you're breaking my heart."

Heather glared at him.

"Look," said Stranahan, "I've seen his Visa bill. Swanky restaurants, designer clothes, a diamond here and there—you made out pretty well. Did he mention he was going to fly you away on a tropical vacation?"

"I remember him saying something about Costa Rica, of all places."

"Yeah, well, don't worry. The trip's off. Rudy's had a minor setback."

Heather said, "So tell me what's going on."

"Just consider yourself damn lucky."

"Why? What are you talking about?"

"Rudy killed a young woman just like you. No, I take that back—she wasn't just like you, she was innocent. And he killed her with a nose job."

Heather Chappell cringed. Unconsciously her hand went to her face.

"That's what this is all about," Stranahan said. "You don't believe me, ask him yourself. He's on his way."

"Here?"

"That's right. To save you and to kill me."

"Rudolph? No way."

"You don't know him like I do, Heather."

Stranahan went from room to room, turning off the lights. Heather followed, saying nothing. She didn't want to be left alone, even by him. Carrying a Coleman lantern, Stranahan led her out of the stilt house and helped her climb to the roof. The windmill whistled and thrummed over their heads.

Heather said, "God, this wind is really getting nasty."

"Sure is."

"What kind of gun is that?"

"A shotgun, Heather."

"I can't believe Rudolph is coming all the way out here on a night like this."

"Yep."

"What's the shotgun for?"

"For looks," said Stranahan. "Mostly."

33

Al García was feeling slightly guilty about lying to Mick Stranahan until Luis Córdova's patrol boat conked out. Now Luis was hanging over the transom, poking around the lower unit; García stood next to him, aiming a big waterproof spotlight and cursing into the salt spray.

García thought: I hate boats. Car breaks down, you just walk away from it. With a damn boat, you're stuck.

They were adrift about half a mile west of the Seaquarium. It was pitch black and ferociously choppy. A chilly northwesterly wind cut through García's plastic windbreaker and made him wish he had waited until dawn, as he had promised Stranahan.

It did not take Luis Córdova long to discover the problem with the engine. "It's the prop," he said.

"What about it?"

"It's gone," said Luis Córdova.

"We hit something?"

"No, it just fell off. Somebody monkeyed with the pin."

García considered this for a moment. "Does he know where you keep the boat?"

"Sure," said Luis Córdova.

"Shit."

"I better get on the radio and see if we can get help."

Al García stowed the spotlight, sat down at the console and lit a cigarette. He said, "That bastard. He didn't trust us."

Luis Córdova said, "We need a new prop or a different boat. Either way, it's going to take a couple hours."

"Do what you can." To the south García heard the sound of another boat on the bay; Luis Córdova heard it, too—the hull slapping heavily on the waves. The hum of the engine receded as the craft moved farther away. They knew exactly where it was going.

"Goddamn," said García.

"You really think he did this?"

"I got no doubt. The bastard didn't trust us."

"I can't imagine why," said Luis Córdova, reaching for the radio.

Driving across the causeway to the marina, Chemo kept thinking about the stilt house and the monster fish that had eaten off his hand. As hard as he tried, he could not conceal his trepidation about going back.

When he saw the boat that Rudy Graveline had rented, Chemo nearly called off the expedition. "What a piece of shit," he said.

It was a twenty-one-foot outboard, tubby and slow, with an old sixty-horse Merc. A cheap hotel rental, designed for abuse by tourists.

Chemo said, "I'm not believing this."

"At this hour I was lucky to find anything," said Rudy.

Maggie Gonzalez said, "Let's just get it over with." She got in the boat first, followed by Rudy, then Christina Marks.

Chemo stood on the pier, peering across the bay toward the

amber glow of the city. "It's blowing like a fucking typhoon," he said. He really did not want to go.

"Come on," Rudy said. He was frantic about Heather; more precisely, he was frantic about what he would have to do to get her back. He had a feeling that Chemo didn't give a damn one way or another, as long as Mick Stranahan got killed.

As Chemo was unhitching the bow rope, Christina Marks said, "This is really a bad idea."

"Shut up," said Chemo.

"I mean it. You three ought to get away while you can."

"I said shut up."

Maggie said, "She might be right. This guy, he's not exactly a stable person."

Chemo clumped awkwardly into the boat and started the engine. "What, you want to spend the rest of your life in jail? You think he's gonna forget about everything and let us ride off into the sunset?"

Rudy Graveline shivered. "All I want is Heather."

Christina said, "Don't worry, Mick won't hurt her."

"Who gives a shit," said Chemo, gunning the throttle with his good hand.

By the time they made it to Stiltsville, Chemo felt like his face was aflame. The rental boat rode like a washtub, each wave slopping over the gunwale and splashing against the raw flesh of his cheeks. The salt stung like cold acid. Chemo soon ran out of profanities. Rudy Graveline was no help, nor were the women; they were all soaking wet, queasy, and glum.

As he made a wide weekend-sailor's turn into the Biscayne Channel, Chemo slowed down and pointed with the Weed Whacker. "What the fuck?" he said. "Look at that."

Across the bonefish flats, Stranahan's stilt house was lit up like a used car lot. Lanterns hung off every piling, and swung eerily in the wind. The brown shutters were propped open and there was music, too, fading in and out with each gust.

Christina Marks laughed to herself. "The Beatles," she said. He was playing "Happiness Is a Warm Gun."

Chemo snorted. "What, he's trying to be cute?"

"No," Christina said. "Not him."

Maggie Gonzalez swept a whip of wet hair out of her face. "He's nuts, obviously."

"And we're not?" Rudy said. He got the binoculars and tried to spot Heather Chappell on the stilt house. He could see no sign of life, human or otherwise. He counted a dozen camp lanterns aglow.

The sight of the place brought back dreadful memories for Chemo. Too clearly he could see the broken rail where he had fallen to the water that day of the ill-fated jet ski assault. He wondered about the fierce fish, whatever it was, dwelling beneath the stilt house. Inwardly he speculated about its nocturnal feeding habits.

Maggie said, "How are we going to handle this?"

Rudy looked at her sternly. "We don't do anything until Heather's safe in this boat."

Chemo grabbed Christina's arm and pulled her to the console. "Stand here, next to me," he said. "Real close, in case your jerkoff boyfriend gets any ideas." He pressed the barrel of the Colt .38 to her right breast. With the stem of the Weed Whacker he steadied the wheel.

As the boat bucked and struggled across the shallow bank toward Mick Stranahan's house, Christina Marks accepted the probability that she would not live through the next few moments. "For the record," she said, "he's *not* my boyfriend."

Maggie nudged her with an elbow and whispered, "You could've done worse."

Chemo stopped the boat ten yards from the dock.

The stereo had died. The only sound was the thrum of the windmill and the chalkboard squeak of the Colemans, swinging in the gusts. The house scorched the sky with its watery brightness; a white torch in the blackest middle of nowhere. Christina wondered: Where did he get so many bloody lanterns?

Chemo looked down at Rudy Graveline. "Well? You're the one who got the invitation."

Rudy nodded grimly. On rubbery legs he made his way to the bow of the boat; the rough, wet ride had drubbed all the nattiness out of his L. L. Bean wardrobe. The doctor cupped both hands to his mouth and called out Stranahan's name.

Nothing.

He glanced back at Chemo, who shrugged. The .38 was still aimed at Christina Marks.

Next Rudy called Heather's name and was surprised to get a reply.

"Up here!" Her voice came from the roof, where it was darker.

"Come on down," Rudy said excitedly.

"No, I don't think so."

"Are you all right?"

"I'm fine," said Heather. "No thanks to you."

Chemo made a sour face a Rudy. "Now what?"

"Don't look at me," the doctor said.

Chemo called out to Heather: "We're here to save you. What's your fucking problem?"

Suddenly Heather appeared on the roof. For balance she held onto the base of the windmill. She was wearing a gray sweatsuit with a hood. "My problem? Ask him." She pulled the hood off her head, and Rudy Graveline saw the bandages were gone.

"Damn," he said.

"Let's hear it," Chemo muttered.

"I was supposed to do some surgery, but I didn't. She thought—see, I told her I did it."

Maggie Gonzalez said, "You're right. Everybody out here is crazy."

"I paid you, you bastard!" Heather shouted.

"Please, I can explain," Rudy pleaded.

Chemo was disgusted. "This is some beautiful moment. She doesn't want to be rescued, she hates your damn guts."

Heather disappeared from the roof. A few moments later she emerged, still alone, on the deck of the stilt house. Rudy Graveline tossed her the bow rope and she wrapped it around one of the dock cleats. The surgeon stepped out of the boat and tried to give her a hug, but Heather backed up and said, "Don't you touch me."

"Where's Stranahan?" Chemo demanded.

"He's around here somewhere," Heather said.

"Can he hear us?"

"I'm sure."

Chemo's eyes swept back and forth across the house, the deck, the roof. Every time he glanced at the water he thought of the terrible fish and how swiftly it had happened before. His knuckles were blue on the grip of the pistol.

A voice said: "Look here."

Chemo spun around. The voice had come from beneath the stilt house, somewhere in the pilings, where the tide hissed.

Mick Stranahan said: "Drop the gun."

"Or what?" Chemo snarled.

"Or I'll blow your new face off."

Chemo saw an orange flash, and instantly the lantern nearest his head exploded. Maggie shrieked and Christina squirmed from Chemo's one-armed clasp. On the deck of the house, Rudy Graveline dropped to his belly and covered his head.

Chemo stood alone with his lousy pistol. His ears were roaring. Shards of hot glass stuck to his scalp. He thought: That damn shotgun again.

When the echo from the gunfire faded, Stranahan's voice said: "That's buckshot, Mr. Tatum. In case you were wondering."

Chemo's face was killing him. He contemplated the damage that a point blank shotgun blast would do to his complexion, then tossed the Colt .38 into the bay. Perhaps a deal could be struck; even after splurging on the car phone, there was still plenty of money to go around.

Stranahan ordered Chemo to get out of the boat. "Carefully."

"No shit."

"Remember what happened last time with the 'cuda."

"So that's what it was." Chemo remembered seeing pictures of barracudas in sports magazines. What he remembered most were the incredible teeth. "Jesus H. Christ," he said.

Stranahan didn't mention that the big barracuda was long gone—off to deeper water to wait out the cold. Probably laid up in Fowey Rocks.

Chemo moved with crab-like deliberation, one gangly limb at a time. Between the rocking of the boat and the lopsided weight of his prosthesis, he found it difficult to balance on the slippery gunwale. Maggie Gonzalez came up from behind and helped boost him to the dock. Chemo looked surprised.

"Thanks," he said.

From under the house, Stranahan's voice: "All right, Heather, get in the boat."

"Wait a second," said Rudy.

"Don't worry, she'll be all right."

"Heather, don't!" Rudy was thinking about that night in the fireplace, and that morning in the shower. And about Costa Rica.

"Hands off," said Heather, stepping into the boat.

By now Christina Marks had figured out the plan. She said, "Mick, I want to stay."

"Ah, you changed your mind."

"What—"

"You want to get married after all?"

The words hung in the night like the mischievous cry of a gull. Then, from under the stilt house, laughter. "Everything's just a story to you," Stranahan said. "Even me."

Christina said, "That's not true." No one seemed particularly moved by her sincerity.

"Don't worry about it," Stranahan said. "I'll still love you, no matter what."

Rudy cautiously got to his feet and stood next to Chemo. In the flickering lantern glow, Chemo looked more waxen than ever. He seemed hypnotized, his puffy blowfish eyes fixed on the surging murky waves.

Heather said, "Should I untie the boat now?"

"Not just yet," Stranahan called back. "Check Maggie's jacket, would you?"

Maggie Gonzalez was wearing a man's navy pea jacket. When Heather reached for the pockets, Maggie pushed her away.

There was a metallic clunking noise under the house: Stranahan, emerging from his sniper hole. Quickly he clambered out of the aluminum skiff, over the top of the water tank, pulling himself one-handed to the deck of the house. His visitors got a good long look at the Remington.

"Maggie, be a good girl," Stranahan said. "Let's see what you've got."

Christina took one side of the coat and Heather took the other. "Keys," Christina announced, holding them up for Stranahan to see. One was a tiny silver luggage key, the other was from a room at the Holiday Inn.

Chemo blinked sullenly and patted at his pants. "Jesus H. Christ," he said. "The bitch picked my pockets."

He couldn't believe it: Maggie had lifted the keys while helping him out of the boat! She planned to sneak back to the motel and steal all the money.

"I know how you feel," Stranahan said to Chemo. He reached into the boat and plucked the keys from Christina's hand. He put them in the front pocket of his jeans.

"What now?" Rudy whined, to anyone who might have a clue.

Chemo's right hand crept to his left armpit and found the toggle switch for the battery pack. The Weed Whacker buzzed, stalled once, then came to life.

Stranahan said, "I'm impressed, I admit it." He aimed the Remington at Chemo's head and told him not to move.

Chemo paid no attention. He took two giraffe-like steps across the dock and, with a vengeful groan, dove into the stern of the boat after Maggie. They all went down in a noisy tangle—Chemo, Maggie, Heather and Christina—the boat listing precariously against the pilings.

Mick Stranahan and Rudy Graveline watched the melee from the lower deck of the stilt house. One woman's scream, piercing and feline, rose above the uproar.

"Do something!" the doctor cried.

"All right," said Stranahan.

Later, Stranahan gathered all the lanterns and brought them inside. Rudy Graveline lay in his undershorts on the bed; he was handcuffed spread-eagle to the bedposts. Chemo was unconscious on the bare floor, folded into a corner. With the shutters latched, the lanterns made the bedroom as bright as a television studio.

Rudy said, "Are they gone?"

"They'll be fine. The tide's running out."

"I'm not sure if Heather can swim."

"The boat won't sink. They'll all be fine."

Rudy noticed fresh blood on Stranahan's forehead, where he had been grazed by the Weed Whacker. "You want me to look at that?"

"No," Stranahan said acidly. "No, I don't." He left the bedroom and returned with the red Sears Craftsman toolbox. "Look what I've got," he said to Rudy.

Rudy craned to see. Stranahan opened the toolbox and began to unpack. "Recognize any of this stuff?"

"Yes, of course . . . what're you doing?"

"Before we get started, there's something I ought to tell you. The cops have Maggie's videotape, so they know about what you did to Vicky Barletta. Whether they can convict you is another matter. I mean, Maggie is not exactly a prize witness. In fact, she'd probably change her story again for about twenty-five cents."

Rudy Graveline swallowed his panic. He was trying to figure out what Stranahan wanted and how to give it to him. Rudy could only assume that, deep down, Stranahan must be no different than the others: Maggie, Bobby Pepsical, or even Chemo. Surely Stranahan had a scam, an angle. Surely it involved money.

Stranahan went out again and returned with the folding card table. He placed it in the center of the room, covered with the oilskin cloth.

"What is it?" the doctor said. "What do you want?"

"I want you to show me what happened."

"I don't understand."

"To Vicky Barletta. Show me what went wrong." He began placing items from the toolbox on the card table.

"You're insane," said Rudy Graveline. It seemed the obvious conclusion.

"Well, if you don't help," Stranahan said, "I'll just have to wing it." He tore open a package of sterile gloves and put them on. Cheerily he flexed the latex fingers in front of Rudy's face.

The surgeon stared back, aghast.

Stranahan said, "Don't worry, I did some reading up on this. Look here, I got the Marcaine, plenty of cotton, skin hooks, a whole set of new blades."

From the toolbox he selected a pair of doll-sized surgical scissors and began trimming the hairs in Rudy Graveline's nose.

"Aw no!" Rudy said, thrashing against the bedposts.

"Hold still."

Next Stranahan scrubbed the surgeon's face thoroughly with Hibiclens soap.

Rudy's eyes began to water. "What about some anesthesia?" he bleated.

"Oh yeah," said Stranahan. "I almost forgot."

Chemo awoke and rolled over with a thonk, the Weed Whacker bouncing on the floor planks. He sat up slowly, groping under his shirt. The battery sling was gone; the Weed Whacker was dead.

"Ah!" said Mick Stranahan. "The lovely Nurse Tatum."

A knot burned on the back of Chemo's head, where Stranahan had clubbed him with the butt of the Remington. Teetering to his feet, the first thing Chemo focused upon was Dr. Rudy Graveline—cuffed half-naked to the bed. His eyes were taped shut and a frayed old beach towel had been tucked around his neck. A menacing tong-like contraption lay poised near the surgeon's face: a speculum, designed for spreading the nostrils. It looked like something Moe would have used on Curly.

Stranahan stood at a small table cluttered with tubes and gauze and rows of sharp stainless-steel instruments. In one corner of the table was a heavy gray textbook, opened to the middle.

"What the fuck?" said Chemo. His voice was foggy and asthmatic.

Stranahan handed him a sterile glove. "I need your help," he said.

"No, not him," objected Rudy, from the bed.

"This is where we are," Stranahan said to Chemo. "We've got his nose numb and packed. Got the eyes taped to keep out the blood. Got plenty of sponges—I'm sorry, you look confused."

"Yeah, you could say that." Scraggles of hair rose on the nape of Chemo's scalp. His stomach heaved against his ribs. He wanted out—but where was the goddman shotgun?

"Put the glove on," Stranahan told him.

"What for?"

"The doctor doesn't want to talk about what happened to Victoria Barletta—she died during an operation exactly like this. I know it's been four years, and Dr. Graveline's had hundreds of patients since then. But my idea was that we might be able to refresh his memory by re-enacting the Barletta case. Right here."

Rudy fidgeted against the handcuffs.

Chemo said, "For Christ's sake, just tell him what he wants to hear."

"There's nothing to tell," said Rudy. By now he was fairly certain that Stranahan was bluffing. Already Stranahan had skipped several fundamental steps in the rhinoplasty. He had not attempted to file the bony dorsum, for example. Nor had he tried to make any incisions inside of Rudy's nostrils. This led Rudy to believe that Stranahan wasn't serious about doing a homemade nose job, that he was merely trying to frighten the doctor into a cheap confession.

To Chemo, of course, the makeshift surgical suite was a gulag of horrors. One glimpse of Rudy, blindfolded and splayed like a pullet on a bed, convinced Chemo that Mick Stranahan was monstrously deranged.

Stranahan was running a forefinger down a page of the surgical text. "Apparently this is the most critical part of the operation—fracturing the nasal bones on both sides of the septum. This is very, very delicate." He handed Chemo a small steel mallet and said, "Don't worry, I've been reading up on this."

Chemo tested the weight of the mallet in his hand. "This isn't funny," he said.

"Is it supposed to be? We're talking about a young woman's death."

"Probably it was an accident," Chemo said. He gestured derisively at Rudy Graveline. "The guy's a putz, he probably just fucked up."

"But you weren't there. You don't know."

Chemo turned to Rudy. "Tell him, you asshole."

Rudy shook his head. "I'm an excellent surgeon," he insisted.

Stranahan foraged through the toolbox until he found the proper instrument.

"What's that, a chisel?" Chemo asked.

"Very good," Stranahan said. "Actually, it's called an osteotome. A Storz number four. But basically, yeah, it's just a chisel. Look here."

He leaned over the bed and pinched the bridge of Rudy Graveline's nose. With the other hand he gingerly slipped the osteotome into the surgeon's right nostril, aligning the instrument lengthwise along the septum. "Now, Mr. Tatum, I'll hold this steady while you give it a slight tap—"

"Nuggghhh," Rudy protested. The dull pressure of the chisel reawakened the fear that Stranahan was really going to do it.

"Did you say something?" Stranahan asked.

"You were right," the surgeon said. His voice came out in a wheeze. "About the Barletta girl."

"You killed her?"

"I didn't mean to, I swear to God." Between the pinch of Stranahan's fingers and the poke of the osteotome, Rudy Graveline talked like he had a terrible cold.

He said, "What happened was, I let go of her nose. It was

. . . terrible luck. I let go just when the nurse hit the chisel, so—''

"So it went all the way up."

"Yes. The radio was on, I lost my concentration. The Lakers and the Sonics. I didn't do it on purpose."

Stranahan said, "And afterwards you got your brother to destroy the body."

"Uh-huh." Rudy couldn't nod very well with the Number 4 osteotome up his nostril.

"And what about my assistant?" Stranahan glanced over at Chemo. "You hired him to kill me, right?"

Rudy's Adam's apple hopped up and down like a scalded toad. Sightless, he imagined the scene by what he could hear: The plink of the instruments, the two men breathing, the wind and the waves shaking the house, or so it seemed.

Stranahan said, "Look, I know it's true. I'd just like to hear the terms of the deal."

Rudy felt the chisel nudge the bony plate between the eye sockets, deep in his face. He was, understandably, reluctant to give Mick Stranahan the full truth—that the price on his head was to be paid in discount dermatological treatments.

Rudy said, "It was sort of a trade."

"This I gotta hear."

"Tell him," Rudy said blindly to Chemo. "Tell him the arrangement with the dermabrasion, tell—"

Chemo reacted partly out of fear of incrimination and partly out of embarrassment. He let out a feral grunt and swung the mallet with all his strength. It was a clean blow to the butt of the osteotome, precisely the right spot.

Only much too hard. So hard that it knocked the chisel out of Stranahan's hand.

So hard the instrument disappeared entirely, as if inhaled by Rudy Graveline's nose.

So hard that the point of the chisel punched through the brittle plate of the ethmoid bone and penetrated Rudy Graveline's brain.

The hapless surgeon shuddered, kicked his left leg, and went limp. "Damn," said Stranahan, jerking his hand away from the blood.

This he hadn't planned. Stranahan had anticipated having to kill Chemo, at some point, because of the man's stubborn disposition to violence. He had figured that Chemo would grab for the shotgun or maybe a kitchen knife, something dumb and obvious; then it would be over. But the doctor, alive and indictable, Stranahan had promised to Al García.

He looked up from the body and glared at Chemo. "You happy now?"

Chemo was already moving for the door, wielding the mallet and neutered Weed Whacker as twin bludgeons, warning Stranahan not to follow. Stranahan could hear the seven-foot killer clomping through the darkened house, then out on the wooden deck, then down the stairs toward the water.

When Stranahan heard the man coming back, he retrieved the Remington from under the bed and waited.

Chemo was panting as he ducked through the doorway. "The fuck did you do to your boat?"

"I shot a hole in it," Stranahan said.

"Then how do we get off this goddamn place?"

"Swim."

Chemo's lips curled. He glowered at the bulky lawn appliance strapped to the stump of his arm. He could unfasten it, certainly, but how far would he get? Paddling with one arm at night, in these treacherous waters! And what about his face—it would be excruciating, the stringent salt water scouring his fresh abrasions. Yet there was no other way out. It would be lunacy to stay.

Stranahan lowered the gun and said, "Here, I think this belongs to you."

He took something out of his jacket and held it up, so the gold and silver links caught the flush of the lantern lights. Chemo's knees went to rubber when he saw what it was.

The Swiss diving watch. The one he lost to the barracuda.

"Still ticking," said Mick Stranahan.

34

At dawn the cold front arrived under a foggy purple brow, and the wind swung dramatically to the north. The waves off the Atlantic turned swollen and foamy, nudging the boat even farther from the shore of Cape Florida. The tide was still creeping out.

The women were weary of shouting and waving for help, but they tried once more when a red needlenose speedboat rounded the point of the island. The driver of the speedboat noticed the commotion and cautiously slowed to approach the other craft. A young woman in a lemon cotton pullover sat beside him.

She stood up and called out: "What's the matter?"

Christina Marks waved back. "Engine trouble! We need a tow to the marina."

The driver, a young muscular Latin, edged the speedboat closer. He offered to come aboard and take a look at the motor.

"Don't bother," said Christina. "The gas line is cut."

"How'd that happen?" The young man couldn't imagine.

It was a strange scene so early on a cold morning: Three women alone on rough water. The one, a slender brunette, looked pissed off about something. The blond in a sweatsuit was unsteady, maybe seasick. Then there was a Cuban woman, attractive except for an angry-looking bald patch on the crown of her head.

"You all right?" the young man asked.

The Cuban woman nodded brusquely. "How about giving us a lift?"

The young man in the speedboat turned to his companion and quietly said, "Tina, I don't know. Something's fucked up here."

"We've got to help," the young woman said. "I mean, we can't just leave them."

"There'll be other boats."

Christina Marks said, "At least can we borrow your radio? Something happened out there." She motioned toward the distant stilt houses.

"What was it?" said Tina, alarmed.

Maggie Gonzalez, who had prison to consider, said firmly: "Nothing happened. She's drunk out of her mind."

And Heather Chappell, who had her career to consider, said: "We were s'posed to meet some guys for a party. The boat broke down, that's all."

Christina's eyes went from Heather to Maggie. She felt like crying, and then she felt like laughing. She was as helpless and amused as she could be. So much for sisterhood.

"I know how that goes," Tina was saying, "with parties."

Heather said, "Please, I don't feel so hot. We've been drifting for hours." Her face looked familiar, but Tina wasn't sure.

The Cuban woman with the bald patch said, "Do you have an extra soda?"

"Sure," said Tina. "Richie, throw them a rope."

Sergeant Al García bent over the rail and got rid of his breakfast muffins.

"I thought you were a big fisherman," needled Luis Córdova. "Who was it told me you won some fishing tournament."

"That was different." García wiped his mustache with the sleeve of the windbreaker. "That was on a goddamn lake."

The journey out to Stiltsville had been murderously rough. That was García's excuse for getting sick—the boat ride, not what they had found inside the house.

Luis Córdova chucked him on the arm. "Anyway, you feel better now."

The detective nodded. He was still smoldering about the patrol boat, about how it had taken three hours to get a new pin for the prop. Three crucial hours, it turned out.

"Where's Wilt?" García asked.

"Inside. Pouting."

The man known as Chemo was standing up, his right arm suspended over his head. Luis Córdova had handcuffed him to the overhead water pipes in the kitchen. As a security precaution, the Weed Whacker had been unstrapped from the stump of Chemo's left arm. Trailing black and red cables, the yard clipper lay on the kitchen bar.

Luis Córdova pointed at the monofilament coil on the rotor. "See that—human hair," he said to Al García. "Long hair, too; a brunette. Probably a woman's."

García turned to the killer. "Hey, Wilt, you a barber?"

"Fuck you." Chemo blinked neutrally.

"He says that a lot," said Luis Córdova. "It's one of his favorite things. All during the Miranda, he kept saying it."

Al García walked over to Chemo and said, "You're aware that there's a dead doctor in the bedroom?"

"Fuck you."

"See," said Luis Córdova. "That's all he knows."

"Well, at least he knows *something*." García groped in his pocket and came out with a wrinkled handkerchief. He put the handkerchief to his face and returned to the scene in the bedroom. He came out a few minutes later and said, "That's very unpleasant."

"Sure is," agreed Luis Córdova.

"Mr. Tatum, since you're not talking, you might as well listen." García arranged himself on one of the wicker barstools and stuck a cigar in his mouth. He didn't light it.

He said, "Here's what's happened. You and the doctor have a serious business disagreement. You lure the dumb bastard out here and try to torture some dough out of him. But somehow you screw it up—you kill him."

Chemo reddened. "Horse shit," he said.

Luis Córdova looked pleased. "Progress," he said to García. "We're making progress."

Chemo clenched his fist, causing the handcuff to rattle against the rusty pipe. He said, "You know damn well who it was."

"Who?" García raised the palms of his hands. "Where is this mystery man?"

"Fuck you," Chemo said.

"What I can't figure out," said the detective, "is why you didn't take off. After all this mess, why'd you stay on the house? Hell, *chico*, all you had to do was jump."

Chemo lowered his head. His cheeks felt hot and prickly; a sign of healing, he hoped.

"Maybe he can't swim," suggested Luis Córdova.

"Maybe he's scared," García said.

Chemo said nothing. He closed his eyes and concentrated on the soothing sounds of freedom: the wind and the waves and the gulls, and the ticking of his waterproof wristwatch.

Al García waited until he was outside to light up the cigar. He turned a shoulder to the wind and cupped the match in his hand.

"I called for the chopper," said Luis Córdova. "And a guy from the M.E."

"Gives us what, maybe half an hour?"

"Maybe," said the young marine patrolman. "We got time to check the other houses. Wilt's not going anywhere."

García tried to blow a smoke ring, but the wind sucked it away. The cusp of the front had pushed through, and the sky over Biscayne Bay was clearing. The first sunlight broke out of the haze in slanted golden shafts that fastened to the water like quartz, lighting up the flats.

"I see why you love it out here," García said.

Luis Córdova smiled. "Some days it's like a painting."

"Where do you think he went?"

"Mick? He might be dead. Guy that size could probably take him. Dump the body off the house."

García gnawed skeptically at the end of the cigar. "It's possible. Or he could've got away. Don't forget he had that pump gun."

"His skiff's sunk," Luis Córdova noted. "Somebody blasted a hole in the bottom."

"Weird," said Al García. "But I had to guess, I'd say he probably wasn't around when all this happened. I'd say he got off the house."

"Maybe."

"Whatever happened out here, it was between Tatum and the doctor. Maybe it was money, maybe it was something to do with surgery. Christ, you notice that guy's arm?"

"His face, too," said Luis Córdova. "What you're saying makes sense. Just looking at him, he's not the type to file a lawsuit."

"But doing it with a hammer, that's cold." García puffed his cheeks as if to whistle. "On the other hand, your victim ain't exactly Marcus Welby . . . whatever. It all fits."

That was the main thing.

A small boat, a sleek yellow outboard, came speeding across the bonefish flats. It was headed south on a line toward Soldier Key. García watched the boat intently, walked around the house to keep it in view.

"Don't worry, I know him," said Luis Córdova. "He's a fishing guide."

"Wonder why he's out here alone."

"Maybe his clients didn't show. That happens when it blows hard—these rubes'll chicken out at the dock. Meanwhile it turns into a nice day."

Just south of Stiltsville, the yellow skiff angled off the flats and stopped in a deep blue channel. The guide took out a rod and casted a bait over the side. Then he sat down to wait.

"See?" said Luis Córdova. "He's just snapper fishing."

García was squinting against the sun. "Luis, you see something else out there?"

"Whereabouts?"

The detective pointed. "I'd say a quarter mile. Something in the water, between us and that island."

Luis Córdova raised one hand to block the glare. With the

other hand he adjusted his sunglasses. "Yeah, now I see it," he said. "Swimming on top. Looks like a big turtle."

"Yeah?"

"Grandpa loggerhead. Or maybe it's a porpoise. You want me to get the binoculars?"

"No, that's okay." García turned around and leaned his back against the wooden rail. He was grinning broadly, the stogie bobbing under his mustache. "I've never seen a porpoise before, except for the Seaquarium."

"Well, there's still a few wild ones out here," Luis Córdova said. "If that's what it was."

"That's what it was," said Al García. "I'm sure of it."

He tapped the ashes off the cigar and watched them swirl and scatter in the sea breeze. "Come on," he said, "let's go see if Wilt's learned any new words."

Epilogue

BLONDELL WAYNE TATUM, also known as Chemo, pleaded
guilty in Dade Circuit Court to the murders of Dr. Rudy Graveline and Chloe Simpkins Stranahan. He later was extradited to
Pennsylvania, where he confessed to the unsolved slaying of
Dr. Gunther MacLeish, a semiretired dermatologist and pioneer
in the use of electrolysis to remove unwanted facial hair. Because of his physical handicap, and because of favorable testimony from sympathetic Amish elders, Tatum received a
relatively lenient sentence of three seventeen-year terms, to be
served concurrently. He is now a trusty in charge of the winter
vegetable garden at the Union Correctional Institution at Raiford, Florida.

MAGGIE ORESTES GONZALEZ pleaded no contest to one
count of obstruction for lying to investigators after Victoria Barletta's death. She received a six-month suspended sentence, but
was ordered to serve one hundred hours of community service
as a volunteer nurse at the Dade County Stockade, where she
was taken hostage and killed during a food-related riot.

HEATHER CHAPPELL continued to appear in numerous
television shows, including *Matlock*, *L.A. Law* and *Murder, She
Wrote*. Barely five months after Dr. Rudy Graveline's death,
Heather quietly entered an exclusive West Hollywood surgical
clinic and underwent a breast augmentation, a blepharoplasty,
a rhinoplasty, a complete rhytidectomy, a chin implant, and
suction lipectomies of the thighs, abdomen, and buttocks. Soon

afterward, Heather's movie career was revived when she was offered—and accepted—the role of Triana, a Klingon prostitute, in *Star Trek VII: The Betrayal of Spock*.

KIPPER GARTH never fully recovered from his *pelota* injuries and retired from the law. His lucrative personal-injury practice was purchased by a prominent Miami Beach firm, which sought—and received—permission to retain the use of Kipper Garth's name and likeness in all future advertising and promotion.

The Dade County Grand Jury refused to indict JOHN NORDSTROM for assaulting his lawyer. Nordstrom and his wife pursued their malpractice claim against the Whispering Palms Spa and Surgery Center and eventually settled out of court for $315,000, forty percent of which went straight to their new attorney.

MARIE NORDSTROM'S contractured breast implants were repaired in a simple out-patient procedure performed by Dr. George Ginger. The operation took only ninety minutes and was a complete success.

The seat held on the County Commission by ROBERT PEPSICAL was filled by his younger brother, Charlie. The zoning rights to the Old Cypress Towers project were eventually picked up by a group of wealthy South American investors. Ignoring protests from environmentalists and local homeowners, the developers paved over the ballpark and playground to construct a thirty-three-story luxury condominium tower, with a chic rooftop nightclub called Freddie's. Nine weeks after it opened, the entire building was seized by the Drug Enforcement Administration in a money-laundering probe that was code-named "Operation Piranha."

The popular television show *In Your Face* was canceled after the disappearance and presumed death of its star, REYNALDO

FLEMM. The program's executive producers soon announced that a $25,000 scholarship in Reynaldo's name would be awarded to the Columbia University School of Journalism, from which, ironically, he had been twice expelled.

Exporter J. W. KIMBLER received a personal letter from the vice-chancellor of the Leeward Islands Medical University in Guadeloupe. The note said: "Thank you for your most recent shipment, which has become the highlight of our spring semester. On behalf of the faculty and of the future surgeons who study here, accept my deepest gratitude for a superior product."

For his dramatic videotaped footage of Reynaldo Flemm's cosmetic surgery, cameraman WILLIE VELASQUEZ was offered—and accepted—his own news-documentary program on the Fox Television Network. *Eyewitness Undercover!* premiered in the 8 P.M. time slot on Thursdays, and in four major markets decisively beat out *The Cosby Show* in both the Nielsens and Arbitrons.

CHRISTINA MARKS declined an offer to become a producer for Willie's new program. Instead, she left television and took a job as an assistant city editor at the *Miami Herald*, and with it a pay cut of approximately $135,000. Soon after moving to Miami, she purchased a second-hand Boston Whaler and a nautical chart of South Biscayne Bay.

The parents of Victoria Barletta were puzzled to receive, via UPS, a black Samsonite suitcase containing approximately $118,400 in cash. A letter accompanying the money described it as a gift from the estate of Dr. Rudy Graveline. The letter was signed by a retired investigator named MICK STRANAHAN and bore no return address.

About the Author

Carl Hiaasen is an award-winning columnist and reporter for the *Miami Herald* and the author of *Double Whammy* and *Tourist Season*. He is a native Floridian.